Finding Forever

The Lost & Found Series

Kristen Casey

www.GallantFoxPress.com

ISBN-13: 978-0-9994045-7-7

Cover Design ©2018, 2021 Tugboat Design

Author Photo ©2016 Kathleen Oristian Photography

EST 2016

GALLANT FOX
PRESS

The Lost & Found Series

Girls Night Out

Finding Home

Finding Love

Lost in Love

Lucky in Love

Christmas in Cambridge

Finding a Husband

Heroes & Husbands

Finding Forever

Forever and a Day

Forever Starts Now

The Flynn Sisters Box Set

The O'Connell Sisters Box Set

About this Book

Twelve years is a long time to wait for the one you love.

Mina's husband Grey was a problem long before he died, but the realization that it's been two years since she buried him still startles her. She's been so busy learning to fend for herself—learning to leave Grey's ugly legacy behind—that Mina's barely noticed her efforts were turning her into an empty shell of a woman. However, when a sexy friend from her past comes to town, she can finally recognize that *she* isn't the one who died. There might be a lot of life left to live—if she's willing to look behind a door she's never dared to open.

Mack has always maintained a strict hands-off policy when it came to his buddy's delectable wife Mina. Sure, he *noticed* her—a guy would have to be dead not to notice Mina. That didn't mean Mack could do anything about it, though. For twelve long and painful years, he's had to sit on the sidelines, watching the lousy way Grey treated her. But now that Mina is free, Mack knows he won't pass up the chance to be with her himself. He wants it all—except there's a very real possibility that the woman he hungers for can't give him what he needs. Mack has no idea what happens then.

Can Mina and Mack seize their shot at forever, once and for all? Or will the demons Grey left behind sink them both?

Chapter One

MINA PLOPPED A couple more cherries into the cocktail shaker and poked at them with a wooden spoon. She'd already smashed some mint leaves in the bottom of the shaker, as well as a little habanero chili. But now the recipe said to "muddle" the berries, and she wasn't entirely sure what that meant. She read ahead. The instruction to add ice and rum was easy—Mina could certainly manage that. However, to finish off the Porch Crawlers, she would need something called simple syrup, and she had *no* idea what that was.

She rifled through her sister-in-law's liquor cabinet. It was well-stocked, but it didn't seem to have anything resembling her mysterious drink ingredient. Mina re-checked the print-out she'd brought with her, looking for clues, and realized she'd also forgotten to bring club soda. *Rats.* She gnawed at her lip and tried to think of a work-around—maybe ginger ale would do the trick? She knew she'd seen a can or two of that in the pantry.

A car door slammed outside, and Mina cursed under her breath, "Damn it." Sadie and Trent had shown up too early.

She'd been hoping to greet her hosts with the cocktails right when they arrived, then shoo the couple out to the lawn chairs so they could watch the sunset together. Mina and her little nephew

Monty could pop in a video for a while, and then she would get dinner started for all of them. It seemed the least she could do, since the Bly family had insisted she join them at their bay house, Winthrop Farm, for the long weekend. They hadn't wanted Mina to be alone for the anniversary of her husband's death. She supposed she couldn't blame them.

It didn't seem possible that Grey had been gone for two whole years already. In some ways, it was like he'd never existed—an unhappy dream that had happened to some other person. There were still days, though, when it felt like Grey Whitney's shade followed Mina around with a persistent, wolfish hunger. Never letting go, never letting up, always wanting to consume her. Those days were fewer and fewer, though. Mina had worked hard to get to this point, and she was so much better than she'd been.

She even thought she would be able to stay in this big old house with her dead husband's family, without any of them ever knowing what he'd put her through. His sister Sadie had always been kind to Mina, despite the way Mina and Grey had gotten together. And, if the extended Whitney family preferred to think that Mina's marriage to Grey had been a happy one, then so be it. They could have that illusion—they'd earned it. Mina would mark the anniversary of his death with them, and when she returned home in three days, she would raise a glass to herself for surviving it. *All* of it.

The screen door creaked opened, and she turned with a smile. "You're here!" she called. She planted her feet, getting ready for little Monty to charge her and leap up for a hug.

But it wasn't Sadie and Trent Bly and their toddler son, who stood in the front hall. It was Mack Bolton. Mina's heart began knocking haphazardly around in her chest, and her breathing didn't seem to be working quite right. She waited until she was sure her voice would be steady before she spoke.

"Well, well. Look what the cat dragged in," Mina finally drawled. Frantically, she glanced over his shoulder to the gravel drive beyond and spotted no minivan and no fancy Volvo station wagon—just Mack's big white pickup truck and her little silver sedan. They were alone.

"Hey, kid," he said. He dropped a duffel near the bottom of the stairs which sure made it look like he planned to stay a while. "What's new?"

"Uh…" Mina shrugged, begging her brain to catch up with this new reality. "Sadie and Trent invited me out for the weekend," she explained. "Are you, uh…"

Mack jammed his hands in the pockets of his shorts and waited for her to finish. He looked amused by her discomfiture.

"Did they invite you, too?" she asked.

"As a matter of fact, they did. Sounds like Monty got sick and they couldn't make it."

"*What?*" Mina wouldn't panic. There was no need to panic about her and Mack Bolton staying alone in this house together. If things got too heavy, all she had to do was *leave*. It was that simple.

"They felt bad and didn't want to cancel," he explained. "So, they gave me a buzz and asked if I would come over and get things situated for you. Maybe take you out on the boat, that kind of thing."

Mina gaped. "Are you shitting me right now?" She had to remind herself that Sadie Bly did *not* know about her history with Mack. *No way* could she know. This was merely a crazy coincidence, that was all—not some devious master plan to get them to hook up.

"Nope." He lifted his chin at the big metal cocktail shaker in her hand. "What are you making?"

"I was trying to make them a drink called a Porch Crawler, but I'm missing a couple of ingredients." Mina huffed, "You'd think they would've let me know they weren't coming."

Right on cue, her cell began ringing on the kitchen counter. "Ten bucks says that's them," Mack laughed.

She turned, set the cocktail shaker precisely beside her, and picked up her phone. Sadie blasted her with a wall of words the moment Mina connected the call. She nodded at Mack—he was right.

"I'll go down to the basement and turn on the circuit breakers," he whispered.

Well, that certainly explained why the blender and the ceiling fan wouldn't work. Mina held the door for him and watched him trot down the stairs into the dark.

"Please don't go home because of us," Sadie pleaded in her ear. "Promise you'll stay."

"I—"

"There's a market right up the road. You remember where it is. Run up there now and then you won't have to leave for the rest of the weekend."

"Don't worry, I'll be fine," Mina assured her. She watched the basement door for Mack to reemerge again.

"One more thing," Sadie said in a rush. Mina could hear Monty crying in the background. "Trenton didn't want you to have to be alone. We sent—"

"—Mack Bolton to check on me?" Mina inquired.

Sadie groaned. "He's already there, isn't he?"

"Yep, he sure is."

"I'm so sorry! I meant to call earlier, but then Monty barfed all over his car seat and we got distracted. Is it going to be too weird having him there? You know him, right? He's a really good guy, I promise."

"It's okay, Sadie. Mack's cool—he and I have known each other for a very long time." Which was probably one of life's bigger understatements.

"I figured, since he and Grey were such good friends. So, you don't mind?"

Mack sauntered into the kitchen, washed his hands, then opened the cocktail shaker to take a sniff. He raised an eyebrow at Mina.

"No, I don't mind." *Much.*

Sadie asked, "Can I talk to him?"

Mina handed the phone over. "She wants to talk to you," she explained.

"Hey, Sadie," Mack grinned. He listened for a minute, then walked over to open a drawer in an antique sideboard. He lifted out a set of keys, jingled them at Mina and said, "Got 'em."

Mina could hear Sadie talking a mile a minute. Mack listened carefully before his eyes crinkled at the corners and he gave Mina a very obvious once-over.

"She seems fine to me," he said into her phone.

Mina rolled her eyes and gestured for him to hang up. He nodded, but then turned and stepped outside, cradling her cell against his shoulder as he pulled a couple grocery bags from the bed of his truck. At least *one* of them had been smart enough to stop at the store before arriving.

Mina wondered again if her sister-in-law could have arranged this on purpose. Would she actually try to throw her and Mack together? Sure, the Blys had encouraged her to start dating again, but a fix-up seemed unlikely—especially *this* weekend.

The spark between them had always been there, of course, but Mina had buried it deep and always hidden it from others. Sadie was pesky that way, though. She had an unnerving way of figuring stuff like that out.

Mack finished up and handed the phone back to her. She put it up to her ear, and immediately noticed the faint smell of his cologne. "Sadie?" she asked.

"She hung up," Mack said. "Are you sure you don't mind if I stay? I don't have to—I only live a few minutes away. If you wanted, I could just stop by if you needed anything."

"It's fine," Mina scoffed. "There's plenty of room for both of us."

Mack's amber eyes roved over her face. His hair was longer on top than the last time she'd seen him, and he'd grown a short, trim beard. He looked impossibly handsome.

"Tell you what," he said. He reached into one of the bags, extracted a bottle of margarita mix, and thunked it onto the counter. "Why don't you fire up that blender and make us a couple of these? I'll meet you out there," he pointed at the Adirondack chairs on the lawn facing the water, "Once I bring the rest of my stuff in."

Now that the electricity was on and the blender would actually work, whipping up some margaritas from a bottled mixer sounded way easier than unraveling the ambiguities of simple syrup. Besides, Mina was going to need every brain cell she had to figure out what to do about Mack. She dumped the contents of the cocktail shaker down the disposal, skimped on the tequila, and soon found herself staring down two glasses of icy-green liquid courage.

She could do this. Mack was a good, easy-going guy, who clearly didn't think anything crazy or life-changing was happening. They were old friends. Old friends hung out sometimes. Simple. Nothing to get worked up over.

Mina tucked her book under her arm, snagged the glasses, and headed for those lawn chairs. Mack's heavy tread was clumping around upstairs, and with any luck he'd take his time. Then she could have a couple minutes to take a few sips, read a few pages, and hopefully get her head straight before she had to make innocuous small talk with the man she'd had a raging crush on for twelve freaking years.

When Mack finally wandered out, he smiled down at Mina, sank into his chair and sighed happily. Other than thanking her for the drink, he didn't say much. Mina pretended to keep reading, and Mack lazily watched the boats sailing by.

The sun was setting—streaking the sky in sherbet colors over the water, which mirrored the colors right back again. Their glasses dripped condensation on the wooden armrests. Mina's hand and Mack's were inches apart, each holding onto their glass like a lifeline. Or…maybe that was just Mina.

She wondered how long he intended to stay quiet. He couldn't possibly think that she could still see well enough to read in the fading light, could he?

Finally, she broke the silence herself. "I think this may be the nicest place on earth."

"Agreed," he said. "I don't know how they found it. One of the perks of working in real estate, I guess." Sadie had sold houses for years, but as far as Mina knew, she had given it up once Monty was born.

"Hmm. No kidding," Mina agreed.

The slightest of touches feathered across her hand—the tip of Mack's little finger just grazing hers. Out of the corner of her eye, Mina looked down, but it was hard to tell if it was on purpose or not.

Mack said, "Maybe we should start thinking about dinner."

She dragged her eyes up from his hand to his face, but he was still looking at the water and made no move to acknowledge touching her.

"I hadn't really thought that far ahead," Mina admitted. She was talking too fast but couldn't seem to stop. "Sadie and Trent were going to bring the groceries when they came, so I can't vouch for what might be in there right now."

Mack shrugged. "That's okay, we can go out. What do you feel like?"

That was an easy one—even someone as distracted as Mina could figure it out. "It's fall on the bay, Mack," she beamed.

He grinned back. "Steamed crabs, it is. Smart girl."

Mina looked down again. Mack was *definitely* brushing her fingers with his. When she caught her eye, a faint laugh passed his lips and he jumped up.

"Come on, I'm starved. Let's eat," he said.

KING'S KRABS WAS right on a marina, a looming bright-blue structure with a boozy local clientele that was rabidly devoted. In a nod to the cool evening, the crab house had set up standing heaters around the perimeter of the covered patio. Coupled with the little flickering candles on the tables and the strings of twinkling lights zig-zagging overhead, they provided a welcoming aura of light in the dim dining area. The atmosphere was relaxed and happy, and Mina figured if she couldn't act normal there, she probably couldn't manage it anywhere.

They'd missed the big dinner rush, so the waitress was able to seat them at a table right next to the water. A line of sailboats and smaller yachting craft were docked a few feet away, and as they bobbed in the water, their fittings clanked softly. Thick brown paper covered the table, and the air smelled of seafood, beer, and bay water.

Mack sat across from her, slouching easily. Mina realized that she'd been trying so hard to play it cool that she hadn't really gotten a very good look at him yet. His worn-out gray T-shirt showed off his tan biceps, and his shoulders and chest looked broader and stronger than she remembered. He'd changed into an old pair of jeans and his hair was longer than usual, beginning to show just a hint of the glossy dark waves it would curl into if it wasn't trimmed regularly. Almost like a woman's hair, Mina thought, silky and thick. Soft-looking. Usually, Mack's hair was cropped too short to notice anything other than the color, and the strong shape of his neck and skull—*not* that Mina had ever obsessed about *that*.

A few large tin lights hung from the ceiling, but their bulbs were so weak they didn't contribute much light. They swung a bit in the breeze, mimicking the motion of the sailboat masts, and their hazy spotlights moved in circles across the wooden floor.

Mina said, "This is great. The last time I was here was for a big 50th anniversary party. It was hard to enjoy myself."

Mack took a swig of his beer, and she noticed his neck again. Watched him swallow while he watched her. "Why?" he asked.

"I was usually a wreck at Whitney family get-togethers," Mina admitted. When Mack looked puzzled, she explained, "All those aunts always keeping an eagle-eye on me, waiting for me to screw up."

He nodded, unable to deny it. Mack probably knew Grey's family better than Mina did. "Luckily, this isn't a family get-together," he said.

In Mina's opinion, that was a good thing. So why did Mack sound faintly irritated? "You're right. I can smile at you—or even flirt with you—and no one here would even care."

Mack's eyes perked up at that and he grinned at her. He definitely liked that. "I will admit, I am partial to the idea."

It seemed she was still a sucker for his random little compliments, Mina thought ruefully. There'd been a time where she'd had to force herself to stop following him around at gatherings, like a stray dog hoping for another table scrap. It had gotten pathetic.

She drank another margarita, this one much stronger than the one she'd made at the house. The waitress delivered orders of hush puppies and dumped a pile of steamed and spiced blue crabs in the center of the table.

Mack mostly watched Mina eat as he drank his beer. It was a challenge to make eye contact when he had that seductive smolder aimed her way. Whenever she shoveled a piece of crab or hush puppy in her face, Mack got this little half smile that made Mina want to either smack him or kiss him—it was a bit of a toss-up.

"Will you knock it off?" she demanded. "I can't eat when you keep looking at me like that."

"Like what, kiddo?"

"Like I'm dinner."

Mack laughed out loud at that, and the sound of it just made the heat pooling low in her belly even worse.

"Come on. Help me out here," Mina begged. "You've hardly eaten any of these things."

Thankfully, he relented. "All right, you. Stand back and let a pro show you how it's done." He set about dismantling the crabs with efficiency and determination, and before long he had decimated the pile between them.

The waitress kept switching Mina's empty margaritas out for full ones, but Mina figured that was okay. Between the feast on the table and the way the tequila was keeping her nerves quiet, she wasn't about to complain. She had been on a few dates since she'd buried Grey two years ago, but not one had felt like *this*.

Could this even be considered a date, anyway? It seemed like one, but Mack was one of Grey's oldest friends. Maybe all his flirting over the years had been meaningless, and he'd never seen Mina as anything more than his buddy's wife.

Hah. And pigs could fly.

DESPITE STUFFING HER face, Mina ended up a little woozy when they finally decided to head out. The parking lot was dark, and a sandy, rocky mess—picking her way across the uneven ground in her thin flip-flops was more of a challenge than it had been before. Mina tried for dignity, but she still managed to turn her ankle on a hidden curb as they neared the truck. Unsurprisingly, Mack was quick to catch her.

He led Mina the last few steps to his truck with an arm around her waist. She propped herself against the passenger side to take the weight off her foot, giggling a little sheepishly while Mack dug his keys out of his pocket. He leaned toward Mina, trying to reach around for the door handle so he could open the door for her.

"Sorry," he murmured. "I just need to..." But when he got closer, he trailed off.

Mina's giggle died in her throat. Mack was so close now—she would only have to tilt out a couple of inches if she really wanted to close the distance between them.

As if he could read her mind, Mack froze in place and turned to look at her. His burning gaze at such close range wiped any last vestiges of humor from Mina's face. He was even more handsome up close, his eyes so dark they looked black, his jaw firm and scent tantalizing. Mina thought Mack was going to kiss her, and her heart kicked into overdrive at the notion—even with those dates a few months ago, she hadn't kissed another man besides Grey since she was nineteen years old.

Instead of going for it, though, Mack simply closed his eyes and grazed her cheek with his own. His beard was soft against her skin. The caress was tender and affectionate and totally unexpected. Mina's breath hitched, and she slid her hands under his soft t-shirt to keep him near. Along his waistband, Mack's skin was hot and hard and begging for closer exploration.

The contact seemed to jerk him awake. He took Mina's arm, guided her aside, then yanked the truck's passenger door open. He helped her hop up into the seat before shutting her in without a word. Mina might have imagined it, but it seemed to take Mack an awfully long time to cross behind the truck to the driver's side. *Someone* wasn't as cool a cucumber as he liked to pretend, and that made her feel better.

The ride back to the house, through the dark and quiet streets of town, felt awkward after their near miss. Mack's radio was playing soft country music but turning up the volume seemed wrong to Mina. Acknowledging that loaded moment back in the parking lot felt clumsy, too. Mina's head buzzed, and she tried to decide what to do. She wanted a taste of Mack Bolton—there was no denying that. But maybe she should discover if he felt the same first.

Mack glanced quickly at her, just as they left town behind and headed down the tree-lined road that led to the Bly property. He cleared his throat, then said, "It should be criminal how good you smell."

Mina snorted. It was the last thing she'd expected. "Like beer and crab carcasses?" she wondered.

Mack chuckled, but it sounded strained. "Yeah, that's it," he retorted.

Silence reigned for the rest of the drive.

MINA WATCHED MACK through the kitchen window. Once they'd gotten back, he'd gone out to sit on the back patio while she washed their glasses from earlier. He'd wanted to help, but Mina had needed a few minutes to herself. Mack only accepted being waved away when Mina finally directed him to Trent's humidor on the side table.

Now, puffs of cigar smoke were drifting around outside, and Mina couldn't find anything else to do in the kitchen. It had seemed like a good idea to dock her phone and play music while she cleaned up, but her playlist had shifted from pop and country to something far more sultry and dangerous.

Languid guitar and harmonica whined from the speakers and tangled mercilessly with the smoke and the night. Mina was hot and bothered, and pretty sure she wouldn't be able to prevent going outside to join the man out there. *Why* had she had so many margaritas at dinner? And how many had she had, anyway? Three? Usually one was more than enough for her, but now she had no impulse control left *at all*.

Mina tried to think. How outrageously had she been flirting with Mack over dinner? It had definitely been a while since she'd been around a man like him. As gorgeous as Mack was, no one could really fault her for it. Her moves were obviously pretty rusty—the inept moment in the parking lot and her complete failure to maintain a normal conversation on the ride back were evidence of that. Mack had probably been relieved to retreat out back by himself. That way, he could hide from Mina, so she wouldn't embarrass herself anymore.

With most of the windows closed, it was stuffy in the kitchen. Mina knew it would be so much cooler outside in the breeze. She fanned her face ineffectually with her hand and looked around for the ceiling fan switch but couldn't find it.

Mack really wouldn't mind a little company—would he? If Mina kept a decent distance away and didn't chatter nervously, it would be totally *fine* to go out there. Hell, she probably couldn't even enunciate well anyway—it was always the first thing to go when she'd been drinking. So, she would just be quiet and companionable, from a good, safe, neighborly distance. And Mina would *not* look at Mack Bolton's mouth, sucking on that cigar. Her face flushed. Nor should she even *think* about it, apparently.

Mina's feet carried her straight out the French doors and right to him. That's when the real trouble started.

Chapter Two

AT KING'S, MACK nursed his cold beer—its label gone soggy with condensation—and watched Mina eat across the sticky table. He'd noticed the gloriously uninhibited way she ate before then, of course, at so many dinners and parties over the years. For some reason, it had always charmed him.

However, once his mom and Grey had called Mack out about the attention he was paying Mina, he'd had to switch to watching her surreptitiously. Mack had guiltily eyed her from under lowered lids, over people's shoulders, and around flowery center pieces whenever he got the chance. He couldn't stop—Mina was simply *that* fascinating to him.

Which meant that Mack had been bowled over when he got the call from Grey's sister that morning. Sadie had been a couple years ahead of them back in school. Now, Mack ran into her around town sometimes, when she and her family were staying at their vacation house. Once in a while, Sadie called Mack and asked him to check on things, when they couldn't make it down or bad weather was coming. He'd never before been asked to look after a human being, though, much less one as mesmerizing as Sadie's sister-in-law.

The opportunity to spend a few unchaperoned days with Mina had been too tempting to resist. Just the two of them, with no one to sit in judgement of how they acted with each other—Mack couldn't have turned that down if someone had paid him a million bucks.

He gazed at Mina in open appreciation now, as she handily dismantled crab after crab from the fragrant, steaming pile between them. Her lips were swollen and red from the Old Bay and the salt rimming her margarita glass. Mina sucked on each crab leg before she discarded it, then licked the spices thoroughly from each finger.

When Mina had said she was hungry, she hadn't been kidding. She clearly had no qualms about eating—really eating—in front of a guy. Mack liked that she was that comfortable around him. He contemplated all the other places he could take her out to eat next—barbecue joints and ice cream parlors, or maybe something involving lollipops. Mack hoped he wouldn't have to stand up any time soon, though, or Mina was liable to get ideas about some other things in the vicinity he'd like her to take a bite of.

When she went after that margarita straw, hollowing her cheeks and humming low in her throat in happiness—Mack was sure he'd lose his mind. Then she did it all over again, and it took every ounce of concentration he had not to groan out loud. He couldn't look away. It was certainly one of the more captivating images he'd ever seen.

His ex-wife Carolynn had been the opposite of Mina—a dainty eater, and perpetually on some diet or cleanse or restricted regimen. She was, therefore, eternally engaged in a tortuous cold war with her food—surpassing any effort to be healthy and settling deep into the zone of disorder. At the time, Mack hadn't realized how depressing that had been. It meant that any real enjoyment of food by him had been…fraught. Seen as a denial and rejection of *her*, like so many other things he'd done and said.

He blinked away the past with effort. Mina had stopped eating and was staring expectantly at him, a tiny grin playing at the corners of her mouth. Her eyes flicked to the side—Mack followed her gaze and finally noticed the waitress hovering impatiently nearby. They'd asked him something, but what?

"No thanks," he guessed, draining the last of his beer and handing the waitress the empty bottle. He must've guessed correctly, because she took it and sailed away without comment.

Mina ate more slowly now as she considered him. "Are you okay?" she finally asked.

He nodded. If Mack kissed her right then, she'd taste bewitchingly briny, and he wondered—would Mina kiss like she ate, with whole-hearted enthusiasm? But he already knew the answer to that, and unfortunately always had. It was yet another fact about her that he'd buried deep, trying to smother it into submission by keeping it locked down tight in the dark.

Sadly, ignoring things hadn't worked terribly well, though Mack had tried to convince himself it had. His problem currently was that all the obstacles to he and Mina being together were simply…gone. And now that they were, Mack didn't know how the hell to proceed. Mina, it seemed, had no such difficulty. It didn't take her long to show him exactly what she was capable of.

HE MADE IT through her first salvo in the parking lot of King's relatively unscathed. Even though Mina had been draped on him like a tipsy, beguiling vine—even though her huge brown eyes had been fairly begging him for a kiss—he'd managed to keep things above board. But only just.

Once they got back to the house, though, Mack ran into more difficulty. Mina wasn't very subtle about her desire to be alone for a few minutes. So, he'd taken the hint, grabbed one of Trenton's cigars as a prop, and high-tailed it outside. Sadie's husband rarely smoked the things—they were more of a relic from bachelor parties past than anything else—but even Mack had to admit it seemed to fit the evening.

Mina bustled around the kitchen, though there wasn't much to do. The window over the sink was open, and Mack absentmindedly listened to her sing along to her playlist. Her voice was alternately high and sweet, then low and suggestive. He tried to push from his mind how all the lyrics suddenly seemed to be loaded with innuendo—that was almost definitely a product of his own dirty mind, and nothing resembling reality. Mina couldn't be teasing him on purpose. She *wouldn't*. Would she?

Tendrils of smoke drifted around as Mack studied the view, the stars, the dark water lapping at the seawall across the lawn. He willed himself to stay put in that chair, where he couldn't do anything irrevocable. It had been too close of a call in the parking lot of King's. Until Mack had a better idea of where Mina's head was at, getting busy with her was going to have to take a back seat. He had to be sure of her, before he made his move.

Mina was irresistible, though. She'd *always* been irresistible. How was Mack going to put the image of her chocolate eyes laughing at him across the restaurant table out of his mind? Or, for that matter, the image of her long bare limbs tangled in his sheets?

Focus on the cigar. If Mina came out there…but no way, she wouldn't. Not if he was still smoking. Every woman he'd ever met despised the smell of cigars. It wasn't like they were wrong—people died from hideous cigar-induced diseases all the time, for God's sake.

So, Mack would simply stay out there as long as it took to cool his overheated blood, using the stogie as his shield. He shifted in the deck chair and tried—unsuccessfully—not to think about Mina's mouth. It was fixing to be a long damn night, though.

Then, suddenly, she was *there*. Mina appeared in front of Mack like an alluring apparition. He looked up and her gaze was intense. His eyes drifted to her mouth—*no*. He could *not* look there. Mack inhaled deeply, then blew out. The cigar smoke curled around her, and Mina did what she used to do with friends, when he'd first met her all those years ago.

She bummed a smoke. Mina reached for his cigar, and Mack felt the corner of his mouth twitch into a smirk. So much for believing the cigar would be a deterrent. This woman was one of a kind, all right. He'd do well not to forget that.

"Sorry. I guess I'm blocking the view," Mina murmured, puffing on the cigar.

Mack's obsession with her lips quadrupled. "Right now, you *are* the view," he retorted, then immediately castigated himself. If his goal was to hold off getting horizontal with this woman, his methods needed some serious refinement.

Mina gazed down at him and took one slow puff, then two. On the third, Mack watched his own hands snake around her bare knees and drift up the back of her thighs with the lightest of touches. He hadn't meant to do it, and thought if he didn't touch her very hard, maybe it wouldn't count. Mina's eyes flickered, but never left his face.

She bent and carefully stubbed out the cigar, then took the ashtray off the armrest and placed it on the flagstones beside his chair. Mack pulled her closer, and then—like the best, sexiest kind of magic—Mina was straddling him in the deck chair, her eyes heavy-lidded and dark with desire. Her fingers curled into the hair at the base of his neck and *Lord* did she ever smell good.

Mina's light vanilla scent had probably been imprinted on his soul for all eternity, but here and now, Mack felt like he could devour her for it. They held still, both seeming to realize that once they lit the match it was going to be an inferno.

As many years as Mack had ached for this woman, he marveled at how he could be in no particular hurry to lock lips with her now that she'd ended up in his lap. His fingers drifted up and down Mina's bare arms, across her hairline, then down around the neckline of her tank top. Mack questioned her with his gaze. Testing, he bent and kissed Mina's shoulder and the side of her neck, then pulled back to look at her again.

Her eyes dragged opened reluctantly, hazy with want. And that was it. Mack had absolutely no resolve left—really hadn't had much to begin with, if he was honest about it. His lips hit hers, and that was all the effort it took from him. Mina was suddenly on fire, passion and heat rolling off her in waves as he explored her mouth with his tongue.

The music shifted to something darker, something hotter. Mack couldn't have planned it better if he'd tried. Mina must have felt it too—she arched under his hands, and he had her tank top up and over her head in half a breath. She gasped when his fingers pushed the straps of her bra off her shoulders. The breeze kicked up, feathering over her back and into Mack's hair.

Was she moaning? Mack wanted to growl with the satisfaction of it. He'd do anything—anything at all—to hear that sound again. The kiss went on and on, their hands seemed to be on concomitant search-and-destroy missions, and it became very obvious that this crazy attraction of his wasn't all in Mack's head. Mina wanted him, too.

How long had he been craving her touch, anyway? Ten years? All twelve? He'd buried the idea so deep down, refusing to ever acknowledge it in the light of day, that it was hard to say how long it had existed.

At that thought, a small note of panic entered the current of his reverie. Mack belatedly realized that he had no exit strategy. If he got in too deep and Mina took off again, it was going to sting like a bastard. Maybe even worse than before.

Mina faltered, too. The kiss slowed, and cooled, and she froze in his arms. Mack forced his fingers to loosen their grip on her hips, but there was no hiding the boat mast in his shorts—he'd been pressing it against the scorching heart of her for the last several minutes. Mina shifted back on his thighs, to get away from it. Mack tried to keep his eyes on her face, and not the glorious vision of lace-covered breasts right under his nose.

"What am I doing?" she whispered.

He pulled back. "Hey. It's okay." Mack pressed a light kiss onto her forehead.

Mina started to tear up and began blinking furiously to stave off the onslaught. She'd been right there with him, until suddenly she wasn't anymore. Mack released his hold on her and white-knuckled the armrests instead.

"I'm sorry. Did I do something wrong?" He couldn't imagine what it had been. Maybe he'd moved too fast, or maybe she'd had too many margaritas? The tears were sliding down her cheeks faster, and Mina's expression looked horrified. This was bad—*really* bad.

She shook her head and looked frantically around for her tank top. Mack dug it out from under his thigh and helped Mina pull it back over her head. He reached out tentatively, afraid to spook her further, and wiped at her cheeks with his fingers.

"Mina, what happened?" Mack asked, his concern for her not dousing his ardor in the least. His whole body cried out for her. He hated the sudden deprivation of the feel of her skin, her scent so close and perfect, his senses flooded with her face, her hair, her long tan legs. After so many years of denial, he finally had Mina right where he'd always wanted her, and he'd only succeeded in making her cry. *Damn.* That extinguished him quick enough.

Mina levered herself off his lap while Mack sat like a stone, trying to comprehend what had gone wrong. She'd been liquid fire under his hands only moments ago.

"I am *so* sorry," Mina whispered, her voice cracking. She rushed inside, swiping at her wet face as she went, and stumbled a little on the threshold.

"Wait," Mack called, confused. "Sorry for what?" He was too late, though—Mina was already gone. He sat there and frantically tried to remember every last thing he'd done.

Mina had come to him. Mack had already resolved quite emphatically not to accost her, but he hadn't needed to. She'd come out *to him*. Her lips had closed around the cigar, right where his own had been.

True, Mack hadn't been able to keep his hands away from the tender skin behind her knees. Every time Mina had walked in front of him that day, he'd wanted to touch her there, and when she stood so close, well...shit happened.

Mack was certain that Mina had felt the smoldering attraction between them, too. Maybe she'd suspected that all his years of pretending had begun crumbling into dust. Maybe her walls were coming down, too. She *had* kissed him back—fiercely. Mack was sure he hadn't imagined that.

Hell, maybe he'd just moved too fast. That had to be it. If he hadn't taken her top off, maybe...but damn it, Mina had been even more beautiful than Mack could have imagined, warm and willing, half-clothed and straddling him in the moonlight. He couldn't make himself regret it.

The truth was that he couldn't resist her, even though he ought to. Especially not when she was so close. He'd let himself get caught up in the music and her singing and the balmy night air. It was a heady rush being alone with her, with no judgmental eyes assessing the propriety of their every move. Mack had ignored his instincts and plowed headlong into things, when Mina obviously wasn't ready yet. And the truth was...Mack didn't *want* to resist Mina, not anymore.

He stared out over the water, feeling like the worst sort of ass. His mind drifted again, replacing the sight of the dark, glassy sheet of the bay with his memory of the silken expanse of skin stretching from her neck to the low waist of her shorts. The way that lacy little bra had lifted her beautiful breasts into a display that seemed meant only for him and his questing tongue.

Mack cleared his throat and jumped up. After all she'd been through, Mina deserved better from him. The temperature was dropping now that the sun had been down for a while, and it was time for Mack to take a long, chilly, punishing walk. Hopefully, he could also get his brain back online. He hoped he wouldn't break his neck in the dark while he did so, but it would probably be only fitting if he did.

Chapter Three

MINA SPENT THE night cowering in her room, wondering how the evening had spun so far out of control so fast. What must Mack think of her? *So much for being a grieving widow*, she thought. She'd been drunk and horny and come on to him like an afternoon thunderstorm. And then, as if that wasn't bad enough, she'd panicked and fled right when things were getting interesting.

In the morning, she dallied upstairs as long as she could. She brushed her hair and her teeth, then pulled on her most flattering bathing suit. Mina stepped into a loose pair of denim cutoffs, then slipped her short white pool coverup over that. It was a little sheer, especially with the black suit underneath, but not *too* revealing. Mack already had reason enough to think she was a tease.

The light of day had brought her a little perspective, at least. She'd freaked out for so many reasons the night before. Sour memories of Grey had intruded without warning, and Mina's total lack of recent experience with dating and sex had made her a bit edgy.

And then there'd been the overwhelming realization that Mack Bolton was not only holding her, but *into it*. She'd thought she could handle being with him, but apparently that had been overly optimistic.

There was no question she had to apologize to him, but Mina was uncertain how to word it. Bringing up her dead spouse seemed like the last thing she was supposed to do when she wanted to jump a new guy's bones—especially if that spouse happened to be an old friend of the guy's. Explaining that Mina hadn't knocked boots in what felt like an eternity also seemed completely graceless.

Which left...coming right out and *telling* Mack that she'd been carrying around an illicit crush on him for years, but still might not have the guts to do anything about it. *Ugh*.

Clearly, none of those would work. What was more, Mina's reckless comment the night before—about flirting without the family watching—only complicated the issue.

One way or another, she'd have to tackle her *mea culpa*, though. So, she finally headed downstairs and braced for the worst.

Despite dragging her heels, she still got to the kitchen before Mack. Mina looked around for some inspiration to aid her cause and came across the vodka and Bloody Mary mix in the pantry. Well...the booze hadn't done her any favors the prior night, but she didn't have a ton of options. She grabbed some eggs and bacon out of the refrigerator to round things out and hoped Mack wouldn't be too hard on her if he had a full stomach and a small buzz.

A few minutes later, he wandered into the kitchen warily, scrubbing a hand across his beard and looking unsure of his reception. His voice came out low and rusty when he mumbled, "Morning."

Mack's dark hair was a little disheveled, his t-shirt rumpled, and he smelled like toothpaste. He was a hot, sexy mess, and under different circumstances, Mina would've tackled him straight back into bed.

Instead, she handed him that drink. "Good morning. Hair of the dog?" She smiled at him, so he'd know she'd regained her sanity, then turned to finish brewing the coffee. "Though I'm probably the one who needs it, not you."

Mack looked a bit confused, but that was understandable. He set the glass beside him on the counter without taking a sip. "How are you doing?" he asked.

"I'm fine. I took a couple aspirin and I'm good as new." Mina hesitated, fussing with the egg carton. The seconds ticked by.

Finally, they both blurted out, "I'm sorry."

She laughed and held up a hand. "Me first. Look—I'm *really* sorry for running away last night. I shouldn't have done that."

"No, I'm the one who's sorry," Mack insisted. "I pushed you too fast. I swear it won't happen again." He looked so ashamed that Mina's heart clenched tight in her chest.

"Mack…it's okay. You didn't do anything wrong. I just," she shrugged, struggling for the right words. "Got caught up in the moment, and then kind of panicked for no reason."

He stepped closer and rested his hands on her shoulders. "I should've realized you needed me to slow down."

"How could you have? I didn't know I needed that myself, until I was back upstairs."

Mack caressed her cheek, and she couldn't resist leaning into his warm hand. "Still," he whispered, "I'll do better next time. I promise." He dropped a gentle, minty kiss on her mouth, then stepped back. "I don't want you to be scared of me."

Mina shifted forward, winding her arms around his waist and kissing him softly, so he'd know she wasn't. Mack's lips lingered on hers, but he didn't part them—didn't take the kiss deeper. He just held her head between his hands and brushed her mouth with his.

Too soon, he pulled back again.

"Thanks for being so understanding," Mina whispered.

"Anytime." Mack glanced over her shoulder at the counter. "It smells good in here. What're you making?"

"Bacon and eggs. Is that okay?"

"Of course. What can I do?"

"You can make some toast if you want."

He busied himself feeding slices of bread into the toaster while Mina beat the eggs and added butter to the frying pan.

"So. What should we do today?" he asked after a while.

"It's going to be warm out again. I figured I'd sit by the pool for a while, maybe have a picnic for lunch. How's that sound?"

"Sounds perfect. But I was thinking—the water's really calm right now. Why don't we take the boat out after we eat, and then hit the pool after lunch?"

"Deal," Mina said.

THEY SAT NEXT to one another in the gleaming white cabin cruiser, Mack scanning the water as he navigated the bay behind the Bly property. He took it slow for Mina, and the boat bobbed from the tide and the wakes of the other craft.

There was a light breeze blowing small clouds across the bright blue autumn sky, and it made the sunlight seem to flicker over them. Mina couldn't believe they'd gotten so lucky with the weather—it could just as easily have been cold and gray at this time of year.

While they sailed through sun and shade, she leaned back against the console and admired Mack in pieces, so it wouldn't seem like she was staring. His faded orange ballcap fit his head perfectly, shading his eyes from view. Mina wouldn't have been able to see his expression anyway—Mack wore a pair of mirrored sunglasses, too. His t-shirt looked old and soft, and stretched across his shoulders. His arms were brawny and brown from the sun.

Mack lounged back in the captain's chair as he steered, relaxed and capable. He'd been mostly quiet, so she assumed that guiding the boat required most of his attention. It didn't matter. She was amusing herself with the scenery quite well, thank you very much.

Mina found her eyes returning again and again to the tantalizing dark space under his splayed knees, where his cut-off khaki shorts draped off his thighs. What would he do if she touched him there? After the way she'd botched things last night, did she even want to risk it? Mack might knock her hand away, or get really mad, and then she would be mortified.

When he suddenly broke the silence, it was a surprise. Mina flinched guiltily.

"Do you have any idea what it does to me when you stare like that?" he chuckled.

"Do you feel trapped?" Mina teased, unnerved that he'd guessed her thoughts so accurately.

"Uh, no."

"How about squeamish?" She was being deliberately obtuse, she knew, but Mack had such a frank way about him. It was disconcerting. She didn't have much practice talking directly about anything—her family tended to get side-tracked into emotional outbursts rather than deal with issues head-on. As for Grey—she'd only learned obfuscation and redirection from him.

"*No*," Mack retorted firmly. "But if *you're* getting seasick tell me now."

"I'm not," Mina capitulated. Abruptly, she felt awkward about her joking. And…she wanted to know what he'd been intending to say. She gnawed on her lip and studied him, trying to figure out how to get Mack to continue.

He grinned, and it was blindingly gorgeous. "*That*," he laughed. "What you're doing right there. Guaranteed to get me hot and bothered."

She paused, assessing the way those plainly-spoken words made her feel in return. *Molten* certainly came to mind. "I am a bit of a captive audience," she bristled. "What else am I supposed to do?"

Mack shook his head. "Not buying it. You could be looking at the water, the shore, the birds, the sky…but no. You're over there checking out *my* homely mug. Like always, I might add."

She sighed dramatically, to cover up how that threw her. "Am I *that* obvious?"

"Let's just say…" He snuck a measuring peek at Mina before returning his attention to the water. "It's been entertaining over the years, never knowing when I might get ensnared by one of your *looks*."

This was getting out of hand again. Mack could not possibly be giving her crap for something he was just as guilty of. "What looks?" she demanded.

"The *I'm gonna drag you into a dark corner and rock your world* looks."

"Rock your world?" Mina smirked. "What year is this?"

"My original thought was much raunchier," he retorted primly. "I'm trying to be a gentleman, though."

Her smile faded. "You don't have to clean it up for *me*, Mack. I'm hardly some shrinking violet."

"I know that. But sometimes it's easier if I clean that shit up for *myself*. That way I don't have to beat myself up later for the inappropriate things that came out of my mouth."

Mina scoffed, "You have never said an inappropriate thing in your life."

"Says you," Mack fired back.

"Besides…" She wondered what she was doing, admitting to these things. It felt weird and unnatural, after keeping them on lockdown for so long. Mack had always been able to pull things out of her, though. "If I *did* give you looks like that—and I confess nothing—then it would only be because you were asking for it."

"Oh, is that right?" he laughed.

"Mack, admit it. Every party. Every get-together. You planted yourself across the room and watched me. I could *feel* your eyes on me." Was Mina insane to say that out loud to him? She'd barely let herself believe it.

"That's very interesting, Mina," he said. Mack sat up straight and stared right at her. "In order to notice that, you would have had to be watching me right back."

Her mouth popped open to deny it, but based on Mack's smug expression, he knew he had her cornered. Mina pried her chin up off the deck and forced her mouth closed again. There had been days, in those last few miserable years with Grey, when Mina had trailed Mack around parties like a forlorn puppy, longing for just one of his tossed-off compliments. Those one-liners had sometimes been enough to keep her going—enough to believe that she still mattered. When Mack gave her one, she was giddy. When he didn't…

"You…you…" she stuttered, struggling to regain her footing.

Mack snorted. "Oh, man. I could barely drink a beer when you were in the same room. I lived in constant fear that I was being too obvious. That someone would call me out."

To learn his side of their history was fascinating. "Did they?" Mina whispered.

His face changed immediately. "Only once," he mumbled. Before she could ask about it, though, he barreled on. "After Carolynn left, I came hunting for you at barbecues a couple times. I had to tell you what you were doing to me. Make sure you knew what I was going through." Mack snorted. "I don't know what I expected. It wasn't like I could make some big declaration or anything. Someone would definitely have noticed *that*."

Mina certainly didn't remember many times after her marriage when they'd been able to speak together alone. And she'd written off most of Mack's attention as wishful thinking on her part, projecting her feelings onto him. "So, what happened?" she asked.

"I think there must have been some kind of group effort to keep us away from each other. Who knows? All I know is that someone always seemed to get in my way at the critical moment."

"That was probably just Grey being Grey. He was pretty possessive. Territorial, even."

Mack sighed, and his laugh this time was edged with something dark. "Who could blame him? Anyway, it was for the best. You looked like you had your hands full—you didn't need me stirring the pot."

"It's all right. You managed to get in a few good compliments, at least."

"You too. Fat lot of good it did us, though."

The light changed, opening up and growing brighter. With a start, Mina realized that they had rounded the tail end of a cluster of tiny islands and were already cutting through the open water of the bay, back toward the Blys' dock.

They fell silent, each weighing the twelve long years of unspoken thoughts between them. Mina wished it could be easy, falling into an affair with a gorgeous man who had always made an effort over the years to let her know he thought highly of her. But she hadn't ever stopped to consider that the interval had taken a toll on Mack, as well as her. She was going to have to be very, very careful if she went ahead with this.

MACK MANEUVERED THE boat skillfully next to the dock, then jumped off to tie it up. He handed Mina onto the rough wood planks and held onto her arm to make sure she was steady on her feet.

"We should probably think about what we want for dinner," he said. "I didn't get a ton of stuff at the store yesterday. What do you feel like doing?"

Mina was happy for the change in topic. "Why don't I cook something? Tell me what you love to eat. Something you haven't had in a while."

They made their way across the lawn toward the back of the house. "You don't have to do that. I can just pick up some steaks to grill or something."

"I really don't mind. I love to cook," Mina told him.

"In that case…" Mack considered her offer. "What about homemade pizza? My grandma used to make the thick Sicilian kind—in the deep pan, you know? Her kitchen smelled amazing all day from the rising dough."

"I can do that. No problem. I think I even saw some yeast in the pantry yesterday." Mina tried to hold herself together, but each new detail she learned about Mack felt like a decadent truffle melting in her mouth. "Was she Italian?"

"Very. Came here in her twenties and married my grandfather a year later. This will be so cool—I haven't had her pizza since she died a few years back. I'll run to the store after lunch and get what we need."

"I hope I don't screw it up," Mina worried.

"Nah. I'll show you what to do. You'll do great."

They headed into kitchen to get their picnic lunch together, since they'd been on the boat for so long. Mack had mostly purchased happy-hour snacks and breakfast food at the store the day before, but as Mina perused the contents of the fridge, she found cold cuts and olives for an antipasto. She sliced tomatoes from the garden and gathered the sun tea she'd brewed on the patio while they were out. Mack found a large basket in the mudroom to pack everything in, then carried it outside. There was some shade under a stand of trees at the side of the lawn, so Mina spread the blanket for them there.

The birds sang quietly in the branches. The leaves were beginning to turn yellow and orange but hadn't started falling yet. A few cicadas still buzzed that late in the season, and the water of the bay lapped softly at the seawall. It was serene and pretty.

Mina picked at her food and made awkward small talk—and tried not to notice the way Mack was watching her. If she wasn't careful, she'd end up repeating her antics from the night before all over again. In his current mood, he was difficult to resist, though.

He apparently thought the same about her. After a while, Mack reached forward, took her glass of tea, and set it aside. He braced himself on one hand, trailed his other up her arm, then wrapped his fingers around the nape of her neck.

"Mina," he murmured. "Let me kiss you again."

She closed her eyes, swayed forward, and then his mouth was on hers. Why had she bothered resisting? He tasted insanely good—salty and sweet and one hundred percent Mack.

His tongue dove deep, and his fingers threaded into her hair, holding Mina in place. She couldn't catch her breath, and she didn't care. The man kissed like some kind of sex-starved pirate back from a long sea voyage—like Mina was the only thing in the world that could satisfy him.

Mack pushed forward, and she found herself flat on her back with his large body covering her. His thigh pressed between her legs, his erection firm against her hip—Mina raked her fingernails up and down his back and thrilled at the way it made him groan into her mouth. He broke away to kiss a line across her jaw, to nip at her earlobe, to lick her neck. When she gasped at the contact, she was rewarded by him chuckling darkly in her ear.

"What are you *doing* to me?" Mack breathed.

"Me?" Her breath caught in her throat when he licked her again. "Which one of us is pinned to the ground here?"

He reared up on his forearms. "Tell me to stop. I will if you say so."

Mina scowled, "Don't you dare."

Mack laughed and shifted his pelvis against her, and her eyes nearly rolled back into her skull. "Well, then," he murmured. "Let's see what else I can do."

He kissed her senseless for a while more, until Mina made the mistake of trying to pull his shirt up and over his head. He grabbed for her hands—to help her or stymie her, wasn't clear. Either way, they ended up clipping the jar of iced tea, which washed across the blanket and soaked their sides in a freezing, sticky rush.

"Ahhh!" Mack howled, rolling away.

Mina sat up giggling and scooted sideways to get away from the wetness.

"You did that on purpose," he accused, getting to his feet and trying to wring out the side of his shirt.

"No, I didn't!" she protested. She took Mack's hand and let him help her to her feet. "I didn't even remember it was there!"

He nudged the empty tea jar with his foot and looked dubious.

Mina checked her watch. "Besides, we probably have to go in anyway. If we don't get the dough going, we'll be ordering pizza instead of making it."

"The idea has its merits," Mack grumbled.

"No, it doesn't. Come on. Help me clean all this up, and we'll get started."

INSIDE THE HOUSE, he trotted up the stairs to change his clothes, while Mina inspected herself in the bathroom. Mack's body had shielded her from the worst of the spill, but not all of it. After a quick internal debate, she decided to shuck her shorts and leave on her bathing suit and coverup. It seemed pointless to change when she was just going to get in the pool anyway, and her shorts had borne the brunt of the tea deluge.

When Mack returned, his eyebrows climbed up his forehead at the sight of her, but he didn't comment on what she was—or wasn't—wearing. All he did was instruct Mina how to make the pizza dough and steal peeks at her ass when he thought she wasn't looking. They got the yeast and the flour mixed that way but watching her knead the dough seemed to break Mack's resolve.

With pained groan, he came up behind her and caged Mina against the counter. "Why is that so damn sexy?" he murmured hotly against her ear. "I can't keep my hands off you."

Mack kissed a trail down Mina's neck while his hand slipped under the hem of her coverup, skittered up her back, and slowly pulled loose the bow of her bikini top. Mina clutched her top against her chest with her forearms and tried to keep her doughy hands off herself.

"*Mack*," she breathed, stunned and aroused all at once. So much for thinking she'd proceed carefully.

"Mmm," was his only response. His blazing hands crept around her ribcage toward her breasts. He sucked her earlobe hard into his mouth.

On the end of the island, his cell rang loudly, startling them both. Mack looked gloomy as he released Mina and went to see who it was.

"It's work," he grouched. "I'm sorry. I have to take this."

He scowled so hard Mina thought he might punch something. Mack readjusted himself in his shorts as he stepped outside and spoke brusquely to whoever was on the line.

She knew there was no saving the mood, though. She cleaned off her hands, then slipped into the guest bathroom to re-tie her top and pull herself back together. When she returned, Mack was still on the phone, but obviously distracted.

His eyes kept drifting back to Mina, following her around the kitchen and roving over her body. Her heart was pounding in her chest. Despite all her good intentions, Mack was going to be the death of her.

Mina finished up in the kitchen right as he finished his call. He dampened a dish towel and draped it over the bowl of dough for her, then set it inside the oven to rise.

"I'm sorry about that," he said again, turning to her. "It's just one interruption after another today, isn't it?" Mack slid his hands around Mina's waist and pulled her against him.

"It is," she agreed. "I'm beginning to think your conspiracy theory has some merit."

He frowned. "Why? What have you heard?" Mack looked around dramatically. "Do you think we need to take evasive action?"

Mina smacked him in the chest. "Stop it."

He laughed, "Why don't I head out to the market while you sit by the pool?" Mack paused to plant a hard kiss on her mouth. "When I get back I can help you make the sauce and stuff."

"Sounds like a plan," Mina agreed. When this weekend was over, it was going to be very hard to give him up, but she would have to. For her sake, as well as Mack's.

Chapter Four

WHEN MACK RETURNED, Mina was asleep on one of the large teak chaise lounges by the pool. The Blys had clearly spared no expense on the things. Each one had plush red and orange-striped cushions, and a few were shaded by a big, red canvas umbrella. If Mack didn't know for sure that he lived fifteen minutes away, he'd have thought he'd wandered into a luxurious resort somewhere.

The sunbathing beauty in the tiny black bikini merely added to the effect. When he stood over Mina, his shadow fell across her face while his eyes skimmed her curves. Sweat shined temptingly in the creases where her thighs met her hips, and along the insides of her elbows. The furrow between Mina's breasts glistened, as did the dip of her navel. Mack was positive he'd never wanted to lick someone so much in his entire life.

"Mina," he called softly.

She woke slowly. When she turned her head to smile sleepily up at him, Mack knew for sure he was a goner. His chest constricted at the thought. No way was he getting out of this weekend in one piece, not unless Mina magically fell head over heels for him, too. If she was going to, Mack hoped she'd do it fast.

"It's hot out here, kid," he told her. "You're going to singe yourself if you lay there baking much longer."

"Oh really?" she shaded her eyes with her hand, and Mack tried not to stare at what that did to her beautiful breasts. "What else do you suggest?" she inquired.

Mack stripped off his ball cap and sneakers, then his old t-shirt and gym shorts. In two steps, he reached the deep end of the pool and dove into the sparkling turquoise water in his briefs. The shocking cold took his breath away—the pool was definitely not heated, and the sunny day hadn't done much to warm the water after the cool nights they'd been having.

Before he could warn her, Mina was laughing and jumping in feet first, too. She came up gasping and sputtering.

"Oh my God!" she shrieked. "I hate you!"

Mack hadn't prepared himself for sight of Mina shivering in a wet bikini. She splashed toward the stairs at the shallow end and darted for her towel, droplets of water sparkling like diamonds on her skin. The rear view was nearly as beguiling as the front had been.

It seemed to defy natural law that Mack was that hard in such cold water. If he got out of the pool right then, there would be no hiding his arousal, either. They still had half the afternoon and dinner to get through, though—and Mack didn't want to put Mina off. So, he dipped under that icy water and pushed off from the wall, forcing himself through as many laps as he could manage before he finally had to call it quits.

By then, Mina would've had to be a succubus to get a rise out of him. Still engulfed in her huge towel, she padded over to the ladder, then stood waiting to hand him a towel, too.

"Thanks," Mack told her, wrapping the terrycloth tight around his crotch, just in case. "The breeze didn't seem so bad before I got in there. It's flipping freezing now."

Mina's eyes flickered over his torso, but she quickly blinked away her interest. "No kidding," she said. "I'm going to head in and try to thaw out in the shower."

Mack had just gotten himself decent. He would *not* think any thoughts whatsoever about Mina in a shower. None. Whatsoever.

"Smart idea," he said. "I'll be in soon. Save me some hot water, would you?"

WATCHING MINA COOK him dinner turned out to be nearly as provocative as watching her knead dough. He'd tried to pitch in to keep his mind off it, but she insisted that Mack simply sit at the counter and keep her company. He had nothing to do *but* watch her, really. How could a man have a woman like that in his life, in his *home*, and not hang on for dear life? Not for the first time, Mack wondered what the hell Grey had been thinking.

When Mina reached to pull the pizza out of the oven, her pot holder slipped.

She hissed, "Ow, ow, ow," before dropping the pan heavily back on the rack.

Mack was up and off his stool before he'd thought twice about it. "You okay?"

"I burned my finger on the side of pan," she said, wincing. She turned on the tap and stuck her finger under the cold water.

After a couple minutes, Mack took her hand, so he could examine the burn. It was already red and swelling into a nasty blister, but Mina would be okay. He brought her finger to his lips and kissed it, but then, unable to resist, he sucked the finger next to it hard into his mouth and grazed it with his tongue. Mina's brown eyes went wide, then dark with desire. Mack released her hand and pulled her mouth up to his for a kiss that rapidly turned volcanic.

She pushed him away with two hands on his chest. "Wait! If we don't take it out, the pizza will burn!"

Mina looked as if she might try to grab it again herself, so Mack shouldered her aside. He pulled the large pan out of the oven, then set it carefully on the stovetop to rest before they cut into it. He inhaled the fragrant steam hungrily—it smelled exactly like his grandmother's.

"I'm going to run upstairs and put something on my finger," she told him.

"If you don't find anything in your medicine cabinet," he told her, "Look in mine. I'm sure I saw bandages and ointment in there."

While she was gone, Mack went out on the back patio to set the small table there. He found little jars in the pantry with votive candles in them, so he added a few of those and lit them with the long matches he found next to the fireplace. He poured wine, tossed the salad, and carried it all outside. The crickets were singing their hearts out, and the moon was just starting its ascent over the water.

When she came out to join him, Mina had donned a little blue sweater over her tank top and swingy knee-length skirt. She looked demure and feminine, and oh so lovely.

And her dinner was delicious—for her first try, it was incredibly close to something his grandma might've made. Mack didn't stint on telling her so.

When they were stuffed to the gills, they took their wine out to the Adirondack chairs on the lawn, to look at the stars. Mack didn't ever want the night to end, but eventually Mina sighed and shivered a little.

"Getting cold?" he asked.

"Yes, but I hate to go inside."

"That's all right. It'll still be here tomorrow for us to enjoy."

"I suppose so." She sounded pensive, though.

Back inside, Mack washed the dinner dishes while Mina sat on the counter, swinging her bare feet back and forth as she sipped her wine. Once he finished, Mack came to stand in front of her. Leaning his hands on the counter on either side of her, he dropped his head to rest his forehead against hers and noticed an angry red streak on one knee.

"What's this?" he asked, running his thumb lightly over it.

Mina gave him an embarrassed little laugh. "I think I got a splinter," she said.

He couldn't imagine why that would be funny. "How'd you get one there?"

Her cheeks turned pink. "From the..." Mina paused and cleared her throat. "...the chair."

Mack frowned and tilted his head, perplexed.

She waved toward the kitchen window. "Outside. Last night."

Comprehension dawned. Outside, last night, while she'd been straddling him. While he'd had his tongue tangled with hers and was pushing his raging hard-on against her body for all he was worth. Mack's jaw locked tight with the sudden, grinding need that swept through him at the memory.

He lifted Mina off the counter and stood her up, then knelt on the floor in front of her. Resting his hands on her ankles, he lightly kissed that knee, then leaned closer to suck on it. Mina made a small sound, and her hands dropped to his head to hold him in place. Mack glanced up at her.

He'd gotten carried away again, but it was hard to care too much. Half of him worried over her well-being—but the other, greedier half was tortured by how delectable every inch of Mina's skin promised to be. Mack leaned forward tentatively and pressed another light kiss higher on the inside of her thigh, right under the hem of her skirt. Mina exhaled on a sigh, flexing her fingers into his hair.

"I want to taste you," he admitted against her leg.

Her answer was soft, but he heard it loud and clear. "*Yes*," she breathed above him. "You should definitely do that."

Mack gathered her skirt and pushed it up over her hips. Mina didn't protest, she just held the skirt for him and leaned back against the counter. He brushed his lips across her panties and was rewarded with her quick inhale. That thin strip of cotton was already hot and damp, but Mack made it wetter. He pressed his tongue against her until Mina was moaning and her thighs were quivering, and then he yanked her panties down her legs and tossed them aside.

Mack dragged his tongue through her folds and groaned at the way she melted for him. He slid one finger deep, then added a second when Mina's knees buckled.

"God, Mina," he murmured against her. "What you do to me." He gripped her thigh and wedged his shoulder under it to help keep her upright. Mack nipped the inviting flesh of her inner thigh, where it was pressed against his cheek, then turned and proceeded to bring Mina up and over the precipice.

When she stopped shaking and the fingers in his hair changed from pulling to stroking, Mack let her go. Mina looked like she'd be okay with sprawling across the kitchen floor for the night, but he had far better ideas. He stood, hooked one arm behind her back and the other under her knees to lift her against his chest, then made for the stairs.

As it turned out, Mina wasn't terribly interested in his ideas. He'd barely set her on her feet in his room before she was desperately peeling his clothes off him. Mack had her out of her own outfit and laid across the bed in moments. Braced on his forearms, he tried to slow her down with some more kissing, but the woman was on a mission, and wasn't going to be denied.

"Please, Mack," she begged, wrapping her long legs around his hips. Mina was so sexy, like a live wire beneath his hands. He didn't know how he was going to last more than a couple minutes, at most.

"Wait," he urged, "Mina, wait." He tried to pull away. Things were escalating fast.

"What? No…" She held tight to him. "Don't go."

"Condoms are in the bathroom, honey. Wait here. I'll be right back, I promise."

Mack levered himself off the bed to go get what they needed, then grabbed a few extras from his toiletry bag just in case. He took his time, sucking in several calming breaths and letting his heart settle down.

When he returned, the cable box cast a dim blue light across his room, and in the bed, Mina reached for him like a sea siren. Mack tossed the condoms on the night stand, ripped open one of the packets, then knelt on the edge of the mattress to roll it on.

Mina pulled him close. The sensation of her stretched out beneath him, skin to skin, was almost too much to bear. He breathed in her addictive, bewitching scent, and placed a careful line of kisses along her collar bone. Her busy hands grazed over his chest and back and ass, then reached between them to wrap around his cock.

Mack froze, every last brain cell he possessed shorting out so his body could focus on that one point of contact. Mina guided him to her entrance, then urged him inside. He supposed he didn't have to worry about a repeat of the night before any longer.

Mack tried to go slow. He did. He was a big guy, and he didn't want to hurt her. So, he pushed a couple inches into Mina, pulled out, then slowly thrust back in a little bit farther. She made a noise of frustration and clutched at him. On his third push, Mina pulled her knees up, locked her ankles against his spine, and forced Mack tight against her. His eyes rolled back in his head at the sudden, engulfing bliss.

Seated deep in her glorious, scorching heat, he groaned when she started writhing around, trying to get him to move faster. Mina's palms skittered across his shoulders, then gripped his neck a little too tightly while she tried to devour him with her mouth. Mack grappled for her hands, laced his fingers between hers, and pinned her arms to the bed.

"Settle down, you," he ordered. "I'll give you what you want, I just need a need a minute, okay?"

Mina moaned, "Mack, I don't have a minute. *Please.*"

He ravished her mouth with his own and started up a relentless rhythm. In minutes, Mina was sobbing out each breath, and then—quick as lightning—her body was pulsing around him. Her climax went on and on, clasping him tight and kicking off his own quaking release.

Mack buried his face in Mina's neck and hung on for dear life. Now that she'd gotten what she wanted, the little minx laughed and nipped him on the shoulder. It was hard to believe she was the same person who'd fled crying only twenty-four hours earlier.

"Dear God, woman. You're going to be the death of me," he mumbled into her hair.

"But what a way to go, right?" Mack could feel Mina's smile against his neck.

He loosened his grip on her hands, but he couldn't quite force himself to roll away just yet. His legs and hips seemed to be locked in place.

Mina wasn't in any hurry to get rid of him, either. She'd wriggled a little lower and was feathering her tongue across his nipple. An electric jolt shuddered through him.

"Mercy," he pleaded.

Mina pushed against his chest, so Mack rolled onto his back. It was fair to say he was completely gob-smacked by his miraculous good fortune. Mina, in his bed, wanting more. Who would have thought?

"Mercy? Mercy's no fun," she claimed. Then she proceeded to show him what *was*.

WHEN MACK WOKE late the next morning, he was disappointed to find himself alone in the bed. The sheets on Mina's side were cold, and his room was empty.

They'd made love again and again the night before—hungry, uninhibited, insatiable. Twelve years of yearning, it seemed, could counteract any amount of fatigue. Inconceivably, Mack was still half hard when he staggered into the bathroom.

After a hasty shower, he searched the house and backyard for Mina, with no luck. She'd made coffee, but no breakfast. There were no damp towels next to the pool and no mugs out by the Adirondacks. It wasn't until Mack climbed onto the bright green

4x4 and made his worried way across the side acreage that he found her.

Mina was walking determinedly down the dirt path leading into the woods, her earbuds in her ears and shiny brown ponytail swinging back and forth. He drove up behind her carefully—she clearly hadn't heard him yet, and he didn't want to scare her. Still, since she'd slipped out without a word that morning…he had to be sure she was okay.

"Mina?" he called.

She jumped, then spun around—and stumbled a bit at the sight of him riding high on the utility vehicle.

"Hey," she said. All signs of warmth from the night before were gone. Maybe Mina had needed a bit of space, just like that first night. Mack had been so anxious to find her that he hadn't considered the possibility. He wondered if he'd made a huge mistake in following her.

"You forgot your vest," he told her, wishing he didn't sound so much like a chiding schoolteacher. "Remember?"

They'd talked about the bird-hunters yesterday, about how they sometimes drifted onto the Bly property from neighboring spreads. Just to be safe, Mack had asked Mina to wear an orange vest if she went in the woods—and Mina had promised she would.

But she'd forgotten, and it spoke to her current state of mind. Mack winced—his fault, probably.

"Sorry," Mina muttered contritely, shrugging it on over her t-shirt. "I guess I forgot." She started off again with a little wave.

"Hey," he called.

Mina halted and turned back.

"Are you okay?"

"Fine," she said. "I just thought I'd work off some of that pizza. Let's have breakfast when I get back, okay?"

Every instinct Mack had screamed out that Mina was anything but *fine*, but what was he supposed to do? Call her a liar?

"Sure," he told her retreating back.

He watched her stride away from him for a minute or two, her shiny black running tights and neon sneakers incongruous amidst all the tangled brown vegetation. What on earth had happened between the time they'd fallen asleep with their lips still touching, and now? For yet another time that weekend, Mack felt really worried. His heart was in a world of danger from that woman— *again*. He wasn't sure if he could take it a second time.

He turned the 4x4 off the small path and headed for the wider perpendicular track, snaking through the grass parallel to the edge of the woods. The two brown stripes had been packed hard by the vehicle's heavy tires, and marked the trail between the storage barn and the tiny beach where the Blys kept their kayaks and canoes.

If Mina came back to the house in a better frame of mind, Mack thought he could take her out on the water again, this time on one of the smaller boats.

She was headed home later. Before she did, he wanted Mina to look at him with happiness once more. Perhaps it would make it easier to say goodbye when the time came.

Somehow, all those years ago, Mack had blown his first shot with Mina. She'd been so young, and so had he. She'd chosen another guy over him and left Mack without a backward glance— though to be fair, Mina might not have even realized Mack was a viable choice. She'd refused to discuss what she was doing, so he couldn't be sure precisely *what* she'd known. For a long time that part had stung more than almost anything else.

But Mack was a different man now than the boy he'd been. Mina had changed too, grown and settled down. Life had undone the choices they'd made and handed them a new opportunity.

Mack couldn't stand it if he screwed up this chance. But maybe the greater concern was—would Mina? Could he trust her with his heart one more time?

Chapter Five

Twelve Years Earlier

MINA MET GREY Whitney was she was only nineteen years old. She'd been waitressing at a diner in town and sneaking into bars with her fake ID at night.

She'd had to be careful about that last part, though. Occasionally, she'd spot her mom in some dive or another and have to slip out the back, so she didn't get busted—or worse, actually have to trawl the bar *with* Elaine.

On the night she met Grey, Mina was *supposed* to be home taking care of Molly, but her kid sister was already fifteen and plenty independent. Molly didn't need Mina to take care of her, even though she liked the company. Besides, with the way Mina and her mother had been butting heads lately, Molly totally understood Mina's need to get away sometimes.

Their dad had taken off two years earlier, back when they were still living in Mystic. Now that they'd landed in Annapolis—yet another new town to adjust to—Mina had had it up to *there* with the shenanigans of the adults around her. She was young, and she wanted to live her own life. She wanted to make her own decisions.

Mina thought Grey Whitney had to be the hottest guy she'd ever laid eyes on. The young Marine was brash and funny and seemed to know so much about life, about the world, about *everything*. Grey knew what he wanted and wasn't shy about asking for it—and from the moment he walked up to her in that crowded bar, he wanted Mina.

They made out on the dance floor all that first night. On the second night, Mina snuck out to get busy with him in the back of his car, on the side of some dark road in the middle of nowhere. Grey went back to his base a few days later, but texted and called her whenever he could.

By the time he returned several weeks later, Mina thought she'd learned all there was to know about the young Marine. He liked to call the shots, for one thing. Mina didn't mind—it was nice to have someone want to take care of her for a change. Until she met Grey, she hadn't quite realized what a burden she'd been carrying since her dad had flown the coop—half the time her disconsolate mom and kid sister acted like *Mina* was the parent, instead of Elaine or Skip.

She would've made a bigger fuss—tried to get some help from someone—if she weren't so worried that Molly would get taken away from Elaine and tossed into foster care. Grey fed the fire, calling the situation appalling.

He said Mina ought to be thinking about college, not waiting tables to help feed her family. Elaine's unabashed husband-hunting was an embarrassment, he claimed, when she ought to be home with her daughters instead. Grey thought Mina deserved so much better, and Mina longed to believe him with all her naïve heart.

That particular night, Mina and her mother returned home from the bars within moments of one another, both drunk and angry. They fought something fierce, woke up Molly, and said awful, irrevocable things to each other. Mina rushed into the bedroom she shared with her sister, dug an old backpack out of the closet, then threw in all the clothes she could fit. It was time to leave. It was *more* than time.

Mina told Molly she'd see her soon. She hated to abandon her sister to pick up the pieces alone, but this time Mina was truly irate. Beyond the pale. She thought she was likely to do more harm than good by staying—the way she was feeling, Mina worried that the argument with her mother might turn violent before long. But even that was okay, because for the first time in her life, Mina had someplace better she could go.

She threw off Elaine's clutching hands and took off. Hiking down the dark road, Mina called Grey and asked if she could stop by his apartment. She knew it would seem like an odd request after only leaving him an hour before, but she promised she'd explain once she got there.

Grey didn't seem fazed. He simply gave her the address and asked if she needed a ride. Mina needed to burn off some steam, though, so she would be calm and thinking clearly once she saw him. She walked the six miles using the navigation app on her phone, and it took her nearly two hours to get there.

Grey met her on the stone steps of a big old building. Mina pretended not to feel utterly defeated. She explained in a rush that there'd been a dustup at her house, glossing over the more sordid particulars.

She couldn't go back home, she said. Mina knew it was late, but could she possibly crash on his couch just for one night? In the morning, she would call around and find a friend she could stay with.

She said all that knowing Grey, knowing he'd never turn down the chance to have Mina in his bed for an entire night. Up until then, they'd only been able to steal moments alone in his car, and it was driving Grey out of his mind. Mina hugged him close on that staircase, let her body melt against his, and silently begged him not to turn her away.

He let her stay, of course. They walked up the steps and through the apartment building's doorway. The floor in the lobby was an old, scuffed marble, a faded reminder of the building's former elegance. The banisters were solid wood—thick, curving things that looked like they could support more than one shaking teenager. Once, this had probably been an opulent place to stay. Now the carpets were worn, and the surfaces were scratched and faded. It was the kind of shabby place Mina probably belonged.

There was no problem, none at all, with her staying, Grey told her. There was just one tiny *thing*…

"What thing?" Mina asked.

"Well," Grey swung the apartment door wide. "*This*." She stepped into the mostly-empty apartment and looked around. There was one crappy futon in the center of the room, piles of books against the wall, and a lamp plugged into an outlet. Nothing else. Nothing.

Mina turned to Grey with wide eyes. "What happened?" she breathed in horror.

She and her mom and sister didn't have much, but this was something else entirely. She spun to take in the utter lack of any furniture, any creature comfort, *anything*. There were pale rectangles on all the walls, marking the former positions of posters and frames. The windows were bare, without shades or blinds of any kind. Outside, the night was dark, but the lights from the streetlamps intruded harshly into the rooms.

Mina moved further into the place to peer in the open bedroom doors. One had only a camo sleeping bag and a military rucksack on the bare floor, likely Grey's. The other contained a messy tangle of sheets and blankets, and neater piles of clothes stacked around the perimeter. Mina had the sudden, sinking suspicion that she might have jumped from the frying pan into the fire.

"This is my friend's place," Grey rushed to explain. "He finally convinced his mom to let him move off campus, but he thought he was renting a furnished apartment. There was a mix-up, I guess."

Mina snorted. "I'll say."

Grey told her the friend studied engineering at the community college and had been too busy to put anything else together yet. The landlord had felt sorry for him and lent him the futon and the lamp.

"Mack lets me crash here when I get leave," Grey continued. "So I don't have to deal with my folks looking over my shoulder. He totally won't care if you stay, too."

Mina wondered if Mack would say the same, but it was only for the night. In the heat of the moment and her rush to get away from Elaine, it had never once occurred to her that Grey lived on a military base and wouldn't also maintain his own apartment in town. It was a foolish and reckless oversight, but tomorrow she could figure out something more permanent.

Grey grabbed his wallet and keys from the kitchen counter and insisted on taking Mina back to her mom's house to pick up the rest of her stuff. He'd take care of her, he said—Mina wouldn't have to worry about anything anymore. He'd look out for his woman. She *was* his woman, wasn't she? Mina had better not be using him or jerking him around.

She knew by now that Grey could be impulsive. They both could. But this—this felt like a real opportunity. The idea of never having to see either of her parents again felt like Mina could *breathe*. At last.

So, she and Grey tiptoed into her mom's apartment and gathered Mina's few remaining possessions. Some things she left for Molly, as a peace offering. The rest, Mina spirited away in the dead of night—right past Elaine, who was passed out on the couch. Her wine glass lay on its side on the carpet next to her. Mina was stone-cold sober, by then.

She didn't meet Grey's friend that night, but she heard him come home. At that point, she and Grey were already tucked into the spare room he was using, *celebrating* her freedom. For the first time—of what would turn out to be many—Mina discovered how good she was at pretending with Grey. Pretending that she was hot for him and overjoyed to be in his arms, and not physically and emotionally spent. Acting like she wasn't freaking out that she'd just run away from home, leaving her little sister to deal with Elaine alone—and all for a completely unpredictable future.

The next morning, Mina was restless and up at dawn. Drawn by the aroma of coffee, she wandered into the kitchen to introduce herself while Grey slept in. She discovered that Mack was oddly calming and easy to talk to, so Mina didn't try to pull one over on him. She simply…explained.

He was grave and reserved, but she trusted him instantly. He had none of Grey's flash or charm, but Mack was clearly a rock-solid guy. He assured Mina she could stay for a few days, no sweat, until she got her feet under her. As long as she kept things on the up and up and didn't bring anything illegal into the place, they'd be fine. Mina had to agree to be quiet when he was studying, but otherwise Mack was cool.

The next couple days were giddy. Grey slept half the day while Mina was at work, then took her out on the town at night. They made drunken love on his sleeping bag until she couldn't stay awake any longer. She told herself that what she was doing was completely different than what her mother and father had done in their youth, and she almost believed it.

The longer Mina stayed away, the more impossible it seemed that she could ever go back. Other than calling her sister once or twice to let Molly know she was okay, she tried not to think about her family at all. Grey liked that—he only wanted her to focus on their future together.

When Grey finally had to return to base again, Mina assured him she'd be fine. She couldn't join him there without them being married, so it made sense for her to stay put in Annapolis. She'd find somewhere to crash, save some money, and together they could plan what they'd do next. Grey hinted that he was going to be making some big changes soon but didn't give her any details.

After he was gone, Mack sat Mina down on the futon and made her an offer.

"Why don't you stay here," he suggested. "You can pay a little rent, help with food and utilities and cleaning. It seems pointless to turn you out when I was going to find another roommate anyway."

"I don't know what to say," Mina admitted. She'd had zero luck finding anywhere else to live so far, but how would Grey feel, knowing that she was here with his buddy? "Can I think about it?"

"Sure," Mack agreed. "Could you let me know by the end of the week, though? There's a guy in one of my classes that's looking for a place, too. I thought I'd offer him the room, but only if you don't want it."

Mina called Grey that night to see what he thought. "Good idea," he said. "Mack's probably the one guy on earth who wouldn't try to steal you."

BIT BY BIT, Mack acquired more stuff: a hand-me-down couch and chair and a rickety table for eating and studying. He got a big king-size bed for himself, that he mostly slept in alone.

He even found a mattress for Mina, which she discovered on the floor of her room one day after she'd worked a double-shift. Mack refused to accept a dime for it—likely knowing she wouldn't eat that week if he did. Her own boyfriend hadn't even thought of that, so in return Mina neglected to mention the gesture to Grey.

Grey called and texted every day, but otherwise Mina didn't see much of him. Mack may have always been studying, but at least he was *around*. Once in a while, he came home late and a little buzzed. Even more rarely, he stayed out all night, and returned the next day smelling like another woman's shampoo. Often, though, Mack sat with Mina on the couch, eating a dinner they'd cooked together and watching movies. It was nice.

Gradually, she made friends with Mack, and pointedly ignored how handsome he was, how level-headed and reliable. He was like a brother to her—someone whose good qualities she could appreciate, without feeling the need to indulge herself.

Mina was high on her sudden, unexpected autonomy, drunk on the pretty picture Grey painted in her head every night of their future…drunk *period* half the time. Mina didn't want someone steady, now that she was finally free. She wanted to *live*. Mack understood. He *always* understood—he was so good that way.

Chapter Six

Twelve Years Earlier

MACK LEFT THE redhead at the bar, even though he was pretty sure she'd been angling for him to take her home. He couldn't, though—not when he knew Mina would be there. Maybe listening in, maybe judging him or coming up with a crack about the girl to tease Mack with the next day.

She did that sometimes—specifically came out to meet a woman he'd brought over, just so she could needle him about it later. Mack didn't think Mina was trying to be cruel, but he guessed she had no idea how much it hurt. He'd never bother with anyone else if she would only give him a shot. If she would only look at him the way he knew he must look at her. Mina was oblivious, though, and usually that was for the best.

Not today. Mack had finally been accepted to the four-year engineering program down in Norfolk, and he'd learned that he could transfer that fall. He'd saved his mom a ton of money by doing his first two years at the community college, but now he was excited to start taking all the ocean and coastal classes he'd only read about up till then.

If all went according to plan, Mack would move back to the Eastern Shore after graduation, open his own firm, and actually be able to help out his mother and siblings for once—not to mention the community in his hometown.

He was both happy and terrified to tell Mina about it. He'd stopped by the bar on his way home hoping to tip the scale more toward happy, but it didn't work. And now…now Mack had to figure out if Mina would consider coming with him.

She'd given him no sign that they were some hot-and-heavy item, other than the fact that she was happy as a clam shacking up with him day after day. Mina didn't appear to miss Grey all that much, but she sure had a way of wanting to know where Mack had been if he stayed out too late. He couldn't be sure how obvious his feelings about her were, but as perceptive as Mina was, he had to assume she at least suspected.

So. All he had to do was tell Mina his plan. Move to Norfolk. Find another apartment. Stick together and see what happened. If the conversation went especially well, Mack planned to suggest that Mina apply to the university herself.

As far as he could tell, she'd been out of school at least a year, and he had no idea what her grades had been like. But, Mina was smart as a whip, meticulous, and industrious. No way should she be skipping college to trail around after a dickhead like Grey Whitney. It was a total waste of her potential. She had never said a thing about it, but she *had* to know that.

When Mack let himself into the apartment, the light over the stove was on, but that was all. It was dark and hot, and only the faintest breeze rattled the blinds on the window over the kitchen sink. Mack sighed. He'd hoped the A/C would be fixed by now— the landlord had sworn it would be.

Mina's door was open and quiet music drifted from within. Mack dropped his keys on the crate they used as a coffee table and wandered over. She was lying on top of her sheets in the same tank top and thin cotton pajama bottoms she'd worn the night before, and Mack couldn't tell if she was asleep or not. Sounds from the street outside mixed with the persistent thick buzz of the cicadas—the sound so tightly braided in his soul with the hot and humid Maryland summers that Mack would probably feel the absence of those bugs like a missing limb.

Over all that filtered Mina's music, her stereo churning out fifty-year-old blues like sticky molasses. The entire scene was far more tempting than anything that redhead—Serena?—had been throwing at him in the bar.

"You're home earlier than I expected," Mina said suddenly from the bed.

Mack shrugged, though he doubted she could see it. "And you didn't go out at all?"

"Nah. It's too hot. I'm trying not to move, but I'm not sure it's helping."

"Want me to grab the fan from my room for you?" Sometimes it bothered Mina when he tried to do stuff for her. He'd learned not to try too often, but occasionally he couldn't seem to help himself.

"No, Mack." She sounded irritated that he'd offered. "You keep it."

Whoever was singing had to have been delivered to their apartment straight from the depths of hell. Howling Wolf or Muddy Waters—or whoever it was—sang like sin itself. Mack was harder than he thought he'd ever been in his life. After weeks of Mina tripping around the place in her cutoff shorts and tank tops, that was really saying something.

He leaned against the door jamb, disgruntled with himself—with his own weakness. Mina was not yet his to lust after, but sometimes that fact was damnably hard to remember.

"God, what the hell is up with your music?" he muttered. He ought to go to his room, but it felt like he was stuck there, caught in her web.

"Shut up." From her tone, she obviously thought he was being sarcastic. "If you don't like it, I'll put some headphones on."

"No, don't." What came out of his mouth next surprised even Mack. "Dance with me." The command was unmistakable, and Mina would probably balk instantly. But ever since he'd started teaching her some basic self-defense—after a knucklehead at the diner got a little rough with her—all Mack could think about was touching her.

"What?" Mina sat up and Mack could see her eyes, the faint shine where the light from the kitchen hit them. He couldn't see her expression—it was too dark for that. But, the streetlight on the road outside her window backlit her torso enough that he could make out the shape of her shoulders and the sides of her breasts.

He stepped all the way into her room and pulled her up by the hand. "Seriously. Just—dance with me."

Mina didn't say a word as she stood, only sagged against the front of him when they started swaying slowly to the music. Her body felt electric, hot and alive through the thin material of his t-shirt. Her bare feet brushed against his, an oddly erotic sensation in its own right. Mack was glad, at least, for the heavy material of his cargo shorts—maybe it would shield Mina from his aroused state a bit.

She sighed and laid her head against his pec, melting into his arms. The weight of her skull resting there made Mack aware of each rise and fall of his chest—each breath he took, while he fought to keep from laying her down on that bed. He wondered if Mina could hear how his heart thundered. He wondered if she found it funny. Mack's hand drifted up her slender back and pulled the elastic loose from her ponytail. He allowed himself one stroke of the satiny strands before he forced his palm back down to the arch at her lower back.

The temperature in the room seemed to be climbing. Mack felt like heat was pouring off him in waves, scorching her. A fine sheen of sweat gathered in the bend of his elbows and in between their palms, where his hand held Mina's. They shuffled back and forth in the dark like they were at a junior-high cotillion, but she didn't complain or try to pull away.

Naturally, she was the one brave enough to break the spell. "It's so hot," she said.

"Sticky, too," Mack agreed. His tongue felt thick in his mouth. Probably unrelated.

"You should take off your shirt," Mina suggested sleepily.

"What?" He was startled from his lazy reverie and went a bit tense. She felt it.

"Please?" she asked. "I'm not trying to be weird. I just thought it would feel nice."

"Mina—"

"It's okay," she rushed to say. "You don't have to."

But Mack was already stepping away from her, pulling the t-shirt over his head and dropping it behind her onto the mattress. He doubted if he'd be able to deny Mina anything when she was like this. Or ever, really.

Mack reached for her and pulled her into his arms again. She rubbed her cheek against his skin like a damn cat, and her soft fingers travelled lightly over his shoulders and biceps.

Mack pressed a kiss to the top of her head as gently as he could manage, afraid she'd mock him for it. His breath was coming faster, waiting for her inevitable rejection. She wasn't his to hold. He shouldn't be there.

Mina wound her arms around his waist and trailed her fingertips up and down the hollow of his spine.

"Mina," he whispered again, hardly able to bear it. "What are you doing?"

"I don't know," she admitted. "Do you—do you want me to stop?"

"No," Mack begged, desperate for her, as usual. "*God*, no." Then he leaned down and kissed her. It felt—it felt like the gears of the universe suddenly locked into place and began churning forward, such was his overwhelming sense of perfect rightness.

Mack had been the one, months ago, to point out Mina in that bar. He'd been the one that was transfixed by the beautiful young brunette with the world-weary eyes. He'd mumbled something about being in love, he remembered, but Mack took too long to get out of his seat and go after her. He'd simply never expected Grey to approach her, to chat her up. God damn it all, to *win* her.

The guy who was supposed to be his friend had brought Mina right to his doorstep, flaunting his victory in Mack's face with unbridled glee. And all this time, Mack had never said a word. But Mina should have been his. There was no way she could kiss him like this and not know it. There was no way that this wouldn't change everything.

Was it five minutes, or five hours that they stood there like that, lips and bodies locked together? Mack would probably never know. All he did know was that eventually, the front door of the apartment banged open, and a clumsy, half-in-the-bag Grey staggered in. Mack was barely able to get his shirt over his head and his body out of that room before Mina's boyfriend spotted him. Mina's boyfriend—Mack's old childhood *friend*.

"Dude," Grey drawled, grinning like the village idiot. "Pay your fucking electric bill." Then his supposed buddy staggered over to Mina's doorway and closed himself inside.

Mack sank down to the couch, in shock. Should he go in there? Would Grey come storming right back out and want to fight? His hands trembled while he waited, but neither of those things happened. Instead, Mack had to flee to his bedroom with his tail between his legs, when the noise from their love-making became too much to endure.

While Grey got jiggy with Mina, Mack tried to channel his hurt—and his fury—into something more productive. He sat at his desk and got caught up on two weeks' worth of homework.

IN THE MORNING, Grey was manic and full of plans. Mina wore a small engagement ring on her finger and steadfastly refused to meet Mack's eyes. Maybe, like him, she was thinking about how her life would be so misspent by hitching her wagon to a guy like Grey—but somehow Mack doubted it. On their way out the door, Grey reached back and slipped Mack a piece of paper from his pocket.

"Here," he smiled, "It's the phone number of that bartender from The Wheel House. Keep her warm until I get back, will you?" Then they were gone.

Mina and Mack had been living together for months—cooking dinner in the evening and making coffee for each other when they woke up. When he finished his homework and she came home from the diner, they sat on the couch in the dark and watched TV together. Being tired and lazy with her was the best part of his day.

Mack had thought…no, he'd foolishly *hoped* that Mina was falling for him the same way he'd fallen for her. After all, it'd gotten awfully domestic in that apartment lately. What was Mack *supposed* to think? He had been right on the verge of telling Mina about the university in Norfolk. He'd been right on the edge of asking her to come with him when he transferred in the fall.

He was an idiot. Mina had become important enough to Mack that she felt like the beginning of his adult life. When she walked out his door without even a backward glance—well, that felt like the end of the world.

Chapter Seven

WHEN MINA WOKE up in the morning it took her a moment to understand what she was feeling. The crisp white sheets, the heavy male arm draped across her hip...Mack's position behind her was so uncannily reminiscent of her early days with Grey, that Mina suffered an excruciating minute of pure, undiluted terror. She couldn't believe she didn't wake Mack when she panicked and scrambled from the bed.

It was two years to the day since her husband had gone to his final reward, whatever that was for him. To Mina, it seemed entirely possible that Grey's ghost had chosen that exact moment to return and punish her.

She knew she didn't love him anymore, by the end of their marriage. If he'd lived, Mina doubted she could have managed to stay together much longer. Perhaps now that Grey was dead, he knew that ugly fact, too. Maybe his ghost could tell exactly how disloyal and capricious she truly was and had come to let her know how he felt about it.

Mina forced herself to turn around and look down, but the only man in that bed was Mack. She tried not to hyperventilate as she watched him sleep, baffled that he could be so unaware of what was happening. He looked long and lean and carved from muscle. Bare-chested, with the sheet tangled around his hips, he resembled a Greek statue in a museum—a fallen angel that had somehow gotten mixed up with the wrong worthless mortal.

For so long, Mack had been the shining proof in Mina's life that good men still existed. Kind men who stayed kind, men who conducted themselves the same behind closed doors as they did everywhere else.

Knowing him had always been a double-edged sword. On the one side, Mina was lucky to have his friendship—to know him at all. On the other, having Mack to compare Grey with over the years didn't exactly make the unravelling of her relationship easier. Meanwhile, Mina herself had existed as nothing so much as an object lesson in wasted potential.

Even looking at Mack, serene in his skin—even repeating to herself that Grey was dead and not coming back—Mina still couldn't slow the pounding of her heart. She forced herself to relive as much of her night with Mack as she could remember, but it wasn't enough to dispel her feeling of unease. The guilt that Grey had apparently never felt while he was alive? Mina felt it then, and it infuriated her.

She grabbed some clothes, then dressed hurriedly in the downstairs bathroom. She let herself out the back door and walked away from the house as fast as she could. There were paths all over the property—if Mina went far enough, eventually she would hit one, and then she could follow it for as long as it took to clear her head and act normal again in front of Mack. It was their last day there. Mina didn't want to ruin it.

IF SHE'D BEEN thinking clearly, she would've left him a note, but Mina hadn't been thinking—she'd been fleeing. She should've known that Mack wouldn't let her disappearance go. She should've realized he would track her down. She also should have known that when he did, Mina wouldn't find the right words to say. She could tell from Mack's expression that she'd only made things worse.

Instead of going back to the house with him, she trudged into the woods, through the trees to the tiny beach, and then followed the narrow strip of sand until it nearly disappeared. When she spotted Mack fussing with some kayaks arranged on a rack up ahead, Mina doubled back to return the way she came. Just inside the tree line, she took off the bright orange vest and sat on a fallen log. She watched Mack return to the house, then step back out onto the patio to drink his coffee.

That man was honest and smart and honorable. Rationally, Mina knew she could trust him. That didn't make it any easier for her heart to do it, though. After last night, she thought she might be more afraid of Mack than she'd ever been of Grey. He was capable of reaching into places inside her that Mina had thought were safely firewalled. Mack Bolton was too dangerous for her peace of mind.

Eventually, Mina forced her feet to carry her back across the emerald lawn, back into the pretty white farmhouse, and back into Mack's presence. She squandered most of the day on busy work, stripping the beds and washing and folding their sheets and towels. Mina scrubbed away any vestiges of her presence from the bathroom and kitchen, then packed her bag. As the afternoon waned, Mack tried to entice her into one more boat ride, but she managed to weasel out of it like the coward she was.

She needed to get back to Annapolis. Back to the safety of her little home, and the job that she'd earned all by herself. There, she had friends who had never known Grey, and her therapist was only a phone call away. Mina knew who she was in Annapolis. She knew what people expected of her. She didn't have to worry about men from her past stirring up weird feelings or acting so irresistible that Mina couldn't help but fall for them.

It was easier when Mina was the one to decide how things went. When she withdrew first, didn't call, didn't follow through…then she could keep people at arm's length. They might not believe her when she protested that she was okay, but at least they didn't press her on it.

At home, there wasn't anyone who had a hold on her, such that if they dropped off the face of the earth that day, it would wreck her for anyone else. Mina knew if she didn't let anyone in, they couldn't take more of her soul than they deserved, and they couldn't ruin her from the inside out.

IT TOOK TWICE as long to get from St. Michaels to Annapolis as it normally did, but two hours later, Mina was finally there. When she walked through her front door that evening, the sensation she'd had earlier—that Grey was somehow back and haunting her—grew stronger. It was difficult to ignore. But other than an odd, rusted red hatchback parked two doors down, everything else about her street and her home looked the same. The car, while strangely familiar, was an anomaly. Grey's shade was not.

Despite her therapist's efforts to wean Mina off her tendency toward negative self-talk, it was like she could *hear* her husband's voice in her head, egging her on—chanting that *He mattered, not her. She was irresponsible. Unmoored. Only someone with big problems would try to physically manipulate him like she did. How little class did she have, anyway?* Mina had learned the refrain by heart over the course of her marriage.

It was ironic, really. Some of the same qualities that had attracted Grey to her in the first place—the very things that he'd been so infatuated with in those early years—had been Mina's spontaneity and her affection. He'd reveled in those traits when they were newlyweds in Chapel Hill. Mina had always thought that was what had helped Grey straddle the bizarre line he'd walked—husband and veteran, but also college student and fraternity brother.

By the end of their relationship, though, Grey had twisted Mina's assets into character flaws. Now that she had the regular insight of a mental health professional, it wasn't lost on her that when she did try to act responsible or pragmatic—like working to get her degree through the military's online university—that was when Grey threw his biggest fits. It had been convenient for him to keep Mina down, because that way he kept all the power. It was convenient for him to turn his failings into Mina's fault.

Her therapist Claudette had explained to Mina that her current pattern of perfectionism was a direct result of being so powerless as a kid—subject to the whims of two temperamental alcoholics who could never be counted on to keep their word. The problem was exacerbated once Mina became a wife. Grey's impulses were what had counted, and Mina was merely along for the ride. She hadn't had any say in where her parents moved the family, or where the Marines decided to station Grey. Mina hadn't had any say in almost anything about her life.

She coped now by controlling what she could, like her home environment. Everything had its place in her house, and Mina was comfortable with that. She had purposely kept very little from her life with Grey, because she'd been so desperate for a fresh start. She'd needed a safe place that held few reminders of him, that Grey hopefully couldn't infect from beyond the grave.

Likewise, Mina was careful about who got to know the full, unedited version of her. Right now, that kept her mostly isolated, but it was fine. She could deal with it, and it was uncomplicated. But it meant that she hadn't touched a man in at least three years. Not casually, she didn't mean that. Mina worked and socialized with several men she was fond of.

But intimate touching—that was another story. After the way her marriage had plunged so precipitously from hot to cold, she hadn't been eager to dip her toe in that treacherous water again. Grey's erosion of Mina had been that complete.

At least she'd been careful, and there were no kids to worry about. For those first months in Annapolis—and then those years in student housing while she helped Grey get through UNC—Mina had been vigilant about birth control. It wasn't until he'd graduated and gone back into the Marines that they'd really entertained the thought of having kids. It was hard to time it right, though—Grey was often deployed, and Mina mostly wallowed in their depressing apartment outside Quantico by herself.

Eventually, Grey decided to move her to the Eastern shore, so Mina could be closer to his family when she finally conceived. They bought a little house with an extra couple bedrooms for the kids they planned, but the rooms stayed empty. By the time Mina realized something was really wrong—that nothing remotely baby-related was going to happen—Grey had come home for good.

He was full of accusations, of course—full of reasons why their lack of children was Mina's fault. Grey complained that she didn't put out enough, and that she was always too tired. He thought maybe Mina had become sterile from some previous STD, contracted before him and not treated until the damage was done. When she tried to protest, Grey took it as evidence of her guilt.

When Grey came home so altered from that final deployment, all Mina's silly hopes for a family died. She went back on birth control, and at some point, they simply stopped having sex. Oh, sure she hugged him occasionally. Grey would lay a hand on her back out in public, staking his claim if he thought other men looked a little too interested in his wife. But they never kissed, and they certainly never slept together.

It had been shockingly easy to do. Mina, after all, hadn't *wanted* to. Not with a man as disappointing or volatile as Grey. Over the years, he'd managed to hijack and kill every joyful impulse she had ever entertained, it seemed. He'd stolen her youth and turned her to stone, and Mina refused to forgive that.

But Grey was gone now and had been for a while. Apparently, he'd been gone long enough for Mina's body to remember that it was still alive, and to wake up from its long, numb sleep. Once or twice, she'd seen something on a man—a tanned collarbone slick with sweat, maybe, or a particularly masculine wrist—and felt her whole system perk up in curiosity. Once or twice, she'd even considered touching herself before she fell asleep at night. But those moments were fleeting—drifts of fog that rapidly burned off when exposed to the sun.

Mina might have managed to ignore them entirely, if it weren't for Mack Bolton. Over the last twelve years, he'd stood as a constant example of what a man could be—of what her own husband was not. Over the last three days, he'd managed to remind her of every time she'd ever set eyes on him and *wondered*. Every time Mack had slipped a compliment into a conversation or winked at her across a room. Every time Mina had lain awake in bed, vaguely jealous of the woman who eventually landed him.

Well, *she* was that woman, now. Driving back over the Bay Bridge on her way home earlier, Mina had considered how ironic it was that life had worked out the way it had. She'd somehow found herself single at the same time as Mack. She'd even been gifted with an extraordinary weekend as the recipient of his blazing kisses and panty-melting skills in the bedroom. He'd made her completely forget *why* she was at that house at all—to mark the anniversary of her husband's death. What kind of woman did that make her, anyway? Thank God he hadn't known.

This thing with Mack had been an utterly amazing fantasy come true—better, actually, than anything Mina was capable of conjuring. But it was foolish to think it could continue. For one thing, a guy like Mack had to have his pick of women. The last thing he needed was to saddle himself with Mina. She had a rocky relationship with her parents, and her bond with her sister was only just recovering from the damage Grey had inflicted. Mina already had one blinding failure of a marriage under her belt—to Mack's childhood friend. She'd be no good at all for him. Mack might not realize it yet, but he would.

And that led to the other problem. There was a distinct possibility that when Mack got to know the real her and came to his senses, he was going to break her heart. Mina had worked so hard to get strong—to get to a place where she felt emotionally stable and safe. Risking it all for a man destined to ditch her seemed like a very bad strategy indeed. Mack stirred up reminders of Grey, and the way Grey had molded her into a person she didn't recognize. Mina had assumed many of those memories were dead and buried, and it was unsettling to realize that they weren't.

She'd been given a new beginning, and she was desperate to hang onto it. Mina could *not* afford to dredge up the quagmire of her past. She refused to trudge through all that muck again. She could not be the uncertain girl who'd been married to Grey, not ever again—not even for Mack Bolton.

In one of life's cruel twists, Mack had let her leave earlier without saying a single word about getting together sometime soon. Maybe he'd gotten what he wanted, and never wanted to see her again. Or maybe Mack had known exactly why Mina was at that house and thought only the worst kind of woman would fall into bed with a new man on such an occasion. Either way, she was in way over her head, and had absolutely no idea what to do about it. She shouldn't want him, but she did.

Men were trouble. Mina should've just stuck to her original plan and kept avoiding them for a while longer. She would, now. She wouldn't judge herself too harshly for falling for all of Mack's many charms—she doubted too many women would be able to resist temptation like him, anyway. But she wouldn't let herself pretend that they had any kind of a future together, either.

WHEN MACK'S CALLS and texts began trickling in over the next week, Mina figured she better ignore them. It was hard, certainly, harder than she'd anticipated. It was best for all concerned, though, so she tried to stick to her guns.

Mack proved to be formidably tenacious, however. He chipped away at Mina's resolve day after day, until Friday morning came, and he finally won the standoff. The main line rang at the law office where she worked, the receptionist transferred the call back to Mina's desk—and then Mack's warm, deep voice was washing over her.

He sounded reasonable and not the least bit perturbed that she'd been ducking him all week. He was in town for a meeting and had brought something of Mina's that she'd forgotten at the bay house. Could he take her to dinner? The restaurant he suggested was ten minutes away—she could probably walk there after work, if she wanted.

Once he'd wheedled an acceptance out of her, Mina didn't even bother asking what she'd left behind. She figured it was either her heart or her sanity, and neither option boded well.

Chapter Eight

MACK TRIED TO keep the spark alive after Mina returned to Annapolis, but his phone may as well have been a brick for all the response he got from her. He tried calling. He tried texting. He tested every new option until each had failed—and it became clear that Mina wasn't merely busy or tired, she was actively avoiding him. Then Mack did what any self-respecting engineer would do, and he went back to the proverbial drawing board until he thought up a fresh plan.

Finally, frustrated by her silence, Mack did a little online searching and came up with the information he needed—the number for her office. He called Mina there on Friday morning, not wanting to give her too much time to think about her response. He did hope to surprise her, though, and hopefully get her to agree to see him. The receptionist was extremely helpful and transferred Mack directly to her.

"Mina O'Connell," she said.

"Hey, sweetheart. It's Mack."

"Mack *Bolton?*"

"Do you know others?"

"Um…no, actually. I think you might be one of a kind."

"So they say." Then he waited.

Mina wasn't the most patient woman Mack had ever known. It didn't take long before she blurted out, "What can I do for you, Mack? You probably realize that I'm at work right now, since you just called me here."

"Right. Well, I'm in town for a meeting, and wondered if I might take you to dinner."

"Tonight?" she squawked.

Mack grinned at his computer monitor. He'd been struggling all week with the design of particularly tricky new dock for a fishery at the edge of town, but suddenly it didn't seem so hopeless. "Yes, tonight. How about 6:30? There's a little Italian place right on the marina that's got good pasta, I hear."

"You mean Carlo's?"

"Yup."

"At 6:30."

For brevity's sake, Mack assumed her acquiescence. "Do you want to meet me there, or should I pick you up?"

"Wait, I—"

"Oh, and I forgot to mention you left something at the Blys'. I brought it with me." He almost hadn't. When Mack spotted that tiny scrap of a bikini hanging on the back of the bathroom door, he'd had a wave of longing wash through him that made him want to keep the thing. Seemed a little pervy to hang on to it, though.

Mina stayed quiet for a minute, and Mack started to worry. Would she refuse him?

"Come on, Mina. Meet me for dinner. Please?"

She sighed. "All right. I'll meet you there, okay?"

"Can't wait."

There was no way Mack was going to let Mina vanish into the wind for another decade. As it was, waiting two years after Grey passed seemed like cutting it a little too closely. What were the chances that she'd stay single for much longer?

Mack had wondered how Mina was doing nearly every day since that miserable funeral. But he had to be sure she was ready. After those first nights on the bay, Mack had been certain he had his answer. Mina was cheerful and affectionate and sexy as hell. But when Sunday dawned, he'd been less convinced she was really over Grey. She'd been distracted and on edge.

Even so, he had to see her again. He knew in his soul it was right—the only question was whether he was timing this correctly.

Mack typed some notes in the dock file and saved it for later. Then he made his way upstairs to pack a bag, just in case he didn't make it home that night. He left for Annapolis way too early, but luckily was heading over the bridge in the opposite direction of the weekend traffic. To kill time, he drove past his old apartment building and looked around for some of the places he used to hang out.

When it was time to meet Mina, Mack circled for ages around the marina lot, trying to find a spot to park his truck. She was in the restaurant waiting when he arrived. He waved off the hostess the second he spotted her—her face was shining like a beacon from a booth in the back corner.

"Hey, stranger," he said, sliding into the opposite seat and grinning at her. "Sorry I'm late."

"It's okay. I just got here," she replied. Then her sarcasm kicked in. "Seems like I haven't seen you in *ages*."

"Six days and thirteen hours," Mack replied, taking a sip of his water. "Not that I've been counting."

Her eyebrows shot up. "That long, huh?"

"Mm-hmm." He studied Mina's face for some sign of what was going on with her. "How you been?"

"Oh, you know. Same old," she demurred. "How about you?"

"Busy week. It's nice to see you, though."

"Aw. Aren't you sweet." Mina toyed with her napkin, and Mack groaned silently to himself. Last weekend had been like a dream—a fantasy come to vivid, pulsing life. Were they really going to be reduced to soulless small talk *now*?

Mina squinted at him. "So…you said you had something of mine?"

Mack dug in his pocket and whipped out her black string bikini, dangling it from his index finger over the center of the table. He'd never expected something so scanty to end up being the only way he could snag her attention again. "Look familiar?" he smiled.

The waitress took that moment to approach, glancing quickly at the bathing suit before forcing her eyes down to stare uncomfortably at her order pad. "What can I get you guys?" she asked.

Even in the low lighting, Mack could see Mina's flush. He grinned wider, she scowled—then snatched her suit off his finger and jammed it into her purse. Without meeting the other woman's eyes, she said primly, "I'd like a glass of the house Malbec, please."

Mack had to fight down his laugh. Mina was utterly, completely delicious—and he wanted to kiss her senseless. He turned his grin on the waitress, who blushed a little as well. Apparently, he was on *fire* tonight. "I'll have the same, thanks."

"Okay, um…can I get you started on any appetizers?"

Mack looked at Mina, who shook her head.

"Just some bread," he told the waitress. She scurried away.

He contemplated Mina across the table while she nibbled industriously at a breadstick from the table that was probably so stale it could be classified as a relic.

"I tried calling," he said, as calmly as he could.

She looked guilty. "Yeah, I saw that. I'm sorry—I was at work and couldn't talk."

"Tried texting you, too," Mack pointed out.

"Mack." Mina looked pained. *Good.*

He couldn't take pretending anymore. "What happened, Mina? After last weekend, I thought…" His bravado petered out—he'd intended to work up to this more smoothly.

Mina set down the fork she'd been holding. "What? What did you think?"

"I thought we had something good going, you know? I thought…you were right there with me."

"I was, I swear," she soothed. "I guess I just figured once you got home, that would be it. You scratched the itch, so what else was there to do?"

Mack gaped at her. "Mina, are you for real right now?"

"What?" she blinked, acting all innocent.

He could tell it meant something to her though. She looked hurt.

"Who are we kidding?" Mina asked him. "You don't need to bother with me."

Mack frowned. "You thought I would want to cut things off, so you went ahead and made the decision for me?"

"No, I—"

"Yes, you really did. But hey, how about letting *me* decide what's best for me? You're certainly free to figure out what's best for you, but I'd like the chance to weigh in on what I want."

"Oh. Okay."

Mack went with honesty. "Mina, I *never* thought I'd have a chance to be with you. Do you honestly believe that one roll in the hay is all I would want?"

Mina shrugged, damn her. "I don't know."

Mack tried to settle his temper. Getting angry at her obliviousness wasn't going to help. "But you thought ignoring me all week was the best way to find out?"

She blew out a breath. "I'm so sorry, Mack. I guess I kind of choked," she admitted.

"Why, though?" Mack took a deep breath and tried to chill the heck out. In what he hoped was a gentler tone, he asked, "Was I not clear about how I feel? Or did I do something wrong?"

"No, of course not." Mina smiled sheepishly. "Would you believe me if I said, 'It's not you, it's me'?"

He chuckled. "That's what they all say."

"To be fair…you didn't actually *say* you wanted to see me again," she pointed out.

"Of course, I did. I remember it. I said—" Mack paused. "I said…" What *had* he said?

Mina raised her eyebrows at him, and he realized he'd truly blown it.

"Apparently, I'm an idiot."

"It's okay," she smiled. "If it helps, it's nice that you're here now."

Mack didn't want to pester her about why she hadn't taken the lead and started that conversation herself—because Mina was far more skittish than he'd realized. He should've seen it right from the get-go, but he'd lost whole days last weekend to a haze of unbridled lust.

As excuses went, it wasn't great, but twelve years was an awfully long time to carry a torch for someone. Finally getting kissed by them tended to screw with your wiring.

Mina was worth that discomfort, though—all that and more. Winning her trust might be the hardest thing he'd ever attempted, but Mack wanted to try. He had to.

The waitress came with their wine and the bread basket, then took their orders and left again.

"So…you really want to hang out again?" Mina asked shyly.

"If that's a euphemism for hooking up every few weeks, then no," Mack said.

"*Damn.*" At least she had the grace to look disappointed.

"Ha," Mack smirked. "Mina, listen. I want to give *this*," he gestured between them, "A go. I want to get to know you and I want to do stuff together. *And* I want to hook up with you, again and again and again—"

She cut him off with a laugh. "I think I get the picture."

"Great. Then what do you say? Do you want that, too?"

She stared at him with her hands pressing down on the tablecloth beside her plate. Mack held his breath. Was it really such a hard decision? Did she actually think he was that bad of a bet? For him, it was the biggest no-brainer in the universe. Apparently not for Mina, though.

"Okay," she said finally. "I'm in."

"Oh, thank you baby Jesus," Mack breathed. "You kind of had me sweating there for a minute."

Mina's face bloomed with another rosy blush. "Was I really *that* good?"

"Girl, you have no idea," he told her. The best he'd ever had, and he had a feeling that had only been the beginning.

Dinner passed in a blur. Before Mack could blink, the restaurant was closing for the night and they were standing out front, shivering in their light jackets.

"Thanks for dinner," Mina said softly.

"Thanks for agreeing to see me again."

Mack leaned down to do what he'd driven there for—and he kissed her goodnight. He'd meant for it to be a sweet thing, something casual to show her she had nothing to fear. But once Mina's lips touched his and he felt the heat of her tongue, everything went haywire. The kiss snapped on every one of Mack's circuits, and had them firing off urgent messages to every relevant port. In seconds, he was a sizzling, sparking mess of male wiring.

Mina broke free with a gasp. He hung onto her waist and tried like hell to clear his brain.

"Where are you staying tonight?" she asked.

"I thought I'd find somewhere before dinner, but I ran out of time," he said. "I'll just drive back home tonight. The traffic probably won't be bad by now."

"Mack, it's already 10:30," Mina frowned. "That doesn't seem like a good idea."

Her concern touched him. In two steps, he backed her against the wall of Carlo's. Mack nuzzled her warm, enticing throat, then kissed a line back to her mouth. Mina wrapped her arms around his neck.

"Stay with me," she urged.

He kissed her, deep and hard. "You sure?"

"Hell, yes."

The way Mack saw it, their history could be the steel frame for him to build on—and last weekend, the first few blocks of the foundation. If he got more time like this with Mina, the future he had in mind would stand tall for a hundred years. He took one of her hands, then kissed each fingertip.

"Eena, Mina, Myna, Mo," he smiled. He let her pinkie slip into his mouth.

Mina grinned wickedly back. Her other hand drifted south and gave Mack a neighborly squeeze in the junk. "Kiss the boy and watch him grow," she said with a wink.

Mack groaned. A hundred years with her. Maybe more. "Sweetheart, you are trouble with a capital T."

"I'm comfortable with that."

"Strangely, so am I. Why don't you lead the way, and I'll show you what this bad boy—" he covered her marauding hand with his own for a moment, then pulled it away. "—can do."

Chapter Nine

MACK FOLLOWED HER back to her duplex in his truck and was right on Mina's heels coming through the front door. She hung up her coat, and Mack's heavy khaki work jacket.

Mina gestured around the small front hall, but there really wasn't much to see. "So...this is it."

He stepped in front of her, looming over her and intent on her mouth. "Nice place," he said, not even pretending to look.

"Thank you."

He leaned closer. "Seems good and private," he said.

"Oh yeah?"

Mack kissed her, hot and deep. She wound her arms around his neck and when he straightened, he brought her body up with him.

"Yeah," he growled. He grabbed Mina's thighs and wrapped her legs around his waist. "Hey, Mina?" He shifted her body higher, but not before she felt how much he wanted her.

"Yes?"

"Please point me toward a bed, honey." His voice brooked no argument.

With a rush, every moment of their first night together flooded her brain, and Mina forgot the reservations she had about getting together with Mack.

"Straight up the stairs, first door on the left," she said quickly.

Mack kissed her again, his tongue delving deep and tangling with hers. At the top of the stairs, he broke off to nudge her head back, so he could kiss her neck.

In her bedroom, Mack used one arm to push her failed outfits from that morning onto the floor, then sat on the edge of her bed. Mina's knees hit the mattress, her chest smashed against his, and her core made contact squarely with Mack's erection. He groaned.

"Oh God. I missed you," he said. His hands held her head in place, so he could kiss her again.

Mina let her flats fall to the ground and set about pulling Mack's button-down free from his pants. He braced his feet on the ground and slid back farther, widening Mina's legs with his thighs and grinding up into her while she worked on his buttons. He let go of her only long enough to shed his pristine white undershirt, and then he was falling backward with Mina in his arms. What was it about Mack's skin? It was smooth and soft as velvet, and hot as a diner's flat top. Mina wanted all of it, all over her.

She disentangled herself from Mack's grip, pushed his arms flat on the covers, and sat up. While she pulled off her sweater, Mack fumbled with the zipper on her skirt. He worked the garment down over her hips, then prodded Mina off him so she could kick it free.

Then he rolled over to tuck Mina beneath him, planting kisses on her sternum and around her navel.

"Scoot up," he told her.

Mack arranged Mina's pillow under her head, took a long, assessing look at her body, then moved lower. He hooked his fingers in the waist of her panties and slid them slowly off. Mack's feet hit the floor, his lips hit her pubic bone, and Mina couldn't help the yearning sigh that escaped her lips. Grey had stopped going down on her about five years into their marriage and hadn't been particularly good at it to begin with. Mack, though—Mack needed no instructions.

His shoulders were broad, and he used them to nudge her legs wide. Mack kissed the inside of each thigh, checked her face to make sure she was still okay, and then set to work. He didn't waste time, and Mina didn't need him to. Mack merely worked her body with efficient, single-minded determination until she was arching up off the bed and begging.

"Please," she heard herself whisper. "Please."

Mack braced her hip to hold Mina still. His tongue landed squarely on the spot she needed him, and he slid two long fingers deftly into the heat of her. That was all it took—five minutes of Mack's attention, and she was spiraling off into the most earth-shattering orgasm Mina had felt in years. Possibly ever.

"Condoms?" he barked, his forehead pressed against her thigh.

"Night table," she said. Mina tried to remember if that was true, if she still had any. It wasn't like she'd had much use for them.

While Mack fished around in the drawer, Mina tossed her bra aside, then worked her way under him to pull his belt free.

Mack handed her two condom packets with a disgruntled, "That's all there is."

She blinked at him, then at the gaping front of his pants. "Are we going to need more than two?"

Mack scoffed. "Hell, yes, we are," he told Mina. He stood and shucked off his chinos, boxers, and shoes in one urgent push before climbing back on the bed. "I left my bag in the truck, but I have more in there."

"Might want to put your pants back on, then," Mina laughed. Her neighbors would freak. Absolutely *freak*. She'd never hear the end of a nude Mack sighting.

"Later," he muttered. Mack scrabbled around in the sheets until he found one of the foil packets, ripped it open, and rolled it over his impressive length. Mina tried to process the entirety of his magnificence—his wide shoulders and chest, arms thick with muscle, and flat abdomen. How had she ever thought she could resist that? Mack Bolton was a work of art.

And wonder of wonders, he wanted *her*.

MINA WASN'T ENTIRELY sure what to expect when she awoke the next morning, but Mack was already in her kitchen drinking coffee when she shuffled groggily downstairs.

He was using her favorite mug himself, the one she drank out of every morning before work. Mack handed her a different mug. The color was pretty, which was why she'd bought it in the first place—but the handle felt all wrong in her hand. Mina frowned. The coffee was really strong. *Too* strong.

"Morning, kid. I hope I didn't wake you."

"No, I didn't hear a thing," she said. Mack's appearance finally registered on her sleepy brain. He was showered and dressed for the day and looked like he'd been that way for a while.

"I'm sorry I can't stay," he went on. "But I've got to take off soon. I blew off half the day yesterday, so I have some work to catch up on."

"On a Saturday?" Mina slumped into her usual chair at the small kitchen table before Mack could steal that too. She gazed longingly at the mug in Mack's hands, and wished she'd added more milk to her coffee before she sat down. If she got up again now, it would only make it obvious that he'd gotten it wrong, and Mina didn't want to seem ungrateful for his effort.

"Yeah, I'm trying to help this little family-run fishery get their facilities up to code. They got dinged in their last inspection, but the place is way too busy during the week for me to do what I have to do."

"Ah." Mina blinked at him, waiting for the fog to clear from her brain. With the high-octane brew she was sipping, that would hopefully happen twice as fast as it normally did.

"Can I make you some breakfast?" he inquired.

"No, I'm good with coffee for now." There was no way Mina could shovel down eggs yet, even with the calories she and Mack had managed to burn off the night before. She glanced at Mack's lap quickly and felt her face heat when he busted her.

He grinned. "Now I'm really sorry I have to go." He got up and looked like he was coming for her.

"Do not come over here!" Mina squeaked. "You're all clean and I badly need a shower!"

"Simmer down," Mack chuckled. "I'm just gonna run up and grab my bag. I'll be right back."

When he was gone, Mina jumped up and darted for the fridge. She poured more milk into her cup, then stuck it in the microwave to heat it again. She felt a little less exposed behind the barrier of her kitchen counter and considered whether it was worth it to go upstairs and get her robe, too.

Being in the same room with Mack and that bed again could only mean trouble, though. It still boggled her mind how she could decide to protect her heart one minute and end up knocking boots with the man the next. How many times had it been, anyway? Mina had no idea. It appeared that all the logic in the world was no match for Mack Bolton's sexy smile, or his spectacularly gifted hands.

Mack jogged down the stairs and dropped his bag next to the front door. He sauntered to the other side of the counter and leaned his hip against it.

Before Mina could even blink, he snagged the large canning jar full of little chocolate candies in his hand, cracked it open, and poured out a handful. He popped them in his mouth in twos and threes, chewing happily.

Mina gasped. "I don't eat those!"

Mack stopped chewing and examined her. "Why?"

"Because."

Because...they had been mailed to her in the weeks after Grey's funeral, sent from a friend of Molly's and her sister. Mina had met Meg and Morgan Flynn only once—but their gift was incredibly important to her.

She'd picked up some extra hours once, working a wedding for the catering arm of the restaurant where she was a waitress. With the extra three hundred dollars—a windfall at the time—Mina had flown up to Boston to see her sister at college, without ever saying a word to Grey.

He would've expected her to pay bills with the money or come up with some semi-important reason that he needed to use it for himself. Instead, Mina had enjoyed a full weekend crashing with Molly in her sublet room and exploring a new city.

While she was there, Molly and her pal Meg had insisted on taking their two older sisters out on the town. Mina and Morgan had hit it off like crazy, even though Mina had never really found a connection like that with other women before. Morgan had made her promise to keep in touch.

But when Mina returned home, the glow of happiness had worn off and she knew she couldn't maintain the friendship. She'd never be able to explain to Grey how she'd met the other girls, for one thing—and they'd never want to stay friends with someone so utterly...*weary* before her time. There'd been a handful of emails that gradually tapered off, then stopped altogether. It was disappointing, but so much was in those days.

When Grey died and the box of goodies arrived, it was wrapped in pretty paper and bows, and contained two heartfelt notes without an ounce of anything other than simple goodwill. Mina had been moved to tears. She'd been so flattered to be remembered. So...overwhelmed to be thought part of such a lovely little club. Morgan and Meg said the candies referred to their collected initials and their one giddy night together—four

"M" names that had been hilariously impossible to enunciate with a few drinks in them.

Mina could no longer remember what she'd written in her thank you note. She hadn't been able to eat a single chocolate, but the sight of them there—every day beside her sink—had gotten her through more than a few rough patches when she felt like no one knew her anymore, no one cared, and no one ever would. They were a talisman against darkness.

However, in the last week, that special jar had been opened and plundered by two different men. First Dimitri—her friend from the bereavement group she attended—had grabbed a huge handful and dropped the candies into his mouth all at once. He'd just done her a favor—stopped by to fix Mina's running toilet, so she wouldn't have to wait for the landlord to get around to it. But she'd still stood there gaping at him, stunned and speechless. She'd had to leave the room and remind herself that he was being nice, just so she wouldn't yell at him.

And now Mack—who poured his moderate helping placidly into his hand, sorted through the colors thoughtfully, and ate them bit by bit while Mina watched. While Dimitri had been largely clueless about his transgression, Mack could tell he'd done something wrong.

"What'd I do?" he asked.

Mina slid the jar away from him and closed the latch again. "Those aren't for eating," she said. "I just keep them for decoration." Thankfully Mack didn't question her on her absurdity, merely swallowed the rest of his haul with a grunt and then brushed his hands against his jeans.

It seemed appropriate that nothing would be sacred with the two guys. They each had an uncanny ability to step right over every wall Mina had thrown up in the last couple years. It was unsettling to say the least.

She felt like she couldn't quite relax. At least Mack was going home soon. She wouldn't have to pretend she was okay for much longer.

That candy was supposed to be hers. One thing only for Mina, that proved she could make and keep friends, even despite Grey's best efforts to the contrary. It had been one thing that Grey couldn't touch, couldn't co-opt into something about him, even from beyond the grave.

Mina snatched the jar from the counter, rolled it on its side to watch the candies swirl like a kaleidoscope, then shoved it into the lower cabinet with her pots and pans. From now on, if anyone was going to eat those candies, it was going to be her, and *only* her. She'd earned every last one of them.

"Sorry, Mina." Mack came around the counter, and when Mina straightened he pulled her into his arms. "Any chance you can forgive me?"

When he kissed her, Mack tasted like coffee and chocolate, and something even darker that belonged only to him. Mina sighed. Resistance was futile. "I suppose," she smiled.

Mack smoothed his hands down her back and over her rear end, using his grip to pull her tight against him. "What do you think, sweetheart? Same time next week?"

By next weekend, Mina was almost certain she could behave like a normal human woman again. "Sounds like a plan," she agreed.

"All right. I'll call you later. Maybe actually pick up the phone this time, okay?"

Mina punched him in the arm, he kissed her again, and then he was gone.

It looked like she was in a new relationship whether she was ready or not. It was okay, though. Mina was still alive, still young, and still had almost her whole life ahead of her. Her mistakes were mostly in her past and she wouldn't let memories of Grey keep her from moving forward anymore.

Mack Bolton wanted her, at least for the time being—and Mina couldn't ask for a better return to living than that. He'd hung in there like a champ while she'd attempted to avoid him— and even remained unperturbed when she acted all persnickety and OCD this morning. He deserved a little something back in return—so Mina decided that next weekend, she would be the one driving back over the bridge to him.

THE WEEK FLEW by. Mack texted her often, at random, and about everything from what he was eating for lunch to which body part of hers he'd like to kiss next.

Mina finally had to admit to herself that she couldn't wait to see him. All week, she'd somehow managed to avoid nailing down a specific time and place, hoping to surprise him in his lair—but she hoped Mack hadn't had the same idea.

By Friday afternoon, there was only one more task Mina had to complete before she left for St. Michaels, and that was her weekly call with her mother. The phone rang right on schedule at two p.m.

"Hey, Mom."

"Mina! How are you?"

"I'm fine. I was just heading out, though."

"Oh. Well, I don't have a lot to talk about. I just thought you might want to hear about Rob's award he got last week. They had the *nicest* dinner for him."

"Who's 'they'?"

"The Chamber of Commerce, of course. This is the third year in a row they've voted him the town's top volunteer."

Mina had only met her stepfather a handful of times, but that had been plenty to form an opinion. The crappy way he'd treated her baby sister told Mina everything she needed to know about what kind of person he was.

"You must be so proud," she said, dry as dust.

As always, Elaine was oblivious to her daughter's sarcasm. "Oh, I am. I wore my aubergine dress—do you remember it? It turned out to be so appropriate and funny, because at the cocktail hour they served this wonderfully exotic dip with eggplant in it. What was it called? Bama something. Bamafanook? Baga...ga...zoof?"

Mina rolled her eyes. "In-A-Gadda-Da-Vida?" Who knew why she bothered—she was only amusing herself. Her mother probably couldn't tell an Iron Butterfly song from a hole in the wall.

"Nooooo," Elaine sounded doubtful. "I don't think that was it."

"I'm just kidding, Mom. It was probably *baba ganoush*."

"Oh! Yes, that was it! Have you ever had it?"

"Yes, Mom. Along with the rest of creation."

Smugly, Elaine pointed out, "It matched my dress."

"Which I suppose would come in handy if you spilled some on yourself?"

"Why would I do that?"

Mina groaned. Their conversations these days never seemed to follow any discernable path, though she supposed it was an improvement over the drag-out fights they'd once had.

"Mom, seriously. I've really got to get going," she said.

"Where are you off to in such a rush?"

"Nowhere special. I'm driving down to St. Michaels for the night."

"Again? Molly said you were there two weeks ago."

Mina decided that playing dumb was her safest bet. "No, she must've gotten mixed up. I'm going this weekend."

"But—"

"And I have to go, Mom. *Now*. I'm already running late."

"But who are you going to see?" Elaine persisted.

"A *friend*, Mom."

Her mother was undaunted, naturally. "A *male* friend?"

"*Mom*." Had she thought that their talks were aimless? Scratch that—their conversations could always veer down the matrimonial road.

"Well, you can hardly blame me for asking, Mina Louise."

Mina cringed at the sound of her full name. What kind of lunatics named a baby girl *Mina Louise*, anyway? She knew the answer, though—the kind who'd thought Ginger from "Gilligan's Island" was the sort of role model a girl could really look up to. Her dad had spent the first ten years of Mina's life quoting silly lines from the television show to her—to which she'd always replied, *It's Mina, Dad. Not Tina.* Hadn't helped, sadly.

"I can blame you," she told her mother. "I *do* blame you."

"Mina, you're not getting any younger. God rest his lovely soul, but poor Grey has been gone for years, now. *Years.* It's time for you to get back on the horse. Before you know it, you'll just be a dried-up old husk, and no one will look twice at you then. Trust me, I know."

Lovely soul, her ass. "Oh my God, Mom. You're a real piece of work, you know that?" One who sounded unnervingly like her former son-in-law.

"Thank you," Elaine said sweetly.

"That wasn't a compliment!" Mina cried, exasperated and not a little spooked. "And I have to go!"

"*Mina*—"

"Hanging up now!"

"Mina!"

"Bye, Mom!" Mina slammed down the receiver, breathing hard. Why did she pick up the phone every week? Why did she *ever* pick up that goddamn phone?

She marched out of the house, threw her bag in the back seat, and drove quickly away. Mina fumed for the first twenty minutes of the drive, but once the radio station hit a decent block of no-commercial music, she was relatively good to go.

She made it all the way over the Bay Bridge before she realized she had no idea where, specifically, she was headed. Mina pulled into a gas station, did a quick internet search for *Mack Bolton, engineer*, then plugged the address she found into the mapping app on her phone. Mack seemed to have quite the website, and she resolved to take a closer look at it the next time she was on her computer. Photos of him in hard hats and tool belts were definitely not to be missed.

Half an hour later, she found his office—an adorable lime-washed brick house with a big white porch. From a decorative pole out front, an elegant arched sign swung in the breeze, with *Matthew Bolton, D.CE – Coastal Engineering* spelled out in shining brass letters on either side. Mina parked on the street, walked up the brick path, and ran her hands over the blue enamel sailboat at the top of the sign. She hoped that her arrival would be welcome.

She sat on one of the pretty black benches flanking the front door and sent Mack a text:

> Hey. Want to grab a cup of coffee?

His response was gratifyingly immediate:

> Always. When did you have in mind?

Mina smiled—she had him. She tapped out:

> Now's good.

Before she could lose her nerve, she stood up and pushed through the shiny black front door. A little bell overhead tinkled when she walked in. The large front room was airy and attractive, with more lime-washed brick on the walls, vaguely nautical-looking bronze light fixtures, and huge framed photos of his various projects hung in ruler-straight lines.

She heard the creak of a desk chair and heavy footsteps, and then Mack stuck his head out of an office toward the back.

"Mina? What are you doing here?"

She shrugged and tried to brazen it out. "Thought you might be up for some java."

Mack crossed the scuffed wood floor in three strides, and engulfed Mina in a huge bear hug. His mouth connected with hers a second later. It was hard to miss his enthusiasm.

"Is that a T-square in your pocket or are you just happy to see me?" she joked.

He grinned, and she noted a tiny dimple beside his mouth she'd somehow never noticed before. "Oh, make no mistake. I am very, very happy to see you."

"Hmm. It seems you already taste like coffee." If she had stuck around for either of the mornings they'd had together, Mina might have already grown accustomed to that flavor. Had she realized how sexy it was, she might have found a way to get better acquainted.

"Don't worry. I have more in the back. Come on."

Mack led her through another set of doors, then into a large, open kitchen and great room at the back of the house. The mug he poured for her had the same logo printed on it as the sign out front.

He dropped onto a brown leather loveseat and gestured to the couch. "Have a seat."

"Thanks." Mina felt unaccountably shy in the face of his handsomeness.

"To what do I owe the honor?"

She raised her mug and toasted him with it.

"How long are you staying?" he tried.

Mina smiled. "As long as you want, I guess. I can get lost until you're done with work, and then we could get some dinner. Or I can find a B&B tonight and meet you in the morning."

"Or we can seclude ourselves upstairs now and not come out till Sunday," Mack suggested.

"That depends," Mina hedged. "What exactly is upstairs?"

"Why don't you come and find out?" he said. Mack stood, took her cup and set it on the coffee table, then held out his hand. He grasped hers tight and led Mina up a set of stairs at the side of the room.

If the last two weeks had shown her anything, it was that avoiding Mack upset her equilibrium nearly as much as being with him did. When he'd shown up at dinner seven days ago and acted all logical and reasonable about them being together, Mina had essentially folded like a deck of cards. From there, falling back into bed with him had been as easy as breathing.

In moments, it became clear that not only did Mack have more living space upstairs—but it included a big bedroom with a large antique canopy bed. The perfectly-made sheets were just begging to be messed up, and that seemed like something Mina was uniquely capable of. If she was going to keep this connection with him up, she might as well make it count.

Chapter Ten

"IS THAT SHIPLAP?" Mina asked, the minute Mack got her into his personal space. She looked around the upstairs hall with wide, curious eyes.

"Yes, but maybe we can table the home decorating discussion for a later time," he answered.

Mack steered her into his bedroom and with no prompting whatsoever she perched on the side of his big wood bed—like an enticing fairy come to grant all his dirtiest wishes.

He braced his arms on either side of her hips, then leaned in to get another taste of her maddening, addictive mouth. He'd been hungering for Mina all week to such a degree, that he'd begun to think he might be going a tad insane. She was *that* amazing.

And to think, all those years she'd been sashaying around right under Mack's nose. If he'd been smarter somehow—or at least cleverer than Grey—Mack might have been kissing Mina O'Connell for years instead of only weeks.

Nevertheless, now wasn't the time for self-reflection. Mack dropped his khakis to the floor, stepped out of his boat shoes, and followed Mina farther onto the bed. He let his weight press her lower body into the pillow-top mattress and nibbled along her jaw.

"I take it you missed me?" she laughed.

"Every day. Every hour," Mack murmured against that silky, mesmerizing skin. "Every *second*." He unbuttoned the top few buttons of Mina's shirt and licked along the lace edge of her bra. She quivered, and he *loved* it. So, Mack undid the rest of the buttons, peeled the top off her, and threw it aside.

"Don't you have to get back to work?"

"Shop's closed for the rest of the weekend," Mack replied. He should probably run back down and lock up the office, just in case.

But—her bra was some insidious combination of pale blue and white lace, and he hadn't known before that instant it was a weakness of his. He wondered if Mina's panties were going to match.

Her hands slipped under the hem of his shirt set his blood simmering. Mack tore the shirt off, so she could touch him some more. He felt her legs rubbing against his, breathed in her light, fresh scent...then bit the tendon running between her shoulder and neck, because Mina was so edible. She shrieked loud enough that he couldn't help laughing at her.

And then, distantly—Mack heard someone come in the screen door at the back of the house, and his mother calling his name. She must have heard *them*, too, because almost immediately her footsteps sounded on the creaky wood staircase.

His bedroom door was open. It was a scant few feet from the top of the steps.

"Hang on," Mack warned Mina, then rolled them together off the far side of the bed. They landed heavily, but he thought he'd shielded her from the worst of the impact. Her face was a startled mask of good humor, but he worried that once the *stunned* part wore off, she'd start giggling again.

Mack jumped to his feet before he realized he was standing there in his boxers, with a virtual boat mast tenting the front of them. Mina wriggled under the bed before he could even think of what to do about her—and he stood there dumbly, wondering how *she* seemed so cool under pressure. He toed the crazy pile of her clothing under the bed with her and sent silent thanks up to the god of bachelors that he owned a bedframe with so much blessed room under it.

Mack refused to say thanks for his mother's shaky knees—even though they were no doubt slowing her procession up his steps. She eventually hit the landing with a relieved exclamation.

Mina must've managed to pull his pants and shoes under the bed with her as well, because her hand swiftly pushed his rumpled pants back out near his toes. Mack dove for them. He yanked them up and zipped them, right as his mom stepped through the doorway.

He felt like his face was on fire, but he rested a hand on the edge of the mattress as casually as he could. Hopefully it would mask his rapidly-waning erection. And—seriously? How could this kind of thing still be happening to him in his thirties?

"Geez, Mom," he complained. "Don't you knock anymore?"

She blinked at his tone. "I'm sorry, hon. I rang the bell about four times."

Mina's hand darted out to tickle his ankle, and Mack glanced down to see what she was up to. Her flowery shirt was stuck half under his heel, so he frantically kicked at it, getting it under the edge of the pleated bed skirt just as his mom rounded the foot of the bed.

"What's wrong, Mack? You look flushed."

He coughed in case Mina took that moment to snort, or laugh, or otherwise make trouble. Casting around desperately for some believable excuse, his eyes fell on a couple of dumbbells in the corner of the room.

"I was just lifting a couple weights," he said. Fortunately, any blatant evidence of his actual activities was now a distant memory, so Mack stood up straight and faced his mother like the adult he supposedly was.

She placed a hand on his cheek and searched his face. "I don't know," she murmured. "You feel pretty warm. Do you think you might be coming down with something?"

Yeah, Mina Fever, Mack thought morosely.

"I'm fine," he said aloud, "But I was just about to hit the shower. Why don't you head to the kitchen and grab some lemonade from the fridge? I'll be down in a couple minutes."

"Sure," she said, as agreeable as ever. "Have you had lunch yet? I could make us some sandwiches."

"Um…" Mack's mind spun. If his mother got to making lunch, he'd never get rid of her—and he'd likely end up with a monster under his bed, instead of Mina. "I'm meeting a friend in a little bit. Let's hold off on the sandwiches, okay?"

"All right." She turned and began making her measured way back down the stairs. Mack stomped into his bathroom and turned on the water, just in case she was still paying attention. When he was sure she was out of earshot, he dropped to the floor and lifted the edge of the bed skirt.

Mina's mischievous face grinned back at him, her cheeks wet with tears of hilarity.

"Oh my God!" she breathed merrily. "How old are we right now?"

"Jesus, Mary, and Joseph," Mack muttered. "I'll try to get rid of her as fast as I can. This is ridiculous."

"It's *hilarious*," she gasped, beginning to giggle again. "Saintly Mack Bolton. You're in so much *trouble*!"

"Shush," Mack commanded her. "Don't you start." He darted a hand under the bed and poked at her.

That just made Mina squeak and laugh harder. "Don't *you* start," she fired back. "Something you can't *finish*!"

Mack banged his forehead on the floor a few times, but it was no use. Now he was cracking up, too.

"Okay, seriously. I'm going to get wet real quick," And…now everything he said was coming out sounding dirty. "And then I'll go get rid of my mom. Don't move."

Tears streamed down Mina's face, and her whole body shook with silent laughter. She waved him away, apparently unable to muster any other sassy words for him.

Mack pushed to his feet and lunged for the shower, struggling to come up with a viable way to jettison his mother, or to explain the extra car parked out front right then. Why did insanity have a way of following Mina O'Connell? And why didn't he care more?

Mina was sitting on the floor next to his bed when he came back out, hugging her knees. Mack mourned the fact that she was all put together again, but at least she still looked cheerful.

"Maybe you can distract her," she whispered. "I can sneak out the front."

He felt like he'd stepped into a goofy mystery cartoon, but he gave Mina his hand and helped her get to her feet.

"And then what?" he whispered back. "Your car's out front." Trying to explain his budding relationship with Mina to his mom—while Mina was standing right there—was *not* how he'd planned to spend his afternoon. He didn't expect his mother to be much of a sport about it.

"I'll think of something," she told him confidently. "Just watch for my signal."

Oh, Lord. Now he was watching for signals. But, since Mack had no brainy ideas of his own, he had to work with what was available.

"*Fine*," he griped. Feeling sullen, he grabbed one more desperate kiss from Mina, then made his way downstairs.

In the kitchen, his mom was mixing up a new pitcher of lemonade to replace what she'd poured for the two of them. Mack plopped onto one of the barstools and watched her for signs that she knew what was happening.

"You look much better now," she said.

Mack snapped, "I told you I was fine."

"Are you mad? I'm sorry I didn't call first."

He pushed aside his frustration. It wasn't his mother's fault he'd suddenly started to get lucky every weekend. "No, it's okay. You just surprised me, that's all."

"Are you sure you don't have time for a quick lunch?" his mother asked.

"I'm sure." Mack sipped from the glass she passed him and wondered if she was feeling lonely. Usually she kept pretty busy, but sometimes she needed a little extra attention. How long had his dad been gone, anyway? Fifteen years or so? Abruptly, Mack didn't want to make his mom leave, but…he'd promised Mina.

Mina. Shoot, he was supposed to be watching for her signal. Mack stood and rounded the island, pulling his mother into a tight hug that faced her toward the cabinets.

He looked over her head and sure enough, there was his girl, waiting on the stairs. She grinned and gave him a thumbs-up, then crept across the room as quickly and silently as a wraith.

Moments ticked by, but finally Mack released his mom. She smiled sweetly up at him, and then they both heard the bell over the front door jingle.

"Mack? You back here?" Mina called.

"Yeah!" he shouted. Based on his mother's expression, she suspected things were about to get interesting.

Mina pushed through the doors with a large brown paper bag in her arms. She looked happily surprised to see Mack's mother. "Mrs. Bolton! How are you?"

Mack thought his mom was just as surprised. "Mina? Oh my goodness, I haven't seen you in ages!"

While the two women hugged, Mack took a peek inside the mystery bag. Sandwiches? Where had Mina gotten subs so fast? Or rather—where *could* she have gotten subs that his mother would find believable?

"What's in the sack?" Mack asked, hoping he looked like this was exactly what he'd expected to happen.

"I grabbed some sandwiches, so we could eat here instead of meeting out—I hope that's okay. I'm sure I got enough to share," she said.

"Mina Whitney, as I live and breathe," his mom sighed. She settled into one of the kitchen chairs and got comfortable. "I thought I heard you'd moved to Annapolis."

"Oh, I did, a couple years ago. I came down to visit some friends, though, and ran into Mack at the coffee shop this morning."

Mack was slightly annoyed that Mina hadn't corrected his mother about her name change, and he toyed with the idea of doing it himself. That would probably be too obvious, though.

"That's wonderful! What are the odds?" His mom smiled toothily.

"Right?" Mina blazed on. "Anyway, he wasn't available until lunch, so I parked my car here and wandered around town for a while."

"Looks like you hit Mia's," Mack supplied, unpacking the paper-wrapped subs.

Mina sent him a grateful glance. "Yes. I got a little bit of everything. I wasn't sure what you'd like."

More kisses from her—that's what Mack would *like*. At the moment, it wasn't what he was going to get, though. He grabbed some plates and cups and brought everything to the table.

"Well, it is very good to see you again," his mother told Mina. She squeezed Mina's arm, then took half a club sandwich and put it on her plate. "Almost like old times."

"Almost," Mina agreed, but her mouth looked a bit tight at the edges.

As he was tucking into a meatball sub, his mother inquired, "Did Mack have a chance to show you around yet?"

"A little bit," Mina assured her.

Mack choked on a piece of provolone. If that little bit included the areas above *and* below his bed, then yeah, he had.

"Maybe he can show you more after we eat. He's got some wonderful old antiques in this place. Light fixtures and tables and..."

Mack nodded along, watching Mina's rapt face.

"...and that gorgeous Amish bed he and Carolynn brought home from Pennsylvania one time," his mother finished.

Mina's eyebrows shot up. "Bed?" she squeaked.

Why did his mom have to bring up the god-forsaken bed *now?* Minutes earlier, Mack had been blessing its very existence. Now, he cursed it. He'd gotten rid of literally *every other* reminder of his ex-wife, except that one.

"Oh yes," his mother agreed blithely. "It's this enormous oak monstrosity that they fell in love with one year. They took a trip up to Amish country for some reason—"

"Anniversary," Mack muttered.

"Yes, that's right. And next thing we knew, Mack had found a way to disassemble it and cart the whole thing home in the bed of his truck. He had to rebuild it in the bedroom, of course. It wouldn't have fit up those stairs otherwise."

"Wow," Mina said. She wiped her mouth with a white paper napkin. "I will have to take a look at that." She wouldn't meet his eyes any longer.

Mack thought he'd maybe like to strangle his mother. Perhaps send her to live in Katmandu for a while, in a nice lock-down facility for wayward parents.

As for Carolynn's whims, they had usually blown over pretty quickly—her affection for Mack being the primary example—but even Mack had been impressed by the craftmanship of that bed when they found it. It had cost them a fortune, but it was worth every penny. It was made to be an heirloom, to soothe many generations of a family into sleep. Thank God, Carolynn hadn't attempted to ask for it in the divorce. She had to have realized it wasn't going anywhere any time soon.

"I'll show you later," Mack promised Mina. He polished off his sub and drank some lemonade.

"Can't wait," Mina fired tartly back.

Mack's mother looked back and forth between them, her forehead wrinkling up.

"I should probably get going," she said.

Mack feared it was far too late for that—no frisky mood had ever been killed more swiftly.

"So soon?" Mina asked.

She really was an incredible actress. Mack would be a little afraid of her, if he wasn't so relieved she'd managed to finesse the motherly pop-in quandary.

"Yes. You two should catch up," Mack's mom said. "Mack, honey, I'll call you later."

"All right, Mom. Thanks for stopping by."

When she'd driven off, Mack turned to Mina. "I am so sorry about that," he said. "It's bad enough that she showed up out of nowhere, but then to bring up…"

Mina stopped him with a hand on his chest. "Mack it's okay. Don't worry about it. It's not like I don't know you were married before. I was at the wedding, for crying out loud."

"I know. But the fact that I had you up there like half an hour ago, couldn't have felt awesome."

"No. It doesn't feel awesome. But let's not talk about it anymore. Why don't we get out of here and do something else for a bit? Take our minds off it."

Mack didn't know what to do. As much as he'd worried about the ghost of Grey lingering between him and Mina, he hadn't even considered that Carolynn might wedge herself in there, too. And that wasn't all.

He'd been so intent on his end goal of winning Mina, that he'd glossed over most of the ways he could screw this thing up before it even got off the ground. If Mack didn't want to lose Mina all over again, it was time to get his head out of his ass and do some serious strategizing.

Chapter Eleven

Eight Years Earlier

M INA STOOD IN an empty library at the back of the inn, gazing out the window at the lawns bordering the bay. The families were out on the grass and in the other rooms—milling around tending to the various old and young among them and preparing for Mack and Carolynn's wedding.

Mina and Grey had driven up from North Carolina the day before, leaving at five in the morning and driving nearly eight hours through dreary rain in his muscle car. Today was beautiful, though—the sky washed clean and blue, and the air fresh. The inn Mack and Carolynn had chosen was a lovely, elegant place and Mina knew she should be happy for them. Instead, she was hiding out alone to nurse a suffocating bout of melancholy.

The sunshine felt like it had a rusted edge to it and Grey was probably half in the bag already, as he tended to do when he had a party to go to. Mina hadn't spotted Carolynn yet, but she'd heard her—laughing raucously with her girlfriends behind a closed door in one of the ground-floor salons. There'd been no sign of Mack, but that was just as well. He was observant enough that Mina doubted if she'd be able to hide her gloominess from him.

As if she'd conjured him by her thoughts alone, Mack appeared out of nowhere, walking silently across the carpet to stand next to her. His hands were jammed in his pockets, but otherwise he looked handsome and polished in his dark navy-blue suit. How on earth had he found her there? She would've thought he had better things to do at the moment.

"I didn't get a chance to say hi at the rehearsal last night," he said. "Was your drive up okay?"

"Oh, it was fine," Mina assured him. "Long and rainy, but no issues."

"How about your room? I told them to give you one with a nice view."

"It's really nice, thanks." Nicer than their student apartment at UNC, that was for sure.

Mack turned to look at Mina's face. "Hey, you doing okay?"

And there it was—Mack's inconvenient perceptiveness. Mina had never met a man more capable of gauging other people's moods. It was like he had ESP.

She felt like she should say something—explain why she was tucked away there by herself—but how could she? You didn't tell a man who wasn't yours that you were jealous of his future wife. You couldn't say that you were afraid you were about to lose him, not when you didn't have him to begin with. Mina had no right to those feelings at all.

Instead of giving voice to the unspeakable, she said, "That might be heaven out there. It's so pretty."

"Looks like it to me," Mack agreed. "Of course, if it *is* heaven, it has one or two plot twists that I never expected from the afterlife."

Mina could feel his eyes on her.

"Unexpected twists? In heaven?" she murmured, forcing herself to meet his gaze. "Is that even allowed?"

"Probably not," he admitted, holding her hostage with his scrutiny. "But sometimes the curveballs life throws at you can be hard to see coming." Mack leaned his shoulder against the window and would've been a study in nonchalance if anyone else was looking at him. To Mina, he looked tense—coiled tight like a spring.

She took a step back and thought about what he'd said. "I guess all you can do is duck and hope the ball doesn't clock you in the head," she replied.

It seemed like an odd conversation to be having on the morning of his wedding and Mina wondered what they were really talking about. Themselves? The few times a year that she saw Mack, their conversations tended toward the enigmatic, with hidden layers occurring to her hours after the fact. She was always…wrong-footed around him these days.

Their former easy repartee had developed roots somehow and grown laden with meaning. Consequently, the banter had gotten much harder for Mina to deliver. When had this thing between them begun to matter so much? Why did Mina care like she did? It wasn't seemly. It wasn't wise.

Mack smiled a sad little smile and reached out with his fingers to brush her sleeve. "Don't worry, kid. I've got pretty good reflexes."

"I don't," Mina grumbled.

He chuckled. "You do fine."

"If you say so."

Mack straightened up and squared his shoulders. "Mina, listen. I need to say this before…you know."

She didn't pretend to misunderstand—he meant, before the wedding. "What?"

"I wish…" he trailed off, took a deep breath, and looked away.

Is was probably incredibly wrong of her, but Mina *had* to know. "Mack? What do you wish?"

"The way I feel about you—" He ground to a halt again, winced, and shook off whatever he was going to say. "You sure you don't have a sister?" he smiled, but it was strained.

"Of course, I have a sister. You know that. But Molly's too young for you, and besides…" Now it was her turn to freeze up.

"Yeah?"

"I'm bad at sharing," Mina said in a rush. "Especially with her."

Mack scoffed, "But you think you can do it with *Carolynn*?"

"It's hardly up to me."

Mack deserved to have a nice life, and if he thought he could do it with Carolynn, then Mina was not going to stand in his way. She'd already made *her* choice, after all.

Mack studied her, then turned to gaze out the windows again. "She can't hold a candle to you," he whispered, so softly Mina wondered if she'd misheard him. "No one can. Say the word and…"

"Mack, you know I can't do that!" Mina hissed, furious at him for delivering that kind of blow so cavalierly. Who did he think she was? Not the kind of woman who could steal a groom from the altar, that was for damn sure. "I will not say one word," she reiterated.

"I say you can. If you want to."

"Well you're wrong."

Someone called his name from the other room, and with a little sniff of amusement, Mack moved away and turned toward the door.

He was drunk again, like he'd been at the rehearsal dinner. He had to be—there was no other reason a man like Mack Bolton would proposition a woman, moments before he got hitched. It made things so much worse to realize he didn't mean a word he was saying. Mina's chest ached with it.

Mrs. Bolton stuck her head in the door and yelped in relief. "Mack! There you are! Come on, hon, we're getting ready to start." When she noticed who he was standing with, a deep divot formed between her brows, but she didn't say anything else.

Mack grimaced at Mina and straightened his cuffs. "Well, here goes nothing," he said.

"Knock 'em dead, big guy," she smiled. She hoped he wouldn't hate her for refusing him.

Mack strode after his mother, and only looked back once—right before he slipped out the door. Mina blinked hard and turned back to the windows, fighting not to let a single illicit tear fall. When she felt like she could grit it out, she stiffened her spine and exited the library through the French doors that opened onto the lawn, prepared to enter the fray.

Grey was standing near the back row of the folding white chairs, and he waved her over impatiently.

"Where have you been? The ceremony is about to start."

"Sorry. I ran up to the room to touch up my makeup," Mina lied.

"I told you before that you looked fine," he countered, irritated with her.

They walked up the aisle and took the seats that the usher indicated. Grey was flushed and sweating in his Marine dress uniform, despite the temperate day. Mina worried that he'd gotten even drunker while she'd left him alone. His grip on her hand was a hair too tight to be comfortable.

Grey locked eyes with the curvy maid of honor when she strolled up the petal-strewn aisle, and his stare stayed on her throughout the service. Mina watched the boats on the water and the birds wheeling in the sky—anything to avoid thinking about what Mack had just told her in the library, or about the vows being spoken under that arch of white roses.

THE RECEPTION WAS pretty rowdy—something Mina used to enjoy, and Grey still did. The bride's father gave a long, rambling speech that alluded in several places to his daughter's promiscuity. Carolynn repeatedly interrupted her maid of honor's speech with corrections, denials, and shouted commentary that no one else understood.

Mack stood next to his teenaged brother Bodhi while the boy
stammered through his best man speech. The kid had scribbled
his thoughts on notebook paper that trembled noticeably while
he read. Mack steadied him with an arm around his shoulder, and
at the end, they hugged and pretended they weren't choked up.
Grey made fun of Mina for crying, too.

A hundred strings of twinkling lights crisscrossed the party
tent's ceiling, and votive candles flickered on every table. The
lilies in the centerpieces made it smell like a funeral instead of a
wedding.

She drank too much with dinner. In part, that was because the
caterers kept refilling her glass with a really good red wine. It also
took the edge off of the way Grey was working the room, glad-
handing other young men so he could follow Carolynn's maid of
honor around the dance floor at a discrete distance. Did he really
think no one would notice?

Mack kept mostly to the head table, while person after person
stopped by to congratulate him. Carolynn was in constant
motion, though—a vivid white whirlwind who laughed and
danced and did shots with her guests but didn't seem particularly
interested in the groom she'd just married. Mina tried very hard
not to hate her, for Mack's sake.

Grey stopped by briefly, to slow dance with Mina when the
DJ played their song, but then he disappeared again. Mina danced
a few more songs with cousins and friends she'd met before, but
finally had to concede that she was not quite drunk enough to
enjoy their slurred compliments and wandering hands. Before
long, Grey was likely to spot something he didn't like and pick a
fight with one of them. They might as well be at one of his
fraternity parties, instead of an elegant wedding. The vibe was
certainly the same.

What Mina needed was some space to breathe. She slipped out
the side of the big white tent, stepped over some bundled
extension cords, and picked her way across the dark lawn. There
was a block of fancy portable toilets set up in a row nearby, with

a few guests lingering in line for them. Caterers rushed around with stacks of plates and cases of wine, but off near the water, the lawn was deserted.

Mina made for a line of white Adirondack chairs facing the bay, her heels sinking into the grass. She dropped into one with a sigh, but when she did a deep voice chuckled from the other end of the row, startling her. She hadn't noticed anyone else out there.

Mack leaned forward and grinned at her. He was in his shirtsleeves and had an untouched piece of cake near his elbow. "Mrs. Whitney, if I didn't know better, I'd think you were snubbing my party," he said.

Damn. Mack was not a spiteful guy—if he was calling her Mrs. Whitney so soon after essentially offering to run away with her, he must still be drunk. Mina, on the other hand, suddenly felt unspeakably sober.

"You're the one out here by yourself. A case could be made that you're snubbing your own party."

"Pshhhh." He swayed a little in his chair.

"Jesus, Mack. Look at you—you're a mess."

"No, I'm not. I'm just a little dishembled. Dis…dish…*disheveled*." He struggled awkwardly over the word, but it didn't dim his giddy smile. "I'm glad you're here. I want to say something."

"Oh, I don't think that's a good idea," Mina said.

"Yes, it is," Mack protested. "I planned it all out and everything, and I didn't get to finish before." He was as petulant as a stubborn four-year-old.

Mina was surprised by the bark of laughter that escaped her, since this didn't feel remotely funny. "God! What is it about you? I just can't, um…" She stopped—she'd have to be very careful about what came out of her mouth next, even if the odds were good that Mack wouldn't remember it later. He had his whole marriage ahead of him—if Mina admitted too much now, it could ruin everything.

"You can't what?" he grinned. "Can't stop thinking about how much you *like* me?"

"Stop it," she demanded. This was totally getting out of hand. "I can't tell you what I think about you!"

Mack looked as innocent as a child when he asked, "Why not?"

"Because it's *way* too inappropriate!" she cried, then immediately cringed. Too much information. Retreat!

"No. *Shit*," Mack agreed emphatically. He nodded his head and kept nodding it. He looked as solemn as if she'd just dropped the most revelatory piece of knowledge on his head that mankind had ever heard.

She eyed him with interest. The cat was out of the bag, now—might as well pet it. "I can't help wondering sometimes, you know?"

Mack swallowed, and she watched his Adam's apple bob in his throat. "You mean—what if we had met each other first?"

"Yeah," Mina admitted. "I know it's wrong."

"I know, honey. Me, too." With a rueful little smile, Mack rose unsteadily to his feet, and then turned to watch the commotion across the lawn. "I guess that's what I wanted to say, but there's no fixin' it now. We're both good and stuck."

He came closer and squeezed her shoulder, then shuffled erratically across the grass, back toward the reception. Older guests were beginning to leave in groups of two and three, as well as the parents lugging babies and sleeping toddlers. The caterers were stacking their dinner ephemera in large boxes outside the tent, and the DJ had given up on slow tunes and was playing popular dance hits at top volume. Mina got up and moved to Mack's vacated chair, so at least she could eat his forgotten cake.

After a while, she knew she had to return, if only to make sure that her husband didn't embarrass himself—or her. Just outside the tent, Mina stopped to look for Grey and hoped she wouldn't see him doing something awful. All she saw was Mack, though, swaying absently while Carolynn gyrated against him. Mina grabbed onto a tent pole for balance, reached down to slip off her painful heels, and forced herself to go in search of her husband. He hadn't spared her more than a word or two in hours and was none too pleased when she found him and interrupted his conversation with a guy she didn't know.

"All right, man," Grey told him, "I'll catch you later." They shook hands, and Mina caught the smallest flash of something passing from one palm to the other.

After the other guest walked away, she asked, "What was that?" even though Grey hated to be questioned.

"What?"

"You gave that guy something."

Grey examined her face in that way that always made her want to squirm. "Just my number," he told her. "He's interested in joining the service. I told him he could call if he had questions."

Mina turned and looked for the other man, spotting him in conference with a few other guys outside the tent. He seemed too old to be interested in the military, and too…preppy, somehow. He belonged in a yacht club, not a boot camp. Something didn't seem right.

"Let's get out of here," Grey said. "I'm whipped."

Mina couldn't wait until she could crawl under the covers. Hidden by the darkness, she'd finally be able to think about everything that had happened that day, without being concerned that someone might read her disloyal thoughts on her face.

It wasn't until the next afternoon, thinking back, that it occurred to Mina to worry if anyone had overheard her and Mack—and to fear that they might say something about it.

Chapter Twelve

Eight Years Earlier

THE NEXT MORNING, Mack and Carolynn dragged ass to his mom's house for the post-wedding brunch. It took him a while to work his way through the guests—but whether that was because Mack was seeing double from the booze's aftereffects, or because there were more people than he expected, was anyone's guess.

He was, frankly, exhausted. After the reception had eventually died down, he and Carolynn had staggered up to their suite, carefully extracted each other from their fancy get-ups, and made a perfunctory sort of love that Mack refused to get depressed over. It had been an incredibly long day, they'd both had a bit too much to drink, and they were dead on their feet by the end of it all.

The fact that sex with his brand-new wife had felt more like an obligation than an undeniable explosion of passion—the way he'd always envisioned his wedding night—well, Mack wasn't prepared to be concerned *just* yet. Their life together was only beginning. There was plenty of time to work out the kinks—or to work *in* some kinks, as the case may be.

Once Carolynn had fallen asleep, Mack laid awake next to her, staring at the ceiling and replaying the evening in bits and pieces of fuzzy memory.

The ceremony was a total blur and may as well have happened to someone else for all Mack remembered of it. Instead, he thought about his father-in-law's incredibly awkward speech at the reception, and the way people had laughed uncomfortably at his dicey descriptions of the bride. Mack thought about Carolynn shimmying up to various teenaged cousins on the dance floor, then laughing hysterically when she made them blush.

His mother wept through the service and kept weeping off and on the rest of the night. Mack had thought they were happy tears, but it was sometimes difficult to tell.

And then Mina—Mina speaking softly to him in the inn's library and on that deserted lawn in the dark. Had he really suggested that he would walk away from it all for her? Yes, Mack supposed he had. Before he took as big a step as marriage, he'd had to be sure there was no chance for them.

IT TOOK SOME concerted searching, but Mack eventually found Mina hiding in the kitchen. She was singing softly along with the radio his mom kept near the phone and was elbows deep in the sudsy sink. His mother must have stepped outside for a moment, because Mack knew there was no way she'd allow one of her guests to wash dishes otherwise.

Mina looked about as tired as Mack felt. He wondered when she and Grey were leaving to go back to North Carolina. The way things were going, he might not see her again for months, if not years.

He leaned on the counter next to her and crossed his arms. "I hadn't remembered the caterers being quite so well-dressed," he told her.

Mina had switched out her shimmery pink frock from the night before with a ruffled skirt that brushed the tops of her knees. She had on sandals and a tank top, and her thin little sweater was draped on a chair nearby. She smelled good enough to eat, and that sensation ratcheted up exponentially when she smiled mistily at him.

"Mack…" she hesitated. "You know I adore you." She cleared her throat and pushed on. "I'm happy for you. And I hope—I hope everything works out for you guys."

That sounded too much like a goodbye, so Mack decided to employ a little selective hearing, in an effort to lighten the mood. "You adore me?"

Out of the blue, it all felt deadly serious, but he didn't want to freak her out. So, he raised an eyebrow and smirked at her. Mina splashed him with some suds.

"Oh please. I'm transparent and we both know it. It's no secret that I care what happens to you." Mina nodded to herself, and then said, "I want you to promise me you'll try to be happy with her."

Her words sounded so rehearsed. Had she stayed up all night crafting what she wanted to say? Why? The wedding was *over* now. He'd given her a chance and she'd turned him *away*. Mack grabbed a half-empty Bloody Mary from the counter next to him and drained it. He was not feeling particularly strong that morning, and a wave of fury was threatening to swamp him.

"I stand by what I said yesterday," he muttered. "And I will continue to do so for the rest of my days." He stared out the propped-open back door, his mind too chaotic to even really see the guests milling around his mom's yard.

Mina apparently couldn't resist a dig. With a fake look of horror, she said, "You still want to hook up with my sister?"

Mack fought for control. "*No.* The other part."

"Good, because I like you far too much to inflict my sister on you." Mina rinsed off a platter and set it on the drying rack, then wiped at her forehead with her wrist. "Or my mother. Or any of my shady family, come to think of it," she added grumpily.

Mack had met her mother once or twice, back when Mina was staying with him. She'd struck him as something of a floozy, but essentially harmless. "What's up with them?" he asked.

"We're having a bit of a rough patch," she sighed.

"Oh?"

"I don't think Molly likes Grey very much. And my mom likes him *too* much, if that makes any sense. They're like wild animals, my family. They either cling like grim death or lash out and try to maim whatever makes them feel vulnerable."

"That seems harsh."

"Yeah well, apparently me being settled and happy freaks them out. It's as exhausting as it's always been."

Was she? Either settled or happy? Mack wondered. "That was yet another masterful deflection of what I was trying to talk about, Mina."

She nodded but wouldn't look at him. "I am attempting to keep Pandora's box tightly shut now, *Mack*," she muttered. "Not like yesterday."

He frowned at the chastisement. "I'm not asking you to do wrong. I just want you to know that—"

She cut him off. "—*because*, if I were to say what I really think and feel…"

Mack held his breath expectantly, his heart launching into an ungainly gallop.

"…I'd probably end up going to hell in a handbasket," Mina finished. She pulled the plug in the sink drain and concentrated mightily on wiping her hands dry with a dishtowel.

Each time Mack thought she was putting him in his place once and for all, Mina managed to backpedal and muddy the water. It was like she was at constant war with herself—wanting to tell Mack she felt the same, but pissed about it, too.

He examined her face. The overarching theme seemed to be that she was a bad person for even admitting to what swirled between them. If that was the case, Mack must be Hell's own overlord for what he'd said and done, just in the last couple of days.

When Mina broke the silence once more, she echoed his thoughts eerily. "I was much better at sinning when I was eighteen," she sighed heavily. She sounded apologetic. "I must have used up a lifetime's allotment back then, and now I have nothing left. I hope you can forgive me." With that, she walked out the door.

Mack stood there feeling like a grade-A dunce. He hadn't even been married for twenty-four hours. What was he doing, trying to goad another dude's wife into declaring...*what*, exactly? Did he want to force Mina to admit she liked *him* best? Did he want her to break her marriage vows, vows she'd sworn to one of his oldest friends? Mack had no idea. He knew he needed *something* from her.

Whatever it was, he couldn't have it, and it wasn't fair to anyone to keep needling Mina about it. She was married. *He* was married, now. The die was cast. The bed was made. All the metaphors about finality applied right there, right then, and Mack was going to have to grow up and accept that shit like a man. He sighed and spun to head deeper into the house, away from other people.

Grey pushed himself off the door jamb where he'd been leaning and shuffled casually into the kitchen. Mack swallowed. It *figured*. But how long had the guy been standing there? He had his answer soon enough.

"What the fuck do you think you're doing?" Grey asked silkily.

"Pardon?" Playing dumb wasn't the most artful thing to do, but it would buy time to think.

"I seem to keep finding you holed up with my wife," the man scowled. "*My* wife."

Mack chuckled at his brio. "We were just talking, bro. Stand down. Besides, I have my own wife now, in case you didn't notice." What did they say? A good offense made the best defense? It was harder than it looked.

"I did notice that, actually. I noticed your new wife drinking mimosas by herself outside, wondering where the fuck you were."

It was impossible to tell how much Grey might have heard. Mack should have remembered the way his buddy kept such a careful watch on Mina. It was easy to get lulled into the idea that Grey was mostly concerned with himself—to forget that part of his narcissism involved making sure Mina was focused on him, too.

"Dude, I brought some dirty plates in and found Mina washing dishes. We got to talking for a minute, and then she left. No big deal."

Grey peered into Mack's face, and Mack gave him a once-over of his own. He was freshly showered and shaved, with a tiny nick on his neck from his razor. His hands were balled into fists and jammed into the pockets of his khakis. His anger was palpable, but Mack knew it had a way of blowing in like a summer storm, then blowing out just as swiftly. He simply had to keep Grey from throwing any punches before that happened.

"Grey, man," Mack said, calculating his odds of succeeding with this salvo. "Mina is…" Loyal. Steadfast. *Too damn good for you.* "She's head over heels for you. She always has been. You can't possibly think any of us knuckleheads could change that?"

It was a gamble. On the one hand, Grey might go for the ego stroke. On the other, he might take umbrage at the hint that he was acting stupid. Mack watched his buddy slowly decide what he was going to do. Maybe Grey was making some calculations of his own, too—could he get away with decking the groom at the wedding brunch? Could he simply laugh off his suspicions and still save face?

"I know you've always been jealous of what I have," Grey said grimly. There was that ever-present megalomania Mack had expected. "But Mina is *mine*. She'll always be mine. Keep away from her."

"Whatever you say," Mack drawled. "But I swear you have nothing to worry about."

Grey set his empty glass in the sink, grabbed the celery, and took a big crunching bite, right in Mack's face.

What *was* this? A hammy fighter pilot movie from the Eighties? Mack closed his eyes and tried to keep his frantic laughter from spilling out. When he opened them again, Grey was gone, but his mom had appeared.

"What was that all about?" she asked. She handed him a fresh Bloody Mary.

"Just Grey being Grey," Mack sighed. He drained half the glass in one gulp, but it did nothing to settle his jumping nerve endings. He'd like to follow that dick outside and clock him right in the teeth.

Carolynn waltzed in, a mimosa in each hand. "I know that guy's your friend, babe, but he's kind of an ass. Alyssa said he was dogging her all day, yesterday."

Mack struggled to keep his head. It was all right for Grey to hit on the maid of honor, but Mina couldn't even *talk* to someone she used to room with? What kind of twisted shit was that?

"Mack?" Carolynn asked, "Did you hear what I said?"

Mack slipped an arm around her waist. She'd been sloppier with her makeup that morning than she usually was, and for some reason it was endearing. "I did. Do you want me to go talk to him?"

"No, Alyssa's fine. It's not worth it. But...isn't he here with his wife? I feel sorry for *her*."

Mack's mother piped up, "I'm sure Grey didn't mean anything by it. He's always been social like that."

Carolynn frowned, and started to protest, "That's not social, that's..." Mack squeezed her hip. Hard. "Maybe I misunderstood," she finished lamely.

"That's probably all it was," Mack's mom agreed. He could hardly blame her—she'd known Grey Whitney since he was in diapers. "Once you get to know him better, you'll see how terrific he is."

Mack tried not to gag. *Terrific.* Yup, that's what Grey was. It was one thing to be friends with a guy like that—you could simply choose to keep your distance when he got out of hand. But Mina was *married* to him. What the hell was she supposed to do? And if she stayed with him, would Mack even be able to help?

"Come on, Mack," said Carolynn. "Let's go back outside. I want you to meet my cousin Vanessa. She's really, *really* terrific."

Deep in thought, Mack let her lead him away.

Chapter Thirteen

MINA HAD HOPED that all the endorphins flooding her system—courtesy of her newly-burgeoning sex life—would counteract the total lack of sleep she'd been getting every weekend, but she was wrong. The receptionist at work showed up on Monday sounding like she was trying to cough up a lung, Mina developed her own fever by Tuesday night, and by Wednesday morning, she knew she was done for.

Mina definitely remembered calling in sick to work that day. And she knew, at some point, she must have told Mack that she was ill, because her cell kept chirping with texts asking how she was. Other than that, the thirty-six hours that followed were a hazy, miserable fog.

But now, her fever had finally broken and her sore throat had improved enough that Mina thought she might be able to choke down more than water or tea.

She managed to take a much-needed shower, and that helped—but it exhausted her. She crawled back into bed with wet hair, so she could rest for a few minutes before she attempted to go downstairs and make real food.

Her cell rang insistently. Mina groaned when she saw who it was.

"Hello?"

"Mina, it's Claudette. How are you?"

"I've been laid up with the flu all week. I am so sorry—I forgot to cancel my appointment, didn't I?"

"Yes, and then you weren't at group, either. Don't worry, I understand—but since you've never done that before, I wanted to make sure you were okay."

"I'm not gonna lie. The last couple days were pretty awful. But now that my fever seems to be gone, I feel more human," Mina told her.

"Oh good. Well, do let me know if you need any help. And you know who to call if you want soup," her therapist said. Marie, from the bereavement group Claudette ran, had a habit of bringing soup to the other members, for any and all reasons. Which would be sweet, if she were any good at making it.

"Believe it or not, Marie's bland soup might be just the ticket right now," Mina admitted. "Maybe I'll call her."

Dr. Mercer chuckled. "All right. Well…you get better and let me know in a few days if you want to reschedule."

Mina thought about Mack, and the way their histories with other people—and with each other—kept intruding on her thoughts. "Yes, I'll do that," she said, before hanging up.

She closed her eyes, sank into the damp pillow, and drifted for a few minutes. She had to eat, and probably ought to change her sheets, but Mina just couldn't work up the energy.

Downstairs, her doorbell rang. She whimpered. Was the whole world trying to kill her? Why couldn't everyone just let her die in peace? She shoved herself off the bed and shuffled to her bedroom window, then peeked out the blinds at the stoop below.

In the orange pool cast by the porch light, Dimitri stood holding a big paper bag of what looked like groceries. Mina didn't know whether to cry or kiss him, but either way, she couldn't let him see her like this. So, she knocked on the window and waved him away, hoping he'd get the hint. Dimitri stepped back from the door, glared up at her, then yanked his phone out of his jacket pocket. On the street behind him, a small, faded red car drifted slowly by, and she frowned. Where had she seen that before?

On her nightstand, Mina's cell pinged with a text.

What is this? Romeo + Juliet?

She typed back:

Go away. I'm too busy dying to have visitors.

Her friend scowled and wrote:

Come down here right now and tell me you're okay, or I'm calling the cops for a wellness check.

Damn it. Friends were a total pain in the ass.

I'm okay, all right?? I'm just sick + pathetic + don't want u to catch this!

Down below, Dimitri stared at his phone, but Mina recognized his expression. She couldn't remember why she'd ever thought he was a decent person instead of a stubborn mule. His jaw set, he resolutely tapped out:

Stop screwing around and open up.

Mina sighed. There was no getting around it. Besides, she was a tiny bit curious to see what he had in that bag. She made her way down the stairs on shaky legs, then unlocked the door.

"You can come in," she told Dimitri. "But you might want to wear a surgical mask. And you probably don't want to touch anything." She looked up and down her street, but the red car was gone, replaced by a shiny black sedan idling at the stop sign on the corner. While she watched, the brake lights dimmed, and it made a slow left down another side street.

Mina stepped inside and locked her door. It wasn't like it was a bad neighborhood, but it did seem like there were more strange cars around than usual. Whatever that meant.

"If you were this sick, why the hell didn't you call me?" Dimitri grumbled. He looked her over. "You look like shit."

"Thank you, doctor, I feel like shit," she told him. She shambled over to her kitchen table and dropped heavily into a chair. "And I was too unconscious to make calls, anyway."

He put the bag on her counter. "You were too proud, you mean."

"I'm not kidding. I was out cold," Mina argued. "What's in the bag?"

Dimitri began unpacking tea and honey and cans of soup. There was also bread, eggs, milk, and bananas. "I don't know. Basic stuff," he mumbled. "I wasn't sure what was *wrong* with you, so I had no idea what you might *need*." He frowned at Mina again.

She frowned back. "Dimitri, why are you even here right now?"

He stared down at his hands, clutching a carton of orange juice. "You weren't at group. I asked Claudette afterwards, and she said she hadn't heard from you. No one had."

Mina deflated in embarrassment. The poor man was worried about her. "I'm sorry," she told him contritely. "I should have told you."

Dimitri shrugged. "Next time." He began putting things in her fridge. "When was the last time you had something to eat, anyway?"

Mina tried to think, but it was hard. She was so tired. "I don't know. Tuesday morning, maybe?" She crossed her arms and laid her head on them. If she weren't so hungry, she could probably sleep for another twelve hours.

"What do you want?" Her friend stood there, hands on his hips, looking ready for anything. A rush of affection pulsed through her. His father ran a Greek diner, and Dimitri had worked many a summer there. Food was love to him, and right now that was probably what Mina needed most.

"You don't have to do this," Mina told him. "I can just make some toast or something."

"You can't even stand," he fired back. "So, toast. What else? Can you handle some eggs?"

Mina's stomach seemed to like that idea. "Scrambled? With cheese?" she smiled.

Dimitri laughed. "You got it. Why don't you go lay down and I'll let you know when it's ready?"

"Don't have to ask me twice," Mina muttered. She staggered over to her couch and flopped onto it, pulling the fleece throw off the side to cover herself.

She must have fallen asleep, because it only seemed like a second had passed before Dimitri was waking her again. Mina pushed herself upright and accepted the plate of food he held out to her. He walked back to her kitchen, then returned with a steaming cup of tea for her, and a mug of coffee for himself.

While she ate, he told her a little bit about what had happened at the bereavement group meeting that afternoon—but he was obviously more curious about the way her cell phone kept buzzing on the coffee table, than in rehashing how everyone else was doing. Finally, he broke off and jerked his chin at it.

"What's going on?"

Mina checked the screen, even though she was pretty sure she knew. *Mack.*

"It's just this guy I know," she said.

Dimitri tilted his head and smiled. "Just this guy? Who likes to blow up your phone?"

"Oh, don't you start," Mina threatened. "You may make a mean plate of eggs, but I'm not scared of you."

"You haven't seen what I can do with a grilled cheese," Dimitri fired back. Mina's phone vibrated again. Her friend gave her a *look*.

"All *right*. Look—this guy and I have known each other for a really long time, okay? He was going to come for a visit this weekend, and he's bummed that I waved him off." Mina swallowed a big bite of toast—it scratched like hell going down her throat, but her desperate stomach rejoiced anyway.

Dimitri shrugged. "So what?"

"So...I feel bad. I don't want him to be upset."

"Well, that's kind of his problem. If he doesn't like it, tough. Why didn't *you* want him to come?"

"Because he'll probably show up and want to clean and do laundry and stuff," Mina complained. "He'll want to take care of me, I know it."

Dimitri sipped his coffee, and eyed Mina over the edge of the mug. "I'm not sure I see the issue. He sounds cool. Why not let him help? You let me."

"I don't *know*," she whined. "It seems like he's always helping everyone. For some reason I don't *want* him to do it with me."

"Is it because of how Grey was? Lording shit over you all the time?"

"Maybe? I like being independent."

"Or..." Dimitri studied her face. "Maybe it's that you don't want to be lumped in with everyone else he knows."

Mina's breath caught in her throat. She hadn't considered that possibility, but now that she did, it felt true. She stayed silent, holding the thought close to protect it.

"I think you've earned the right to some help, bud," Dimitri said softly. "Don't make things harder on yourself than they need to be."

Mina scraped up some eggs and chewed them slowly, stalling while she thought. "It's kind of new between us. Old, but new, too. I know it sounds precious of me, but I'm not sure I want him to see me all gross so soon. I do have *some* pride."

"And...there goes *my* ego," Dimitri snarked. He laid a hand over his heart. "Always a bridesmaid, never a bride."

Mina rolled her eyes. "Oh, for the love of God. Don't be ridiculous."

He grew serious again. "If the guy's going to be an asshole about something as simple as you being sick, better to know that sooner rather than later, right?"

Well, yeah. Grey had taught her that. Still, Mina was dubious. "I do want to see him, I just..." She watched her phone buzzing on the table and bit her lip. She wasn't used to people taking care of her—her parents certainly never had. Letting Mack coddle her felt let an admission that things between them were more serious than a few orgasms between friends.

"Will you answer that man?" Dimitri pleaded. "Dude sounds like he's going nuts over there."

This was the sort of thing Mack excelled at. He had helped her and Grey find a place to live when they moved back from North Carolina. He'd helped Mina cart home a second-hand treadmill she bought one time when Grey was deployed, transporting it to her house in his pickup truck.

There were other things, too, other times Mack had stepped up. He was a *helper*, plain and simple—he saw a problem, and then he figured out how to fix it. Mina wasn't so sure she wanted to be a problem that needed fixing, though. She already had her mother for that.

"*Mina.*"

"Okay, fine," she conceded. "But if this goes wrong, I'm blaming you."

"I can take it," Dimitri told her. He stood and took her empty plate. "Now what else needs to be done?"

"Not a thing."

"Lies. Always so many lies."

Mina sighed. There was no way she could face changing her sheets tonight, but there was also no way she wanted to sleep on them again after two nights of fever sweats.

"Maybe you could change my sheets," she admitted. "If that's not too weird or disgusting."

"Now we're getting somewhere," he smiled. "Where are the fresh ones?"

"Linen closet is at the top of the stairs on the right," she said. "But you better have a decontamination suit stashed away in your car or something. No kidding—this disease is deadly."

"I'll be fine," he called over from the kitchen. "Already got my flu shot. I bet you wish you had, too."

"Now is not the time to gloat, Dimitri," Mina growled. She looked at the screen of her phone. Five missed texts. Damn it.

Her friend headed toward her stairs, juggling some yellow rubber gloves and a container of antibacterial wipes.

"Will you please tell Prince Charming he can come slay the dragon? I'll be upstairs playing Cinderella," he said.

"It's a good thing you're handy," Mina told his retreating back. "Otherwise you'd be out of here so fast your head would spin."

"Promises, promises." Dimitri's voice filtered down the stairs. A minute later, Mina heard the squeak of the linen closet door and the thump of his heavy footsteps down the hall.

In the space of one hour, her therapist had called to check on her, Dimitri had shown up at her front door with food and helping hands, and Mack had texted her five—no six—times to see how she was. Mina didn't know what she'd ever done to deserve the kindness of people like that in her life, but it sure did make a girl feel nice.

She looked down at her phone again. With shaking hands, she opened up her texts and considered what to say.

Chapter Fourteen

MACK WAS ANXIOUS for the entire drive to Annapolis on Friday evening. Mina had apparently been sick all week, and had wanted to cancel their plans for the weekend. While that made sense, he'd also been worried for days about how bad she sounded, and desperately wanted to get eyes on the situation—maybe even take her to a doctor, if need be. The fact that Mina had so readily resisted his offers to help kind of hurt.

It had taken days of pleading—then some mild, empty threats to show up unannounced—before Mina finally agreed to let Mack come see her.

There was probably an unpleasant word for the way he'd pushed, but if he got there and Mina seemed truly unhappy to see him, then Mack knew he would leave. For the time being, though, he was loaded down with bags of provisions, and hopefully he'd thought of everything.

She answered the door of her small duplex wearing loose, white flannel pajamas. They were emblazoned with large navy-blue anchors, and smaller, vivid red lobsters. He wasn't positive yet, but Mack thought maybe one or two of those little crustaceans had Santa hats on. He grinned, cocking one amused brow at her while he stood on her doorstep. Christmas was months away.

"What?" Mina demanded. "Surely you didn't expect me to greet you in *Wicked West's*?"

To be fair, she hadn't as yet greeted Mack at all. Nor had she invited him in.

"The fact that you even know what *Wicked West's* is…" he began, struggling to banish the suddenly lurid images of the lingerie and sex toy shop flooding his cerebral cortex. *He* shouldn't even know what that store was.

Mina rolled her eyes so hard, she was lucky they stayed in her head. Mack decided he needed to regroup.

"You know what, sweetie?" he told her, "On second thought, I wouldn't put it past you."

Her narrowed gaze snapped to his, suddenly alert.

He continued, "But that's what's always been so damn enticing about you, I guess. The fact that you can pull off—" Mack gestured expansively at her get-up, "*Those*, in addition to some crazy-ass corset with laces and studs and shit…"

His mouth went dry, and Mack realized that he'd better freeze that train of thought right in its tracks before it ran the hell away with him.

"A guy never knows what he's going to get with you, he just knows it's gonna be damn good," he finished. His chest puffed out. There—that ought to gain him entry.

Mina stood in her doorway blinking rapidly at him, shock etched into every feature of her face. Two small splotches of red adorned her cheekbones, standing in stark contrast to the rest of her too-pale skin.

"I come bearing gifts," he added softly, breaking the silence that had fallen between them. He lifted the plastic bags in his hands to show her, since she hadn't noticed them on her own.

It seemed to jog her out of her paralysis. Coloring slightly more, Mina moved aside and held the door wide for him, then closed and locked it once Mack stepped inside.

He strode into her kitchen and unloaded six-packs of beer and hard cider onto her counter, while Mina unpacked the containers of Korean take-out he'd brought.

"I rented a couple movies," she offered shyly, straightening the neck of her pajama top. "You'll probably hate them. They're all romances."

"First germs, and now this?" Mack complained.

Mina hesitated. "I should go change."

"No, you shouldn't. Those pajamas are great," he smiled. She was swimming in them and it was adorable. "Besides, that was the deal, wasn't it? I told you I'd bring you food, so we could veg out watching bad movies in our jammies. Didn't I?"

"Except you're not wearing jammies," Mina complained, shifting on her feet. "I feel stupid."

"First of all, I'd get arrested if I went out in public in what I normally sleep in," Mack said. He gazed at her while the significance of *that* sunk in. "Second of all, I'm a grown man. You can't really expect me to pick up booze and take-out in pajamas."

"Or lack thereof," Mina mused.

"Or lack thereof," Mack confirmed. He hoped she remembered sleeping nude in his bed together, because he sure did. Shame about that flu.

She shifted her gaze so fast it startled him. "Is that *kimchi*?" she blurted out, valiantly changing conversational direction without warning.

"It is. I have *bibimbap* and green tea for you, too. You'll be feeling 100% in no time with this stuff. Loaded with garlic and antioxidants. Or something."

"At minimum, it will clear out my sinuses," she agreed, laughing. Mina started coughing then, and Mack winced at the deep chest rattle he heard. She got it under control after a minute or two, but her eyes were watery and it was clear it hurt like hell.

"I almost forgot. There are these, too." He dumped out the last bag—the one from the pharmacy. Four kinds of cough drops skittered across her countertop, plus both day and night-time cold medicine.

Mina took one look and slumped in relief. "Ohhh. Bless you, kind sir," she murmured. "You're the best person I know."

THEY ONLY GOT through one sappy clunker of a movie before her medicine kicked in and Mina started nodding off. She'd hadn't made much of a dent in her dinner, so Mack brought it all into the kitchen to stick in her fridge. He'd been dubious when she voted for the spicy Korean food, and maybe he'd been right. If she let him stay, he'd make her something plainer in the morning—something her recovering system could handle better.

Back on the couch, Mina was awake again and starting a new Regency rom-com, but she looked melancholy. Mack checked the screen—people in old-fashioned tuxes and gowns were twirling around a ballroom flirting with each other.

Mina said, "Grey and I never did stuff like that."

"What?"

"Well…we almost never got all dressed up to go out anywhere," she said. "But also—we never paid much attention to each other when we were out. He was more interested in mingling. Talking to people he knew…meeting new people. Half the time, I felt more like a prop than someone he actually wanted to spend time with."

Mack clenched his jaw. Grey, again. That *asshole*. Mack couldn't comprehend having Mina on his arm and wanting to pay attention to anything else in the universe.

"We should do it," Mack suggested, since anything else he said would probably come out as, *Dickhead is lucky he's dead, or I'd kill him myself.* "Go somewhere fancy, sometime."

"It's funny you should say that." Mina coughed for a bit, but Mack would've bet his last dime that it was a stalling tactic that time, and not the real thing.

"And why is that?"

"Now that I've softened you up with *bulgogi* and probably infected you with my virus…" Mina began.

"Oh, this ought to be good."

She grimaced. "I'd like to apologize in advance for the crummy thing I'm about to ask of you."

"Don't bother. Nothing could be crummier than giving me tuberculosis."

Mina dropped her head into her hands and groaned, but that just kicked off another round of horrible coughing. It took a while before she could talk again—that bout sounded real enough.

"Sorry," Mack said. "Let's try this again. How may I be of service?"

"I got invited to this thing next week. I *really* don't want to have to go alone."

"Done."

"Just like that? Trust me, you probably want to hear what it is before you agree."

Mack peered at her. "It'd better not be a bachelor auction. I did one of those in college one time, and I will *never* do that again. Huge mistake. Completely humiliating."

Mina laughed, then coughed, then laughed some more. Her eyes were streaming. "No, it's nothing like that. But—Lord, tell me there's video somewhere of that auction. I'd pay good money to see that, and I bet I'm not the only one."

Mack scoffed, "It took a whole team of hitmen to suppress that evidence. You think I would just *hand* it over to you?"

"Please?" Mina wheedled. "It would save the soul of a sick and wretched woman."

"Pshh. Not on your life," Mack said. "Now—where are you dragging me next week?"

Mina hid her face behind a throw pillow. "Please don't kill me. It's *so* awkward. I can ask a friend. It's okay—I'll just ask a friend."

Mack yanked the pillow down and gestured for her to get on with it.

"The veterans group in St. Michaels is giving Grey some kind of posthumous award at their annual ball," she blurted out in a rush. "They asked me to be there to accept it."

"Shouldn't they have done that *last* year?" he wondered.

"Apparently they didn't hear he died in time."

Mack winced. "You're right. That it not my favorite idea."

"It's so much worse than you think," she whimpered. "It's black tie. You'd need to wear a tux."

Mack scrubbed at his face. "I mean...really? What did I ever do to you? Why do you hate me so much?" Tuxedos were even worse than regular suits—they had those stupid cummerbund things that never seemed to line up correctly with his waistband, and tiny studs instead of normal buttons. All that, before you even got to the damn bow ties.

"I swear I don't hate you," Mina promised. "I'm just the world's biggest chicken. On the bright side, there will be dinner and dancing, and I promise to wear a *very* pretty dress."

Mack eyed her speculatively. "Hmm. Well that's something, I guess." To his knowledge, *Wicked West's* didn't sell ballgowns, only underpinnings. But maybe, since they'd been talking about it, Mina would...

"So, you'll do it?" She looked pathetic in her pajamas, with her red-rimmed eyes and pale skin, and tissues crumpled all around her. Mack couldn't have denied her if he'd tried.

He sighed. "Fine. I'll go. Will that pretty dress be very short and very tight?"

Mina smiled wide, generous in victory. "How about *long* and tight?"

"With a plunging neckline?"

"Let's say—a slit high up the side instead. But that's my final offer."

Mack crossed his arms on his chest and slumped low on the couch, scowling. "*Fine.*"

She scrambled across the couch and launched herself at him, hugging him tight. "You're my hero, you know that, right?"

If only. "I try," he said, which was truer than either of them was likely to admit.

Jesus Lord, had he really just agreed to accompany Grey's widow to a military ball, so she could accept a posthumous award in his honor? Had Mack gone *insane?*

"I'm going owe you big time for this," Mina said. She shimmied down on the couch and laid her head in Mack's lap.

"Don't worry. I'm sure I'll think of something." Mack stroked her soft hair over and over, watching until Mina fell sound asleep again.

"Do you know?" he whispered quietly to her. "Do you have any idea what you do to me?"

Chapter Fifteen

S ATURDAY MORNING, MACK had called to suggest that Mina pack a change of clothes for the night, so they could stay at his place instead of having to drive all the way back to Annapolis after the ball. In all of her nervous fluttering getting ready, though, she completely forgot to do it. When Mack came to her door looking hot as sin in his tailored black tuxedo, Mina pretty much forgot her own name, too.

"Hey, beautiful," he said. "I see you held up your end of the bargain."

Mina had barely found the silver satin dress in time, only spotting it on the clearance rack of the department store during her lunch hour two days ago. It hugged her curves, had a dangerously low neckline, and a slit cut high up her leg. She smiled. It was too racy by half for the place they were going, but her date proclaimed it perfect.

Mina hurried upstairs to throw some things in a bag and took the opportunity to quickly change out of her misguided skin-colored slip and into the one set of lacy black lingerie that she owned. At least if Mack got her out of her slinky dress later, he wouldn't find an ugly wetsuit underneath—and Mina's superhero name wouldn't have to be *Skin Girl*.

She worried that the black lace would show through, but Mack *had* been angling for something stimulating. And, after agreeing to go with her, the man certainly deserved that much.

Mina quickly searched her bureau drawers, but she didn't have anything even approaching sexy pajamas to pack. True, she hoped she wouldn't actually *need* them, but if this thing she was making Mack attend got tricky, sex might be the last thing on his mind, anyway. Mina chose a pair of flannel bottoms and an old concert tee instead, grabbed her toothbrush, and zipped up the bag.

In his truck on the long drive there, the silence was loaded. Mina fiddled with the stereo, crossed and uncrossed her legs, and fussed with her hair in the mirror. She'd only agreed to attend this event out of sympathy for the kindly old veteran who'd phoned her, after she'd ignored the paper invitation in the mail. Had she really needed to drag Mack there, too?

Around the time they left the Bay Bridge behind and hit Kent Island, it became obvious that he was—for the moment, at least—untroubled. Mack grinned swiftly at her and glanced at Mina's legs.

"I'm not sure whether to pray this event runs long, or hope the whole place gets evacuated five minutes in," he admitted, clutching the steering wheel. "Seriously, Mina. That dress is dangerous."

She let out a startled laugh. "You're a bad seed, Mack Bolton." James Bond over there was one to talk—his tuxedo looked like it had been made especially for him and would make nearly any woman's mouth water.

He grinned wider. "Pots and kettles, Mina. Pots and kettles."

MINA HAD BEEN told that the event to honor the fallen servicemen and women would be part of the veteran organization's annual ball. But upon their arrival, she was apprehensive to discover that the posthumous "award" Grey was receiving would be bestowed at the very beginning of the dinner, giving her no time to get settled and prepare herself. She and Mack were hardly in their seats for five minutes before a group of older men beckoned her and a handful of others to the small stage.

After a brief introduction, each veteran solemnly read the names and biographies of two locally-born servicemembers who had died recently, while Mina and the other family members stood stiffly off to the side. She was, by far, the youngest person on the stage, and possibly also the biggest fraud.

Once they'd finished, a sweet old man kissed Mina's cheek and handed her a certificate, and minutes later she was back at their table, stunned she'd driven all that way for something so...brief.

Mack seemed to understand her confusion. He set down his water glass, slung his arm around Mina's shoulders, and pulled her in for a bracing hug. When she settled back in her chair again, Mack's eyes were worried.

"Doing all right?"

She leaned close to whisper, "I'm sorry. I can't believe we came here just for this."

"It's okay," he murmured back. "You didn't know. Besides— look at these guys. This is important to them."

"I know. And they think it's important to me, too, but..." Mina stopped and looked around. "I feel like an imposter. A lot of these people are really upset. Rightfully so."

"Yeah, well...they weren't married to Grey."

She nodded. *That* was why she'd wanted Mack with her, instead of coming alone or taking Dimitri. Mina could count on Mack to understand the private hell of pretending to miss someone who hadn't been terribly *nice* to her anymore. A man she hadn't loved any longer.

She looked into Mack's face, and found his eyes drifting over the black lace edge of her bra, which kept peeking out of her dress's neckline when she shifted the wrong way. Mina sat up straight and discreetly readjusted herself while Mack smiled, knowing he'd been busted. Perhaps there was hope for later, after all.

Across their table, a large, florid man slammed his beer down and raised his voice.

"I don't care!" he told his wife. "That whole thing was an embarrassment."

"We can go," the woman said. "Let's just go." Mina recognized her as the mother of Lieutenant Alex Hoffmann, one of the other soldiers that had been commemorated.

"Like hell! I'm not going! I paid my dues like everyone else here," the man grouched.

He glared at the next table, where a handful of middle-aged soldiers stood comforting the teary-eyed civilian man in their midst. The mourner wore round tortoiseshell glasses, shaggy hair and an ill-fitting tuxedo, and looked like a professor who'd taken a wrong turn into tragedy—and maybe he had.

"Doesn't mean I have to sit quietly while they all cry over my imbecile son," Mina's angry tablemate said loudly.

She wondered to Mack, "If that's how he feels, why did he even come here?" She thought she'd spoken under her breath, but apparently not.

The man checked her place card. "My son was a flaming faggot, Mrs. Whitney—a panty-waisted faggot. He wasn't *valorous*," he sneered, "Someone just got rid of him, that's all. God's way of doing some clean-up for the rest of us. I can't imagine why the Corps is going through with this farce. It certainly isn't the same outfit as when I served, that's for damn sure."

Mina gaped at him in dismay. When she managed to snap her jaw shut again, she protested, "God wouldn't do that."

At the same time, Mack growled, "Don't bring God into this."

The man snorted and shook his head, muttering, "Or what? I already got saddled with a queer for a son. What else are you going to do to me?"

Mina turned to look at Hoffmann's mother, but the woman merely stared stonily down into her martini glass, clutching her dead son's certificate in her lap. Whether her silence was in support—or defiance—of her husband's vitriol was unclear. Eventually she pursed her lips, shook off her paralysis, and took a long draught of her drink.

Mack's hands were balled into white-knuckled fists beside his plate. While Mina's objections to the elder Mr. Hoffmann's comments were of a general nature, Mack's offense seemed a bit more personal. He stood abruptly, making the wine and water glasses on the table clink and rattle.

"It sounded like your son was a fine officer, sir, and clearly a good friend to these people." Mack gestured at the soldiers nearby. "And he'll be remembered for that, whether you like it or not."

He nodded to Alex's mother, intoned, "I'm sorry for your loss," then stalked away.

Mina yelped in surprise, shot to her feet and grabbed her purse, then hurried after him.

"Mack? What the heck was that about?" She grabbed his arm and stopped him on the dance floor.

Mack pulled Mina into his embrace smoothly and began swaying to the music. The curious eyes trained on them eventually fell away, little by little.

"My little brother is gay," he gritted out. "When he came out, there were a bunch of people who thought it would be funny to tease me about it," Mack scowled. "Like I was supposed to be embarrassed of him? That kind of shit drives me nuts."

"I'm sorry," Mina said, rubbing his back. She'd met Bodhi at his wedding and cried right through his heartfelt speech about the big brother he adored. "We'll go sit somewhere else. Or we can leave—do you want to get out of here?"

Before Mack could answer, though, a man came striding toward them with an amazed expression wreathing his face.

"Mina? Mina Whitney is that you?" His voice was delighted, but Mina froze in place. Even after changing her name back to O'Connell last year, she still ran into people who didn't know she was a widow. She still had people scold her for shedding Grey's name like a pair of too-small shoes.

When Mina turned warily to see who it was, Mack's hand fell from her lower back and left her cold. She vaguely recognized the soldier standing there holding a sweating beer but couldn't quite put a name with the face.

He stuck out a hand, saving her the trouble. "Chris Leigh. You probably don't remember me, but—"

Now she had it. He'd been one of the Marines from base in those first days of her marriage, before Grey had left active service and they'd moved to North Carolina for college. Chris was younger than she and Grey, and always a tad drunker and more boisterous than anyone else. That was quite an accomplishment, since as Mina remembered it, many of the young enlisted guys had spent most of their off-hours hammered.

Mack wasn't that way, though, even then. Solid, steady Mack often had a beer in his hand at those old parties in Annapolis and Baltimore, but Mina didn't have a single memory of him ever getting wasted. He'd even tried to keep her and Grey out of trouble, too.

Mina shot an anxious glance at him, but Mack's expression was hard to read. She could hardly expect anything else—it wasn't like the whole night had been a blast, or anything.

"Of course, I remember you. But I, uh—I go by O'Connell now." She shook Chris's damp hand and studied his face. "How have you been?"

He had new lines around his eyes and mouth, making his cheerful party-guy mien seem strained. He'd gotten a little pudgy, too—his dress uniform fit snugger across his midsection than it should have.

Mack, in contrast, was as trim and fit as he'd ever been. If that fine-looking tux was a rental, it was certainly a good one.

"Good, good," Chris replied distractedly, looking around. "Just got out a couple months ago. Staying with my folks until I figure out my next move."

Mina nodded. Chris then seemed to realize that he'd only greeted one of them.

"Oh, hey. Mack, right?" They bumped fists. "Good to see you, man."

"Likewise," Mack murmured, but offered nothing else.

"So, yeah. Geez, it's been ages," Chris continued awkwardly. He took a gulp of his beer. "What's it been? Like ten years or something?"

Twelve years, almost exactly, since she'd married and buried a manipulative, controlling prick.

"Just about," Mina agreed. She sighed.

Chris looked around the room again, perplexed. "So, uh…where's Grey? He here?"

Damn—he must have arrived late and missed the ceremony. Mina blinked her eyes to buy some time, but for some reason they stayed closed on the last one. Damn, damn, *damn*. When she was finally able to force them open again, she found Mack gazing at her, telling her without words that he'd handle it if she wanted him to.

Mina shook her head. She could do it. She had so *much* practice doing it.

"No, he's…" she trailed off. Swallowed. Tried again. "He died, Chris."

"*Shit*, are you serious?" His mouth hung open. "When? What happened?"

Mina's face felt stiff. Her body held in place like a mannequin, but it may as well have been across the room, for all she felt like she was actually inhabiting it.

"There was a car accident," her mouth said. She'd had to utter those words before, but it didn't get easier with practice.

She wondered how much worse it would be if she also had to say that he'd taken his own life. It didn't seem likely to happen—

as far as she knew, she was the only person to even suspect it. And Mina only let herself do that when she was very, very angry with Grey.

"Aw hell," Chris breathed, looking green. He seemed suddenly aware of how uncomfortable Mina was. "I'm sorry," he added weakly. "I didn't know."

"It's okay," she said, wishing she had Mack's arm around her waist again to steady her. "It's been a while. Two years."

Two years, in which she'd discovered that Grey had cheated on her not once or twice, but chronically. Two years of learning that not only was her dead husband an alcoholic, but likely hooked on pills, too. More than seven hundred days of wondering what had really happened overseas, and what really happened on that dark road the night of his death. And last, but not least—two years of regularly hearing how wonderful her dear, departed husband was. How perfect. How *missed*.

Chris stepped forward to envelop her in a sweaty, too-close hug.

Bad touch, Mina's chaotic brain protested.

"He was a good man," Chris lamented next to her ear. "A damn good man."

Mina felt like she'd been carved from stone. In that last year, when Grey had gone on inactive duty and was spinning his wheels at home, their house had started to resemble a fraternity basement. Mina had taken to stashing trash bags in closets and drawers all over the place—the better to clean up the empty beer cans and burger wrappers that ended up everywhere.

She'd taken to locking doors in her own house, too—never knowing when she might find some previously-unknown service buddy of Grey's sleeping on their couch...or what that buddy thought about the bonds of matrimony. That wasn't the work of a *damn good man*.

Mack moved in and pried Chris off her. "We were just heading to the bar to get a drink," he said briskly. "Can we get you something? Another brew?"

That was a lie, although Mina couldn't fault Mack for it. They'd been dancing—or leaving—but liquor sounded just about perfect right then.

Chris looked back and forth between them, a little shell-shocked, a little mortified. "No, um…" He held up his half-empty bottle and clutched it like a lifeline. "I'm good," he said.

Mack put a hand on Mina's arm and exerted gentle—but unrelenting—pressure to steer her away.

"Well, it was nice to see you again," she told Chris politely.

"Yeah, you too," he said.

Mack gave Chris a small wave, and they were free. Six feet away, maybe eight, and Mina chanced a quick peek over her shoulder. Lieutenant Christopher Leigh was powering across the room in the dead opposite direction from her. Well, at least there was that—the man would be avoiding her like the plague for the rest of the night. They always did.

Chapter Sixteen

BETWEEN THE SAD piece of paper they'd handed Mina earlier, and the confrontation with the homophobic father at their table, Mack hadn't thought their evening could get much worse. That was before Chris Leigh popped up out of nowhere again, and cornered Mack near the restrooms.

"Hey, Chris," he sighed. He'd been sort of expecting this, but Mack had hoped to avoid it.

Chris had always been too nosy for his own good. "So, you and Mina together now or something?" he asked.

"Yeah. I guess you could say that."

"Grey always said you had a thing for her, but I thought he was just fucking around, you know? He got like that sometimes, but he wasn't ever serious. At least—I didn't think he was."

"He wasn't serious, Chris," Mack said. At this rate, Mina was going to owe Mack her first-born child by the time this night was over. Not that Mack had a problem with that. "Besides, it's not like they're together now."

"Still, dude—banging your boy's wife. That's crazy, man." Mack remembered Chris as being a bit of a lush, but he hadn't figured he would be nearly so persistent. Lack of much else going on in his life, he supposed.

"Crazier than not even knowing your boy was dead?" he inquired.

It was a direct hit. "What? I wasn't even around, man. I only got back to the States last spring. How was I supposed to know?"

Mack shook his head. A real friend would have been in touch. A real friend would've known, would've already checked in with Mina to see if she needed anything. But this guy was just like all the other random a-holes that had always swirled around Grey. Just like *Grey*, come to think of it. People there for the party, but not for any of the crap that came after. If Mack knew one thing, though, it was that there was no fixing stupid.

"You weren't," he told Chris. "Forget I said anything." He clapped the guy on the shoulder and turned back toward the ladies room, wondering what on earth was taking Mina so long.

"Aren't you worried about what people will say?" Chris asked him.

Like Mack had any control over that? You couldn't build any kind of a life around shit like gossip and innuendo. He was abruptly furious and spun to let the other man know—and whatever was on his face must've been good and ugly, because Chris took two unsteady steps back.

"Listen, you sorry little fuck—I knew Grey Whitney a lot longer than you did, so whatever allegiance you think you're paying him, you can stow it, all right? And as for Mina...what is this, Victorian England? She's mourned Grey plenty for the last two years—more than he earned—and if that woman wants to move on, that's her business and her right. She doesn't need any commentary from some asshole who drinks too much and lives in his parents' basement. You got me?"

Chris looked over Mack's shoulder and went a sickly sort of white. "Yeah. I got you. My bad." Then he scurried away like the sewer rat he was.

Behind Mack, Mina cleared her throat. He turned to see her smoothing her hands down her dress.

"Hey, Mack," she said. Her eyes flicked between him and Chris's departing carcass.

"How long have you been standing there?" He straightened his posture, attempting to look respectable.

She smiled, though. "Long enough, tough guy."

Mack let out a long, resigned breath. "I'm sorry. I just—" he shook his head, out of words.

"Don't apologize. I get it," Mina said. She sidled up close to his side and slipped her hand into his jacket, resting her warm palm against his thumping heart. "Thanks for defending me."

"What a night, huh?" he said shakily. Everywhere Mack tried to rest his hand, he encountered either slick satin or bare skin, but now was definitely not the time to dwell on it.

"How about we get the heck out of here?" she asked smoothly. Mina's light perfume drifted up, and he breathed it in deep.

That devilish dress she was wearing was making it hard to think—to focus. It was the only possible explanation for why he'd been slavering over her for the last hour and a half, his mind rolling down erotic paths of what might happen once he got her home. Somehow, despite ample reminders, Mack kept losing sight of why the hell they were there to begin with. He had lost his ever-loving mind, and that was a fact.

He *hated* that Mina would be tied to Grey Whitney's name and memory forever. He hated that men still existed who would so baldly defame their warrior son's memory. And more than anything else, Mack hated that Grey was the one who'd teased him the worst about Bodhi being gay—and that Mack had never punched him hard enough to cave his face in over it. He could not, for the life of him, remember why he had ever stayed friends with Grey.

It couldn't have been sentiment, or nostalgia—there weren't enough uncontaminated memories for that. It was more likely force of habit...or access to Mina, he supposed.

Delectable Mina, who was his very enticing date for this very miserable evening. What a waste of a perfectly indecent dress.

Even supposing Mack *could* get in the mood later, no way in hell would Mina be up for some sheet shenanigans after all this. And that was a crying shame.

MACK DIDN'T LIVE far from the ball's venue. He and Mina rode the short distance quietly, not saying much except to confirm to each other how much worse than a lousy college bachelor auction the night had turned out to be. There weren't enough apologies in the world for it, and after her first couple attempts, Mina didn't even try.

Mack parked his truck in the detached garage out back, went around to help Mina out, then grabbed her bag from behind her seat. She held tight onto his arm as they walked the short brick pathway to the house, then stood aside so he could unlock the kitchen door and turn off the alarm.

He held the door for her, and Mina didn't dither. She marched right up the last two steps, strode across the family room, and headed directly for the back stairs.

Mack chased after her, not coming to halt until she was perched daintily on the foot of his bed. Her expression was intense, but not upset.

He dropped her bag next to his dresser with a thump, then reached behind himself to close and lock the door. Based on the look on Mina's face, Mack didn't want to take any chances that his mom—or anyone else on earth—might show up unannounced again.

Her hands smoothed back and forth across his down comforter. "So," she said. "Your ex-wife's bed, huh?"

Mack took two steps closer. "To be fair, I liked it too. I wanted it, too."

"Why?"

He shrugged. "It looked very…enduring. It's literally the only thing that I kept from back then, besides the house."

"I see." Her hands moved back and forth again, like she was making an invisible snow angel. The silvery dress only added to the effect.

Mack told her, "I stripped and sanded the wood after she left. Re-stained it, got a new mattress, and all new bedding."

Mina's eyebrows shot up in amusement. "That seems a little extreme."

He moved even closer. "If I was going to keep the bed, I needed to make sure there was no residual…negative energy left over." It sounded nuts when he said it out loud, but at the time, Mack had worked like a man possessed to get the job done. He'd scrubbed every last vestige of Carolynn from his house and his life, and it had made him feel better.

He took the tail end of Mina's thin satin sash and let the material slide through his fingers.

"I'm sorry," Mina joked. "Did I just hear the logical engineer say *negative energy*?"

Her voice was casual, but her eyes were fixed on his hand. Mack caught the satin ribbon before it could fall and pulled the drooping bow at Mina's waist free.

"Negative energy is a real thing," he told her. "You don't want it lingering around, infecting your life."

"I'm pretty sure there's none here," Mina breathed.

Mack slid the length of the ribbon through his fingers again and studied Mina, sitting on his mattress between the two sturdy bedposts. Two more solid columns flanked the head of the bed. What Mack ought to do was tie her to his bed with that silky sash and keep her from running away from him again. Keep her all to himself. Maybe tonight wasn't the best night for that, though.

Mina blinked at him with wide eyes, as if she could read his thoughts. He let the ribbon flutter to the floor, and said, "Not anymore. Not ever again."

Then he kissed her. Her mouth was lush and eager, and Mack wanted to feel its dark promise *everywhere*. He nipped at her full bottom lip, and Mina answered by sucking his tongue deep into her mouth.

She stood and pressed herself against him. Mack ran his hands over her firm rear end—slippery through the material of her dress—and felt the edges of her panties underneath. He wanted to see them. He *needed* to see them.

In between kisses, Mack searched Mina's quicksilver form for some sign of a zipper. He sucked on her neck while he tugged at the shoulder straps, to no avail. He groaned in frustration—was the damn thing painted on? For lack of a better option, he gripped at the skirt and began pulling it up.

She batted his hands away with a husky laugh. "Let me," she said. Her arms folded behind her, Mack heard the zipper come loose, and then suddenly Mina's gown was sliding down her body like a rippling river of mercury.

"Mina," Mack breathed, stunned into submission.

These were not the girly undergarments she'd worn before. The slightest scraps of black lace covered her breasts. Mack had caught glimpses of that bra all night long—whenever Mina leaned over, and her neckline gaped—but if he'd known how little there was to the thing, he might have combusted on the spot. A complicated network of ribbons held it all together. Inverted chevrons capped the lace with small bows, then connected to the straps over her shoulders. Other ribbons crisscrossed under her breasts and around Mina's ribcage.

Mack worked his fingers under a couple of them to test their tensile strength—flimsy enough. He could probably snap them if he wanted to, but Mina looked so unbelievably sexy. Maybe he could save that kind of thing for some other bra, something less special.

His eyes drifted down. The bottoms rode low on her hips— tiny, insubstantial things constructed from more sheer bits of lace and narrow black ribbons. A little bow was sewn dead-center on the top edge, and he touched it carefully with one trembling fingertip. He glanced up at Mina to find her brown eyes dark and avid, and her lips parted.

He looked back down. Mack watched his thumbs hook under the sides of her panties and slide them down over her hips. He knelt in front of Mina, pushed the lace off her legs, and wrapped one arm behind her. Mack pressed a light kiss to the velvety skin of her stomach—she smelled warm, like vanilla.

Mina sighed, dropping her bra next to him on the floor and pressing her hands to his skull. He kissed each hip, then stood and took the tip of each lovely breast into his mouth, gratified to hear her sudden gasps. She was pliant and willing, that much was clear. Mack grasped her waist and lifted Mina onto the center of his bed.

He shrugged off the tuxedo jacket and hung it on the bathroom door, trying to settle his galloping pulse. Mack pulled open a drawer, fished out a couple condoms, and threw them on the bed, too.

Once he touched Mina again, he had a feeling he wouldn't be able to stop, not for natural disasters, or nuclear bombs, or even an alien invasion. He stood at the foot of the mattress and regarded his prize while he tried to get undressed.

Mina wasn't making it easy. She stretched her arms high over her head while she watched him struggle with his shirt studs and flexed her knees restlessly.

It figured. The one time Mack needed to get naked fast, he found himself in the most complicated rig a man could wear. One of his cufflinks clattered across the wood floor. He resolved to look for it another time.

Mina's legs shifted around. "God, Mack," she murmured. "Look at you." She stared at each inch of skin as it was exposed. He couldn't seem to expose it all quickly enough.

His arousal was throbbing and too sensitive when he rolled on the condom—Mack had to pause and steady himself, close his eyes and hold his breath until he was sure he could continue at a decent pace.

Up near his pillows, Mina's breath hitched. He wanted those long legs of hers locked around him. He wanted to sink into her sweet heat and never emerge. When Mack opened his eyes and saw Mina wet her lips, he thought she might want that, too.

He had to be sure, though. His voice came out sounding rusty when he said, "It's been a long night. You sure you want to do this now?"

He let go of his erection and set his hands on the mattress, so he could press a kiss to one of her slim ankles. Mina's toes were painted a red so dark it was nearly black. He kissed one of them, too, then trailed the tip of his tongue across her foot to tickle her high, delicate arch. She jolted like he'd shocked her.

"I am as sure as sure can be," she told him.

Mack chuckled at that, then crawled toward her. He planted open-mouthed kisses in a few select locations along the way, and by the time he and Mina found themselves face-to-face, she was breathing hard. Hell, so was he.

Holding her gaze, Mack twined his fingers with hers, flexed his hips, and pushed into her. Mina's gasp was louder this time, and she squeezed her eyes shut.

Mack immediately hated that, his soul screaming a long, drawn-out *No*. After the ghosts of their past had swirled around them so much that night, he had to be sure Mina knew who was loving her. He needed to see that Mina *knew*.

"Open your eyes," he demanded. Mack drove in and out, until at last Mina did as he asked. Her eyes looked drowsy and hazed with desire. Her hair was a silken mahogany pool on the white comforter. She was his, in more than body, though he doubted that she understood.

"Who am I?" Mack asked. "Who?" He doubted if he'd ever been with a virgin—but he'd never before felt so frantic to erase a woman's memory of other men.

Mina pulled her hands free of his, so she could cup his face. "I know who you are," she reassured him.

Mack needed to hear it, though. "Say it," he begged. He didn't know how much longer he could hold off—Mina just felt so damn perfect around him.

Her eyes were soft with understanding. "Mack," she said. "It's just you and me, Mack."

Relief and gratitude rushed fiercely through him. He took her mouth, tasted red wine, and thrust harder. Faster. There was no holding off the onslaught any longer—not where Mina was concerned. She turned him into something wild and uncontrolled, something untamed.

Before long, her body was tightening around his, pulsing and pulling him into her release. Mack gasped Mina's name into her neck and finally let himself go. He didn't think he'd ever get enough. How could he possibly ever get enough of her?

THEY HELD EACH other for a long time, then slept for a bit. Mack blinked awake too soon, right as the sun was peeking over the edge of his bedroom windowsill, painting the sky in streaks of pink and gold.

Mina was still draped across his chest, boneless and beautiful. The furnace had kicked on sometime during the night, so the bedroom felt cozy. Mack pushed the sheet the rest of the way off her body and let his hands pet her skin.

He stroked her back softly with his fingers, and caressed the lower curve of Mina's rear, right where it met the top of her thighs. Mack had never suspected that was such a sensitive area, not until a deep shiver worked its way down her spine. She came awake with a start. Mack could feel her mouth shift into a smile against his chest.

"Stop tickling," she mumbled groggily.

"I love your ass," Mack told her. "I've been pretending not to notice it for so long, I could probably recognize it blindfolded."

"Oh please," she scoffed.

"No really," he insisted. "You have no idea the dirty things it makes me want to do."

Mina propped herself up, so she could scowl at him. "Like *what*?" she demanded.

Mack laughed. "Not *that* dirty. Geez, Mina, you're so suspicious." He spanked her lightly, making her wriggle against him again. "I'm a small-town guy, kiddo. My imagination is *not* that good."

"Well, I don't know," Mina huffed. "You could've been cooped up and festering all this time, coming up with all sorts of degenerate fetishes."

"Oh, now I'm a degenerate?" he squawked, indignant.

"You know what I mean!"

Mack shook his head. "Mina, the only fetish I have is the complete inability to think about anything but you."

Her body, certainly—Mack could spend hours wallowing in every feminine curve of her. But that wasn't the only thing he loved. He also loved the way her voice went high and girly when she spotted rabbits and cows in the fields, and when she saw herons near the water. He loved the way Mina still cried at commercials and smelled all the flowers, despite the uppercuts life had thrown at her. Hell, Mack just plain loved *her*.

No one could fault him for that. Mina O'Connell had invaded his entire system from the first moment he'd lain eyes on her. Now that he'd had the chance to get to know her better, to share time and space and kisses with her, he guessed he was probably ruined for any other woman. Maybe he always had been. Unfortunately, Mack doubted he could tell her that. Not yet, at least.

Chapter Seventeen

Five Years Earlier

T HEY HADN'T BEEN back in Maryland long before Grey found a new group of friends to spend his free time with, in addition to the old coterie who still hung around. Mina had barely unpacked the moving boxes and set up their new place, before Grey was home on leave and the poker nights and bar hopping began again in earnest.

That particular week, he'd coerced a large group into attending a football game together over the weekend. Mina—of course— had taken care of the particulars. She arranged carpools and ticket purchases, and the food sign-ups for the tailgate Grey wanted to have. She collected money for the parking passes and the keg and made sure there would be enough tables and chairs.

The day had arrived and as expected, everyone socialized for hours in the parking lot of the stadium before the game. The Whitney cousins were there as well as all their friends from the neighborhood, with their assorted wives and kids in tow.

Watching them all, Mina was stunned by the peculiar sort of pain she felt, seeing Mack Bolton dote on his oblivious wife. When his hand rested on Carolynn's hip, his fingers crept under the edge of her shirt to caress her skin. Mack's arm stayed draped across her slim shoulders and his mouth kept kissing her hair.

Mina had trouble understanding what he saw in the woman. Carolynn was pretty enough, she supposed, with her long dyed-auburn hair and tanned skin. She was slim and dressed fashionably, but she was also loud and brash. From what Mina could tell, the woman fed off being the center of attention, the ring-leader.

Mina hadn't warmed to Mack's bride at the wedding but had assumed at the time it was because of her own jealousy. Now, in more casual circumstances, she wondered if she'd been on to something.

Despite Mack's displays of affection, he did not look happy. Even though he'd promised Mina he would try with Carolynn, he seemed instead like a man who was merely enduring—someone going through the motions to keep his spouse happy. He looked tired.

What exactly had happened here, while she'd been living in North Carolina? Mina frowned. She'd been so busy worrying about her own problems, she hadn't taken a single minute to think about whether anyone else was okay. Not Molly, not her old friends from Annapolis, and not Mack. And if that was true, it just made Mina selfish.

As usual, once they got to their seats Grey was more interested in his beer, and in parsing the intricacies of the game with his buddies, than in his wife. Mina people-watched as she always did—soaking in the stadium atmosphere and the cool fall weather in her accustomed, place-holder kind of way. She talked to the kids and helped them with their stuffed animals, and board books, and knit hats.

When she was a mother herself someday, there would finally be people who actually cared about her—who cared what Mina did, and what she thought. She hadn't been on birth control for many months, though, and still hadn't been even one day late. All her adult life, she'd menstruated like clockwork, every twenty-nine days without fail—she'd never guessed that would one day be a source of frustration. For once, she wanted her periods to stop.

Grey was getting testy about the situation. He seemed to think Mina was trying to pull a fast one on him, even though he knew how much she loved babies—and knew how much she wanted one of her own. In the dark of night, she'd begun to wonder whether *he* was the one purposely preventing them from conceiving.

Grey certainly had more to lose. A baby, after all, would throw a serious monkey wrench into his lifestyle. He'd have an awful lot less money and time to spend on himself. To Grey, a baby seemed to represent nothing more than a trophy—something he could brag about, instead of an actual human being requiring love and attention. Mina shouldn't have been surprised. Grey didn't seem to think wives required those things—why would babies?

She wondered how long Mack and Carolynn would wait before having kids. Or maybe they were already pregnant, and that was why he was keeping such a close eye on her. While Carolynn seemed a tad flighty to make a very good mom, what did Mina know? She hardly had any experience with that sort of thing, only the big sister kind of stuff she'd done for Molly.

THE MOMENT WHEN you realized you were stuck with the wrong man was never a good one. Mina's moment just happened to arrive in public, with the worst possible people in attendance. The man she'd married noticed, as did the man she probably *should* have married. Even Should Have's wife cottoned to it—and usually she was only aware of herself.

At least Mina was thorough.

She had noticed Mack eyeing her with concern for a while, but during the third quarter of the game, he found an opening to approach her. Carolynn had gone to the bathroom and Grey had left for the concession stand to get hot dogs and another beer.

Once the coast was clear, Mack slid casually into the seat next to Mina. Without more than a quick glance at her, he murmured in an undertone impossible for anyone else to overhear over the noise of the crowd.

"Listen, I probably only have a couple minutes to say this, but I want you to hear me. I mean really *hear* me, Mina. Commit what I'm about to say to memory and never doubt it, never forget it, okay?"

"Okay," she replied with trepidation. She had no idea what it could be about. It sounded like she was in trouble, but she couldn't imagine what she might have done. She hadn't said two words to him or his wife all day.

"All right, listen. The way Grey treats you—it's not okay. You don't deserve to be ignored. Not by him, and not by anyone."

That was probably the last thing Mina expected to hear. "Why should you care?" she asked. It came out with more of an edge than she intended.

"Don't pretend I don't care, Mina," Mack sighed. "I've always cared. You know that."

She didn't know what to say. He had no reason to protect her, no dog in this fight. "Come on, Mack. You only care about how hot your wife is," she retorted snidely. She hated how nervous he made her feel. Why was he always trying to unsettle her? To make her confront things that couldn't be changed? It wasn't like she could simply up and leave Grey. Mina had nowhere else to go, no one she could lean on.

"I care about Carolynn. Of course I do, or I never would have married her. But she's not you, and she never will be." He'd said something similar on the cusp of his wedding.

"Lucky her," Mina muttered.

"How can you say that, after all that we've said to each other?"

At this, Mina's head jerked up in alarm. This was dangerous territory, especially with Grey somewhere nearby. "I have no idea what you're—"

Mack held up a quelling hand to cut her off. "*Stop.* There's not enough time to play dumb. I know what's going on, okay? Between you and Grey, and between you and me. What I want you to know, without a doubt, is that I feel the same way. Exactly the same, okay?"

She swallowed thickly and could feel his eyes rest on her for a moment. Mack didn't know what he was saying. He *couldn't* know, because Mina had only just realized what a horrible mistake she'd made, herself. Once, there'd been a tiny fraction of time when she might have chosen Mack over Grey, and she had failed to pick correctly. It had never been more apparent to her than right that second.

"Mina—I get that it's totally crazy and there's nothing either of us can do about it now. I accept that you love my friend, and I do love my wife. It's not…*that*. But it is…" At this, Mack paused, seemingly at a loss for words.

Mina passed a yellow crayon to a cousin's daughter from the baggie she held in her lap. She stopped another crayon from rolling away under the seat in front of her, trapping it under her shoe before it got away.

"It is what?" she croaked, not sure she wanted to know. Not daring to look him in the face.

"It's important," he finished. "I get that Carolynn will always be different than you, and God knows Grey and I are total opposites. The lives we have with them are real, and they matter. But I see what you do to yourself when we are all together, Mina, and it's tearing me apart inside."

"What am I doing?" she whispered.

He couldn't have heard her—maybe he'd only read her lips. "You're belittling yourself. You are comparing yourself to Carolynn and deciding that you come up short. You're comparing how Grey treats you and deciding that you must not be worth his attention. I can see it in your face, but you're not right. It's killing me."

Mina shook her head. This couldn't be happening. Mack had always been too perceptive. It was partly why he'd intimidated her so much, all those years ago—probably why she'd walked away so easily. She'd almost never looked back, either. Not until today, anyway.

"Whatever this is between us," Mack continued, "Is real, too. And it *matters* too." He said it with so much feeling. Mina couldn't breathe.

The cousin's kid handed her a completed coloring page, and Mack stared down at the way the paper—clutched tightly in her lap—shook in her hands.

"Please, Mina. I need you to know you're not alone. And I need..." he huffed out a frustrated breath. "I need for you to promise me that you won't forget. Ever."

Mina opened her mouth to protest when Mack's face broke into a wide, guileless grin. His voice changed too, when he called out, "Hey! I was wondering where you guys were! Thought maybe you took a wrong turn or something."

He stood and smiled toward the end of the row, where his wife and Mina's husband were starting to shuffle past everyone's knees and bags and discarded snacks.

"Smile, Mina," Mack instructed under his breath, low and serious. She could only imagine what her face looked like.

Something exciting happened on the field and the crowd surged to their feet with a unified roar. Mina stood along with them, clapping and cheering.

Mack murmured "Good girl," right into her ear. His breath was too warm, and she fought a knee-jerk urge to flinch.

Grey edged past her to get to his seat. Mina, in a panic, blurted out, "I'm glad you're back. I'm gonna run to the bathroom real quick, okay?" She didn't think he heard her, so it came as a surprise when she turned and Grey smacked her hard on the butt, right in front of everyone. He laughed loudly when she glared at him, with a warning sharpness she didn't like the sound of.

Mina peeked down at the back of their heads one more time before she ducked into the concourse. Grey was watching the game, but Carolynn was turned toward Mack, her expression furious and mouth spitting out angry words. Mack bounced a friend's toddler on his knee, his brow furrowed as he listened to her.

She suspects something, Mina thought. Maybe not with any certainty, but Carolynn had guessed all was not as it should be. And if Mack's wife had done that, chances were good that Mina's husband had, too.

In the bathroom, she fought not to vomit up the soft pretzel she'd eaten. She hadn't done anything wrong. Neither had Mack, and they wouldn't. So why did she still feel so awful? So guilty?

When Mina went back to her seat, Grey only made matters worse, picking on her or Mack at every opportunity.

She'd never had any kind of poker face. It made sense that everyone had figured out her traitorous feelings so easily.

By the time the game ended, though, Grey's treacherous mood seemed to blow over. And in the days to come, Mina began to doubt her memory. She must have misunderstood Mack's intent. Maybe it had all been some odd sort of hallucination, or fever dream that she'd mixed up with reality.

Mina wondered if a single one of those significant glances, or any of those terrifying words, had ever actually been spoken by Mack Bolton. Maybe she'd simply created something out of nothing, in order to cope with the wrenching disappointment her marriage had become.

Maybe Mina was kidding herself to think that a different choice so long ago would've resulted in a happier outcome for her. Perhaps Grey was right, and the problem was with *her.*

Chapter Eighteen

M INA HAD SUPPOSEDLY gone to the ladies' room, but she didn't return for a long time. He was worried about her.

While he waited for her to come back, Mack cupped his phone loosely in his hands, scrolling through the photos he'd taken at the tailgate earlier. He paused at one that his cousin had taken of him, which just happened to have Mina's profile directly beside his face. Mack stared—he knew he did. In fact, he couldn't seem to tear his eyes away. Had he ever possessed a photo with the two of them together? And why should that matter so urgently at the moment?

Mack had thought he was the only one who noticed Mina's disappearance—but maybe he was wrong about that. His wife seemed to be aware of her absence, too. Carolynn jostled him and her loudest, most attention-seeking laugh erupted from her. Mack slipped his phone back into his pocket.

He'd mostly ignored his wife's outrageous flirting with Grey, but she'd clearly lost patience with Mack's inattention. For someone so pretty, Carolynn could be cripplingly insecure, and nothing got her goat worse than indifference—she'd rather people despise her than not pay attention.

So, Mack exerted the effort she required—he slung his arm across the back of her seat and kneaded her neck. He kissed his wife's cheek and told her that she smelled nice. Much as he'd once promised he would, Mack *tried*. Affection and compliments were like his wife's lifeblood, and the more public—the more extravagant—the better.

Except this time, it didn't work. Mack's efforts only seemed to irritate Carolynn further, and he wasn't sure why.

Then, just before the fourth quarter, Mina returned to her seat looking quite a bit worse for wear, and Carolynn kicked her performance into high gear.

"Oh my *God*, what is with these crappy seats? My back is killing me," she complained, looking around to gauge her audience. "We should *not* be sitting here. Who bought these, anyway?"

Mack didn't need to look around like she did. With Carolynn's long hair and tan skin, he knew she'd be getting the attention she craved. She always did. As for the crack about their seats, well— that was a direct shot at Mina, who everyone knew had arranged the whole outing.

Mack's wife stretched her arms over her head and arched her back, exposing her flat stomach in the world's most out-of-place yoga pose. For effect, she added a loud exclamation that was better suited to a porn film than a football game—she'd certainly never uttered a thing like that in her marital bed, that was for damn sure. How many beers did she have to drink, anyway?

There were murmurings from some of the people around them. Mack patted his wife's waist.

"Come on Lynn, sit back down and I'll rub your back for you."

She turned to him with narrowed eyes. "Why? Am I *embarrassing* you?" She looked around and rolled her eyes at the growing number of spectators, "Seems like I'm *always* embarrassing him."

What the hell? "That's not true," Mack denied automatically. Though increasingly, it was.

Not a few gazes pinned him with disdain, Grey's among them. Everyone sure appreciated his wife, though. Mack's old buddy let his eyes rake over Carolynn from head to toe, and Mack bristled. It was one thing to steal a girl in a bar that Mack had not officially laid claim to. But if Grey thought he was going to hit on Mack's *wife*, right in front of Mina, no less…

"Mack, face it. You are *no fun*," Carolynn said tartly.

It stung. It always stung, but Mack tried to keep his self-control and not rise to her bait.

"Look, this football game is basically over," he explained. A quick glance at the scoreboard belied his claim—the score was 24-23 with only five minutes left. The home team's left back intercepted the ball, and like every other fan there, Mack paused to watch the ensuing melee.

Once the guy was down, he continued, "Why don't we head back out to the truck?"

Sometimes, diversion worked when Carolynn was in a mood—the promise of some entertainment, where she could hold court and keep people's focus on her, was something she was generally in favor of. But this time, her stormy expression didn't lighten at all. She only snorted and grabbed her bag from under her seat.

Once Mack stood with her, the rest of their group seemed to make the same decision. Cousins and friends gathered their coats and kids and cast-off snack bar trash, then headed for the exit. Out in the parking lot, they stood in small groups near their vehicles and tried to decide whether to head straight home or hit up a restaurant for a late dinner.

Mack searched the faces, but Mina and Grey must have stayed behind to watch the end of the game. He prayed Grey wasn't giving her as hard a time as he was getting.

He unlocked his truck and gestured Carolynn inside, but naturally she wasn't having any of *that*.

"I don't know why you're treating me like this!" she belted out, snaring the eyes and ears of multiple bystanders. "I'm not doing anything wrong!"

Mack stood there motionless and felt his face flame. He'd learned the hard way that trying to debate with Carolynn was a dead end, so he said soothingly, "I know you're not." Too late, he realized how that might aggravate her.

"If you would only loosen up once in a while, none of this would be happening," she hissed.

Mack sighed and scanned the group, relieved to note that several of the families with kids had already buckled up and were pulling away.

Logically, he knew that this argument wasn't really about his ability to cut loose. It had to be about jealousy. His wife had either seen him talking to Mina or had spotted him looking at Mina's photo. He'd put money on it.

Knowing that Mina had once been his roommate—even briefly—had always driven Carolynn berserk. Adding alcohol to the mix meant this was likely to get uglier, but at least the Whitneys hadn't come out of the stadium yet. Mack didn't think he'd be able to keep his composure if his wife decided to make a target out of Mina. And, since the chance of Grey defending Mina was slim, Mack would only grow more infuriated—and probably push Carolynn clear over the edge.

With a lot of their companions gone, Carolynn was left with mostly the people from the surrounding tailgates as her audience. The small groups of young men filtering out of the stadium exits were certainly paying keen attention to Mack's beautiful, overwrought wife.

"Hey!" she called out, spinning around. "My *husband* is no damn fun! But I bet some of you all would like to have a good time!"

She emphasized "husband" like it was a deprecation. Mack swallowed his rage and growled, "*Lynn*. That's enough. Get in the damn truck."

There were murmurs and a couple of catcalls from all around them. Carolynn slipped past Mack and sauntered a few feet away.

"Who's with me?" She grinned over her shoulder at him he wondered if she might be truly evil, instead of merely drunk.

If Mack collared her and shoved her in the truck like he wanted to, he'd look like a caveman. But he could hardly let Carolynn take off with a total stranger, either. What the heck was he supposed to *do*?

Help arrived in the form of his younger cousin, Kevin—a strapping dude only months out of the fire academy. He stepped into Lynn's path and blocked her forward progress, as well as most of the rowdy guys' view of her. With a look at Mack that said *I got this*, he grinned at Carolynn. "I'm game. What do you have in mind, sweetheart?"

Kevin had been born when Mack was in the first grade, and they'd been tight ever since. Mack trusted him, but he was also fairly confident that the young man didn't know what he was in for.

"Kev—" he began.

Carolynn looped her arm through Kevin's and smiled triumphantly. "Where should we go, *Kev*?" she asked, mimicking Mack's tone. "Let's blow this taco stand. It's so lame."

Kevin unlocked his Jeep with his key fob. In moments, Mack's wife was perched high in the passenger seat, looking like the cat that ate the cream.

"You don't have to do this, man," Mack told him.

"No worries, bruh. I'll let her blow off some steam, and then I'll bring her right home. She'll be safe with me."

What was Mack thinking, agreeing to such a thing? But that was a dumb-ass question. He was thinking about how exhausting Carolynn's penchant for exhibitionism could be, and how hard it was to talk her down once she got wound up. He was thinking about the hour-long drive home and the way her shrill voice had a way of caroming around the inside of his truck. Lastly, Mack was thinking about his new business, his new graduate classes, and all the work waiting for him at home.

So, he nodded and stepped back, and watched another man drive off with his wife. Then he slid behind the wheel of his truck and waited. Mack watched the closest stadium exits as casually as he could, hoping to catch one last glance of Mina before he took off to lick his wounds. He'd promised her years ago that he would make an effort with Carolynn. He did try—he listened to his wife's stories, took her on weekend getaways, and brought her flowers for no reason. It never seemed to be sufficient, though.

Mack had tried to explain to Carolynn what it would mean for him to buy that old building in downtown St. Michaels to start his own engineering firm. Mack had triple-checked that she was okay with him going to night school for his graduate degree. He'd thought she was on board and understood all of it, but their life had been nothing but bickering for the last six months.

Carolynn claimed that Mack didn't pay her enough attention. She bitched that he was married to his blueprints and that he noticed other women too often—but *her* eye was the one that always seemed to be wandering.

Once, her brazen flirting had been all for Mack. Once, he'd been enough for her. Mack hadn't anticipated how quickly all that would fade. He hadn't expected that even Carolynn—in all her over-the-top glory—wouldn't be able to make him forget Mina. And the final surprise? Even though he'd thought his feelings for another woman were deeply buried, Mack's wife had turned out to be freakishly good at flushing them out. However, much as he might want to, he couldn't tell Mina any of that.

Mack heard the crowd roar inside the stadium, and the touchdown music blared from the loudspeakers. The cannons fired, the game concluded, and lots more people began streaming into the parking lot.

At last he spotted Mina and Grey, filing through the gates and walking quickly to stay ahead of the departing horde surging behind them.

Grey strode a few paces ahead of his wife, seemingly unconcerned with them getting separated. Mina stared at her feet as she walked, her hair falling in a curtain that shielded her face from Mack. But then a gust of wind blew through, lifting the mahogany waves away—and Mack's heart gave a painful, lurching thump in his chest. She looked so forlorn, so sad. So…alone.

There was a lot wrong in her relationship with Grey. Other than trying to bolster her spirits—to reassure her she was special, that she deserved better, and that Mack cared—he didn't have the foggiest idea what to do for her. He barely knew what to do with himself most days.

Mack pointed his phone as furtively as he could, zoomed in, and snapped one more photo of Mina. Then he put the truck in reverse and got the heck out of Dodge. When Carolynn came home later, there would probably be an even bigger scene—Mack had the feeling he'd be up all night arguing with her.

He needed to get some work done before that happened, and maybe get some rest. He'd need it—there was an exam in one of his classes Monday night, and a meeting with a new client right before that. If Mack could land the account, it would be his biggest project yet, and get his name out to the local building community in a way no amount of advertising could.

Mack was well on his way home when his cell lit up with a text from Grey.

Dude, your wife is the best!

No doubt Grey had already heard about that scene in the parking lot from the others—maybe he'd even heard it from Carolynn herself. Mack fumed, but he didn't respond. It was exactly what that smug bastard wanted, and he refused to give Grey the satisfaction.

Back at home, Mack stood over the kitchen sink and had a shot of whiskey to clear his head, then settled in at his desk. It was hours before he finally understood that Carolynn wasn't coming home.

Kev texted around two in the morning to report that he'd dropped Lynn at her cousin's house, and to point out that Mack's wife was "a handful". Mack didn't even want to speculate on what that might mean, and Kevin didn't elaborate.

IN THE DISMAL months to come, there were friends who suggested that if Mack hadn't spent so much time starting his company or going to night school for his graduate degree, he might have had more time to notice that his wife was unhappy. There were people who admitted that they'd seen Carolynn out in places she shouldn't have been, and ones who mentioned her increased drinking. Mack heard talk about all the attention Carolynn's boss had been paying her.

He couldn't ask his ex about any of it directly, since she never stopped by when Mack was actually home. He left messages on her cell, and Carolynn left notes on the kitchen counter. One day, he returned from class to find that all her stuff was gone—as if she'd never lived there to begin with. The calls from her attorney started then.

Mack's mother was more pointed than the others. She corralled him into her fancy living room, then came right out and told him that any wife would feel slighted if she noticed her husband was eyeing another woman as often as Mack did—not to mention a married lady he had no right to.

"That's not true. Who?" he demanded. "I don't do that!"

"Oh really?" his mom fired back. "Not even to Mina Whitney?"

Mack sat down heavily on the sofa she only used for guests. He knew he must look guilty.

"It's not right Mack. You need to stop," she said. "Your marriage may be over, but hers isn't. Don't condemn Mina, too."

"Mom, I would never do that," Mack protested. This couldn't be happening. This was awful.

He dropped his head in his hands and tried to breathe. Why couldn't he ever seem to leave well enough alone—to simply leave Mina be? Why did he *care* so damn much? His clumsy attempts to help her were only going to wreck her life the same way he'd ruined his.

"*Mack*," his mother persisted. "Listen to me. I'm not the only one who's noticed. Do you understand?"

He looked up.

"You *have* to leave her alone."

Mack nodded and said, "I understand."

Chapter Nineteen

I LOVE YOUR neck," Mack murmured, trailing his fingers over the downy strands at Mina's nape. "It's been bedeviling me for years. I think the harder I tried to ignore it, the worse it got."

"Years?" she laughed dismissively. It was unnerving, the way he seemed to have a knack for uncovering each one of her vulnerable spots. How long would Mina have to wait before he started poking around in the tender spots of her psyche? Of her heart?

"You wear your hair up a *lot*," Mack retorted.

Mina just snorted at that.

"Seriously. Your neck looks so soft and pretty," he tried to explain. "So vulnerable when it's exposed like this." He placed a soft kiss under her ponytail and it quivered down her spine to underline his words.

Mack whispered, "I always felt like I could touch it, you know? Right out in the open with everyone watching, and no one would even guess how intimate it would be."

His fingers tickled Mina and right on cue, she shuddered again. Apparently, necks were a bigger deal than she'd ever realized. Trust Mack to know all about that.

"No one but me," she murmured.

"And me," he agreed.

Mack was fascinated, stroking her gently across the underside of her hair, along the tendons of her neck, then down onto the tops of her shoulders.

"Why didn't you?" she asked, unable to shake the image he presented. "You never did anything like that."

"You wouldn't have wanted me to, for one thing. But also, because no one has that good of a poker face," Mack said. "Certainly not me, and especially not you."

"What? That's not—"

"If I had done this," Mack tickled, Mina jumped, and he ducked to smile into her face. "You would've looked like *this*." He touched her cheek, eyes warming. No, not warming—*burning*. "Then I would've looked like *this*," he chuckled, pointing at himself.

Mina took in his avid expression, and knew he spoke the truth. Grey would've been searching for exactly that sort of thing, too. She shook her head at Mack. He likely didn't know the extent to which her husband had obsessed about them. Grey had never quite discarded his suspicion that there'd been something illicit between his buddy and his wife. The notion that such a self-absorbed man might be so wickedly perceptive—that he might see so deeply inside her heart and her brain—had always unsettled Mina.

Mack misunderstood her silence. "Come on, Mina," he said. "You know all those old aunties had eyes like hawks. But they aren't here now, are they?"

"Nope," she replied dutifully. She tried to keep her voice cheerful.

"And I can touch you all I want."

"You mean, all *I* want," she pointed out.

"In that, I'm going to hope that our interests align," Mack smiled.

THE DAY HAD dawned sunny, but windy and cool. While Mack went down to the kitchen to make coffee, Mina showered and dressed in a pair of dark skinny jeans, tall suede boots, and a turtleneck sweater. She wound her hair into a loose knot on the back of her head and put on her shiny lip gloss that smelled like oranges.

Mack returned, kissed her, and noticed it tasted like oranges, too. He claimed he wanted to undo all of her preparations and tumble Mina directly back into his bed.

"You're insatiable," she giggled. "You promised to take me to brunch."

"I was probably coerced," Mack scowled. "Brunch is overrated."

"Look at it this way—if you don't feed me, I'll rapidly lose the desire to do anything else today."

"Anything?" he murmured, taking her earlobe into his mouth.

"Yup."

Mack drew back, tilted his head, and studied Mina's expression. "You make a fair point," he admitted grudgingly.

"Yes. I do. Now please get dressed."

THE BISTRO THEY went to was pretty, with high ceilings, rugged brick walls, and plants everywhere. Mina sipped a pink Bellini in a tall champagne glass and ordered the eggs Chesapeake. Mack got more coffee and an enormous platter of raw oysters.

They were deep into a semi-serious discussion about the possibly aphrodisiac properties of those oysters when two older women stopped next to their table.

"Goodness, what are you two doing here?" Grey's mother exclaimed.

Mack's coffee went down the wrong way, and he launched into a dramatic round of coughing and sputtering.

"Just catching up," Mina smiled. Her former mother-in-law was supposed to have retired and moved to Florida. Mina couldn't imagine what she was doing *there*, and with Mrs. Bolton, no less.

"Again?" Mack's mother asked.

"*Mom*," Mack warned.

Mrs. Whitney looked back and forth between them.

"I thought you'd left for Florida," Mina said.

"Oh, the buyers moved the closing date back a week. George and I figured we would stick around and get in a few more goodbyes with friends." She and Mrs. Bolton smiled at each other.

Then Grey's mother swiveled toward Mack and laid a hand on his shoulder.

"Mack, dear, I'm so glad to see you. I ran into Carolynn just last week at the warehouse store out on Route 50. I can't imagine what got into you two. You always made such a darling couple."

"Well," Mack sighed. "You know how it goes. People change sometimes."

Her mouth twitched into a small, humorless line. "Not that much. You ought to call her, Mack. She really looks wonderful."

Mina couldn't seem to find a good place to look. She glanced at Mack, thought better of it, and decided on a large Boston fern across the room. Such lovely, fluffy, bright green fronds.

"We don't keep in touch, Mrs. Whitney," Mack said flatly.

His mother cleared her throat. "Well," she exclaimed. "I would ask you two to join us, but it looks like you've already gotten started." She cast a pointed look at Mina's half-empty Bellini.

"Thanks anyway," Mina smiled again. So many smiles—so little actual joy. She battled the urge to pick up her glass and chug down the rest, just to spite them.

"Oh good," Mack said. "It looks like they have your table ready." The hostess stood nearby, holding a pair of menus and two sets of silverware wrapped in striped cotton napkins.

Mrs. Whitney leaned down to place a dry kiss on Mina's cheek. "Grey would be so touched to see you keeping up with his old friends, Mina."

"Would he?" Mina asked faintly. She wasn't so sure.

"Okay ladies!" Mack belted out. He jumped up to kiss and hug his mother, and then steered her toward the hostess. "Better head over. Enjoy your meal!"

Once the women had their backs to her, Mina finished off her drink and ordered another. That would show them.

Mack sat back down, looking stricken. Instead of saying anything, though, he picked up his fork and jammed an oyster into his mouth. Buying time until he could gather his thoughts, Mina supposed. She'd bet her last dime he'd apologize, even though it wasn't his fault.

Before he could do that, or try to spin the women's words into something less cutting, Mina asked, "Mack? What happened with you and Carolynn anyway?"

He blinked at her—she'd taken him by surprise.

"It seemed like one minute you two were good and the next, we heard that she had moved out," Mina told him.

He laughed bitterly. "You don't know? I figured *everyone* knew."

"About what?"

Mack wiped his mouth and set his napkin precisely in his lap again. "About the other guy," he drawled.

"Another guy?" Mina gaped. "*Who?*"

Mack stared at her shoulder, refusing to meet her eyes. "Her boss, I think. That's what they told me, anyway."

"Well, what did Carolynn say?"

"Basically, when she did talk to me, it was to tell me all the ways I wasn't doing it for her anymore," he droned. "She didn't elaborate on what others might be doing."

"Mack." Mina was appalled. "She was *insane*. There's no way you weren't a terrific husband."

He shook his head and looked weary. "Actually, she was mostly on the money."

"Mack, *no*."

"It's all good, though. I learned my lesson." He lifted his eyes and stared right at Mina, grim and intense. "I won't make the same mistakes again," he said.

Mina fidgeted, abruptly uncomfortable. That sounded heavy and serious, and permanent as hell. But she couldn't give anyone that kind of assurance—not with the way she was. Not with the burdens Mina carried around inside her. If Mack thought she could offer him more than what they had right then, he was bound to be disappointed again.

She glanced toward the back of the restaurant and found two pairs of motherly eyes on her. Mina couldn't exactly deny the truth now, she supposed. It was probably obvious that she'd been pining after Mack for years—and Grey must not have been the only one to have guessed.

What was more, those two women clearly knew she wasn't good enough for Mack, not long term. She could see on their faces that they thought she would hurt him.

"Mina?" Mack prodded.

She refused to be the agent of any more heartache for this man. Mack thought he wanted her now, but if he knew the truth about her he'd take back every last promise he'd ever uttered.

He deserved to be happy.

"Well, whoever you end up with will be a very lucky woman," she smiled. Sadly, Mina knew it wouldn't be her.

Chapter Twenty

H E HADN'T PLANNED to spring it on her but running into the moms at brunch had thrown Mina off pretty severely. So, on the walk back to his place, Mack told Mina his big idea. If they were going to manage it, he'd need to make sure she could get time off from work. They'd need to buy tickets and make sure their passports were up-to-date.

"So, my mom has this big family get-together for Christmas every year," Mack said. "I'd love for you to go to it with me. But, after Christmas, what do you say we get away for a little while? If you can get a few days off from work, I thought we could hit up a beach somewhere before New Year's. Hawaii is probably too far," he mused, "But I bet we could find something in Costa Rica or the Dominican Republic."

Mina was taken aback. "Mack, I—"

He slapped his forehead. "What am I thinking? I just assumed that you wouldn't be visiting your mom or dad, but I completely forgot about Molly. Are you going to see her?"

"No, I'm not. Molly's too busy playing house with her formerly-boneheaded—but now rehabilitated—man. No way am I crashing that party."

They arrived home and he let Mina in through the back door. "So, you'll go with me? If you don't like the beach we could do something else. Savannah, or New Orleans, or…" Mina's wan face grew paler and Mack hesitated. "Europe?" he tried.

She stood in the middle of the room and took a deep breath. "That sounds nice, but I can't. I'm, uh…"

What? What else could she possibly be doing?

"I'm going skiing with a friend," she lied.

"A friend. Oh…" He studied her face. Something was off. "Who is it?"

Mina took a deep breath, like she was steeling herself. "Dimitri," she said, with a fake veneer of calm.

Mack jumped up and paced around his family room. "Dimitri is a man's name," he pointed out.

"I am aware."

"Well, who is he?" He wouldn't go crazy. He was not going to go crazy. Women had male friends all the time, without it being cheating. Carolynn was just an anomaly—not the start of a pattern that would take over Mack's life for eternity.

Mina shrugged. "He's just a friend."

"A friend. A male friend, that you are going skiing with for an entire week, alone?" Okay, maybe Mack *was* going crazy.

"I'm thirty-two years old, Mack. I hardly need a father anymore."

"I'm not trying to be your dad, I'm trying to be your boyfriend. And I *thought* we were exclusive. Or monogamous, or whatever you call it." It was incredibly difficult not to sound petty right then, and he wasn't sure why he bothered.

"Mack, we are." She was trying to sound reassuring, but that only made him more suspicious.

He threw up his hands in frustration. "Well, you won't be finding me going out of town with random chicks I know!"

"Dimitri is not some random guy!"

"That's clear." He jammed his hands in his pockets, so they wouldn't keep curling into fists.

Too late, Mina seemed to remember what Mack had told her about his ex-wife. She amped up the soothing tone. "Mack, calm down. I'm not cheating on you. Dimitri is a friend from the bereavement group I go to. We're not…I mean, I'm not…"

"Sleeping with him?" he inquired.

She sighed. "*Skiing* with him. *Or* sleeping with him. I lied, okay? I'm sorry."

Now Mack was just confused. "Why would you do that?"

"I don't know." Mina stalked into the kitchen area. "It just sort of popped out."

He dropped heavily into his favorite armchair. "You don't want to go on vacation with me?" It had seemed like such a good idea. Mack had been dreaming about it for days.

Mina shook her head, though.

"Why?" He thought back over the whole weekend, and only one thing could have put Mina off. "Was it because of what Mrs. Whitney said earlier?"

"No. I can't let myself worry about what she thinks," Mina said, but Mack wasn't sure he believed it. "I think this might be…too much too soon, that's all.

"I see." He didn't. Not really. They'd had twelve years to wait for each other. How much more time was necessary?

Mina smiled weakly at him.

"So…" He had to figure this out. "You feel pressured?" Mack guessed.

"A little."

He winced. His fault. "Jesus, I'm sorry, Mina. I really like you and I want to spend more time with you. That's it. I wasn't trying to be pushy."

"Mack, I like spending time with you, too."

"Just not *too* much," he clarified. He stood up again, restless.

"Essentially," Mina said. "For now."

Apparently, the weekend booty calls were okay with her, just not anything more substantial. Mack didn't think he was on board with that.

"Do you, uh…" He passed a hand over his face, trying to think. "See that changing at some point?"

"Honestly? I haven't thought that far ahead," she claimed.

He stared at his shoes. "We were supposed to go to that concert next weekend. Do you still want to?"

"Of course I do, Mack." Mina came out from behind the counter and put her arms around his waist. "I'm not asking to split up. I'm just not ready to go away with you yet."

She'd hurt him, but he wasn't sure she'd even realized. Mack held her carefully and tried to rally. It wasn't the end of the world, just the end of his vacation idea. He'd known all along that he would have to proceed carefully with Mina, but in his enthusiasm for, oh…everything about her, it was hard to remember sometimes.

"Okay," he told her. "I'm sorry. I guess I got carried away."

"I understand. Do you?"

"Yeah, it's good. I'm good," Mack said. His mind was reeling, though. He wasn't entirely sure what had just happened.

"Are *we* good?" Mina asked.

"Sure. We're fine." But were they?

BY THE TIME the next weekend rolled around, things appeared to be back to normal. Mina had called and texted Mack during the week the same way she always did.

He spent the night with her Friday, and on Saturday, she'd been happy and excited for the chance to see one of her favorite bands in concert that evening.

They'd landed an unseasonably warm day, so she and Mack picked up some sandwiches and beer and drove to the amphitheater early to tailgate.

In the packed-dirt parking lot before the concert, Mack discovered a new place that Mina was ticklish, completely by accident. They were standing near the back of his truck eating and people watching, when he reached behind her for the beer he'd set on his fender—and brushed the delicate skin on the back of her thigh, right where the hem of her cutoff denim skirt landed. Mina nearly jumped clear out of her skin.

Mack watched her eyes go wide, heard her breath hitch, and he was hooked like a trout on a line. It was amazing, really, how many ways you could find to touch a woman there, he reflected. He spent half the concert trying to discover every last one—teasing her until Mina was a trembling bundle of nerves. Frankly, Mack was a little surprised that she didn't suspect something was up.

Maybe she did, though. She was dancing and singing to the music, sure. But she was also hugging up on Mack and sticking her hands in his back pockets, kissing his neck and his ear and generally driving him wild.

If he hadn't been there himself, Mack might've thought their conversation the prior weekend had never happened. He wasn't going to remind Mina about it now, though—not when he couldn't wait to get her home.

Eventually, Mina wanted to duck out and use the facilities. Mack walked her down their row of seats and out of the covered pavilion, but instead of getting in the line for the ladies room, she swiftly yanked Mack into the darkness around the corner of the concession building.

In seconds, Mina was wrapped around him like a weed, hands everywhere and begging him for it. It wasn't like he didn't want to—her kisses were off-the-charts desperate, and the way she pressed against him had Mack ready and then some.

Still, he tried to resist her. He'd spotted the security guys strolling by only ten feet away, and the drifting scents of urine and beer hardly set the most romantic mood.

His reluctance bothered him. Mack hated to sound like a stick in the mud—he always had, but somehow always managed to anyway. His cousins and Grey used to get on him about it, and later, Carolynn did, too. They'd called him "The Voice of Reason" like it was a bad thing.

As much as he didn't want to be *that* guy right then, Mack also didn't want to be the dude disrespecting Mina by taking what he wanted against a concrete snack bar wall.

He murmured something about not having any protection with him, instead. Predictably, it was like he'd poured a cold beer over her head. She abruptly stopped kissing him and set her feet back on the ground. Mack couldn't make out her expression in the darkness, but her body language sent out the message loud and clear.

She sounded a bit sullen when she muttered under her breath, "It's not like a condom's gonna make the difference anyway."

Mack rested his arm against the wall beside her head, feeling her withdrawal—sensing her gathering herself for retreat.

"Why? Are you on the pill?" he asked her. They hadn't discussed it before. Mack had always been prepared.

"No need for that," Mina sulked. "Forget I said anything." She shook her head like she was annoyed, but he couldn't tell if it was with herself or with him. Mina straightened her clothes with a couple efficient yanks, then ducked under his arm and headed back out into the light.

Forget it? That was preposterous. Mack wasn't going to forget something like that. He trotted to catch up with her, but Mina quickly changed course, giving him a small wave and heading into the crowded ladies room. He stood there dumbly, going over everything she'd said again and again while he waited for her.

By the time she emerged again, they'd missed three whole songs and an extended drum solo. He'd bought and eaten a soft pretzel and a hot dog, and Mina's whole demeanor had shifted back to normal again.

It wasn't only that this wasn't the place for some big heart-to-heart, either—it was like he'd dreamed the whole damn thing. That was becoming a bit of a theme with her.

Mack was right back to second-guessing whether he could actually pull off this relationship with Mina. The odds didn't seem great. As skittish as Mina seemed to be, she was bound to get spooked again at some point. Even worse, Mack had the unsettling feeling that she was keeping some big secrets. Things that mattered—things that would take her away from him.

The stakes were ratcheting higher with each kiss Mina gave him, though. Mack wasn't sure he could bear it if she left once more.

Chapter Twenty-One

THE FOLLOWING FRIDAY, far sooner than she expected, Mack texted Mina to let her know he was on his way to Annapolis. He'd had a crew reconstructing a seawall that week, but between bad weather at the shore, a delayed permit, and the town's inspector cancelling on them at the last minute, it seemed he'd called it an early day.

That meant Mina had an hour, maybe an hour and a half, before he arrived at her house and saw that she had pint-sized company. For some reason, she'd been conflicted about telling Mack over the phone. She'd made things a little weird between them when she refused to go on vacation with him, and then…there was the critical matter of her freak-out at the concert.

Mina could've predicted Mack would reject the idea of sex in public, but it had been more reckless of her to let that comment slip about unnecessary birth control. All week, she'd worried that Mack would pester her about it, but so far, he'd stayed quiet. She only hoped that seeing her with Monty wouldn't inconveniently refresh Mack's memory.

Maybe Mina would get lucky, though. Maybe Sadie would finish at her doctor's appointment early and come pick up her kid before Mack got there.

She should have known that wouldn't happen—Mina had never been the fortunate type. Mack must have hit zero traffic and driven like a bat out of hell, because he rang Mina's doorbell no more than fifty minutes after he first texted. It figured.

"Hey, babe," he grinned, when Mina let him in. "How happy am I that you had the day off?" He handed her a large bouquet of orange and yellow mums, then leaned in for a kiss. Mina stepped away before it could get too steamy.

Once she was out of the line of fire, Mack was immediately pelted in the chest with a barrage of foam pellets. He clutched his shirt, dropped to the floor of her front hall, and writhed around a bit in apparent agony.

When he finally opened his eyes, there was an undersized kid in a crooked red cowboy hat smiling down at him.

"Well, well, well," Mack sneered. "If it isn't my old nemesis, Montgomery Bly. We meet again, sir."

Mina covered her mouth to stifle her laugh. He was a *natural*.

"I shots you, Misser Mack!" Monty informed him cheerfully.

Mack sat up and felt around on his chest. "Uh, nope," he told her nephew. "You only thought you shot me. But what you don't know is that I wore my invisible force field today." He jumped to his feet and dusted himself off, superior as can be.

Monty's big blue eyes went round. "You *did*?"

Mina stepped in to explain. "We're being cowboys today, Mack. Not space guys."

"Says you," Mack retorted haughtily. "*Some* of us are space cowboys."

"Oh," little Monty breathed, clearly impressed. "That true, Auntie Meema?"

Mina rolled her eyes. "And here I thought he was just a gangster of love."

Mack scoffed, "It's not an either/or thing, Auntie Mina. All the best guys do both."

Monty's wide gaze had been ping-ponging back and forth between them, but at this he piped up, "Yeah!"

"Duh," Mack winked at her.

"What is she?" Monty pointed at Mina.

Before she could come up with something suitably fabulous, Mack chuckled, "Oh, she's trouble."

Mina stared heavenward, searching for deliverance that didn't look like it was coming. She'd promised Monty she would bring him to the park before he had to go home, though, and no way would he forget. It was time to go.

"All right. Well, *whatever* you two are, we have to get to the park and search for the bandits now, before they have time to take over the whole world."

"And before Mommy comes back, right?"

Mina straightened Monty's hat. "Exactly."

"Misser Mack, are you coming too?"

Mack rocked on his heels. "I don't know. Are there even swings there?"

"Yes!" Monty nodded excitedly, hopping in place.

"Then, *yeah*. Of course, I'm coming," Mack drawled. Mina locked the door, and they were off.

Mina was crazy about little Monty, but it was sometimes hard to keep him entertained for long. Mack made it look so easy. His quips and jokes didn't seem to require any effort at all. He'd slid expertly into the role of World's Best Sitter, and Monty was eating it up.

As they walked up the block, Mack swung the boy up onto his shoulders, then took Mina's hand. "You might've pointed out that you were babysitting when I texted you."

"And ruin the surprise?"

"It was a fun surprise," he smiled, jostling Monty a little and making him laugh.

"Are you sure you don't mind? It's not for long—Sadie is picking him up in about an hour."

"I don't mind," Mack insisted. "Monty's great."

At the playground, there weren't many other people—just one tall man in a janitor's green jumpsuit and the tiny girl with him.

As the girl went down the same small slide over and over—and the man bent each time to catch her—Mina decided he looked familiar.

"Aw! No bandits," Monty cried. "There's just that girl."

Mack set him down and turned to look where the boy was pointing. "Not *just* a girl," he said. "She's obviously a highly trained secret agent. I bet she's only acting innocent to fool you."

Monty looked dubious.

Mina turned away from the janitor and cackled as evilly as she could. "Just like me," she said. She grabbed little Monty, tossed him over her shoulder, and ran in crazy zig-zags across the grass.

The janitor looked up with a smile when they got close, and Mina jerked to a halt. "Hey, that's my friend Dimitri," she exclaimed. She gave him a wave.

Monty squealed and struggled, so she let him down. He scampered right back over to Mack and hugged his leg. "Auntie Meema knows the man!" he declared, red-cheeked and out of breath.

Mack raised his eyebrows when she walked up.

"It's my friend Dimitri," she told him. "The one I told you about. But…he's with a little girl who looks *exactly* like him."

"I believe those are called daughters," he retorted.

"I knew nothing about this daughter," Mina explained.

"Ah," Mack smiled. If he felt any ill will about Dimitri's role in their aborted vacation, he didn't show it. "Why don't you investigate, while Monty and I go conquer some swings."

"Come meet him first," she said. As soon as he did, Mack would see that Dimitri was harmless.

He shook his head, though. "Thanks for that, but it's okay. I'll meet him later."

Mina watched him race her nephew to the swing set, and when she turned back, Dimitri was already making his way over.

"Who's that dude?" he asked. The little girl's hand was dwarfed by his, and when Mina smiled at her, she popped one grubby thumb in her mouth and frowned.

"He's an old friend," Mina told him. "A better question might be, who's this lovely lady?"

Dimitri looked sheepish. In all the time they'd been friends, he'd never once mentioned having a kid, much less one so small. She must have been only a toddler when his wife had passed.

"This is my daughter Lilly. Lilly, this is my friend Miss Mina."

"Pleased to meet you," Mina told her. Lilly bobbed an adorable little curtsy, then pulled free of her father and ran back to the slide.

Dimitri looked distinctly uncomfortable.

"So. You have a kid," Mina said. "What a surprise."

"It never came up," he muttered.

She slanted a doubtful look at him. "On purpose?"

"Probably." After the topics that had been discussed in the bereavement group, Mina could imagine why he thought he'd keep quiet about it. Realizing she didn't know him nearly as well as she'd assumed was upsetting, though.

"And…" She plucked at his jumpsuit. "It seems you're working as a janitor now?"

Dimitri had run a successful development company before his wife had gotten ill. He'd closed up shop to take care of her, but Mina hadn't realized his finances had taken quite that big of a nose dive since.

"It's not what you think. After Anna died, I wanted to keep things as stable as possible for Lilly. Anna had her in preschool at this little private place in town, so when she started Kindergarten, I enrolled her there. But…she was losing her shit every day when I dropped her off. I couldn't deal. I thought if I got a job there, it would help Lilly if she could see me during the day, and know I was nearby."

"That's very sweet, but as a janitor? Why not teach or something?" Mina asked.

Dimitri just shrugged. "Didn't have it in me."

She could believe it. Mina had already been in the group for a few weeks when Dimitri first started coming. She remembered the utter devastation on his face, the ruin that he'd tried so hard to hide.

"Hey, you want to meet my nephew and my friend?"

Dimitri scoffed, "If that guy is just your friend, Lilly over there is the Queen of Sheba."

"So...yeah?"

"Yeah, sure. Lead the way."

The two men sized each other up for a few minutes, but otherwise managed to keep things civil and not come to blows or anything. Mina was quickly exhausted from trying to deflect all the significant looks each one of them kept sending her, though.

"Time to go," she called to Monty.

He came running back, Lilly in tow. "She's not a secret agent, Misser Mack. She said she's a princess."

Dimitri smiled. Mack drew back and looked amazed. "*Whoa.* That's even better." Then he leaned down and whispered loudly, "But just between you and me, princesses can be secret agents, too. And it's not like she could just *tell* you that. You'd have to be clever and figure it out."

Monty turning questioning eyes on Mina, finding that hard to believe. "Don't look at me," she said. "Mack's the expert."

BACK AT THE house, Sadie was waiting for them in the driveway. She got out of her car when she saw them approach up the sidewalk.

"Well, hello there, stranger!" she grinned.

"Sadie! Long time no see." Mack hugged her tight, and then Monty was shoving between them.

"Misser Mack is a space cowboy," he told his mother.

"You know, I think I heard that about him."

"And Auntie Meema is twubble."

Sadie looked amused and raised one eyebrow in Mina's direction. "Now, *that* is news to me."

"Hardly," Mina snorted.

Sadie leaned in to Monty's ear, and whispered conspiratorially, "It's always the quiet ones you have to watch out for."

"Okay," Monty whispered back.

Mack laughed. "Ain't that the truth," he said.

MACK WENT HOURS without broaching the kid topic, and Mina was anxious the entire time. Finally, after a casual dinner out and a hasty bout of lovemaking, she couldn't take the elephant in the room any longer.

"You were so good with my nephew," Mina told him tentatively. "Monty...obviously adores you." She couldn't figure out why it was nagging at her so much.

"He's great," Mack responded. "I get to see him sometimes when they're in town."

He raised her shirt and kissed her stomach, hands holding Mina's hips in place. Mack was smiling and happy.

"You were great too, sweetheart. You're going to make an amazing mother someday." Mack kissed her belly again. "And man, are your babies gonna be beautiful."

There is was, the reason for her discomfiture. With a sickening thud, all of the impossible reasons why she and Mack could never work out snapped into place in Mina's brain. Just. Like. That. Well, what had she expected? She'd walked right into it—started the one conversation with Mack that she was not equipped to deal with.

Mina went stiff. Mack must have felt it too, because he froze in place, lifted his eyes from her navel, and asked, "What?"

She knew she couldn't run, but she couldn't stop herself from scrabbling backwards on the bed, grateful that she at least had on a tank top and some panties and wasn't completely exposed. When she saw Mack's alarmed expression, her panic ratcheted up a notch. Mina floundered her way off the side of the bed, snagged her jeans from the floor, and stabbed her shaking legs into them.

"Mina?" Mack asked, bewildered. "What's wrong?"

She shook her head, slipping on her flip-flops and searching around for a sweater.

"Nothing. Um—" She spotted her navy cardigan under a chair and dove for it. "I just remembered I have a thing, that's all."

"A *thing?*" Mack sat up and scrubbed a hand over his face, dumbfounded. "It's nine o'clock!"

"Yes," Mina affirmed. "I'm sorry. I really have to go."

"Mina—"

"*Shit,*" Mina cursed, looking around. "Where the heck is my purse?" She pulled on her sweater but couldn't make herself meet his eyes.

"On the coffee table," he said reasonably.

She took off, catching the toe of her sandal on the raised board of the threshold, and stumbling.

"Wait!" Mack called. He scrambled off the bed and stalked after her. "Mina, what did I say?"

"Nothing!" she cried, but even she could hear how unconvincing that sounded. Lowering her voice, she added, "Everything's fine." She snagged her purse, dug through it to extract her keys, and headed for the front door.

With a huff of incredulity, Mack lunged for her and caught her hand. Unlike Grey, though, his hold was gentle.

"Everything is not fine! Please talk to me," he said. "What did I do wrong?"

Mina stared at the door, so close to setting her free. "I can't do this right now," she whispered. If she didn't get out of there soon, she was going to completely lose it.

Mack let go of her hand.

Surprised, Mina chanced a peek back at him. When she did, he stood up straight as an arrow, squared his shoulders, and lifted his chin. He looked a bit like Monty, and like nothing she deserved.

"Whatever is happening right now, I'm sorry—okay? I did not mean to upset you. And…" he swallowed with effort. "I hope you'll tell me what's going on, so I don't unwittingly do whatever it is again."

God—he looked so dignified, and so worried. "*Mack*," Mina sighed heavily.

"Mina, if I don't know where the sinkholes are, how can I avoid stepping in them?" he asked, the epitome of calm.

Mack was too nice a guy—too *normal*—to have to deal with all of her baggage. "Don't you get it?" she grimaced. "They're everywhere. You can't avoid them."

Then she left. She wasn't proud of it, that was for sure. But if Mina didn't reach the safety of her car in about two-point-five more seconds, she was going to completely fall apart in front of Mack. There was no way in hell she wanted to do that. He'd never let it rest until he got to the bottom of it, and that was something she couldn't let him do.

At a gas station several blocks down the street, Mina parked her car and tried to get it together. She should have known falling for Mack Bolton was too damn good to be true. But somehow, lost amidst the giddy revelation that he'd been holding a torch for her from the very beginning—lost within the blossoming love she felt for pretty much everything about him—was the fact that Mack was a consummate family man.

He was *made* to be a husband and a dad. His failure with Carolynn notwithstanding, he'd be incredible at it. And, while Mina might be able to take another swing at the matrimony thing…she wasn't going to be the one to make him a father. She'd be damned if she'd give him any opening to try to convince her that it didn't matter. Mack would only be lying, and eventually he'd grow to hate her. Just like Grey had.

Mack texted to ask if she wanted him to leave. He begged her to tell him if she was okay. He wanted to come to wherever she was. It was all too much like the last night Grey was alive for Mina to ignore.

She forced herself to type out some responses: *Yes, she needed him to leave. Yes, she was okay. Yes, she'd explain later. Yes, she'd come home so he could be sure she was safe.*

Reluctantly, she drove home to find Mack's truck idling on the street in front of her townhouse. When she pulled into her driveway, he honked once, then drove away. He still managed to do the decent thing, even when he was up a creek without a paddle. She hung her head.

The indisputable fact of Mack's nature was yet another harsh reality that had come to crash the party like so many others in her life. Mina had no recollection of getting out of her car, but when her front door finally swung shut behind her, she took two steps into her family room, dropped her purse, and fell to her knees. There she stayed, crying hot, furious tears—jagged sobs like she hadn't experienced since she was seventeen—about the total unfairness of it all.

Chapter Twenty-Two

I F MINA HAD expected him to simply leave town after that demonstration, then she was sadly mistaken. Mack had barely been able to leave her alone for the night, given the condition she'd been in.

He'd wanted to respect her wishes, though, so he'd driven around town for a while, until he found a decent hotel where he could crash until morning.

For ten interminably sleepless hours, Mack laid in that sterile room, Mina's nonsensical words zinging around inside his head like an electron cloud gone wild. Once dawn finally broke, he got cleaned up and checked out.

Mack found a coffee shop where he could get some breakfast, and then he texted Mina that he was on his way back over. It wasn't like she'd be sleeping either, and whatever had happened the night before was something big—something they needed to talk about.

When Mack arrived, he wasn't sure Mina would let him in. She did, though, and she looked about as awful as he felt. He followed her back into her kitchen and tried to tamp down his trepidation.

He thought he'd better cut right to the chase. "As far as I can tell," he told her, "You freaked out when I said that you'd make a great mom someday. That's usually considered a compliment. So, why would it make you run for the hills?"

Mina rubbed her hands over her pale face with a heavy sigh. "Mack, you know I didn't have the best childhood. Sometimes stuff still hits a nerve, okay? I'm sorry I lost it, and it was…" She halted briefly. "Extremely cool of you to leave like you did. True, I didn't expect you to actually stay in town—"

"Yeah, no—I was not going to drive back home when you were still so upset," Mack said flatly. "Why don't you fill me in a little more, though? Why does your childhood make you flip out about being a mother?" He plopped into a chair at her table and made himself comfortable.

"You don't know what it was like," she complained. "Before my dad took off, my parents shuttled us around from place to place, and we never got to go to parks or other regular kid stuff. We were, like, hanging around the docks and taverns with my dad all the time. I was only seventeen when he left for good, and instead of being a kid I suddenly had to be the parent for both Molly *and* my mom."

"So…" Mack ventured, "You feel like you've already been a mother? Is that what you're saying?"

"In a way, yes."

"Honey, you're right—I don't exactly know firsthand how that feels, but I can imagine how hard it must have been. And then to get free of that situation, only to end up with Grey…"

"*Now* you're getting it," Mina said sourly.

Mack wouldn't go that far, but he was trying. "I realize that you have baggage. I was there when you acquired some of it. But we *all* have baggage, okay?"

"Oh, sure. Like *you* have baggage." She rolled her eyes.

"You know…" Mack bit back the retort on his lips and tried to deliver a softer version. "I suppose I should be flattered you think I'm so perfect. But the truth is, life gets hard for everyone on this planet at some point or another, and I am no exception."

He didn't think Mina would love hearing about the way her leaving with Grey twelve years ago had wrecked him, so instead Mack went with some history she might understand better.

"When my dad passed away, my mom needed a lot of help. Bodhi and the twins were still in high school, and we all had to pitch in to make sure they got what they needed. I was carrying a full course load in college, so it wasn't like I had a ton of time or money to help."

Mina gazed at him, her brow knitting into a frown. She hadn't been around for those years. Didn't know what he'd been through.

"And later, when Carolynn left…" Mack paused. It was one of those life events that was, in retrospect, both a blessing and curse.

Mina said, "It's okay. You don't have to talk about it."

Mack didn't want to. Not with her, and definitely not right now. "Anyway, my point is that if you could try to step outside your own head for a minute, you'd see that *no one* leads a charmed life. We all have our crosses to bear. And we all handle our messes in different ways. When it comes to me and you—"

"Mack, *that's* what we need to talk about—more than my lousy adolescence. There can't be a 'me and you.' Not in the way you deserve."

He couldn't help noticing that Mina wasn't saying she didn't want him—she never did that. Instead she seemed to think he deserved some amorphous thing in life that was superior to her. Mack tried to take comfort in what he could, and not get bogged down by the impossibility of convincing Mina that—for him— there'd never been *anything* better than her.

"As I said, when it comes to me and you," he continued, "If you would only let me in a little bit, tell me what's going on when you feel upset or vulnerable, then we can work stuff out. Move past it. Together."

"You don't get it. I *can't* do that. I can't give any man—any person—that kind of power over me ever again. Grey made damn sure of that." Mina snorted. "Do you have any idea how often I can hear his voice in my head?"

"Mina, Grey's *gone*. I can do a lot of things, but I can't…I can't fight a dead guy for your affection."

"I'm not asking you to. And you can't ask me to lay all my crap out on the table for you to pick through, either."

Mack shook his head, confounded by her analogy. "Don't you trust me at all?" he asked.

She shrugged. "Trust is not one of my strong points. Don't take it personally, though. I don't trust *me*, either—I tend to make very bad decisions. This is hardly something particular to you."

"I have been consistent, though. From the very beginning, I've made sure you know how I feel about you. It's not hard to figure out." Mack hesitated, but figured if he was in for a penny, he was in for a pound. "I…love you, Mina. I want you to love me."

There it was, out in the open. Mack had hoped for a better moment to break it to her and prayed he hadn't blown everything by saying it now.

"Apparently, so did Grey," she scowled. "I fell for it and look where that got me. Ten years gone and I'll never get them back."

Okay, bitterness was not what a guy usually looked for when he told a woman that he loved her. Mack tried not to feel pissed.

"Except I'm not Grey," he pointed out, for the nth time.

"No, but you *were* lifelong friends with him—with a liar and a cheat and an emotional manipulator," Mina fired back. "Why would you do that? What kind of person does that make *you*? And let's not forget that you already have one divorce under your belt. How can you be so sure you won't have another?"

Mack felt the blood drain from his head. "You—you can't possibly be holding that against me." Why was Mina acting so defensive all of the sudden? He'd only been trying to get her to see reason, and now she was going to turn on him? To lash out? He'd unwittingly wandered into some previously-uncharted hell, that was for sure.

"Listen. I made the wrong choice once," Mina said. "I lost a whole decade to it. And now, I'm only just getting on my feet. I finished my degree and got my own job, and even made my own friends—people who never knew Grey and don't associate me with him. I cannot give all that up for some unreliable future I can't count on."

Mack blinked, struggling to follow her reasoning. "I would never ask you to do that. And you *can* count on me. I have always, always been in your corner. Can't you see that?"

"Mack, I'm reasonably sure that if you were to do something shitty, it would be unintentional. But right now, I'm just not confident in my ability to sort the good guys from the bad."

"Oh gee, thanks."

"I'm even less certain of whether who you are now, is who you'll still be in ten years. Or twenty," Mina went on. She shrugged, "And me sitting around waiting for the crap to hit the fan doesn't sound like a pleasant life to me."

"So, instead, you're going to…what? Sit around alone forever, so you never have to risk your equilibrium? You're going to end this first, before I have a chance to hurt you?" Mack had a long fuse, but this bizarre funhouse conversation had incinerated most of it. "What if I was never going to hurt you?"

"It's not like that."

"Actually, I think it might be."

Mina tried for a placating tone that made him want to punch something. "Mack, the thing is—we both deserve to be happy. Whether you're a good guy or a bad one, or your loyalty and trustworthiness will evaporate like the fog—*you* deserve to have joy in your life. And you won't find that with me. I can't give that to you."

"But I'm telling you that you can. You *do*."

"Maybe right now. But not two or three years in the future."

"Why?" he demanded. "What happens then?"

Mina sighed. "You're a family guy, Mack. It's as plain as the nose on your face. Before long, you'll want to get married, and after that you'll want to make babies. And I cannot be a part of that."

"Mina, I have seen you with babies—with Monty. You can't possibly expect me to believe that you don't want kids someday."

She exploded, "It's not a question of want!"

"Then tell me—what *is* it a question of?" Mack paused and considered. "You *can't*?"

Her voice was so quiet, he almost missed her words. "I don't think so."

This had the stink of Grey's ugliness all over it. God, Mack hated what that man had done to her. "Don't think, or don't *know*?" he challenged.

Mina protested, "Mack, I was married for *ten years*! And I never once got pregnant. Doesn't that tell you something?"

"No, it doesn't, because it leaves out a whole host of pertinent data. It is hardly conclusive proof that you aren't capable—that something is *wrong* with you. But hey, let me take a wild stab in the dark. Grey told you that it was your fault, and that makes it true, right?" Mack knew he was being harsh, but honestly—when would it ever end?

"I don't want to fight about this right now," Mina said.

Now it was Mack's turn to bellow, "Who's fighting?"

She stared mulishly at his face and waited him out.

"Mina, come *on*," he pleaded. "I can't keep doing this. I can't keep doing battle with another man's *ghost*."

"You're not."

"I *am*. One day you're right there with me, and I think everything is great. And the next day, you withdraw into your shell. I don't know what I've said or done to set you off, because you won't *tell* me anything. I have no idea what I'm up against and it's wearing me out."

"And I don't want to do that to you anymore."

"I want to try. I think you're worth it. That *we're* worth it. But this is…not what I expected. I'm banging my head against the wall and I'm not even sure if you love me back, if you *want* this. If you ever will. Because you won't tell me."

"Mack, we need to concede that this relationship isn't meant to be. Call it quits while we still can."

"I'm trying to get you to open up to me—to let me in—and you want to break *up*?"

Mina struggled with her words. "We'll still…be friends. We can talk and…even hang out sometimes, if you want. We just won't be making each other miserable."

Oh, now he made her miserable? She was one to talk. "Jesus," he said. "*Friends*, Mina? You think you'll be okay with me seeing someone new? Because having to watch you with some other guy does *not* sound delightful to me."

"We did it before. We can do it again."

"I don't want to do that again! It sucked!" he sputtered.

"Then I guess the other option is to not see or talk to each other at all." Mina was fighting back tears, and he *hated* it. But Mack couldn't stop now.

"I *thought* the other option was you finally letting me behind the…" Mack waved his hand at her. "The firewall."

"You were wrong."

"No, I wasn't." He felt like he was in school again, bickering with Bodhi or his sisters.

Mina made an impatient sound. "Mack, what's it going to be? Can we be friends, or not?"

"Please don't do this, Mina," he pleaded.

"I have to. For both of our sakes."

He grabbed his keys. "You know, right from the beginning I worried that you'd leave again, but it seemed like you'd moved past all that. I let my guard down, and I guess that's on me. However, if this is what you think you need to do, then I really do feel sorry for you." *Shit.* He probably shouldn't have said that.

Mina blinked back tears. "*Mack*," she implored him.

If he didn't leave, he was going to do something irrevocable, something worse—like crying or clutching at her.

"Fine," he grated out. "You know where to find me. When you're ready to trust me, to talk about what's really going on in that head of yours, then you know where to find me."

Mina reached out, but Mack stepped back, away from her hand.

"I'll call you," she said sadly.

"Just..." He swallowed down the knot rising in his throat. "Give me a few days, okay? I need a little time to wrap my head around this."

"I understand." She twisted her hands together. "And I'm sorry."

Mack paused with one foot out the door. "Not as sorry as me," he said. He forced himself to take the remaining steps to his truck, to get behind the wheel and start the ignition. He forced himself to leave the woman he loved behind, while she stood crying in the window.

He'd known it might happen. Mack had *known*. Didn't make it hurt any less, though.

Chapter Twenty-Three

Two Years Earlier

WHEN SHE WAS nineteen, Mina had left her mother and sister in the dust because she'd yearned to be free. She'd wanted to be young again—to live her life the way *she* desired, without all the pressure and drama.

To Mina, Grey had been the ideal embodiment of that coveted independence. He was confident and fun-loving and ambitious, and together they were going to see the world.

Year by year, he'd chipped away at all her hopes. First, there'd been the surprise of him getting out of the service and enrolling in college in North Carolina so soon after they were married. Instead of being stationed somewhere exotic with her new husband, Mina had been stuck in a dinky campus apartment while Grey went to his classes and joined a fraternity. After graduation, he'd joined up again as an officer, but there was Mina—back in base housing, still doing all of the same boring things.

Ten years ago, Grey had encouraged Mina to ditch her family and marry him, and at the time it had seemed like a no-brainer. How could she have guessed that he would eventually condemn her for being a runaway who didn't know the first thing about family? Mina hadn't seen a single sign that he would abuse her affections, then vilify her for acting cold. He had used her body, then told Mina it was her fault nothing came of it. *Her fault. Her fault. Always her fault.*

She hadn't seen any of the world. Whenever Grey was deployed, Mina stayed home. When he wasn't deployed…Mina still stayed home. She waitressed and hung on, but her husband never made good on anything that he'd promised her. What a fool she'd been. Mina had given up everything for Grey Whitney, done all that he'd asked of her, and gotten nothing but sorrow in return.

He'd made excuses for why she couldn't go to school—then turned her lack of a college degree against her. Grey told Mina she didn't know what she was talking about any time she formed an opinion different than his. He claimed the only reason she'd even gotten within spitting distance of a college was because of him.

When she had the chance, Mina quietly enrolled in the online university the military ran for service members and their families and began plugging away at some night classes. She might not have been able to convince Grey that she wasn't some shiftless dolt, but at least she could prove it to herself.

As with so many other things, she hadn't questioned at first why Grey controlled the purse strings so tightly, even when he was away. Checks Mina wrote to pay the bills sometimes bounced, and occasionally the cable would get turned off for a month or two.

As time went on and Mina trusted her husband less, she realized she'd better give herself some options. With some of the money that she made waiting tables, she opened a secret bank account and began saving a couple dollars here and there from her tips. Just in case. Even though Mina agonized about what Grey would do if he found out, it felt safer to have that small safety net out there.

Still, every time Grey came back from a deployment, Mina tried to meet him with renewed hope. Together, they could tackle their problems, and return to the way things used to be in the beginning—but only if they worked at it. Grey still had to do what the Marines wanted, but if Mina tried hard enough to be what he needed, she could have everything—her marriage and her husband and a family, too. She knew she could fix things. She'd had no idea how naïve she was.

THE LAST TIME he returned home was different, though. Grey came and went at odd hours, didn't sleep or eat regularly, and was even more short-tempered than usual. Mina struggled to keep him on an even keel when she was home. During her shifts at work, she worried the entire time, not having any idea what would be waiting for her at the other end.

On that day, she'd left before Grey awoke. Mina opened at the diner, busted her ass through the breakfast rush, then hurried home. He'd looked pretty haggard before bed the night before, and she wanted to make sure he was okay. But when she arrived, it was as if she'd wandered into the middle of a particularly convoluted argument without hearing the beginning.

Mina stood rooted in the middle of their family room, smelling of hash browns and coffee while her husband said a lot of things that made no sense. She didn't even take off her apron while she attempted to find a thread of logic connecting his random thoughts. But at last, one important detail seemed to float to the top of the stew. Grey was bored.

He blustered hotly about the indignity of being relegated to the reserves, when he thought he should be out fighting like a true Marine. Mina was stunned. She didn't even know her husband had shifted to inactive duty and had no idea when that might have happened.

Before his confession, Grey had been acting like he was merely taking some leave while he bided time until his next deployment—somewhere far away, where Mina *wasn't*. Now that the secret was out, his tirade lost steam and he sagged onto the couch.

Mina left him there and went into the kitchen to start the coffee maker. Without the structure of the military, she wondered how much further her husband might spiral. Having him home every day for good had the potential to make life more difficult...but perhaps it would be a positive thing for them.

Maybe whoever or whatever was bringing Grey down wouldn't bother him anymore, and—with more time together and a regular civilian life—their relationship might recover. Maybe they could even try again to get pregnant.

There was that pesky hope again. Mina tried to stay realistic about their chances, but it was hard. Despite all that had happened, she still didn't want to admit how badly she'd probably botched her life. If she could fix her marriage, it would prove to people that she wasn't a complete disaster—prove that there was still something left that Mina could accomplish, something she could succeed at.

She brought him a steaming mug of black coffee, just the way Grey liked it. It was obvious that he hadn't showered or eaten anything yet, even though it was close to noon.

She was baffled about why he would keep his actual service status a secret, but maybe now that he'd calmed down a bit she could convince him to tell her more. While they sat there on the couch, she managed to convince him to go out on a date with her that night to celebrate.

Treating his retirement as a happy occasion helped to mask Mina's misgivings about why he'd kept her in the dark and seemed to further stabilize Grey's mood. It would be better than bickering about it all day at home, anyway.

THAT EVENING, AFTER a quick glance at her husband, Mina decided it would be better if she drove—something Grey never would've allowed even five years earlier. Back then, he'd always pointed out men riding in women's passenger seats on the road, sniffing derisively and calling them *pussies*. Mina had tried to give him perspective sometimes, theorizing that the man had just had dental surgery, perhaps, or broken a foot.

Behind the wheel that day, she winced when she realized that she never once tried to say anything like: *Maybe that woman likes to drive. Maybe she's in love with her new car. Maybe she's his boss, or his instructor, or a race-car driver for her day job.* Mina never tried, because she knew, without a doubt, what Grey would have said about ideas like that.

What Mina couldn't figure out was how she'd been okay with it for so long. Maybe she fought so hard to justify and fix things between them, because she didn't want to admit that she never should've married him in the first place—and hadn't merely screwed things up along the way.

The outing was nothing major, only a casual dinner at a new restaurant ten minutes away. Grey had showered but didn't shave for their date and had worn a wrinkled button-down shirt over unwashed jeans. He sat through dinner grudgingly and picked sullenly at his food.

Their waiter was an older Italian man, the kind of career restaurant worker Mina had spent most of her adult life around. She'd liked him immediately, but the more the man doted on her, the more irritated Grey got.

Towards the end of the meal, the waiter tried once again to soften up her husband. He laid a hand on Grey's shoulder, then gestured at Mina. "You wife, look at her. So pretty. You a very lucky man. She give you beautiful babies one day, *si?* Make you happy." It was exactly the wrong thing to say.

Grey snorted. "Happy? That's a joke. I think you've got us pegged all wrong, dude. *We* don't get to be happy."

Shamefaced, Mina declined the dessert menu and tried to ignore the concerned look the waiter gave her. Grey paid the check in cash, refused to tip, and unceremoniously ushered Mina out. She could feel her cheeks burning in mortification and questioned why she'd ever thought a date would be a good idea.

Still, once they got in the car, she said, "Maybe that man was right, Grey. We *could* be happy again. If we tried to—"

"Get real, Mina." Grey's voice was thick with scorn, and maybe something even more unsavory. "I don't deserve whatever happiness he thinks I should have. And I don't think you do, either."

It was one thing to be irritable and angry all the time, or to belittle Mina for the mistakes she'd admittedly made. But to suddenly claim that neither of them even *deserved* to be happy was an entirely new angle Grey hadn't touched before.

It spoke to something deeper going on than just regular issues readjusting to civilian life. Mina had to concede it was possible her husband needed more help than she had realized—more than she was capable of giving him.

She stopped on their way home to get gas, delaying the inevitable moment when she'd have to be alone with him again. As soon as she turned off the car, Grey hopped out of the passenger side and lurched through the automatic doors of the mini-mart. Usually, once he'd gone in to pay for the fuel he would come back out to pump it for her afterwards.

Mina didn't want to rock the boat when her husband was acting so touchy. So, she stayed behind the wheel, keeping an eye out for him in the rearview mirror. Grey swaggered out ten long minutes later, but instead of grabbing the pump handle, he merely popped a piece of cinnamon gum into his mouth and slid into the passenger seat.

"Let's go," he muttered.

Mina could taste the bitterness in the back of her throat, the frustration with the way she couldn't seem to acknowledge the writing on the wall.

"I still have to pump the gas," she explained. "I thought you were going to do it."

Her husband's brow creased in irritation. "Seriously—you can't even pump gas, now?"

Mina could pump gas just fine. But she probably hadn't because she was waiting in vain for some glimpse of the white knight he used to be. Which only made her a sucker, something she never was before Grey. She got out without another word and did the job herself.

The little things like that—the cracks in the dam that had begun spiderwebbing out in every direction of her life—were partly what had Mina feeling like she was walking on eggshells all the time. They had her waiting, every moment, for the volcano to blow. It was coming. Any chump could see it.

What *had* happened on Grey's last deployment, anyway? Would Mina ever know the truth, ever understand why the man she'd married went off the deep end for good?

There'd been a brief story in the paper once that he'd refused to elaborate on, but now she pondered whether that even mattered anymore. Grey wasn't merely distracted or anxious, he was downright nasty—and without warning. Mina was beginning to feel…afraid.

On the ride home, she made one last effort to talk to Grey. As gently as she could, Mina suggested they try therapy. Something. *Anything.*

Not only did he refuse, Grey started taking potshots at her again. She could have predicted the refrain—*Mina was only a trashy ho he'd picked up in a bar. A shameless flirt who couldn't cough up the goods. What was the use of having a wife, when she couldn't even give him sons? Someday Mina wouldn't be young and pretty anymore—she'd just be a wrinkled old barfly. And then she wouldn't be any good to anyone.*

Grey's face was flushed, and his eyes were bloodshot—more than they'd been at the restaurant. The instant Mina pulled into their driveway, he bolted from her car and got straight into his. She stood beside his door and begged Grey to come in the house with her, not even caring if the neighbors could hear.

After a long brooding moment, he cracked his window.

"You know what? I'm done with this shit," he told her, never taking his eyes off his windshield.

Mina stepped back, swallowing hard.

His bleary gaze swung to her. "Maybe now you'll finally realize how much I hate you," Grey surmised. He reversed out of the driveway and squealed off down the street, never once looking back.

Mina knew she had to leave—both the house and the marriage—and the sooner, the better. Whatever might have been salvageable between them was long gone now. She went inside, sat down, and tried to make a plan.

THE FOLLOWING HOURS had been rough. As the time passed, Mina had called and texted Grey, to no avail. Later, when the police found the wreck and estimated his time of death, she would realize that Grey had been dead for at least half of her messages.

That was odd. Weren't you supposed to feel it, when someone close to you left the earth? Mina hadn't. When Grey smashed his car into a tree, she'd never felt a thing.

It had been a clear night, the moon and stars and regularly-spaced streetlights providing plenty of illumination. The roads were dry and free of debris, and as far as they could tell Grey's car hadn't suddenly malfunctioned.

He'd had a low level of alcohol in his system—when he took off, it'd still been early enough for him not to be drunk yet, and he'd only had that one glass of wine with dinner. They'd found traces of pills in his bloodstream, though, and questioned Mina about whether her husband had been on any medication recently.

As best as anyone could surmise, Grey Whitney had been startled by a deer bolting from the woods that night. They suspected he'd swerved to avoid it, then smashed his car into a tree instead—the huge oak had totaled Grey's Charger and drove the steering wheel deep into his chest. Deer were plentiful beside that road, especially that time of year. Without any other evidence, it certainly seemed to be the most plausible explanation.

Mina couldn't help feeling skeptical, though. After all, there wasn't a single speck of deer hair on Grey's car, and no hoofprints anywhere beside the road. More damning than that, however, was what she knew of his state of mind. The night her husband left her, Mina doubted if he'd cared one whit about living—but maybe he'd cared a lot about dying.

IN THE TUMULT that ensued, Mina fumbled her way through many things, but one of her biggest mistakes was the decision to forward Grey's calls to her own cell. What had seemed efficient in the moment, rapidly turned disturbing—the constant hang-ups and "wrong numbers" cast a cloud of suspicion on what exactly her husband had been up to in the weeks before he died. Something bad enough to kill him? God only knew.

The female callers who stayed on the line were even worse, though. Mina didn't have to speculate about *their* significance— they were indisputable confirmation that Grey's eye hadn't been the only part of him wandering. She had known he looked, of course, and sometimes even flirted. It was hard to miss that. She just hadn't realized Grey was *actually* cheating on her—a lot, based on the number of women trying to reach him. A Marine with a girl in every port: how clichéd was that?

As Grey's beneficiary, Mina had thought her sudden access to his bank accounts and credit cards would be one good thing about the whole mess. She set about trying to unravel their money situation, but it was even more eye-opening than the women had been.

Mina didn't have a clue what most of the odd sums deposited and withdrawn were. There were so many late fees, transfers to people and companies she'd never heard of, and purchases of merchandise she'd never laid eyes on. She explained what she could in the calls from the police, and on her visits to the station.

The cops weren't the only people curious about Grey. In the week before she buried the man who'd wrecked her life, various individuals within the Marines began to phone her as well—too many to keep track of. On the day of the funeral, though, a new person called.

By then, Mina was ready to strangle her mother, who'd supposedly flown in to "help." Her sister Molly had clearly not given them the full story on her new flame and was mooning around trying to avoid him like a depressing, lovesick marionette.

They'd barely gotten back home from the interment when Mina's phone began ringing again. She ducked into the kitchen to take the call—in case it was another one of Grey's paramours—while Molly and her mom greeted the open house guests.

"Is this My-nah Whitney?" the man asked.

Mina poured herself some wine. "It's Mee-nah."

"Mrs. Whitney, this is Captain Ted Daniels. I'm calling from the Marine Corps Criminal Investigative Division. We have a few questions we need to ask you. Would you be available to talk to us tomorrow at two?"

He was vague about the reason and didn't give her much information, merely pelted Mina with a tangled string of official-sounding phrases that mystified her. Daniels pulled rank and refused to take no for an answer, so before long, Mina found herself agreeing.

It had to be about the toxicology results from Grey's autopsy, she supposed—dying while DUI was almost certainly a violation of the Marine Corps code of conduct.

She hung up and drank some of her wine, but it didn't help her apprehension. Every day she unearthed ugly new details about her husband, and tomorrow would probably be no different. She checked on Molly and Elaine and was relieved to find them clear across the family room. No way could they have heard her conversation from there, and they'd both be gone the next day—

before Mina had to explain anything about her meeting with Daniels.

She watched them arranging casseroles on the buffet table. For some reason, her family kept suggesting that she eat something, though Mina didn't even want to think about food. She supposed she could admit she was a little light-headed—she just didn't think it had much to do with hunger. Still, maybe a couple crackers would get Molly off her back. To get to those, though, Mina was going to have to go out and make conversation with the mourners crowding her family room, and she wasn't quite ready for that madness.

Sanity arrived in the form of the very handsome and reliable face of Mack Bolton. She'd spotted him in the church, tall and strong as a tree, but hadn't been sure he'd show up at her house. As with most things that week, she ought to have known better.

He must have been standing there longer than she realized, because he jerked his chin at Mina's phone, wanting to know what was up with the Marine's call. Of course he did—Mack was always trying to fix things if he could.

Mina told him about Captain Daniels, then confessed, "The guy sounded so mad, but I can't think what I could've done wrong. I'm sure it was something, but—"

"You? Why would they be unhappy with you?" Mack asked.

She speculated, "Maybe I filed something the wrong way? Made a mistake on some form?"

"Mina, Grey was the one in the Marines, not you. If they're unhappy about something, it's probably something *he* did, not something to do with you."

Mack was always so calm—so logical. He had every reason to be thinking clearly, and Mina had every reason not to be. So, she nodded in agreement and thought once again about the business card stashed in her pocket.

During the funeral planning, the priest had carefully watched Mina interact with her mother and listened to the way they talked to each other. He'd obviously come to some conclusions, because later, he'd quietly slipped Mina the number of a counselor—and Mina had been carrying it around like a life preserver ever since.

Maybe…maybe on Monday, after she talked to Daniels, she would finally call. Grey had clearly done a number on her. She should probably hear what this Dr. Mercer had to say about it.

She left Mack in the kitchen and headed for a group of Grey's old fraternity brothers she hadn't spoken with yet. Together with their polished wives and girlfriends, they were exactly the kind of people she'd never felt comfortable around.

Few of them remembered Mina, despite the fact that she and Grey were together the entire time he'd been at Chapel Hill. She'd gone to all the parties, had these men in her home countless times, but—while most had some vague recollection that Grey was married back then—it was as if Mina herself had been a ghost. A yeti-like creature that everyone knew about, but no one remembered actually spotting. It didn't do great things for her ego, to realize how unmemorable she apparently was.

When her phone began buzzing again in the pocket of her black dress, Mina was relieved for the excuse to break away. It was another unknown number, but perhaps the Corps investigator had a change of heart and was going to let her reschedule. Mina stepped away from the group with a mumbled apology and put the phone to her ear.

"Hello?"

"Hey. Who's this?" Didn't anyone have basic manners anymore? Even a little bit?

"This is Mina Whitney. Who is *this*?" she inquired.

"This is Cora. What are you—like, Grey's sister or something?" Mina dropped her head back and stared at the ceiling. Not another one. Not *today*. She didn't need food—she needed another goddamn drink.

"No," Mina sighed. "I'm Grey's widow. We just buried him this morning, so if it's all the same to you—" The line went dead, which was just as well. Mina put her phone back in her pocket and went in search of her sister and some more wine.

Combined with Grey's final, despicable words to her—still rattling around in her brain like a vile handful of dice—the discovery of his rampant infidelity had been another dent to Mina's soul that she really didn't need. She decided to cancel his line as soon as she could and ditch Grey's cell in the Severn River.

Out of the corner of her eye, she noticed a faded red hatchback through her front window, slowly threading its way through all the parked cars on her street. Mina turned to watch, and realized she'd been seeing it pretty often lately—which was strange. A new neighbor on the street, perhaps, or a kid with his first car?

She huffed out a breath. Who cared? Being nosy about her neighbors was probably the *last* thing Mina should be worrying about. She moved on and tried to forget about it, focusing instead on the one tiny pinpoint of salvation her brain could latch onto—Monday, and Dr. Mercer. With therapy would come help. *Finally.*

She felt so freaking gullible, thinking about how hard it had been to endure—when all the time Grey was doing…whatever it was that he'd been doing. Mina's clandestine college classes and paltry little bank account seemed so silly now. They certainly couldn't compete with Grey's secrets. He'd had her snowed, and then some.

Even so, the *one* thing Mina now knew for certain was that each night, she came home to a place Grey would never set foot in again. She could count on the quiet. It was peaceful all by herself, and Mina had quickly discovered that she could almost…breathe again.

She could almost believe that she had somehow survived the unthinkable, and that someday—she might even get to live the life she'd dreamed of so long ago. And all alone in the dark of night, Mina refused to feel one iota of guilt that the miracle had come at the expense of Grey's miserable life.

Chapter Twenty-Four

Two Years Earlier

THERE WERE MORE people at the luncheon after Grey's burial than Mack expected to see, but that was probably just a reflection of his own thoughts on the matter.

He dropped his mom off with Mrs. Whitney in the corner of Mina's little front room and told her he'd get her some coffee—then went in search of Mina herself. Mack was spooked by the way she'd looked at the funeral and interment. She seemed...remote. Checked out.

He found her in the kitchen, huddled in the corner with her back to the doorway and her phone pressed to her ear. She'd slipped off her black high heels for the moment, and they lay on their sides next to her stocking-clad feet.

"I realize that you have a job to do, Mr. Daniels, but..."

Mina didn't appreciate whatever the person had interrupted her to say. Her voice sounded annoyed when she continued, "My apologies *Captain* Daniels. You do understand, *Captain*, that I buried my husband less than two hours ago, right?"

She flipped a couple pages in the planner resting on her counter. "Surely this can wait for a week or two. I have family in town, and—"

Captain Daniels wasn't a patient man, given his propensity for interrupting new widows. Mack stepped back into the hallway and leaned against the wall to give Mina some privacy, but her voice still traveled to him easily.

"*Fine*," she spat out. "Monday at two. I'll be there."

With that settled, she slammed her phone against the counter a bit harder than was probably advisable and let out a sound of frustration.

Mack walked back into the kitchen right as she turned around.

"Mack! Oh man, I've never been so happy to see someone in my life!"

That was nice to hear. He stepped closer to give Mina a hug, then dropped a light kiss on her petal-soft cheek. He nodded at her phone. "Everything okay?"

"Yeah," she sighed. "For some reason, there's like a hundred hoops the Corps expects me to jump through. Grey wasn't even active duty anymore, though. It's so aggravating."

"Huh. You'd think they'd be better at this," Mack mused.

"I know, right?" Mina cried. "It seems really weird. I don't know what's going on." She slipped her feet into her shoes and winced.

"Listen, I don't want to keep you," he lied. "I only wanted to let you know that my mom and I were here. But, now that I have—what can I do to help?"

Mina peered out the doorway at the guests milling around. "Crap, I don't know. My mother's acting insane, as usual. My sister is pretending she's not heartbroken, even though the asshole showed up here with his snooty secret fiancée. There's way more people here than I expected, and every time I talk to them I feel like I've entered some kind of alternate reality."

"Why's that?" Mack frowned.

Mina turned to him and waved her arm around vaguely. "It's like they all knew a completely different man named Grey than the one I was married to. I mean—am I nuts? Did I not even know the man living here?"

Mack shook his head. How was he supposed to answer *that*?

"*You* knew what Grey was like, right? It wasn't just me?" Mina demanded.

He relented. "Mina, I've known Grey since we were little kids. Of course, I knew what he was like." Grey was a chameleon, always changing color to suit the situation as he saw it. He was mercurial, moody, temperamental. The kind of guy who could be cruel for inexplicable reasons. The friend who'd steal your girl right out from under you, just because he could—and then spitefully pretend it was love.

"Then please tell me what has gotten into all of them!" Mina begged. "I don't think even one person has told me something honest this whole day."

Mack said, "People don't like to talk badly about the dead, especially to the widow at the funeral. Come on."

She scowled, then grabbed a wineglass from the counter behind her and took a hefty gulp. "Or maybe Grey saved all his assholery just for me," she muttered sullenly.

And me, Mack thought.

"Knowing him, I doubt that," he told Mina. Given the way she was pounding that wine, she clearly needed some truth. But, too much more of either and Mina would have a whole new set of issues. "Hey, why don't I grab you some food? There's enough out there to feed an army."

"No thanks," Mina demurred. "I'm not hungry." But then, she turned too fast toward the counter and had to catch the edge hard to steady herself.

"I'm going to respectfully disagree," Mack smiled. "How about some chicken salad, to soak up some of that *vino*?"

"Shit," Mina groaned. She stared balefully over Mack's head. "This day already feels like it's lasted an eternity. How long do you think they're all going to stay?"

Mack checked his watch. "Well, the card they handed out at the church said four p.m."

"Four!" Mina squawked. "What the *fuck,* Mack!" If ever there was a woman who sounded like she was on the verge of a meltdown, it was her.

Mack gawked at her, speechless.

Mina made a visible effort to calm down. "*A:* I didn't even want to have the lunch here, but my mother insisted. And *B:* I told that woman no later than three!"

"I'm sorry, kiddo. Again, how can I help?"

She shook her head, looking defeated and so alone. Mack badly wanted to fold her in his arms and protect her from everything in the world that wasn't him—his heart ached with it.

"Um, maybe check with Molly. She's wearing herself out trying to avoid that guy of hers, but she does seem to know what needs to get done," Mina told him. "I should probably get back out there and mingle." She made a face. "Or whatever."

"If you're not up to it, then screw it," Mack suggested. "We'll tell everyone you needed some time to yourself. They'll probably all feel guilty and leave, then."

"That's so tempting. You have no idea. The Dekes are all acting like this is the Kentucky Derby. My mom is confusing everyone by insisting that Grey was in the Navy—not the Marines—and my sister can't seem to keep straight how many years he was even in the service. That doesn't even *touch* the dudes I've never met, who're acting like they were Grey's military BFFs."

Mack chuckled. "Just say the word, sweetheart."

Mina blew out a long breath. "No, I can't. Then I'll be here alone with my mom and Molly, and I'm definitely not ready for that. I'd better stick this out for a while more."

"You don't think you could talk to Molly? She seems all right to me."

"She's the best, but she's also my kid sister. I don't want her to worry, and she totally will."

"All right," Mack told her. "Just give me the nod if you change your mind." He'd stay close to her, in the off chance that Mina actually took him up on it, but he wasn't expecting much.

"Thanks, Mack," she said. "I really appreciate it."

"Don't mention it. I'll find you in a few minutes with that food, okay?"

She nodded and then she was gone, absorbed into a group of preppy men and women gathered near the fireplace. They peered at Mina like she was some bizarre moth pinned to a board. *Butterfly*, Mack silently corrected. *The rarest of beautiful butterflies.*

He poured coffee from an urn into a flimsy plastic mug for his mom, then carried it over to her. She'd found a spot on a loveseat with Grey's mother, and the two of them were paging through an old album of Grey's high school football photos. Mack waved them off when they tried to suck him into their misty-eyed reminisces and headed back to the buffet table.

The chicken salad looked like it had been hit by seagulls, but Mack was able to put together a decent plate of baked ziti and limp-looking salad for Mina. It would have to do. He brought it over and handed it to her discreetly, waiting to leave until she picked up the fork and put some of it in her mouth.

When Mack turned away, he bumped directly into Grey's uncle Nick. Nick was a pipefitter, and a damn good one. Mack had used him on a job or two recently and been struck by his kindness—but mainly by how far from the solid Whitney family tree Grey had fallen.

Nick thumped Mack on his shoulder and murmured sadly, "May his memory be eternal." The man moved on, but the phrase took root in Mack's gut, making it churn.

Memory was supposed to be a lovely, enduring thing. Meant to be a comfort to the grieving at times like this.

But what happened if the memories of the dead became *too* resilient? What happened if the memories, unlike the person, refused to die? What then? After all, not every memory was a good one, and not every person left only charitable feelings in their wake when they passed. For example, Mack's association with Grey Whitney could be divided into two halves—a light and a dark—and neither wanted to bite the dust.

Grey had grown up around the corner from Mack and been one of his best friends when they were kids. He was fun-loving, cheerful, up for any adventure. He was fearless in the woods and out on the water. Grey wasn't afraid of parents or girls, or even their mean old science teacher from fourth grade.

It seemed natural that he'd go into the Marines—*twice* even. It made sense that girls would pick him over a quiet guy like Mack. Most of the time, Grey Whitney seemed larger than life. It was hard not to be impressed by him.

Somehow, though, that long-ago boy had turned into something different during his second stint in the service. He became someone unreliable—someone you couldn't trust. A man who didn't honor his commitments or his wife and was disloyal to his friends. It seemed callous in the extreme to be grateful that Grey hadn't managed to also abandon any kids before he'd died, but Mack couldn't shake the thought. How awful would it have been for them to grow up hearing all the stories about their dad, and never be able to know if any of them were true?

Now that Grey was gone so suddenly and so young, leaving only Mina behind, Mack realized he didn't know how to mourn a man like that. And maybe—maybe he wouldn't. He knew he ought to feel shame about it, but…so be it.

Grey had stolen Mina right out from under Mack's nose, and then didn't even have the decency to treat her right once he'd snared her. Mack might have forgiven him eventually, if he'd seen that Mina was happy. That she'd been loved and cared for.

But looking at what Grey had done with his enormous good fortune—seeing what Mina had become while married to him— well, Mack supposed Grey could rot in hell, for all he cared. He glanced guiltily at the priest, tucked in the corner of the room with a couple of Grey's elderly aunts. Maybe Mack would one day meet Grey there.

Looking around, he thought Mina had a point about the luncheon. Everyone there was lamenting the passing of some beloved guy that Mack barely recognized. The real Grey was far more complicated than anyone was willing to admit, at least on that particular day. Mack drifted around the rooms and wondered how many of those people had secret memories of Grey—memories they'd never share with another and would sooner forget. Odds were, it wasn't only him and Mina.

Mack ended up in conversation with one of Grey's teammates from that last tour in Afghanistan. Like everyone else, Mack had read the papers, and had a general sense of what the group had endured—the warehouse explosion and village firefight.

When they'd all returned, there'd been quiet court-martials, too, but almost no one talked about *those*. Mack didn't recognize the name of the man he spoke with. He supposed that was probably a good thing.

As Lieutenant Moore prattled on about his wedding the year before and his efforts to adopt a kid, Mack's mind wandered again. If he and Carolynn had stayed together, maybe they would've had a family by then. Maybe Mack would be standing there like some of the others, cradling an infant in his arms, or bouncing a toddler on his hip. He couldn't feel sorry that it hadn't happened with Carolynn, but he would feel sorrow if it never did.

Abruptly, he thought of Mina again, and searched the room for her. *There*, near the bay window at the front of the house, head-to-head with her sister. Her plate of food had disappeared, unfortunately, replaced by another glass of wine.

Looking at her, Mack wondered whether Mina wished she were holding a baby that day, too. A piece of Grey and her, something to hold onto and nurture—a seed that they'd planted together and that would one day grow up in the world for everyone to see.

Somehow, Mack doubted it. The very last thing Mina probably needed was more memories of Grey Whitney than she already had.

Chapter Twenty-Five

MINA COULDN'T SAY how she'd made it through the beginning of the week—after Mack walked stiffly to his truck and drove away on Sunday, everything else was pretty much a blur. She'd eaten and slept and showed up on time for work, she knew that much. But as for whether she was still a breathing, functioning human was anyone's guess.

When Wednesday afternoon finally rolled around, Mina gratefully cut out of work early to attend her weekly bereavement group. It was organized and run by her therapist, Dr. Mercer—or Claudette, as she preferred to be called. With any luck, either Claudette or one of the other attendees would have something insightful to say about Mina's horrible weekend. At the very least, she could count on someone bringing dessert and commiserating with her.

The group usually met in the dining hall of the Catholic church, with the uncomfortable plastic and metal chairs pushed into a large circle in the center of the room. When Mina made her way inside that day, she noticed that they had a bigger group than usual. It tended to happen, whenever the holidays loomed on the horizon.

The process was the same every week. Claudette would sit in one chair, holding the weighted metal ball that the group used to recognize a speaker. She'd introduce that week's topic with a few words, then pass the ball to her neighbor. A group member could always choose whether to speak or pass the ball, depending on their comfort level on that day.

Mina thought maybe the small sphere was half of one of those Chinese stress-ball sets. If she was the first to hold it, the ball felt horribly cold and impersonal, the faint machine etching on its surface giving it an odd, rough feel. It always led to an internal debate for her—sit right next to Claudette and hope to absorb some of her comfort and courage? Or risk the counselor passing the ball in her direction to start, before it had been warmed by other sympathetic hands?

Mina hesitated as she glanced around the room, checking to see who else was there. Finally, she chose a seat directly across from Claudette and two chairs away from her friend Dimitri, who was always the first to arrive. He'd been coming to group more often recently but talking even less than usual. Mina thought something might be up with him—more than her suddenly discovering he had a daughter, that was.

After a few more people straggled in, Claudette checked her watch and began. "Today I'd like to talk about moving on," she announced, looking around with a gentle expression. "How do we do that? How do we even contemplate it? And, when do we know we're ready?"

There was some murmuring, and some shifting on the chairs. That day's group had newer widows and widowers in attendance, as well as ones who had been alone for a long while. Neither looked thrilled by the topic.

"Marie, why don't you start?" Claudette handed the ball to the woman on her right.

Marie was emphatic. "No way," she said. "I'll never do it. Phil was enough to last me a lifetime." She handed the metal ball to the next person.

Hannah flushed red, but it was hard to say whether it was from guilt or pleasure. She twisted the rings on her fingers and admitted, "Actually, I already have." She smiled weakly at one or two people. "I met him at our college reunion this summer. I didn't even intend to go, but…I did." Hannah swallowed so loudly, Mina could hear it all the way across the circle. The young woman added softly, "The house was really quiet that day, you know? I had to get out of there."

There were understanding nods all around.

She prattled on nervously, "His name is Tom. We actually dated for a few months back in freshman year, if you can believe that. We totally hit it off again and I'm…" Hannah peeked around at faces, searching for acceptance. "I'm happy."

Claudette smiled at her warmly. "That sounds wonderful. Congratulations."

Hannah smiled and handed the ball to Bill, who—as always—barked, "Pass."

Evan was next. He rolled the ball back and forth between his palms like he was playing hot potato with himself. He was nearly as young as Hannah, clean-cut and fit—and as neurotic a man as Mina had ever encountered.

"Honestly?" he said. "The thought of trying to find someone else seems so hard. Where am I supposed to find another person I like that much? There's like…a *billion* people out there." Evan had told them early on that his husband had died suddenly, felled by an undiagnosed heart ailment within two months of their marriage. He was the only man Evan had ever slept with after coming out in his early twenties.

Claudette nodded slowly. "Yes, when you view it that way, I can see where that might feel overwhelming. Maybe instead of focusing on the whole billion, you could try starting within the circle of people you already know. That way, it's less daunting. Then, when you feel more comfortable, you can branch out a little farther. And so on."

Evan nodded, looking thoughtful, and handed the ball off.

People you already know...Mina had a visceral jolt of recognition, realizing how neatly Mack fit into that category. Mack, with his dark wavy hair and amber eyes. Mack, of the very talented tongue and hands.

Mack—who likely never wanted to talk to her again. Mina was jerked from her reverie by Hannah's chipper squeak.

"Like me!" she announced.

The ball finally made its way to Mina. But when it did, trying to explain her heartache over Mack seemed too big, and too impossible to attempt. Mina shook her head and murmured, "Pass."

Soon after, the ball reached Dimitri at the end of the line. Based on his grim expression, Mina expected him to stay quiet.

Instead, he stated categorically, "Never. I will never get married again, and that's a fact." He was clear. Certain. Nearly defiant.

Claudette's mouth tilted up slightly in a soft smile. Her affection for him was obvious. "Never is a very long time," she commented.

Dimitri jutted out his chin and stared at the curtain behind her shoulder, his walls already back up. Mina's heart hurt for him, and his little girl. The illness that had taken his wife and Lilly's mother had been fast and brutal.

Claudette talked for a bit more, but Mina wasn't listening any longer. There were times when the group felt like the only place anyone understood her at all. And there were other times when the collective psychic baggage of its members was suffocating— a heavy wet fog that Mina couldn't breathe through. Even though she'd been looking forward to the meeting for days, Mina suddenly couldn't wait for the group to disperse.

Dimitri was on to her, though, and cornered her in the hall. Standing next to Mina, he was a full head and shoulders taller than her, lean and stoic as a knight from some old fairytale.

"What was that?" he demanded, pointing in the direction of the meeting room.

"What was *what?*" Mina fired back. She'd been so close to escape. Only three more feet and she would've made the parking lot and the protection of her car.

Dimitri took her arm and led her away from the others—some of them stalking quickly for the exit, and others milling around anxiously, unwilling to leave quite yet.

"You know what," he said quietly, glancing around to be sure no one overheard. He studied Mina's face. "You've never 'passed' before. Not ever. So why now?"

Mina sighed. If anyone would get it, it would be Dimitri. Besides, he'd never let her weasel out of an explanation, anyway.

"Wanna get some coffee?" she asked.

His shoulders relaxed a little at her easy capitulation— apparently, he'd expected her to put up more of a fight.

"Sure," he said. "If you're going to tell me what's going on."

"Well, just remember," Mina warned. "You asked."

They agreed on a place to meet, but after she pulled into a parking spot, Mina sat in her car for another few minutes, gathering her thoughts for the conversation to come. How would she explain? Many of the other group members had loved their dead spouses dearly, including Dimitri.

To admit to them that she didn't so much *miss* Grey, as feel like his memory was stuck to the sole of her life like a piece of moldy gum, felt callous in the extreme. To tell the group that she'd tried to "move on" with one of Grey's oldest friends was even more insane. And that was all before Mina even touched on the issue of whether she could actually give Mack the family he deserved. Claudette would keep them from getting too judgey with Mina, but still…it seemed like it was asking a lot of them.

Dimitri was the only one besides Claudette who *might* hear her out. Keeping everything bottled up inside hadn't worked very well, so Mina was going to have to try. Somehow.

Inside the coffee shop, he wasted no time once she slid into the seat opposite him.

"This is about that guy, isn't it?" he said. "The one from the park?"

Mina groaned. "Yeah, I guess it is."

"Mack, was it?"

She nodded. "It just happened, and I couldn't face trying to explain it to everyone else—not before I've even had a chance to figure out went wrong myself. Things were going pretty well between us...but then I blew it."

"Already? I just met the guy last weekend," Dimitri frowned.

"I know. Some old..." Mina waved her hand around, not knowing how to name the lingering taint of ten Grey years. "Old crud came up after we saw you at the park. I panicked, we argued about it, and then I told him we couldn't see each other anymore."

Her friend's dark eyebrows shot up in surprise, and Mina rushed to elaborate. "I mean, I said we could still be friends. Just not friends with...benefits," she finished lamely. "More like friends who see movies together and stuff. Like us."

Dimitri stared at her for a long moment, shaking his head. He rubbed at his forehead, but finally he spoke. "Mina, you know I love you dearly, but did you *actually* give that poor man the 'let's be friends' speech?"

"Well...yeah," she agreed. "Was that wrong?"

"I don't know, *Friendzone*. Did you also say, *It's not you, it's me*?"

Mina thought back and flinched. "Possibly. In a manner of speaking."

Now it was his turn to groan. "You know, I had such high hopes for you. I mean, I'm clearly a total lost cause, but you—you had so much promise."

"Dimitri, stop. I'm trying my best here. But there's all this wretched *crap* leftover from Grey that keeps coming up whenever I'm around Mack. He's a good guy. He doesn't deserve that. *I* don't deserve that. It's...it's better this way."

"You really like him, don't you?" he asked.

"I really do. But that's beside the point, now. He won't want anything to do with me, after what I said. Not if he's smart, anyway. And he is."

"No, I don't agree. I don't think it is beside the point. Because the man I met last weekend was utterly head over heels in love with you."

"Dimitri!"

"What? You want me to pussy-foot around it? Blow smoke at you? You're obviously scared by what he's making you feel, but that doesn't mean you should run *away* from it. If anything, it means you ought to be facing it head-on. Tell this Mack character about all your worn-out garbage and see what happens. If he's a good dude like you think, he'll take it in stride. If he's not, *then* you can kick him to the curb."

Mina gaped at him. "Who died and made you the boss of me?"

"Seriously?" Dimitri shook his head in disappointment. "Now we're in middle school?"

"The thing is," she admitted. "It might be too late for all that. He was pretty hurt when he left on Sunday. I don't want to keep jerking him around."

"So don't," he smiled slyly. "You forget I saw him with you. Try giving Mack a chance, Mina. I'd bet my right arm that he'll come around."

"I'll think about it," Mina conceded. "Now—how about explaining how you procured a daughter out of thin air."

Chapter Twenty-Six

THE WEEK AFTER Mina gave him the boot was not Mack's favorite in recent memory. In fact, the desolation he felt at her inscrutable rejection was, frankly, pretty excruciating. He struggled to unravel where he'd gone wrong—but, more importantly, Mack could not think of a single thing he could do to make things right again. For good or ill, he loved that woman. And God, did he miss her.

All he felt like doing was sitting around moping He didn't particularly want to go anywhere, but especially not the family picnic in his mother's back yard that weekend. He'd been ordered to. Hopefully, that didn't mean that his mom had lined up more church-going dating prospects for him—Mack didn't think he could face making small talk with a sweet twenty-something right then if someone had a gun pointed at his head.

While he fired up the grill and looked around for a place to set the packages of hot dogs, he scanned the yard. All the usual cousins and neighbors, some folks he didn't know, and...Mack spotted his mother's old pal Ms. Ettie. He had a distant memory that she was a counselor—something to do with alcoholics maybe?

As he recalled, the two women had met in a widows group after their husbands both died, around the time Mack was in college. Sometime later, Ettie had decided to make a career of it. Which conveniently made her the exact person he wanted to talk to today.

He beelined over, red plastic cup in hand. "Hey, Doc," he greeted her.

Ms. Ettie smiled warmly. "I'm sorry." She checked her watch. "Did you have an appointment?"

"No, I did not," Mack laughed. "Forgive me. People must do this to you all the time."

"They do," Ettie agreed. "And I always know it's coming when they call me *Doc*," she chuckled.

"I'm an ass," Mack acknowledged, waving off a gnat buzzing around his face. "And I'll leave you alone now."

"Mack, I've known you since you were nineteen, and you have never once asked me for help. Don't sweat it."

"I probably could've used you after Carolynn left," he admitted.

"And yet you didn't, which means you probably need me desperately by now. Let's hear it, Bucko."

"I'll try to keep it short."

"No worries. I've got nowhere else to be."

So, Mack launched into the saga as best he could. A brief history of how he and Mina met—how she should have been his. A few points about Grey, and what he knew of their life together. His impression of Mina's mother Elaine, who he'd seen at Grey's funeral. The way he and Mina had reconnected and hit it off like gangbusters, and lastly…where they were stuck now. It took slightly longer than Mack expected.

Throughout his entire rendition, though, Ettie nodded sagely. Then, when Mack trailed off helplessly at the end, she cleared her throat.

"I'm sure you've heard from your mom that my parents were raging alcoholics, right?"

When he nodded, she continued, "It's partly why I got into this line of work. I counsel a lot of adult children of alcoholics, and that sounds like what your friend probably is."

"I agree."

"Two things to remember: First, everyone who was *supposed* to take care of your friend only let her down. She likely learned early—and repeatedly—that words were meaningless, promises got broken, and she couldn't believe anything her loved ones told her. Your friend's going to have a very hard time with trust, Mack. You'll need to be very patient."

That made perfect sense. "Patience is not my problem. And I don't want to take care of her," he explained. "She doesn't need it, and probably wouldn't let me anyway. I just want to…be her safe harbor, you know?"

"That's a nice instinct," Ettie commented. "And it ties in with my other point. You have to remember that since your friend has only ever had herself to rely on, giving up control is going to be an issue for her. If—as you suspect—she's also recovering from an emotionally abusive relationship, that's going to go double. She's going to have difficulty letting you do things for her, and letting things happen organically. She'll want to control *how* things happen, so she doesn't get caught by surprise or blindsided by anything unpleasant. That might make her execute some preemptive strikes before they are actually necessary."

"Yeah, I can see that," Mack said. Man, could he ever. "Grey was a real piece of work, too. He treated her like shit, as far as I could tell."

"I'm sorry, did you say *Grey?*" Ms. Ettie was suddenly looking a little green around the gills.

"Yeah. Grey. Mina's husband."

Ettie's hand flew up and pinched the bridge of her nose, and her eyes squeezed shut. She looked like she'd just gotten the headache to end all headaches.

"Ms. Ettie, are you okay? Do you want to sit down?" Mack asked.

"Oh my God, Mack—I'm not an invalid!" she protested. "But I *cannot* have this conversation with you right now."

"Why? We were just having it."

"Listen to me. I. Can. *Not*. Have this conversation with you," she said tersely. "I am *prohibited* from having this conversation with you."

"I…" Mack blinked dumbly at her. Could she possibly be implying what he thought she was? "Seriously?" he asked.

Ettie didn't answer, since his mother and little brother chose that moment to saunter up. Mack peered around the yard—luckily, the twins had taken over the grill, so they were neutralized for the time being.

"Claudette, you old cougar," his mom drawled. Bodhi flinched at the moniker. "How many times do I have to ask you to stop flirting with my boys?"

Mack groaned. "Mom! Why would you say that? Ms. Ettie has never done…*that* a day in her life!"

Inside, his mind was spinning—having a complete freak-out that he'd just been hitting up Mina's probable therapist for advice about her. *God.* Could his life get any more complicated?

Bodhi turned tail and fled, exactly like a skittish deer flushed from the underbrush. Mack gazed after him and wondered when his brother had turned into such a cowardly little punk. They were going to have words about it, later.

When he turned back, Ettie was getting away—whispering with his mother in a way Mack did not like the look of.

"Ms. Ettie, wait!" he called.

She waved him away. "Advice still stands, Mack," she belted out over her shoulder. "Now go away."

Mack stood there gaping like a fish for several long minutes. A couple of his teenaged cousins came running up, giggling and begging him to take them out on the river in the rusted dinghy his brother kept tied to the dock.

Mack barely managed to cough out, "Maybe later," before sending them over to help his sisters work the grill. Seconds later, he was powering back toward the house.

Inside, he trotted upstairs to his old room, flopped onto the narrow sagging mattress, and tried to digest everything that had just happened. He was no closer to finding a solution to the problem of Mina than he'd been yesterday.

And now her therapist was unfortunately well-informed about his side of things. Hell, for all Mack knew, Mina had been talking to Ettie all week. Maybe the doctor already knew about every one of Mack's deficiencies, and was just being polite for his mom's sake.

Bodhi swaggered in a few minutes later. Because of *course*, he did.

"What was that all about?" his brother asked.

"Mind yer bidness," Mack drawled, mainly out of habit, rather than a real desire to keep anything from the kid.

"Let me guess—lady trouble?" Bodhi dropped into Mack's old desk chair, a jumble of lean and gangly arms and legs, along with his sly-dog grin.

"How do you figure?" Mack knew he probably looked guilty, though.

"Oh, I dunno. Maybe because you're a good-looking 34-year-old man, and instead of talking up the single ladies at the picnic, you were out there wasting time with a stern middle-aged woman."

"You know people over fifty aren't like, contagious, right? They have interesting things to say and everything, you little knucklehead."

Bodhi nodded. "Especially when they happen to be licensed therapists."

"Uh—" Mack floundered for a quip that could counter that and came up short.

"So, who is she?" his brother pressed.

"You wouldn't know her."

"Try me."

Mack sighed. Resistance was pointless—when there was gossip to be had, his brother was like a bay retriever gunning for a fat duck.

"Her name is Mina. I've known her for a long time."

"Oooooh yes, the famous Mina Whitney, right?"

Well, that was troubling.

"You know her?" Mack sat up and peered at his little brother. "She goes by her maiden name now, by the way. O'Connell."

"Be that as it may, Mom is *not* going to be happy about it."

"Why should she care?"

Bodhi laughed off Mack's idiocy. "Well, let's see—there's the part where she's hell-bent on fixing you up with someone from her church. And then there's the part where she thanked her lucky stars for years that you weren't the one to get saddled with Mina."

"Wait…what the hell are you talking about?"

Bodhi said, "Mom can't stand that chick. Mrs. Whitney bitched for years about how her sainted son threw his life away for Mina. I guess Mom figured that it could've just as easily been you who ended up with her—especially since you two lived together for a while. Mom used to talk about it all the time back then."

"Are you freaking kidding me?" Mack was flabbergasted. "And, I don't know—like Carolynn was such a step up for me?"

His brother was enjoying this far, far too much. "Oh Lord, no. Mom hated her, too."

Mack dropped his head in his hands. It wasn't like any of it mattered anyway. He might love Mina until the end of his days, but she had made her thoughts on the matter eminently clear. Unless she had some magical change of heart, or Mack came up with the Win-Her-Back Plan of the century…he'd once again lost Mina. And that was torture.

"Hey," Bodhi said, softer now. "What's really going on?"

"Jesus, kid." Mack scrubbed his hands across his face and looked into the unexpectedly kind eyes of his younger brother.

"I'm fucking in love with her, all right? I have been...for a really long time. It's like there's always been this circuit linked up between us, and whenever we're together we keep looping whatever amazing energy is in there, back and forth."

"So, what's the problem? If she's special enough to win you over, Mom will come around."

"It's not that," Mack sighed. "Mina ditched me last weekend. She wants to be *friends*."

Bodhi recoiled. "*Oh*. That's not good."

"Tell me about it."

"So, what are you going to do?"

"I have no freaking idea," Mack admitted.

"Ms. Ettie didn't help?"

"No, as I just discovered, Ms. Ettie may actually be Mina's therapist—something she realized only *after* she was starting to drop some serious science on me."

"No shit?" Bodhi gawked.

"No shit."

"Mack, you gotta, like, talk to Mina or something."

"Tried that." Mack stretched out flat again. It was useless.

"What about—could you send her flowers? Maybe upgrade to the teddy bear and balloon option?"

Mack scowled at him. "Dude, do those lame-ass ideas actually work for you? Because I'm starting to understand why you're *also* single right now."

Bodhi shook his head. "Don't try to change to subject. This is not about me. You're obviously going to have to go DEFCON-2 on this woman."

"I'm afraid to ask." But Mack would, if it came to that. He needed all the help he could get, even if it came from a guy barely old enough to drink.

"Two words," Bodhi said. "Baby kittens."

"Lord have mercy," Mack begged, staring at the scuffs on his ceiling. But he filed the idea away anyway, just in case shit got critical.

Chapter Twenty-Seven

M EENY, I'M SO glad I reached you," Molly whispered into the phone. "I think I have news."

In a lightning-quick assessment that she'd honed over many years, Mina gauged her little sister's tone of voice. Good news, she decided, not bad.

"Oh, really?" she asked. She only bothered with the inquiry to be polite—there was only one thing this could really be about.

"You have to promise not to tell anyone."

"Who am I going to tell?"

"Mom, for starters. Or Dad."

"I haven't talked to Dad in at least seven months," Mina informed her sister. "And you know I don't tell Mom anything. I think your secret is safe with me."

"I haven't even told Jake yet," Molly confessed breathlessly. "I want to confirm it first. But I'm so excited and I had to tell someone!"

"Here I am," Mina said. "Ready and waiting."

"Meeny, I'm late! Like, *really* late."

Yup, there it was. Just as Mina suspected. It was all good, though. Molly and Jake were two adorably happy peas in a pod, and they deserved this good fortune. There was zero reason for it to be sticking in Mina's throat like it was—none at all. Younger siblings got married and pregnant before their older sisters all the time. Mina was happy for her. *So* happy.

"Well, well," she drawled. "Look at you. Molly's gonna be a mommy."

"Oh my God, I think I am," she quiet-squealed into the phone. "I can't believe it!"

"I'm so happy for you. Are you happy?" Mina asked. That was a lot of happies, but she thought she sounded normal. Mostly.

"I'm like—stupid giddy," Molly said. "How am I ever going to keep this secret from Jake?"

"You're not, you goof. Why would you? If it's true, he's going to want to share in your excitement. And if it's not, he'll want to be able to comfort you."

It was ironic how knowledgeable Mina sounded, given how little personal experience she had with a relationship like Molly's. Grey would never have acted like anything but an ass about a baby, even though he'd thought he wanted one. Mack, though— Mina suspected Mack would do everything right.

Molly grew silent while she contemplated her sister's advice. Mina could hear water in the sink, and the clank of a dishwasher opening and closing.

With a big inhale, her sister finally said, "You know what? You're right. I had this whole plan of how I was going to break it to him, but I hate keeping Jake in the dark. I should just tell him, shouldn't I?"

"I think so, but what do I know?" Mina said. She kept her voice light and cheerful, so no trace of angst would filter through. Molly wouldn't suspect anything, anyway—they'd never really discussed the kinds of awful things Grey had routinely said and done. Mina didn't need her sister's pity—the fact that Molly had instinctually never liked Grey felt like enough for her.

"Okay, I'm going to do it!" Molly giggled. "I'll let you know how it goes!"

Please don't, Mina thought. *I can't take it.*

AS LUCK WOULD have it, Mina's regular monthly therapy appointment came less than a day after Molly's call, and only two days after getting coffee with Dimitri. The conversations had been rattling around in her brain like a pocketful of loose change, so when Claudette asked how things were going with her, the first thing Mina blurted out was *not well*.

The therapist had probably known she wouldn't have to ask Mina about "passing" in group earlier that week. As usual, Mina's own guilt and misgivings took care of that.

"My little sister thinks she might be expecting," Mina began. "And Dimitri thinks I ought to be talking more to this guy I know—about, like, my history with Grey and stuff." It was vague and nonsensical, but Mina figured she'd refine it as she went along.

Naturally, Claudette said something Mina wasn't expecting. "It sounds like what Dimitri thinks is important to you."

"It is. Of course, it is." What did that have to do with anything? "Why?"

"Because Dimitri is…steady. I feel like I can count on him, and that's not something I can say about a lot of people in my life," Mina explained.

"Do you think you might be developing romantic feelings for him?"

"Dimitri? Oh my God, *no*," Mina protested. "Not him."

Claudette smiled a little. "You seem emphatic about that."

Mina was flustered. "Well, yeah. For one, I don't like him *that* way. And two—you've met him! That man is *never* going to get married again."

Her therapist watched her for a moment to make sure Mina wasn't going to add anything else. Then she said, "Couple things jump out at me. As I said to Dimitri in group the other day, never is a very long time." Claudette paused.

"I know."

"You also said something else interesting."

Mina frowned. "I did?"

"Yes," Dr. Mercer nodded. "I wonder—if it bothers you that Dimitri thinks he's never going to marry again, does that mean you would like to?"

She shrugged, but her guilty expression probably gave her away.

The therapist came at it from the side, instead of striking head-on. "If you aren't interested in Dimitri that way, then who are we discussing?"

"Oh. Well…" Mina swallowed thickly. She'd known this was coming, so why did she feel so unprepared?

Claudette raised her eyebrows and waited patiently.

"It's this guy I know from a long time ago," Mina explained. "He's, uh…"

"What?"

"An old friend of Grey's," she confessed.

"And of yours?" Claudette prodded.

"I guess you could say that."

The doctor tilted her head. "Is it in doubt?"

"No. Not really." Mina thought about it. "Mack is…even more reliable than Dimitri, if you can believe that. He's always tried to look out for me. I told him I didn't know if I could count on him, but that was pretty ridiculous. Anyone could see that he's as steady as a rock. He always has been."

Claudette coughed and took a couple minutes to clear her throat before she continued, "And Dimitri thinks you ought to be telling Mack more about some of the things that went on between you and your husband? Why do you think that is?" The therapist had an odd expression on her face that Mina had trouble deciphering.

She hadn't told Claudette a thing about Mack yet—not about the days with him at the bay house, or about them spending weekends together more and more, or about the fiasco of the veterans ceremony. She'd been purposely withholding important information, and shifted uncomfortably, feeling like she'd been busted.

"I don't know," Mina lied. "I don't think it matters anyway. Even though it seemed good with Mack for a while, it's not like it could ever last. I told him so, and he really didn't like it," she grumbled.

Claudette leaned back in her chair and studied Mina for a bit. "I can imagine," she said finally. "Why don't you think you have a future with him?"

Mina shrugged. Like this was the second grade, and not a therapy session focused on improving her mental health.

"Could it be because you think he wants to have children someday?" Claudette suggested.

Mina nodded, relieved not to have to say it out loud. "Yes, exactly. He's going to be an amazing father. You should see him with his nieces and nephews. And with mine, for that matter."

"Mina, we've discussed this issue in passing before, but now I have to ask—do you believe that you can't have children because it is true, or because Grey *said* it was true?"

"What do you mean?" she stalled. How many people were going to ask her that same damn question? It was like the whole world was in on it.

"Well, for example—were either you or Grey ever tested by a fertility doctor to determine what exactly the problem was?" the therapist clarified.

That was simple. "No," Mina said.

"Which means there's a fifty percent possibility that the issue was with Grey, and not with you."

Mina shook her head. "The Whitney men are all crazy fertile. That's not possible."

In an uncharacteristic flash of disapproval, the doctor sniffed, "Is that what Grey told you?"

"I…yes." Mina clasped her hands tightly in her lap. *Crud.*

"Do you see where there might be a margin of error involved here?" Claudette raised her palms up. "To your knowledge, are there any hereditary issues with fertility in your family?"

Mina conceded, "I don't really…know."

"There's a large range of possibilities for why you and Grey never got pregnant," Claudette sighed. "It could have been timing or stress. He might have been taking medication or drugs that affected his fertility or contracted an asymptomatic venereal disease. Or, Grey could have been exposed to something in the military that rendered him either temporarily or permanently sterile."

The therapist paused, then went on, "I seem to recall you saying something about you two gradually stopping intimate relations...." She trailed off, waiting for Mina's confirmation.

"Yes, that's true," Mina agreed.

"If Grey was experiencing some negative side-effects— possibly some erectile dysfunction—that could have contributed to both the infertility and the cessation of intimacy."

Mina shook her head again, a thousand new and confusing scenarios swirling around her brain. "I feel so stupid," she whispered. "Why didn't I ever think about any of that?"

"When a spouse has a very forceful personality, as it sounds like Grey had, that's not terribly uncommon." There was no judgement of Mina's failings in Claudette's voice—only calm, reasonable understanding. She'd never come right out and labeled Grey's behavior as emotional abuse, but Mina had to think that would happen eventually.

She took in a big breath, then released it. A glance at the clock on the side table showed Mina that her forty-five minutes were nearly up. She pulled her purse into her lap and dug through it for her keys, avoiding eye contact.

The therapist broke the silence gently. "Mina...we've talked a lot about 'fault' here, haven't we?"

Mina's eyes shot to hers. "Yes," she whispered.

"When you first came to see me, you were hauling around a pretty heavy load. But what have we discovered, you and I?"

"It's not always my fault," Mina intoned. Every week, over and over, that had been one of Claudette's big themes.

"Right," the doctor affirmed now. "Not your parents' divorce, not your mom's other choices, not what happened to Molly, and not even how Grey died."

"Okay. Yes." Mina tried so hard to believe it, but it was *hard*. Taking responsibility for things she had no control over had become something of an entrenched habit.

Claudette seemed to sense her difficulty. "That was a long list of things for you to be burdened with, Mina."

She sighed, "I know."

The therapist studied her for a beat. "Mina...I'd like to point out that this whole question of infertility also belongs on the roster of things that are not your fault."

"But—" A flood of images played behind Mina's eyes—the string of bar hookups she'd had before Grey chief among them. She'd never actually slept with any of them except Grey, but maybe she'd done something wrong. Maybe one of them had given her something bad, something that kept her from getting pregnant. Maybe Mina was just *broken* inside.

Claudette interrupted her thoughts. "*Whatever* the reason for it—whether Grey was sterile or you are, or whether it was some inauspicious combination of your two reproductive systems—none of that would be all your fault, do you see? It would be unfortunate and sorrowful, but not a situation for which you bear the entire blame."

Mina locked her jaw and stared firmly at the wall next to the exit, so she wouldn't cry. She *wanted* to believe what Claudette was saying, but just then, it was totally overwhelming.

"When your friends get upset with you, Mina—and I'm thinking of Dimitri and Mack at the moment—it may be because they are troubled by your instinct to carry more than your assigned load, so to speak. It's possible that they aren't trying to bully you, so much as trying to protect you from yourself."

The timer chimed softly on Claudette's desk, and Mina shot to her feet.

Her therapist settled back in her wing chair, unperturbed by Mina's desire to run. "Let's try to meet again next week, instead of waiting another month. If you'd like, we can talk more about why the state of your fertility matters in the context of Mack, specifically."

"I would like that," Mina agreed. She'd thought she would call the office later to set it up—now she wouldn't have to. "Thank you for fitting me in."

"Anytime. Really," Claudette soothed. "Stop by Kendall's desk on your way out. She'll arrange a time, okay?"

Chapter Twenty-Eight

Six Months Earlier

IT WAS MACK'S mom who got him to sign up for the dating website. She'd said that it had been three entire years since his divorce, and that St. Michaels was too small a town for him to hang around waiting to bump into the right woman, like he was some hapless character from a TV movie.

She was wrong—it had been four years of blind dates and one-night stands—but also right. Mack wasn't meeting anyone. He didn't exactly care, though.

But, as he saw it, if creating the dating account got his mother to stop trying to fix him up with young divorcees from her church, then it might just be worth it.

He applied the minimum amount of effort to his profile before making it live. Despite that, Mack's listing started getting hits in its first few days. Fresh meat, he supposed.

He was able to rule out most of the women with only some half-hearted messaging back and forth, but there was one photo he couldn't dismiss quite so easily. Over and over, the site suggested her to Mack, and it was beginning to get to him.

He was enormously put off by the fact that her name was Caroline—that was far too close to "Carolynn" for his comfort.

Caroline's face was another story, though. It drew him in like a crabber pulling up traps, so Mack finally sent her a message.

She responded within hours and was witty, self-deprecating, and distinctly not desperate-sounding. They talked sporadically online for a couple of days, while Mack searched for everything he could find about her electronically. A few photos from some 5K she'd done, and a blog she wrote about arts and crafts. Nothing ominous. He bit the bullet and asked Caroline to lunch—there was just something about her he couldn't shake.

The morning of their date, Mack had an appointment with a new client. What he thought would be a quick inspection of the guy's tumble-down dock turned out to be much more involved. He'd spent three hours in a smelly pair of waders, investigating the extent of the damage affecting the man's unsound seawall, which stretched along a hundred feet of the pricey bay-front property. The job would be big and well-paying. It was a God-send.

But it meant that Mack didn't have time to run home and change before meeting Caroline. He thought that would be okay, though. Lunch was supposed to be casual, and she didn't seem the type to mind. It would be something to talk about, anyway— a way to tell her about his job and business. Wasn't that a detail she'd probably want to know?

In person, Caroline was similar to her photos, but not *quite* what Mack was expecting. For one thing, she'd said she managed a little gift shop in town, but she showed up wearing a crisp black power suit and heels and reeked of perfume. She looked more like an ambitious realtor than a laid-back shopkeeper.

Before he introduced himself, Mack hung back and listened to her request a table. Caroline's Jersey accent was strong. Her lipstick color was even stronger. There'd clearly been some photo filters applied to her selfies, and he wondered if she'd been honest about her age.

Mack didn't have a clue whether he ought to shake her hand or try to hug her, so he settled for something in-between. He laid a hand on her elbow and stepped closer to get her attention.

"Caroline?"

She turned with a bright smile.

"Hey. I'm Mack," he said.

The smile fell away as she took in his appearance. Mack glanced down at himself, too. He'd reapplied his deodorant and thrown on a clean Henley in his truck before heading over, but he still had on the same worn jeans from that morning. His work boots were pretty beat-up and dirty, but he'd tried to knock most of the mud off them before he came in. Who knew a couple sandwiches would require something fancier?

"Sorry," Mack explained, "My morning appointment ran longer than I expected."

The bridge of her nose crinkled, sending hairline disturbances out across the surface of her makeup. "What are you, a contractor or something?" Mack didn't have to guess what Caroline's opinion of that was.

"No, uh—"

Margie gestured at Mack from the back of the restaurant, indicating the booth she'd just finished busing.

"I'm an engineer." He pointed out their table to Caroline and stood back for her to go first. She tossed that brunette ponytail of hers across her shoulder—narrowly missing his face—and clacked across the wood floorboards in her shiny sky-high shoes. Mack followed in her vapor trail, and his misgivings about the whole idea grew.

Ordering was more complicated than it should have been, especially once Caroline mentioned that she'd already checked out the menu online before arriving. She didn't eat lunch meat or bread—two of the more basic components of a sandwich, as Mack understood it. She wasn't in the mood for soup either, which pretty much left her with a salad. Caroline said she was fine with drinking only water.

Mack was ravenous, so he ordered a Reuben, the house-made chips, and a soda. He felt vaguely guilty about it, though—so perhaps Caroline had more in common with his ex-wife than just her name.

Across the table from his date, he tried to understand why he'd found this woman so tempting. As they attempted to move past the surface-level details they'd already shared with each other online, it became clear they didn't have much in common.

And, after only forty-five minutes together, Caroline was already a bit of a pain in his ass. She lectured Mack about his soda, so he peevishly ordered a second one. She wanted to discuss the fat content of pastrami, so he lied and told her he almost never ate it, but that he'd wanted to treat himself after the morning he'd had.

At the one-hour mark, almost to the second, Caroline said she had to go. Mack told her he'd ask for the check, but she was already standing and sliding her purse onto her shoulder.

"It was so nice meeting you," she told him. Her tone was insincere. She gave Mack's hand a brisk shake when he stood up too, then wiped her palm on her skirt. "See ya."

"You too," he said. "Take care."

Not a word about another meeting, thank the Lord. Mack plopped back down, seeing no reason why he shouldn't stay and finish his lunch.

Online, there'd been something fetching about Caroline. Something...*familiar*. He still didn't know why.

She didn't resemble anyone he knew, not off the top of his head. Long brown hair, sort of short and athletic-looking, and...*aw, hell*. Caroline didn't look like Mina goddamn Whitney, did she? *Crap*—Mack thought she might. He was a total moron.

He drove his truck back home, blazed straight through the office and pushed into the kitchen at the back of the house. He pulled up short at the sight of the big old peace lily on the window sill and groaned. His mom had given him that plant more than a decade ago. Mina had babied it when she lived with him, and when she left…Mack had dragged it from place to place, keeping it alive like it was going to cure cancer someday. He was pathetic. He should just *call* her.

His ex-wife Carolynn had left him for another man four freaking years ago. Mina's husband Grey had been buried a year and a half ago. What could be the harm in calling Mina, just to check in? In fact, Mack probably had a social and moral duty to do so—to make sure she was okay and didn't need anything.

As long as he protected himself and didn't get in too deep, he'd be fine. They'd be fine. Everything would be so freaking *fine*.

He pulled out his cell before he could second-guess himself. Mina picked up on the third ring.

"Hello?" That was her sweet voice, all right. He'd know it anywhere.

"Mina? Hey, kid. It's Mack."

"Oh my God, Mack—how are you?"

"Doing okay. How 'bout you?"

"I'm good." She sat there in silence for an excruciating minute. "So…what's up? Did you need something?"

This was not going the way he'd thought it would, but that was on him. It *never* went the way Mack thought it would with her.

"No, it's just…something dumb. I met someone who reminded me of you today, so I thought I'd call. See how you were doing."

"Mack?" She drew out his name into a long, teasing syllable. "Did you go on a date with a *lady*?"

Oh, God. How had he forgotten the way she used to needle him about girls? Mack didn't think he could take it today, not from her.

"She could've been your cousin," he admitted, against his better judgement. "But she wasn't anything like you."

"Poor you," Mina laughed.

"Exactly. Poor me."

And then Mack saw his opening, yawning in front of him, just waiting for him to step through. So, he did.

"How about hooking a brother up and meeting me for lunch this week? Now that I've suffered through Fake Mina, I could use a dose of the real thing."

True, it might be a case of the cure being worse than the disease, but no one except Mack had to know that. Mina certainly wouldn't know the difference.

"I'd love to, but it might not be as easy as you're expecting," she warned.

Yeah, when was it ever?

"What do you mean?" he asked.

"Well, I heard they're doing some work on the bridge this week. Traffic might be pretty bad."

The bridge? As in, the Bay Bridge? *Shoot.* In his haste to call her before he lost his nerve, Mack had totally forgotten that Mina had moved to Annapolis about a year ago. What the hell was wrong with him? Even the *thought* of her made him stupid.

"No worries," he heard himself say. "I have an early appointment in town on Thursday." Which he would be setting up that afternoon. "We can meet up after that."

"Are you sure?"

The traffic thing was no joke. If Mack didn't leave early enough—like, the night before—it would stretch for miles at a virtual standstill.

"Sure, I'm sure," he said, chipper as a daisy. "Wouldn't miss it for the world."

As HARE-BRAINED IDEAS went, that one was right up there. But on Thursday, as Mack leaned back in his chair in the marina tavern, he couldn't make himself care a whole lot. Mina was picking her way through the tables toward him, and she was as gorgeous as she'd ever been.

Like his date two days ago, Mina wore a skirt and heels, but the effect was totally different on her. Mina looked polished and professional, and sexy as sin. Mack tried not to wonder if she'd have a garter belt on under all that gabardine—and failed miserably.

She grinned at him. "Hey, Mack!"

"Look at you," he said, when she slid into the seat across from him. "What's with the hot librarian look?"

Mina laughed him off and took some time to arrange her purse on the chair next to her.

"Not that there's anything wrong with that," he added. He rubbed a hand over his mouth and hoped it would keep him from uttering any other gems from the Troglodyte Handbook.

She took a deep breath, her hands bracketing her plate, and asked, "How the hell are you?"

"Better now," he smiled back. "It's good to see you. You holding up okay?"

Her smile turned stiff, and she lifted the menu to study it. "I'm better now," she echoed. "Hey, do you mind if we order fast? I only have about an hour, and then I have to get back to work."

"Yeah, sure," Mack agreed. The waitress hurried over, and he rushed through his order. All he could think was, *One hour? That's all?*

Once they were alone again, he gestured. "Looks like you have a good job. Where are you working?"

"At a law firm up the street. I'm really lucky. They're nice."

"That's great. What do you do?" She clearly wasn't waitressing anymore.

Mina shrugged. "I'm just a paralegal."

Mack sat back. When had that happened?

"You look surprised," she said.

"No," he denied. But it was no use—he was a lousy liar. "I'm sorry, I had no idea. I guess I should have. When did you, uh…" Go to school? Find the time? He'd known Mina for more than ten years. Why was he suddenly so bad at communicating with her?

Thankfully, she didn't seem the least bit offended. "When Grey went back into the service, he was away a lot. I had plenty of time to get a degree and get certified through the military's online university."

It had always chafed Mack that Mina had missed out on an education of her own while following Grey all over creation. He should have known better, known she'd find a way to look out for herself, even in Grey's shadow. It made him irrationally proud.

He tossed a balled-up napkin at her. "Good for you, kiddo."

"Thanks. I like it." Mina smoothed the napkin out on the table in front of her. "It's interesting, and there's always something new, you know?"

"That sounds perfect."

She nodded. "What about you? What have you been up to?"

"Same old, same old. My firm is starting to do well. I'm getting a lot of work, so I've been able to fix up the house a bit. Help out my mom and the kids."

"And based on the whole date thing you mentioned, I'm assuming you're still single."

She tried to sound casual, but Mack saw the way Mina's eyes watched him from over the rim of her iced-tea glass. His heart, already thumping alarmingly fast, kicked into overdrive.

"Yeah. I don't meet a ton of people. It's driving my mom berserk."

"Same," Mina agreed. "Dating in your thirties is so…"

"Odd," he supplied.

"Very. I feel like I missed out on some crucial orientation class or something."

"Me too," Mack laughed. "Everyone out there seems to know something I don't. Putting that mess online makes it even worse."

"You're just trying to make me feel better," Mina complained. "You probably have all the ladies beating down your door, you hound."

"Why, Mina Whitney," Mack drawled, his radar ticking into high alert. "Are you flirting with me?"

She snorted, but the clumsy joke seemed to put her at ease. "Incidentally, I go by O'Connell now."

Mack was pleased. The fact that Mina had returned to her maiden name was as good a sign as any that she might be ready to date seriously again. He mulled that over while they bantered back and forth and picked at their sandwiches, but as quickly as it began, the party was abruptly over.

Mack knew that some hours dragged on, while other sped by. This hour, though, hadn't even felt like a blip on the chart. One blink, and it was done. Mina hugged him tight—like she would a long-lost cousin—and Mack offered to walk her back to her job just to have another few minutes with her.

When she said goodbye, she seemed sad. Mina didn't hint even a little bit that she'd like to see him again, and Mack was strangely reluctant to press. He turned away from the building and walked back down the hill, each step feeling heavier than the last. Would he ever stop longing for that woman? Was it foolish to hope that she might someday care? Mack didn't know. What he did know was that fate had granted him a second chance. He only had to watch, and wait, for the right moment.

Chapter Twenty-Nine

Six Months Earlier

ON THE DAY the Marine Corps CID started calling again, Mina was in a pretty good headspace. She'd settled into her job at the law firm and managed to unpack most of the boxes from her move to Annapolis.

Mina had even made enough progress with Dr. Mercer—Claudette—that she could transition to a monthly appointment instead of the original weekly or biweekly ones. She'd made some friends in the bereavement group that Claudette ran, and she felt good. Stable.

She almost didn't answer the phone, since she knew the Corps couldn't possibly still have business with her. Still, curiosity got the best of her, and before long Mina found herself agreeing to meet the new investigator after work the following day.

This Marine turned out to be older than the man she'd talked to right after Grey died. His face was lined and grave, and he came armed with an attaché full of files.

"Major Vasquez, I was already interviewed by your office once—the day after Grey's funeral, I might add. He's been dead for a year and a half. What else do you need to know?" Mina inquired.

Vasquez rested his hands on the file on his lap. "Let's just say, some new information has come to our attention. We needed to follow up."

His demeanor was unsettling. "Okay," Mina shrugged. "But I'm not sure how useful I'll be."

"Mrs. Whitney. Or...I'm sorry, is it Ms. O'Connell now?"

"It is O'Connell," Mina confirmed. Eventually people would finally figure that out.

"Thank you. What can you tell us about how your husband spent his time during his last few months in the service?"

"Not much. Grey was overseas for a lot of it, and when he came home he didn't talk about what he did," Mina replied. "Why are we going over this again? I told them right after his accident I didn't know anything."

The Marine smiled politely and ignored her last statement. His brows twitched together slightly, like he was resisting a frown. "You never asked him what it was like?"

"Of course, I asked him. Grey just refused to discuss it."

Vasquez flipped some pages in his file. "It says here that you told Captain Daniels you believed Grey was training police recruits in the country of Afghanistan during his last deployment. How did you come by that information?"

Mina shrugged again, trying to tamp down the sense that she herself was on trial for something. "I don't know. Maybe because that was what was in the papers."

He raised his eyebrows and didn't seem the least bit impressed with her sarcasm—which was fine, because Mina wasn't the least bit impressed with his arrogance.

"The papers?" he asked, dubious.

She sighed. "The *Post*. The *Sun*. Every other newspaper this side of the Mississippi."

Vasquez gave an amused little sniff. "Reporters don't always do a ton of vetting on things like that. If we hand them something sensational enough—make it look all cloak and dagger—they eat it up. They'll basically print whatever we want them to."

Mina rolled her eyes. This absurdity was too much for words. "Am I supposed to find that reassuring?"

There was a pause. More paper shuffling, then, "So, when your husband returned to the States in April…"

Mina interrupted, "That's wrong. Grey came home in June."

The investigator read out, "Lieutenant Grey Thomas Whitney arrived stateside on April eleventh. He was debriefed on the events his unit participated in and departed two weeks later, accepting an immediate dishonorable discharge in lieu of risking a court martial." He flashed the official-looking document in front of her face, too quickly for her to read.

"But…that can't be right. Grey was still on inactive duty when he died. He still had three years left of his service obligation."

"Can you provide us with documentation attesting to that?" When she stared at him, the Marine tacked on a completely anemic, "Ma'am."

Could she find the paperwork? Mina struggled to remember whether Grey had actually shown her the orders, or whether he'd only *told* her about them. Told her, come to think of it, months after the fact, during a heated argument about something completely different.

Where might documents like that be? She certainly hadn't run across them at home yet, but once she'd cleared out all his clothes and given the sentimental stuff to his mother, she hadn't exactly dug much deeper.

If Grey's discharge really had been dishonorable, it would explain so much—like the way her spousal benefits seemed to be perpetually hung up in red tape, and the way he'd never been able to get a decent job.

As Mina sat there staring through the bay window behind the Marine's head, another piece of his insane statement registered.

"Wait—what exactly was Grey going to be court-martialed for?"

The man's face blanked of all expression. "I'm sorry. That's classified."

More frustratingly twisted paths that never led anywhere. It was classic Grey, except Mina was done with all that. Grey wasn't ever coming back, and she'd finally figured out it was probably her saving grace.

"Well, how about this, pal?" she said. "You can tell me why you people are back here asking me questions right this minute, or you can get the hell out of my house until you have a subpoena. I *know* what kind of man my husband was. You aren't going to surprise me, alright?"

They faced off for long minutes. Eventually, Major Vasquez's expression relaxed slightly. "What kind of man do you think he was?"

"The kind of man whose side women called his widow for months after he died," Mina said sharply. "The kind of man who had mysterious pills in his system when they did the autopsy. The sort of man who had so many secrets that I was only slightly surprised that your office came calling once he was gone. That clear it up for you?"

The Marine grimaced. He closed his eyes for several seconds, then nodded to himself. "There have been other cases that have proceeded after Grey's," he admitted finally, and Mina had never been happier to have him drop the whole *your husband* thing. "Involving the warehouse explosion, and the firefight in the village. Some new evidence shook out, pointing to far more culpability in Grey than we had previously believed."

"And so, you wanted to see what the little wife knew," Mina said sourly.

He nodded once, all signs of hostility and self-importance gone.

"Nothing. I know nothing, and that's the God's honest truth," she told him.

Vasquez cleared his throat, uncomfortable now after his former bravado. "Well, I do appreciate your time," he said. His hands shifted papers back into his briefcase, and his eyes refused to meet hers.

When he stood, he shook her hand firmly and said, "And I'm sorry."

Actually, Mina kind of believed him. How many of these interviews had this man had to conduct? What must his days be like? It seemed to be an incredibly depressing way to live. "Major...if I find anything..."

His face softened a little more and he handed her his business card. "Just give me a call."

"I'll give you a call," she echoed. In three long strides, the Marine reached the front door and let himself out.

At first, Mina couldn't figure out what part of that whole conversation bothered her more. In the end, she decided it wasn't the revelation that Grey had lied to her that stuck in her craw, it was the way being called *Mrs. Whitney* still grated on her nerves. She wasn't Mrs. Whitney anymore, and someday the world would realize that. She needed to let it go.

She was neck deep in the world wide web, trying to find links to those old news stories about Grey's unit—trying to track down the names of the other Marines that had been court-martialed—when the phone rang, and Mack Bolton's name popped up on her caller ID.

A distraction. That was exactly what she needed after the farce of that interview. Without thinking much about it, Mina agreed to meet Mack for lunch later that week. His voice was still as deep and attractive as it had always been, but Mina couldn't let herself go there.

If the Corps was going to keep coming at her every few months, she needed to make sure she discovered as much as she could about whatever Grey had been mixed up in. Once Mina was better prepared, *then* maybe she could spare a few minutes on memories of the tantalizing Mr. Bolton.

She didn't find much online that she hadn't already learned, however. Officially, the Corps reported that an insurgent group had attacked one of the police trainee classes. A team of Marines had apparently tracked the insurgents to a small village near the base, but in the ensuing conflict the village was destroyed, and many civilians were killed. A nearby warehouse had blown up, but it was believed to be unrelated. That was it.

The verdicts of the court martials Mina found hinted that there was more to the story. Phrases like *impeding an investigation* and *providing false testimony* jumped out at her. Something more had happened in that village than the public had been told. And—huge shocker—Mina's lying husband seemed to have been right in the thick of it, along with all the other dirtbags and cheats. No wonder Grey had never wanted to talk about it with her.

Mina sighed. She hadn't yet run out of topics to discuss with her therapist, and she might as well add this to the list at her next appointment. More of Grey's dishonesty uncovered, and another mess he'd left Mina to clean up. The indignities just seemed to drag on and on. Would she ever truly be free of him? Would she ever stop being Mrs. Whitney and have a life that wasn't tainted by Grey's outsized shadow?

One thing she *didn't* want to talk about with Claudette quite yet was her upcoming lunch with Mack Bolton. For one thing, it would take way longer than forty-five minutes to explain their convoluted history—and to make sure that the therapist understood Mack's deep-seated goodness and caring nature.

Mina would hate if the other woman characterized him as some kind of opportunistic vulture, cornering her in kitchens over the years so he could tell Mina she was special. When and if she did tell her doctor about him, Mina would be careful that Mack came out looking like the kind and decent guy he was.

Which got her to thinking. Why on earth had he *really* called her today? Sure, Mack had joked about a blind date gone wrong, but that was hardly cause to ring Mina up out of the blue. He probably had more regular dates than Mina did, and the women would have to be both blind and foolish to screw up a chance to be with him. At thirty-four, Mack Bolton had only gotten better with age.

Sentimentality, Mina decided eventually—that had to be what this was about. Mack was a soft-hearted man, and if that other woman had really made him think of Mina—as he claimed—then he was exactly the kind of guy who'd decide it merited a visit. And if Mina was letting her own silly feelings about Mack get in the way of figuring out his motives? Well, then there was no better way to see what was actually up, than to go meet him.

Chapter Thirty

I N THE DAYS that followed, Mack debated with himself. Should he call Mina and apologize for the things he said? Should he drive by her house to make sure she was okay?

And—in his darker, more self-castigating moments—should Mack change his address, change his number, and change his name, so that Mina O'Connell could never hurt him again?

She waited a couple weeks to reach out to him, and while each second of that time had felt like an evolutionary era, reach out she did.

Sadly, when Mina finally thawed out their relationship deep freeze, it was not because she missed Mack and wanted to get reacquainted with him and his junk—but because she had a pesky reptile-control problem.

It didn't do much for Mack's ego. He tormented himself about whether she'd first tried Animal Control, or even that dude Dimitri she was tight with. Mack agonized over whether he was a third-stringer, or the man Mina couldn't do without.

Nevertheless, when she called him about the snake in her kitchen, he'd dropped everything and come running. That was hardly surprising. Mina's voice had trembled just enough to neutralize any misgivings Mack might have felt. The greater problem was that he had firmly resolved *not* to do crap like that for her, if only to save his own sanity. So why was he?

He and Mina both knew she didn't *really* need Mack to haul over there to get rid of some unwelcome critter. Somehow, the call felt more like a peace offering than an actual crisis. But, to be fair—a snake was a snake. He didn't think it would actually be dangerous, but that didn't mean Mina should have it underfoot.

He drove the hour to her house and listened to her recap, while his eyes hungrily devoured her face. To keep from pulling Mina into his arms and kissing her senseless, Mack dutifully grabbed work gloves and a shovel from her garage and got to flushing the thing out from under her sink.

The snake had taken up a defensive position, coiled tight behind the bottles of cleaning solutions in the dark and the damp. Mack tipped the beam of the flashlight around and made a mental note to fix her leaking sink drain while he was there.

The snake didn't appreciate all the attention. It sprang into motion suddenly, darting out of the cabinet to slither straight across Mina's kitchen floor. She shrieked like a horror-movie victim and knocked Mack flat on his ass when she jumped out of the way.

He scrambled to his feet and grabbed for the shovel, but barely clipped the tip of the reptile's tail before it slid handily under her refrigerator.

"Jesus, did you see that thing?" Mina squeaked, staring at the place it had disappeared. "It was bigger than I thought it was!"

Mack had to admit, it *was* larger-than-normal. But as he'd expected, it was only a garden snake, and therefore essentially harmless.

"Fuck," he muttered. "Now I'm gonna have to move your fridge."

With a sigh, he gripped the sides of the heavy appliance, and worked it away from the wall.

"Let me know if it comes back out," he told her, watching the floor near his feet for movement.

When he finally got the fridge pulled out and felt a chilly breeze along the floor, Mack knew the snake had given them the slip—there was a fist-sized hole low in the wall, punched right through into the garage.

"Oh, come *on*," he bitched.

Mina peered over his shoulder. "Geez. That explains why it was so drafty in here last winter."

"I'll patch it for you later," Mack said. "Let's go find that sucker."

She opened the door into the garage, flicked on the lights, then pointed and yelled, "There!"

"Open the garage door," Mack told her. "Maybe it'll go right out."

Of course, it couldn't be that easy. Instead of heading for freedom, the snake darted to the side—right for a stack of boxes against the wall. Mack peered around. Based on the amount of crap in the garage, he understood why Mina's car was always parked out in the driveway instead of in there.

When he slowly shuffled closer, the snake stretched its length along the base of a big wooden trunk, turned the corner, and began to disappear. Mack rushed forward and pushed away some boxes near the side.

"Shit," he grumbled. "I lost it."

Mina was staring at the olive-painted trunk with an odd expression. She crouched warily, inspected the side, and moaned, "*Damn* it. I think it might've gone *inside*. Look." She pointed out the corner of the trunk, where a small portion was dented inward. It looked like it'd been dropped at some point, breaking the wood. And she was right—the snake could easily have pushed inside.

"Only one way to find out," Mack said. "Where's the key?"

"I...don't know."

He looked closer, and realized the trunk had a faintly military look to it. Something of Grey's, then. He stepped back—maybe this was a bad idea.

"I got rid of most everything else," Mina rushed to explain. "But I didn't know what was in this box. I was afraid there might be...guns or something." She looked pained. "I thought I might find the key when I packed up the house to move, but I never did."

Mack took a deep breath. There were a thousand different things that could be in that box, and he was pretty sure he didn't want to be present for the unveiling of any of them. He doubted Mina did, either. "What do you want to do?" he asked.

"Do you think we could break the lock off?"

"Maybe." Mack bent down and looked carefully. "The lock is pretty new. The metal of the latch looks sound, too, but the wood around it feels old. It's kind of soft."

She stared at the trunk and set her chin in a way he'd seen before. "Give me the shovel," she said.

"Have at it," Mack smiled, and handed it over. Then he watched in fascination as Mina whacked the shit out of that stupid, snake-harboring box.

He wasn't going to *point out* that she appeared to have some pent-up aggression to work through, but...Mina appeared to have to some pent-up aggression to work through. Right when Mack was getting ready to call a halt to the massacre, the lock, latch, and a decent chunk of the trunk's lid clunked solidly onto the concrete floor.

"There," she breathed, satisfied.

"All right, tough guy. Why don't you give me that?" Mack pried the shovel from her grip and stepped forward. "I'll poke around and see if it's in there." With the handle, he prodded at the contents.

No guns—at least, no obvious ones right on top. Mostly, the box seemed to be filled with papers and files and a few odds and ends of old clothing. There were some musty tactical pants and a pair of black combat boots.

Mack nudged one boot—empty. Its twin, not so much. When he shifted it, he caught the slightest bit of glossy movement inside. Mack worked the shovel under the sole, lifted it out, and carried the boot to the yard. He flung it a few feet away and watched the garden snake slither fast toward the woods behind Mina's duplex.

"Got it!" he called. "Once I seal off that hole and fix your drain, you ought to be good to go." Mina didn't respond, so Mack grabbed the empty boot and walked back into the garage.

She was hunched over the open trunk, sifting through the papers with a troubled frown on her face.

"Mina? Did you hear me? We got him."

She jumped up. Mack handed her Grey's old combat boot, she gingerly placed it back in the box, and then she slammed the lid closed before Mack could get another look inside. Mina smiled, but it was stiff and unnatural.

"Thank you so much," she said, walking toward the kitchen door. "I think this calls for a beer, don't you?"

"Yeah," he grunted. Mack rubbed at his chest to calm his racing heart back down.

She hit the button to close the garage, stepped aside so he could go in before she turned off the light, then edged past him.

"Everything okay?" Mack asked, eyeing her. "What was all that stuff?"

"Oh, it's fine. It just looked like a bunch of old papers and junk, but I'll have to go through it to make sure there's nothing important."

He waited for Mina to take two bottles out of the fridge, then he crouched in the niche to quickly measure that hole in the wall. Her husband had been dead for two years. She'd probably thought she was done with that kind of stuff.

"I'm sorry," Mack said. It was weak, but all he could think of.

"That's all right. Once the movers put all that old stuff out there, I kind of forgot about it, I guess."

Mack stood and accepted the beer she held out. "Life gets in the way," he said.

"It sure the hell does," Mina agreed.

He took a long fortifying drink and watched her. After a minute or two, Mina pulled out one of her kitchen chairs and hesitantly sat in it. She gestured, "Do you have time to hang out for a bit?"

"Sure. Yeah," he said. "I should run to the hardware store before it closes, but I can finish my beer at least."

Mack sat. He tried not to stare. Mina looked tired, and too thin. He wondered if she was eating well enough, or if she'd been sick again.

"So how have you been?" they both asked at once.

Mina shook it off with a smirk. "Go ahead," she offered.

"Good, good," Mack lied. "Been busy at work. You?"

"Same." Mina stared down at her hands for a bit, then looked up at him with an expression that would've done a hound dog justice.

"Mack, listen. I'm really sorry about how we left things. It feels like I led you on, and I want you to...know..." Mina stuttered to a halt while her words seemed to get tangled up in her mouth. "I never meant to hurt you," she finally finished.

Mack hadn't meant to get hurt. He just couldn't seem to avoid it around her, though.

"Hey, no sweat, kiddo. I'll be fine." Eventually. He hoped. "You gotta do what feels right."

"So, you don't hate me?"

Her? No. More like himself for being to helpless to resist her. Or Grey, for having ruined her.

"Naw," Mack said. And...that was the sum total of what he could conjure up. He surged to his feet, left his half-full beer on the counter, and looked around for his keys. "I'd better get that stuff. Where's the closest hardware store?"

Mack needed some space if he was going to get through the next hour or two occupying the same room as Mina. Maybe staring at a selection of drywall patches and spackle for a while would break his heart and his dick out of the unfortunate grab-Mina-hold-Mina loop they seemed to be stuck in.

He missed her and loved her—so damn much. Maybe focusing on what he *could* do, instead of what he *wanted* to do, would keep Mack from throwing himself at Mina's beautiful, uninterested feet and begging for mercy.

Chapter Thirty-One

MINA HADN'T BEEN sure how she was going to get rid of Mack once he found that box in her garage. Even after the way they'd left things two weeks ago—the way she'd disappointed him—he'd still come swiftly to help her. It seemed awfully cold-blooded to try to get rid of him again so soon. And all because of a dead man's cast-off things.

In her defense, she *had* called two different pest control companies before texting Mack. They were both closed—apparently critters weren't supposed to come lounge around people's sunny kitchen floors on a Sunday.

Mina had spent a few minutes thanking her lucky stars that she hadn't tripped over the beast in the dead of night—but once her loitering made the snake restless, she'd snapped a quick photo and texted it to Mack.

He'd responded almost instantly and was on the road within half an hour. If anyone could've rid Mina of the disgusting reptile—which looked more like someone's discarded bicycle tire than anything you'd find in your yard—it was Mack. Along with Grey, the man had spent his entire childhood tramping around the woods of the Eastern Shore.

He'd made no reference to their argument and short work of the snake. After a quick run to the hardware store, he'd even gone the extra mile and patched that weird little hole in her wall. Mack had fixed her dripping sink drain, and then inquired if there was anything *else* he could do.

As much as she wanted to—as much as she'd mourned the loss of him—Mina couldn't allow herself to enjoy his company. But, because he'd insisted on being so infernally helpful, she could hardly kick him right back out again.

So, she'd ordered some Thai food and a pay-per-view action movie. She sat on the couch and mocked bad guys with Mack, just like they had twelve years ago. Despite their earlier awkwardness, it had felt like it used to—even the simmering sexual frustration between them had been the same. The whole time, though, Mina's mind was on that wooden trunk, and what she might find inside.

After they watched a second movie and it got a bit late for him to drive back over the bridge, she let Mack crash in her spare room. The sounds of him moving around in there had eventually died down, and she was reasonably sure he'd fallen asleep.

But Mina still sat up long into the night, tormented by all the things she couldn't do. Couldn't be with Mack, couldn't get free of Grey. Couldn't even sleep. She couldn't quite force herself to go back into the dark garage, either—not when the big black snake might return and ambush her.

Mina had briefly considered going to Mack's room. The draw of his presence, the way he lit her up from the inside out, was huge when he was this close. But she knew it would hurt too much afterwards—for both of them. Instead, she waited until morning and made Mack extremely platonic coffee and pancakes, then said goodbye in the driveway with the appreciative half-hug of a friend.

Mina watched him go and wished she hadn't called him—that she'd tried harder to take care of that snake herself. Despite what she'd suggested two weeks ago, it was clear there was no way she could just be Mack's friend. She wanted him too much. It was totally untenable.

But maybe—maybe if Mina finally had some answers about Grey…maybe then they would have a chance. If she could find a way to make peace with her past and lay it to rest like she had her husband, maybe Mina could also find a way to be with Mack again. Claudette certainly seemed to think it would work, and the doctor hadn't steered her wrong yet.

Once Mack's truck turned the corner at the end of the street and she waited another fifteen minutes to be sure he wasn't coming back, Mina called in sick to work. With that accomplished, she lunged for the open garage and that beat-up old box. A firm shove made it clear it was too heavy to lift. One of the leather handles was broken, which was probably how it had gotten dropped in the first place—by Grey himself or by the movers who'd brought her here. Between that handle and the broken lid, Mina doubted the box frame would hold up to her trying to drag it inside the house, either.

She went out back and grabbed one of her patio chair cushions to kneel on, then came back to settle warily in front of the trunk to begin her excavation. Fortunately, her neighbors had already left for work. Mina didn't know what she was about to find and didn't want any nosy eyes around, or prying questions.

Besides Grey's old combat boots, there was a pair of faded and ripped camouflage pants and a few ragged olive-green t-shirts. There were several stacks of papers, some official-looking mail, and a brown accordion file. Mina piled those neatly to the side.

The next layer held two sidearms, thankfully unloaded. There wasn't any ammunition, but there were a few holsters—shoulder, ankle, *and* belt by the look of them. Mina didn't remember those being a part of any of Grey's various uniforms, but she supposed it was possible.

She found a couple of his old political science textbooks from UNC, along with a small plastic baggy of pills. Mina peered suspiciously at them—God only knew what those might be. Knowing Grey, the pills could be anything from vitamin supplements, to antibiotics, to roofies. Most likely they were some illicit vestige of his fraternity years that she'd rather not be acquainted with. Mina shoved the bag into one of his boots and moved on.

At the bottom of the trunk, the thin cardboard liner was warped and water-stained and beginning to curl up at the corners. She brushed her fingers across it and found the mold still damp and alive. Mina stared at the way the liner's base didn't lay flat and studied how it had separated from the frame of the trunk. Heart thumping, she gingerly reached in and lifted the whole thing out. And there it was—the real stuff Grey had wanted to hide.

A small brown notebook, a sandwich bag of photos, and bracketing those—two more olive-green t-shirts, each wrapped around something inside. Mina stared for a long time, hesitant to touch it all. She poked one of the bundles with a finger and felt how hard it was.

This had to be it—the reason why her husband became unhinged in his final months. Anything Grey had buried like this simply had to contain the answers Mina needed.

A memory from six months ago rushed in. The major the Marines had sent to interview her had obviously believed Grey was involved in the case he was investigating. He'd said, *"If you find anything—hear anything—that doesn't fit with what you think you know about your husband, call me. Because if this goes the way I expect it to, you* will *be hearing from me again before long."*

"Is that a threat?" Mina had blustered.

The Marine had been deadly calm. *"No, it's a fact."*

Now Mina swallowed, then reached into the trunk to remove one of the bundles. She'd found two guns already—maybe this was the ammo? But then, why hide it so carefully? She shuddered, remembering yesterday's uninvited visitor. At least this wasn't alive.

She unwrapped the t-shirt, pulled off the thick taupe sock, and extracted a dense brown block of...something. Mina sniffed at it, then set it down quickly, stunned.

She'd never tried anything worse than a joint or two over the years—liquor had always been more than adequate to take the edge off for her. Still, she'd seen enough movies to know what she might be looking at. Drugs.

Inside the house, Mina heard the door between her kitchen and her patio bang shut and nearly jumped out of her skin. She was scared—this was bad. Hands shaking, she scrabbled on the concrete floor for her phone. Mack answered on the second ring.

"Mina?"

"How far away are you? Can you come back?" she pleaded.

She heard traffic noise around him. "What's wrong?" Mack asked.

"I...I found something. Please, Mack? I think it's important."

"Yeah, uh...hang on. I'm almost at the bridge. I need to turn around. I'll call you back in a few, okay?"

"Okay, just—"

Mack cut in and demanded, "*Mina.* Are you okay right now?"

"Yes. Just hurry."

She wrapped the shirt and the sock around the block and shoved it back into the trunk. Mina sorted through the pictures in the bag, but only recognized a few of the men from Grey's funeral.

While she waited for Mack, she flipped through the notebook and read the names and dates and dollar amounts. In the back were two letters from the Corps, folded into quarters—*a torched village, and entire families dead. Use of force deemed inappropriate.* And also—*an explosion in a pesticide warehouse. Troops exposed to burning chemicals, three in particular. Medical follow-up strongly advised.*

Mina grabbed her phone again, and shakily typed in the names of those chemicals. Banned from use in the States and the E.U., they were nasty concoctions with a host of horrible side effects. Cancers. Birth defects. *Sterility.* Someone breathing the burning fumes of a fire like that would be especially susceptible. Her mind spun as she tried to unravel the implications of what she was seeing.

Mack's truck squealed as he rounded the corner onto her street, and seconds later he was throwing it into park behind her car. He rushed over to where Mina was still sitting numbly and squatted beside her.

"What's going on?" His worried eyes took in the mess around her.

"Look." Mina retrieved the bundle containing the brown block, unwrapped it, and showed it to Mack.

Mack frowned, peered closely, then reared back. "Mina, that looks like heroin."

She blew out a breath. "That's what I was afraid of."

"Yeah, but—if so, that's a *lot* of it."

"And there are two."

"*Jesus.*"

"I know. I also found this." She showed him the notebook, and the two memos tucked inside.

Mack sat back on his rear end, his knees bent and legs splayed out in uncomfortable-looking angles while he read. At last, he looked back up at her.

"Mina…this looks pretty bad."

"I know. But maybe it's not. Maybe Grey was only part of the clean-up crew. Maybe he had nothing to do with what happened in that village."

Mack's beautiful amber eyes roved over her face, trying to gauge her mood. She could see him trying to decide what to say. "Yeah," he said after a while. "Maybe."

Even now, the man was going to try to protect her. A wave of affection washed through Mina—Mack was truly one of a kind.

"That wouldn't explain the drugs, though," she pointed out.

He could see the truth as well as she could. Mack shook his head. "Do you know if Grey ever saw a doctor like they suggested?"

"No. He…" Mina remembered something.

"What?"

"That investigator guy said he came back to the U.S. nearly two months before I ever laid eyes on him."

Mack scowled, and Mina hurried on before he could pounce on that ugly fact. "Maybe Grey saw someone then, but…my guess is probably not." She took everything from him and settled it back into the bottom of the trunk. "How sad is this? It's easier for us to believe Grey was a drug-dealing murderer than a decent Marine trying to do good."

"Mina…" Mack reached for her but drew back quickly when she flinched. "I'm so sorry."

Staring into the trunk, she thought about the way Mack had always been so ready to believe the worst of Grey. No matter what she'd told him, he'd never seemed surprised.

"Did you know about any of this?" she asked suddenly.

"No. Of course not!" Mack said. "You guys were in North Carolina for years, and I barely saw Grey in all that time. How could I have known? It wasn't like we were…I don't know, shooting up together, or something."

Mina choked back a sob. "What is *wrong* with me, Mack? How could I…how could I be married to someone like that for ten *years*," she gestured wildly, "And not even know?"

"Shhhh," he crooned, scuttling over and wrapping his arms around her. "There's nothing wrong with you, honey. Grey was an expert at deflecting attention. If he didn't want people to know he was insecure, or afraid, or any of the other things that normal people feel, he just—joked louder. Partied harder. Turned it around on them. He got rowdier and drunker and happier, until everyone else around him got on board. Until they were all so worried about themselves, they forgot to look at him very hard."

"I wasn't just some stranger in a bar, Mack. I was his wife and I fell for it. All of it."

To his credit, Mack didn't point out that Mina was once, in fact, one of those strangers in a bar. "It doesn't mean that he didn't love you," he soothed.

She could only snort at how preposterous *that* was.

"No, really. Grey used to make us all promise not to tell you any incriminating stories from when we were young. He really did care what you thought about him," Mack said.

"Yeah, maybe in the beginning. But it was only because it gave him the high ground when he lectured me. Even I know that's not the same as love."

He raised his eyebrows. "What do you mean, *even you*?"

Mina wasn't going to touch that topic with a ten-foot pole. Mack hated it when she put herself down—it seemed to be a bit of a blind spot for him.

Instead, Mina said, "About six months ago, the Corps sent another investigator to interview me. I'm going to have to call him, obviously."

Mack scowled, perhaps realizing that there was much she'd never told him. He sat up and looked closer at the two guns on the floor. Moving carefully, he checked them both to be sure they were unloaded, then set them into the trunk, along with the rest of the stuff.

"I'd say so," he agreed. "Either him or the cops."

Mina asked Mack the hardest thing yet, "Will you stay while I do it?"

"I can try." He blew out a long breath. "Let me make a couple of calls and see if I can move some stuff around."

He went into the house to charge his cell and make use of her landline, and Mina heard him slam her patio door shut again. She must have left it unlatched when she went to get the chair cushion, but it'd never blown open like that before. Maybe Mack could look at that, too, while he was there.

Mina rifled through that little packet of pictures again, looking at the names penned on the backs. To her knowledge, all were teammates of Grey, though she hadn't met many of them personally. A few had since been court-martialed, if her internet research six months ago was accurate. Of the men she recognized, two had no children that she knew of, and the third had regaled her at the funeral luncheon with the tale of his efforts to adopt. If Mina added Grey and herself to the list, there were no biological children between any of them, despite their years-long marriages.

She cast a quick glance at the door leading into her kitchen, closed tight against the autumn chill. Then Mina unearthed her phone from the blast field surrounding her. It sure seemed like she had one more call of her own to make. The phone rang and rang, and then...

"*Obstetrics and Gynecology,*" the nurse answered.

"Hi, this is Mina O'Connell. I'm a patient of Dr. Davis. I need to make an appointment with her, please."

"Okay, let's see. It looks like you just saw Dr. Davis last March. You won't be due for your next annual for five more months. Is this for something different?"

"Yes, it is," Mina said. She squeezed her eyes closed and forced the next words from her mouth. "I need to have my fertility checked. Assessed, or whatever. It's important."

When she managed to pry her eyes open again, there was Mack—standing in the kitchen doorway staring at her, solemn and stoic as a judge.

Chapter Thirty-Two

MACK STOOD THERE on the threshold, looking at Mina sitting on the dirty concrete of her garage floor. For several long moments, he couldn't seem to make his mouth work right.

When he forced it back into function at last, it was to utter the supremely unhelpful syllable of, "Hey."

"Hey," Mina lobbed back. She held up her phone. "I suppose you heard that."

Was she kidding, or just stalling? It didn't seem to matter either way.

"Yeah, I sure did," Mack replied. He looked out at his truck, parked behind hers in the driveway, then back at Mina. "Mina…"

"Maybe you shouldn't stay, after all," she said, her face going an alarming shade of gray.

"No, I think I should," Mack said. "I think we need to talk, you and I. Don't you agree?"

She stared off into space, probably considering her options. If Mack left now, he had the nauseating feeling it might be for good.

"Mina? Why don't you come inside and tell me what's up."

She got to her feet slowly, then walked carefully and precisely past Mack into her kitchen, where she pulled out a chair and sat down.

He stood next to the other chair and studied her face, trying to assess her stability. After what she'd just found in her garage, Mina would be understandably unnerved. Mack didn't want to make all that worse, but he also didn't want to lose this opportunity to try to reason with her.

He sat down. "Mina, let me get this straight. Did you want to end our relationship because there's a slight chance you might not be able to have biological kids someday?"

"I wouldn't call it slight," she said.

Mack shook his head. "I would. Based on that call you just made, I'm going to assume that neither you nor Grey were ever tested to figure out what was going wrong. You've *admitted* that he tended to blame you for things that weren't your fault. What I don't understand is why you would believe a single thing that ever came out of that lying ass's mouth. And now, with all that stuff in the trunk…"

Mina swiped at her cheeks, smearing the wetness from her tears around.

He reached over, handed her a napkin, and continued, "You just read for yourself that Grey was probably exposed to some nasty stuff in that explosion. How much more proof do you need that the lack of babies probably had nothing to do with you?"

"It's…it's immaterial," Mina murmured. "You don't need to be saddled with all of my effed-up life. I won't ask that of you. It wouldn't be fair. Besides—I just can't handle any more uncertainty."

No matter how Mack tried to explain it to her, she couldn't seem to believe that he wasn't going to hurt her—that he wanted her, body and soul. He could go out tomorrow, bring about world peace and cure cancer by lunchtime, and Mina would still be comparing him to Grey.

"I gotta tell you, kid—I don't think this is about your fertility," he said. "From where I'm sitting, it seems like this is more about whether you think you can trust me not to turn into a dirtbag like Grey did."

Mina dropped her head onto her folded arms and hid her face from him. Why had Mack always liked her so much, from that very first moment? It wasn't because she made it easy to get close, that was for damn sure. He supposed it had to be because she'd felt like the lightness to his heavy. Where Mack was reserved and serious and shy, Mina could be effervescent, and adventurous, and courageous. Her cleverness and passion felt like the perfect complement to his logical, analytical brain.

"The thing is, Mina, I'm *not* Grey. I've *never* been Grey. I don't have his personality or his experiences, and I certainly don't have his demons. I shouldn't have stuck with him as long as I did, but I let nostalgia get in the way of common sense. But you—you can't expect to plug a totally different man into your life and get all the same results. That's not how life works."

"I know that," Mina murmured into her sleeve. She still didn't look at him.

Mack couldn't take her remoteness one more second. He stood up. "I care too much to let you jerk me around," he told her. "Either you're in or you're out. Not this half-assed, 'let's be friends' shit. I need to know for sure if you'll ever be mine. *Really* mine." He hated to play hardball with her, but enough was enough. He wasn't a masochist, for fuck's sake.

Mina stood jerkily, too, and cast around for her purse. "I have to go."

"Seriously? You already tried that the last time. This is your house," Mack balked. "Mina, you've got to stop leaving right when shit gets hard." The second those words left his mouth, he regretted them. There was hardball, and then there was...*that*.

She whirled around and looked staggeringly betrayed. "Is that what you think I do?"

"Well...yeah," Mack admitted. "Kind of. Do you disagree?"

She blinked rapidly, her eyes spilling over again. "I can't believe you actually just said that to me."

"Okay, but I did. It's how I feel." Mack moved slowly toward her and held out a hand. He didn't dare touch her, or she was certain to bolt. "Tell me why I'm wrong."

For a moment, he thought she might. Mina lifted her chin, opened her mouth…and then turned and walked out of her house. It was like her freaking superpower, passed down from her father.

She'd left her mother and sister Molly all those years ago, then swiftly left Mack as well. Mina had already admitted—only somewhat guiltily—that she'd left Molly's wedding reception early, to catch a flight she hadn't really needed to take until the next day. Who knew what else she'd fled from? It certainly hadn't been Grey.

And here Mina was, trying to leave yet again, over something as inconsequential—though understandably daunting—as whether she would have biological kids or adopted ones someday.

Sure, Mack hoped to have a family eventually, too. But it wasn't like he was all rigid about how that would happen. *No one* knew that kind of thing going into it. An awful lot of people assumed, that was for sure, but given the number of things that could go awry when it came to fertility—no one could ever be sure what they'd end up with until the deed was done.

Mack was trying to take it as a compliment that Mina was even thinking along those lines where he was concerned. He was also trying not to burn holes in the panels of her back door from the laser heat of his stare. And he was trying really, really hard to do what Miss Ettie had suggested, and not race right after her.

Mina needed space and time and patience to process stuff, the doctor had advised. Mack would give her that, but he was praying it wouldn't take another twelve freaking years. He wanted her *now*. And he wanted Mina to want him, too.

While Mack remained there, paralyzed and out of ideas, her kitchen door swung back open again. Mina stood staring at him for a long minute, then moved over to the table and sat back down. She folded her hands primly in her lap, changed her mind, and gripped her knees. Mina shook her foot and waited for Mack to sit down, too. Once he did, she started talking.

"When Grey and I were first married," she said. "Things were pretty good most of the time. I mean, everyone knew I'd ditched my family and hadn't been to college yet—because Grey always found a way to tell them—but it wasn't a big deal. At first, he did it because he liked to act like he'd saved me. He liked to play the white knight."

"That sounds like him," Mack said carefully.

"We told everyone in Carolina that I was waiting to go to school until he finished, so it would be less of a strain on our relationship and money, and so on. He liked to pretend that we had thought everything through—planned it all out and weren't making it up as we went along. That way, it wouldn't seem so much like he was rash and impulsive. Like he hadn't married beneath him in some...fit of lust or something."

Mack opened his mouth to refute that one, but Mina cut him off.

"Grey had this one mood that could get tricky, but...it only happened occasionally. He could be mean, but it never lasted long, you know? I thought I could handle it." She fell silent.

To keep her narrative going, Mack asked, "What changed?"

"As time went on, he gradually got worse. He knew I felt guilty about leaving my sister behind, so he started to use that against me. The story changed from him being my Prince Charming—saving Cinderella from her evil family—to me just being some trashy runaway from a dysfunctional home. Grey made me different from him, not...not a part of him any longer. We weren't on the same team anymore."

Mack gritted his teeth. He wanted to rage and break shit, but Mina was telling him things she'd never said before. No matter what, he had to let her finish—for her sake, if nothing else.

"And the college thing?" he prodded.

"At first, it was never the 'right time' for me to start school, even though I helped him with most of his work at UNC and audited a few classes when I could. Eventually, he turned it around on me. Said I was stupid and didn't understand anything. He said a college education for me would be a total waste—like throwing money into a black hole."

"But you still did it," Mack said, even more impressed than he'd been before. "How?"

Mina shrugged in that self-deprecating way she had. "I was mad, and I wanted to spite him. Every time Grey teased me in front of his friends, I was so embarrassed. I wanted to prove that I could do it. So, I enrolled in the military university without telling him and did the work whenever he was away."

"Good girl."

Mina went on, the flood of words rolling out of her. "Later, when Grey started to get really bad, I worked harder to finish. I figured I ought to have a more reliable way to support myself than waitressing, in case he left. I was terrified of ending up like my mom."

"Smart," Mack told her. Not like Mina needed him to tell her that, but he did want to be supportive.

As he thought it through, there was only one more thing she hadn't yet touched on. "That just leaves…the whole kid thing," he prompted.

She took a deep breath, like she'd been ready and waiting for that. "Yeah. You were right that Grey and I weren't actually trying to have kids for the whole ten years we were married. For some of that time, we used birth control. And for other stretches, we weren't even…um…"

Mack felt his eyebrows inch upward. Was Mina suggesting what he thought she was?

"You weren't…"

"Sleeping together anymore," she blurted out.

He sat back.

"Ah." That went against nearly everything he thought he knew about Grey.

Mina gestured insistently. "But for those times that we did try, you have to understand—his message was clear, and relentless. Especially after we moved back to Maryland, especially once Grey came back from overseas that last time. I was defective. I was broken. I was frigid. I came from a screwed-up gene pool. You name it. Let me think…what else?" She rolled her eyes skyward as she thought. "Oh—Grey was *also* paranoid that I was messing around behind his back. So, when we didn't conceive right away, he accused me of picking up some disease that had made me infertile."

"Wow. Talk about classic cheater guilt," Mack mused, amazed.

"Probably," Mina acknowledged. "After he died, I got calls from other women for a long time. Strange cars idling outside the house, that kind of thing."

Mack closed his eyes. Indignity upon indignity, and he'd sat by and done nothing to help her. No one had.

"I'm sorry to hear that," he murmured.

"Anyway," Mina said, resting her hands on the table, "The best thing I ever did was start seeing Dr. Mercer. She helped me learn how to put blame where it belonged, instead of always taking it all on myself. You know what I mean? Like…she said that at age nineteen, it probably wasn't my responsibility to parent Molly—it was my mother's. I had the right to my independence, to my youth."

"Sure you did," Mack agreed. "Dr. Mercer is very wise." He hesitated, but thought it was as good a time as any to confess, "I know her, by the way. Claudette—she's a good friend of my mom's."

"You're kidding." Mina looked alarmed.

"Don't worry," Mack rushed to reassure her. "She would never violate doctor/patient confidentiality. I just…talked to her one time, and she happened to recognize your name. She's pretty awesome, though. In case you wondered."

Mina nodded. "It's easy to see that. And on the one hand, she was right. I did need to split from my family situation. But I probably should've tried to stand on my own two feet for a while before hooking up with some guy I barely knew."

Mack watched her for a time. If she could be brave, then so could he.

"Mina, I have to ask, when you left with him—when you married Grey—did you have any idea how I felt about you? I know I never came right out and told you, but we did...we did make out that one time. I figured it must be obvious."

"I think I..." She considered her answer. "I must have guessed on some level. I was so confused in a lot of ways, but I do think I had the brains to know that if I stayed with you—if I didn't get out of there soon—I would probably be stuck forever. And as much as I liked you personally, that felt suffocating. In contrast, what Grey was offering me felt like escape. Freedom...*Life*."

Mack snorted.

"I know, right?" she laughed grimly. "I am sorry, though. Back then, I just wasn't ready for the anchor that is Mack Bolton."

Mack couldn't resist that lure. "And...now? What about now?"

For the first time, Mina smiled a little, and it seemed to be a happy one. "I think I'm beginning to see the light."

"How refreshing," he smiled back.

"Mack, I came back here to tell you all this, not to gain your pity—but so you'd understand how hard it is for me to say this next part," Mina said.

And here it was—either the end or the beginning. Mack's heart started racing.

"Okay," he said calmly.

Another deep breath, and Mina swallowed hard. "I love you. I have loved you for a really long time, and I probably always will," she admitted. "There is nothing I want more than to see where this goes with you." She gripped her hands together until her knuckles went white. "I have to be truly crazy to even consider something like that again, but I can't seem to help it. Not when you're with me. But Mack, I'm terrified. I'm scared shitless about how much power you already have over my heart."

Mack stood, took Mina by the hand, and led her into the family room. He sat on the couch, pulled her into his lap, and cradled her body against his chest.

"Your heart is safe with me," he told her. He brushed a strand of hair off her cheek and whispered, "I'm going to love you so well, and so long, that it will wash away every last thing that man ever said or did to you."

Mina clung to him and instead of the dribbling tears from before, she began full out sobbing. Mack's shirt was soaked in moments.

"Promise?" she pleaded into his chest.

"Oh God, yeah," Mack told her. "Forever and always."

Chapter Thirty-Three

MACK, SERIOUSLY," MINA mumbled eventually. "I don't know how to do this. I want to—it's just that I don't even know what a normal relationship looks like anymore."

Mack stroked her hair and her back like he was trying to tame a wild animal, and Mina supposed, in a way, he was. Raised by wolves, and all that.

"Luckily, we don't have to do everything all at once," he told her. "We'll just take things step by step, okay? We'll stick by each other no matter what happens and get through what we need to—but we'll do it together."

She huffed out a laugh. "You make it sound so easy."

"Well, I guess it will only be as easy or as difficult as we make it."

"But...I don't even know where to begin." Okay, now she was whining. Mina sat up straight on his lap and dried her face with her shirt.

Mack laughed a little at her obstinance. "All right, how about this? Why don't we get one of the hard things out of the way right now, while we're thinking about it. Do you have a number for that investigator you mentioned? The one who wanted you to call him if you found anything?"

She nodded. His business card was still tucked under some old keys, in the junk drawer in her kitchen.

"So, let's call him before he leaves for the day. Tell him you found something, and then we'll see where we are. Okay?"

One five-minute phone call. That sounded doable, especially with Mack there with her. Mina got up and dug out the card, dialed the number with trembling fingers, and prayed that it wouldn't blow up in her face. Would they accuse her of hiding Grey's stuff on purpose? Lying about it? Being *involved* somehow? All the ways it could go wrong seemed legion.

After the third ring, Mina thought she might get off easy, and only have to leave a message. The CID guy answered on the fourth ring, though, startling her with the sudden tense bark of his voice.

"*Vasquez.*"

"Major, this is Mina O'Connell. We spoke about my husband, Grey Whitney, about six months ago?"

His recognition was instantaneous. "Certainly. How are you, Ms. O'Connell?"

"I'm fine. Listen, I won't bore you with the details over the phone, but I came across a trunk of Grey's in my garage and…" Mina stopped to swallow down her trepidation, while Mack gave her shoulder a squeeze. "I think you might want to take a look at it."

"Really," the Marine said. "Okay, uh—hang on." There was a long pause, during which she thought she heard a muffled conversation, paper rustling, and tapping keys. At last Vasquez came back on the line.

"Are you there?" he inquired.

"Yes."

"It doesn't look like I can get out to you before next Tuesday at the earliest. I'm heading out to San Diego as we speak, to take care of another matter."

"Oh, I…" Mina had hoped to have the trunk out of her house by that evening. To have to wait three or four more days seemed horrible, but she still said, "I guess that's fine."

"Are you able to secure the trunk in a safe place until then?" Vasquez inquired.

"It's in a locked garage that only I have access to. I think it should be okay there." Assuming no criminals were aware of what was hidden in it, that was. Mina supposed it was a good thing snakes didn't talk.

"Great," the major replied, sounding upbeat. "I'll give you a call as soon as I know what time I can come out. Does that work for you?"

"Sure."

"And Ms. O'Connell? Thank you for calling."

After Mina hung up, she told Mack what the other man had said. She considered her options, then begged, "Can I ask you a favor?"

"Anything."

"Can we go back to your place? I don't think I can stay here all weekend, knowing all that *stuff* is out there. It's creeping me out."

"Of course. That works out well, actually—I still have a couple things that I need to finish up in my office before I'll be free for the night. You can hang out for a little bit upstairs, and then we'll grab some dinner. How's that sound?"

"Perfect," Mina said, and meant it.

She threw some clothes in a bag, and they were on their way to the shore within half an hour. It felt good to leave that box behind her, and then—just as they were cresting the bridge—the sun set over the bay in an exuberant wash of red and orange. That felt even better. Mina grabbed Mack's free hand and held on, hoping it was a good omen for the days to come.

ONCE THEY GOT to his house, Mack walked Mina upstairs to settle her with a hot bath and a glass of wine before he went back down to finish his work.

Two hours later, she was dressed again—but half asleep—when he dashed upstairs, apologizing for how long he'd taken. Mack showered and changed, gave her a quick hard kiss, and then led Mina outside.

"I'm starved," he told her. "What do you feel like?" They walked several blocks into the heart of town, holding hands. Mina looked around at the warmly-lit shopfronts, pulled her jacket tighter against the chill, and pointed.

"That one looks good," she said.

Mack had thrown his clothes on quickly, but as he sat across from her at the little round table, she had a chance to really study him. As usual, he wore broken-in jeans and leather laced-up boots, though the boots were nicer than his standard work ones. Mack had rolled his button-down shirt up to his elbows, and the pale blue grid pattern emphasized the lean muscles in his forearms and his tanned skin. Mina smiled, wondering if her smart engineer had chosen the plaid for its distinct resemblance to graph paper.

He'd also worn a fitted tweed vest over his shirt, which merely made his stomach look flatter, and his shoulders broader. He was a mouth-watering specimen, for sure—somehow both rough and sophisticated at once, and Mina couldn't believe he was hers.

As she catalogued his attributes, it occurred to her that Mack would likely be embarrassed if she pointed out any of them to him. He was modest and self-deprecating, and not at all like Grey had been—all shock and awe and *look at me*. Grey would already have listed the ways the shirt flattered him by now. He would've explained about how the boots were some special brand that only he knew about.

Mina had to stop comparing them. She *had* to. As Mack kept reminding her, they were not the same, and never had been. Mack was here and now, while Grey was forever in the past. Thank heaven for that.

Mina was grateful that she and Mack had found a way to work out their differences—she wouldn't have to suffer through any more days without him or pretend like she didn't want him.

She'd managed to open up and tell Mack so much already, which was good. But Mina realized there was one last thing she had to get off her chest. One thing that still weighed on her soul, that she'd never quite let herself admit to anyone else.

After they ordered, she confessed softly, "I think Grey might have killed himself." She'd never said that aloud before. Not to anyone—not even herself.

Mack froze, his beer halfway to his lips. He stared at her, then lifted the bottle to drain half of it in one gulp.

"I think you might be right," he agreed, keeping his voice carefully neutral.

Mina hadn't expected that. She jerked back, knocking her own empty bottle over in the process. "You do?" she hissed. Too loudly, it seemed—the woman at the next table frowned over at her.

Mack nodded. "Why do *you* think that?" he asked.

"Oh, I don't know—maybe because the man was miserable for the last few weeks he was alive?" she said sourly. "Maybe because he told me he hated me and that he was 'done' with us? Or…maybe because there was nothing on that road that night except him."

Mack nodded some more, then lifted his arm to order another beer. Mina picked at one of the mini crabcakes they'd ordered as an appetizer and watched the way he fidgeted.

"Mack? What do you suspect?"

He sighed heavily. "Well, I've been thinking about all that stuff you found. What if Grey knew they were coming for him? Either the other guys that had a stake in those drugs—or the Marines? What if…he felt the noose tightening and decided the investigators were getting closer with each new person that got court-martialed?"

The litany of all the ways *she'd* gone wrong had been so loud, Mina hadn't really considered that aspect. "You think Grey was trying to get out of doing jail time?"

"It's possible," Mack nodded. "He would've hated for you to find out *he* was the one who couldn't have kids. If he was hiding a drug habit, he probably knew that would come out in a court case, too. In jail, he'd probably have to undergo some kind of detox or rehab—and, if his habit was bad enough, that would've been scary."

"I don't know, Mack. Grey was pretty far past caring when he died," Mina mused.

"Well, maybe about some things. But that kind of case would've been very public—it would've made all the papers. His parents and parents' friends would know, and he'd never, ever live down the shame." Mack snorted, "Grey cared about one thing more than any other, as far as I could tell."

Mina raised an eyebrow at him. "Himself?"

"Well, yeah," he laughed. "But also how other people saw him."

"Mack, how could I have been so blind?" She shook her head, feeling dejected.

"You were emotionally abused for ten years, Mina. That wasn't exactly the best set-up for playing Nancy Drew."

"You must've thought I was so stupid," she said.

Mack shook his head. "No, I really didn't. You were just...vulnerable."

"It's funny to hear you say that, because at the time I thought I was so tough."

"In a lot of ways, you were. But what I meant was, people like Grey—manipulators—always gravitate toward the ones that no one is looking out for. People that don't have a support network, you know? No fathers or big brothers or hulking friends to rain holy hell on them if they don't treat their woman right."

"Well, that was definitely me, for sure," Mina muttered.

"Pretty much," Mack agreed. "Grey knew he could say and do whatever he wanted, and no one was likely to challenge him except you."

"And I didn't. Do you think that's why he picked me? Out of all the girls he must have known—was I just the biggest, most gullible doormat?"

NO. GREY HAD picked Mina because he liked to *win*, no matter the cost. And on that long-ago day, in that moment in the bar, he'd wanted to prevail and wanted Mack to lose. God only knew why—Mack had long since given up on trying to figure it out.

To Mina, he simply said, "No, sweetheart. I think Grey zeroed in on you because even he could see what a catch you were."

They paid their check and strolled through the dark, quiet streets toward home. Back at the house, Mina walked into the kitchen to get herself a glass of water, so Mack sprawled in his favorite leather armchair by the hearth and gazed into the empty grate. In a couple more weeks, it would get cold enough for him to start building fires—maybe by Halloween, but almost certainly by Thanksgiving.

Mack thought that hanging out with Mina in his cozy house would feel wonderful, and now he actually had a fighting chance of seeing it happen.

She walked around to stand in front of him, much like she'd done on that very first weekend they'd stayed together. She nudged Mack's knees wide so she could get closer, then ran her fingers back through his hair. A small smile tugged at the corners of her delectable mouth.

Mack rested his hands on her gorgeous hips, flexing his fingers into the meat of them. Mina was so beautiful to him—soft and curved and feminine, with that heady vanilla scent of hers. He wanted to taste her from stem to stern, wanted to feel her and hear her call his name.

She had her own ideas, though. Before Mack could pull her into his lap and peel off her layers of clothes like he was unwrapping the world's best present, Mina knelt on the carpet between his knees and began working on the buttons marching in a line down his chest. Once she had them all undone, Mack shrugged out of his button-down and vest, then helped her get his undershirt up and over his head.

He managed to entice her into a very nice interlude of kissing, but right when things were starting to get interesting, Mina broke it off to trail her tongue down Mack's neck. She kissed a path over his heart and moved south, the whisper of her warm breath against his stomach making his skin erupt in goosebumps and his cock jerk to attention.

Mina's soft fingertips hooked under the waistband of his jeans, sliding toward the button below his navel. As Mack watched, she slipped the metal fastener free and carefully worked his zipper down past his straining erection. Seconds after that, she freed him from his boxers and wrapped her hand possessively around him.

"Oh no you don't, Missy," he chuckled. "You've tried that trick on me before."

"Yes, and as I recall," Mina purred, "It worked like a charm."

Mack could hardly argue with that kind of pro-level reasoning. He dropped his head back and gazed at Mina weaving her spell over his body as long as he could manage it—while she bewitched him like no other woman ever had. Seeing his length slide between her lips had to be one of life's greatest sights. Feeling her tongue stroke him to completion, knowing that she was finally his—Mack could hardly fathom it.

Mina brought him ruthlessly over the edge, and then some. When she'd finished him off, she simply laid her cheek on his thigh and beamed up at him. He lifted one boneless arm to stroke her shining hair, but otherwise, Mack wasn't sure he could budge.

She seemed to understand. Mina helped him out of his boots and pants, then stood in front of him and undressed slowly.

He couldn't take his eyes off of her, but he managed to lean to the side and snag his wallet out of his pants. He extracted the condom inside, wedged it under his thigh, and ran his hand up Mina's strong, pale leg.

"Come a little closer," he urged her. She shuffled two inches toward him, but Mack pulled her forward until her knees hit leather. "Closer," he said.

Mina's mouth could never resist some sass, and now was no exception. While she asked, "Why?" her body was getting with the program and straddling Mack's lap like it was their favorite position—and maybe it was. They'd certainly ended up like that often enough.

He undid the braid in her hair and spread the silky waves over her shoulders. Then Mack nipped at her bottom lip and gave Mina her answer. "Because I want to bite you," he smiled.

She giggled, and it brought every inch of her torso into contact with Mack's chest. Her melting-hot center brushed against the tip of his shaft, jolting it suddenly back to life—and Mack tried not to stroke out from the sensation.

He wished again for a roaring fire in the grate. Its flickering light would outline Mina's body beautifully, turning her golden and fiery in his arms. He wanted to fill his hands with so many parts of her. While Mack's lips got busy with her mouth, his hands smoothed over her full breasts, her curvy hips, and her heart-breakingly rounded ass. Mina was glorious and alive and warm in his arms—a place Mack never thought she'd be.

"I love you," he said against her lips. So much it hurt.

"Love you," she whispered back. Mina tilted her hips and dragged her slick heat along his cock, and Mack knew neither of them could wait much longer.

He scrabbled between the armrest and the cushion for the condom he'd stashed there. Once Mina saw what he was after, she snatched it from his hands and did the honors herself. Before

Mack could blink, his dream woman—his unattainable fantasy, his never-ending crush—positioned herself over him and took him deep inside.

Mina's body was hot and wet, and squeezed him like a fist. She was urgent and needy, but Mack wanted to slow down time, instead. He never wanted that moment to end. He grabbed onto Mina's hips and kissed her slow and deep.

Somehow, she found a way to get with that as well as ride Mack like he was a prize stallion at the county fair. He'd always loved that damn chair, but now that he'd seen what Mina could accomplish with it, that affection skyrocketed. Mack was never going to get rid of the thing, and probably would end up buying another before long—just so they'd have more options.

When he couldn't stave off the storm any longer, he worked his hand between them to hurry her along. Mina didn't exactly need his help to get there, though—with one brush of his thumb, she was going off like a cannon blast from a tall-masted vessel and towing Mack right along in her wake.

He held her tight when she finally sagged against him. They drifted off for a bit like that, but the sweat drying on their skin finally made it too chilly to stay there any longer. Mina disentangled herself to pull on her sweater and her panties, while Mack yanked on his jeans. He seemed to have misplaced a boot, so he switched on the small side table lamp to search for it.

There were smudges marring the dark brown leather of the chair, evidence of their lovemaking. Mack might have tossed a shirt over it and left it for the morning, but Mina wanted to clean it up before it did any permanent damage. She went over to root around under his kitchen sink, looking for paper towels.

Her voice rose up from behind the island. "You have *leather wipes*?" she called in amazement. "Who even buys those, besides you?"

"That's what you're supposed to use!" Mack protested.

Mina returned to his side, holding the canister and smiling sweetly. "Do you always do what you're supposed to do?" she inquired tartly.

Mack took the plastic container from her and tossed it on the chair, then dropped his clothes to the floor and wrapped Mina in his arms. Even after everything they'd just done, she still tasted faintly of the cappuccino and cannoli she'd had for dessert at the restaurant.

"Not always," Mack growled. "And that's when stuff gets fun." He hoisted Mina over his shoulder and brought her to his bedroom upstairs, to demonstrate what he meant.

Chapter Thirty-Four

ON WEDNESDAY MORNING, Mack stood with his arm around Mina in her open garage, while Major Scott Vasquez pulled on a pair of latex gloves and set a stack of evidence bags on the tarp next to where he was kneeling. Vasquez had brought another Marine from the Criminal Investigative Division with him, but other than introducing himself as Warrant Officer Kowalski, the man hadn't said anything else.

Mina watched the investigator with worried eyes. "We went through it all, obviously. That's how I knew I should call you. But...I guess that means our fingerprints are all over everything now, right?"

Vasquez nodded. "It's okay. I understand."

Her phone began ringing in the kitchen, and she excused herself to go answer it.

The major turned to Mack, as Mack had expected he would. "Tell me again who you are?"

"Mack Bolton. I'm the new boyfriend," he smiled, holding out his hand. "I've known Grey almost my whole life, and Mina for the last twelve years."

Vasquez's face was not accusatory—in fact, he looked rather pleased that Mina finally had someone in her corner. "Mind giving me your contact information, in case we need it?"

"Not at all," Mack said. "Though I suspect you already have it. I was interviewed by your office briefly about two years ago, and nothing's changed since then."

"I'll look for the notes," Vasquez said. He glanced toward the kitchen door, then gestured at the broken lock of trunk. "So, what happened here? Was it like this when she found it?"

"No," Mack explained, "Mina said she didn't know where the key might be, so she whacked the crap out of it with a shovel to get it open."

At this, the silent Marine finally cracked a grin. "Oorah," he murmured.

Mack smiled, too, and decided he liked Kowalski immensely.

Vasquez said, "Did Ms. O'Connell say if she'd ever seen the trunk before? Why did she feel like she needed to get into it so fast?"

"Would you believe there was a snake?" Mack chuckled.

The major's eyebrows shot up, and he pulled his latex-encased hands slowly back from the lid.

"Just a garden snake," Mack rushed to add. "Mina had me come over to help get it out of her kitchen, but once we did, the bastard managed to slither right into that trunk."

"How?" Vasquez frowned warily at the box, and Mack was reminded of those prank toys from childhood, where a fabric snake sprang from a can to scare the pants off unsuspecting kids.

"Through that smashed-in corner. It's all good, though—I found the bugger in a boot, and tossed it out in the yard there. So...unless the snake crawled back in sometime since Mina called you, you should be clear."

She came back out just as Vasquez opened the lid. "Ms. O'Connell, can you give me an idea of what I'm looking for?" he asked.

She glanced at Mack.

"After we went through it, I put everything back mostly the way I found it," Mina said. "You should probably unpack it all. There were quite a few items of interest, as far as I could see."

The Marine nodded, and much the same way Mina had the week before, began laying Grey's old things out on the tarp around him. Occasionally, Kowalski would step in to photograph something, or help bag an item.

Mina watched quietly, breaking her silence only to direct the investigator to look inside Grey's old boot for the baggie of pills, and then instructing him to remove the trunk's false bottom to find the worst of the hidden contents.

Vasquez's expression stayed the same whether he was handling a t-shirt, a textbook, or the two blocks of heroin. His companion logged each item on an official-looking form, then—when he ran out of room—in a notebook he'd been using to brace his writing. When Vasquez finally finished his task, the major sat back on his heels and shared a long look with the other Marine.

"So?" Mina asked nervously. "Is that what you were looking for?"

The Marine sorted the evidence bags carefully and didn't answer her at first, but Kowalski locked eyes with Mack and nodded slightly. Mack had to think that Mina's discovery had helped their case against Grey Whitney immeasurably—how could it not? He wondered, though, whether it had also uncovered more sordid layers than they'd been anticipating.

The major said, "All this—this is exactly what we've needed from the beginning but could never find." He stood and looked at Mina. "You did good, Ms. O'Connell. Really good."

She shrugged, as she tended to do. "Call me Mina," she said. "Don't forget—Mack and I both handled a lot of that stuff. I guess our fingerprints are all over everything, but Friday was really the first time we'd ever seen it. I swear."

"Duly noted." Vasquez brushed off his knees and spent a few more minutes cross-checking the evidence bags against the other Marine's log.

"Major Vasquez," Mina said.

"Scott," he answered.

"Scott. You guys are going to take all that with you, right? The…whole thing?"

He nodded. "With your permission, yes."

"Good. It's bad enough that it was here in my garage all this time without me even knowing. I would hate to have it here any longer if I can help it."

"I understand." Vasquez gestured to the other Marine, who opened the back hatch of their large, blacked-out SUV and began laying things inside.

"Will you let me know what happens?" Mina requested. "It sort of looks like Grey was dealing or something, right? Is that what you think? Can you—can you even charge someone for that after they're dead?" Her hands twisted together in front of her.

Mina's voice was cracking, and she was virtually vibrating with anxiety. Mack squeezed her shoulder and murmured, "Down girl."

A flash of red out on the street caught her eye and seemed to distract her. She pulled away to take a few steps into her driveway. "What the hell?" she muttered.

Vasquez stepped up beside her, following her gaze. "What is it?"

"It's just—that car. I know I'm probably paranoid, but I feel like I keep seeing it. It seems really familiar."

"Maybe it belongs to one of your neighbors?"

"No, I don't think it does. In fact…"

Mack came to stand on her other side, eyeing her carefully. Suddenly, it all seemed to click together, and the color drained from her face.

"I know where I've seen that car. I used to see it outside my old house in St. Michaels, too. Right after Grey died, I—" Her eyes swung to Vasquez. Mina was scared, and like Mack, he saw it immediately.

Scott turned to Kowalski. "Get the plate number," he barked.

The other Marine strode up the sidewalk taking photos with his phone, while the little car made a quick turn at the stop sign.

"Got it," he said on his return, then stashed the phone in a pocket of his uniform.

"We'll look into that," Vasquez assured them. "But for now—"

Kowalski nodded at him, and each of them grasped an end of the tarp to lift the empty, rickety trunk into their SUV. The warrant officer smiled at Mina.

"Ma'am," he said kindly, then bumped fists with Mack before getting behind the wheel.

Vasquez told her, "I'll keep you updated. There are other cases besides Grey's, so I might not be able to tell you everything—but I'll try, okay?"

"Thank you, Scott," she said.

"You bet. And thanks again for reaching out. I know it had to be a nasty surprise to find all this, but for us it could be exactly the break we've been looking for. It looks huge. Seriously. You helped us a ton."

"Well, at least there's that." Mina stepped back and slipped her arm around Mack's waist. "Good luck," she told the Marine.

He looked between her and Mack and nodded. His face softened when he said, "To you as well."

"I KNOW YOU probably have to go," Mina said, once the Marines had departed and she and Mack settled into her kitchen once more.

"What? Why would I have to go?" he wondered.

She shrugged. "With all the projects you're juggling, you've got to have stuff you should be working on. There're obviously more important things to do than sit around here holding *my* hand all day."

Mack frowned at her. "Mina, holding your hand was the most important task on the list, trust me. Why else would I still be here?"

"I don't know—surely you have an appointment or something."

"Honey, my firm is in St. Michaels. How many appointments do you think I have in Annapolis, anyway?"

"You always have them here!" she objected. "You've told me *at least* three times that you were in town for an appointment."

Mack laughed. She had him there. "Not for work, Mina. Those meetings were always with you."

"*Me?*" she squawked.

He nodded. "It's always been you. Right from the beginning."

He'd been dancing around that admission for a while now, but maybe it was time to finally let it break free. It seemed like every other dirty little secret was seeing the light of day—why not his, too? Helpfully, Mina played right into his hands.

"You mean when your supposed buddy suddenly saddled you with an economically undesirable roommate, all those years ago?" She tried to laugh it off, but Mina's question hit the mark too well for it to be much of a joke.

"Well before that, kiddo," Mack said. As he expected, her forehead wrinkled up in confusion. There was no backing out, now.

"Mack, when Grey brought me to your apartment was the first time I ever laid eyes on you," Mina told him. "I'll never forget the look on your face. I mean—harboring a runaway wasn't exactly up your alley. I thought for sure you'd throw me out."

Mack disregarded most of what she'd said and mused, "And I'll never forget how you looked the first time I saw *you*, two months before that. Some dive bar—I can't remember the name. The Wheel House, maybe?"

"I'm sorry. *What?*" There was that incredulous screech again.

"You had on this white top with a frilly ruffle thing all around the bottom. And the tightest jeans I think I'd ever seen."

Mina sat there staring at him. "That…sounds right. It was my favorite outfit to wear out."

"It suited you," Mack said.

"You didn't talk to me, did you? I'm pretty sure I would remember that."

"No, I didn't. To my eternal regret."

Mina was no dummy. She could tell there was more to his story. "So, what *did* you do?"

Mack leaned forward and ran a hand gently through her silky dark hair, marveling at its softness. "I sat there like a dope for a while, watching you get hit on by every dude in the place. God, your hair—it killed me even then. I was frozen to the spot by the sight of you."

She studied him some more. He hoped Mina would see that he wasn't merely reminiscing—that this was something that had haunted him for a long time. Dogged him, even. Would she put it together? The thing that had happened two months before she showed up on Mack's doorstep?

"Then what?" she prodded.

He couldn't look into her lovely chocolate eyes anymore. So, Mack dropped his gaze to the little gold M dangling from her necklace, and dropped his voice, too. "Then I turned to my friend. *Look at that girl,* I told him. *She's amazing.*"

Mina inhaled and held her breath. Maybe she already knew where this was going. "What did he say?"

Mack lifted his eyes briefly to hers. "He said, *You're right.*" That same sick feeling settled into his stomach, like it always did—like it had only happened yesterday instead of a decade or more.

"So…did *he* talk to me?"

"Yes," Mack replied.

Mina considered that, then asked, "Did I talk back?"

He smiled. It was a valid question. Then and now, Mina could have the pick of the litter. "Yes," he whispered. He fixed his eyes on her neck again.

"Your treacherous friend stole me from right under your nose? Is that what you're telling me?"

Mack nodded. Then he scooted his chair closer, cupped Mina's cheek, and growled against her lips, "And now I'm taking you back."

When he kissed her, Mack poured every ounce of hunger and urgency that he could manage into it. With the demand of his mouth alone, he pressed Mina against the back of her chair, then gripped the edges of the seat beside her with both hands and held her caged there.

When her lips parted, he dove in, looting and pillaging what should have been *his*. Her reaction was the same satisfying one as always—she melted against him and tried to get closer.

Mack wanted to lose himself in that kiss. Wanted to lift her onto his lap and take her right then. But there was one more detail that Mina needed to know, and her native curiosity didn't disappoint him.

"Mack?" she gasped, breaking away from his ravaging mouth. "What was his name?"

That was the question he'd wanted her to ask, but suddenly he didn't feel ready. "Whose?" He tried to kiss her again.

"You know whose," she chided, turning her head away. "The friend who stole me."

"Ah." Mack stopped kissing the neck she'd so helpfully offered to him and looked back at her necklace. Had her former husband given it to her? Was he close by, even now—even in death?

"His name was Grey," Mack said.

Mina deflated like a pierced balloon. "Oh, Mack. Oh no."

His torment shifted abruptly into fury. "Oh, *yes*. I let that bastard win once, Mina, but no more. He didn't appreciate you when he had you, and now he's gone. Grey doesn't get to have you anymore, you hear me? No more. He lost that right—he had his chance and he fucked it up."

Mina blinked back tears, but at least she wasn't frightened by Mack's outburst. Perhaps Grey had inured her to all that. Could she even imagine what their life would've been like, if she'd only met Mack first? If she'd only chosen him, instead of Grey?

She sighed heavily. "God, Mack. I don't know if I was smart enough to appreciate you back then." It clearly pained her to say it.

And maybe Mack had been too immature to hang on to her. It was a valid point, but he shook it off. He no longer had any interest in regret.

"What about now?" he wondered.

"Now, I'm too—"

Another excuse? After how far they'd already come? Mack interrupted her.

"Mina, I didn't fight for you before like I should have, and maybe you wouldn't have wanted me to anyway. What's done is done. We can't negate the past, but we *can* choose what we want for our future."

"What are you saying?" Mina was stalling, but at least she wasn't running. Mack considered that a win.

"I'm saying, I choose you. Baggage or no baggage. Babies, or no babies. I will always, always choose you, from here on out. What I want to know is whether you're going to choose me, too." It was a risk, putting Mina on the spot like this. There was really no telling what she might do, even after everything.

"*Mack,*" she moaned.

Was it, *Mack don't be silly, you're embarrassing yourself?* Or was it, *Mack, please, you ought to know this?* He just wasn't sure.

"What?" he demanded.

Mina clambered into his lap and the chair beneath him creaked in protest. But her arms were around his neck and her lips were a millimeter from his when she breathed, "Of course I choose you. Best choice I've ever made, too."

Chapter Thirty-Five

JUST SO YOU know," Mack said after a while, "I *tried* to ignore this connection between us. I tried to bury it deep and let it wither—to leave you to your life. I tried to live *my* life with someone else." His voice was beseeching.

"I know you did," she assured him.

"Mina, it didn't work. It never worked. So, now I'm going to do what feels right. I'm opting to spend the rest of my days with your fortitude and your wit, your bravery and loyalty and beauty. Most of all, I'm picking your heart. It's mine. I'm claiming it, sweetheart, you understand?"

Mack laid his big, warm palm on Mina's chest, right between her breasts where her heart was pumping in a thundering rhythm.

"I do," she managed to choke out.

It was difficult to comprehend how something so stupendous could be handed to her like this, but she wasn't going to pass it up—not anymore. Mina reached out with her hands to cup Mack's handsome face, so he wouldn't look away. His skin was warm and vital, and his eyes searched hers.

He smiled softly at her. "This is the part where you tell me if that's all okay with you."

"I…" She wanted Mack. With every fiber of her being, she wanted this man. So, what was her hesitation? The truth was… "It is okay, but I'm scared."

"Of me?"

"Of us. Mack, this feels so *big*, you know?"

He nodded. "For what it's worth, Mina, I'll never stray. I won't ever put another person, or my job—or whatever else crops up—ahead of us. *You* are what matters most to me, and that's not going to change."

"Mack, what if I can't be what you want? What you need? I'm nothing special. I have issues, still. I'm probably going to suck at stuff, sometimes."

He grinned that sexy, taunting grin of his, damn him. "You promise?"

"Mack, *focus*."

"Okay, okay. Look, both of us are who we are. We're only human. Neither one of us is going to be perfect all the time—I do realize that. All I'm asking is that you give us a fighting chance."

"You make it sound so easy."

"Well, if that's what you want, too—it kind of is," he said.

Mina smiled. "Well then, Mr. Bolton, I think we've got ourselves an agreement."

BASED ON WHAT they heard in the ensuing weeks, the Criminal Investigative Division of the Marines was keeping busy trying to unravel what Grey's team had gotten mixed up in during their final tour. Kowalski called periodically to let Mina know how the case against Grey was progressing and to reassure her that she wouldn't need to testify, but it was the beginning of winter before she heard from Vasquez directly.

The morning had dawned clear and cold, with a light dusting of snow on the ground. The minute they spotted it, Mack built a roaring fire downstairs and tucked Mina under a blanket on the couch. He delivered a cup of coffee to her, then wandered into the kitchen to start breakfast, humming happily under his breath.

When the cordless phone began ringing, Mack was standing at the stove in only a low-riding pair of gym shorts, frying up a pan of scrambled eggs while slices of bread browned in the toaster. It seemed too early in the day for it to be a telemarketer. Mina set aside her mug, reached for the phone on the table and answered it.

"Hello?" she said.

"Ms. O'Connell, this is Scott Vasquez from CID. How have you been?"

Mina sat up a little straighter. If Scott was calling her himself, it must mean that he had news. She looked over at Mack. He was still moving the eggs around the pan, but he was watching her for some sign of who it was.

"Hey Scott," she said for Mack's benefit. "I'm good. What's new?"

"Well, first off, I want to apologize. I tried to have the court records for Grey's case sealed, but the judge declined. Which means that come Monday, it's entirely possible that reporters might get their hands on it and start calling you."

"I see." After a beat of silence, Mina asked, "Should I be worried?"

"I don't think so, but…some things came out at the tail end of our investigation. It's about to become public record, and I wanted you to hear it from me first, instead of getting ambushed with it by 'Joe Schmo' at the *Sun*, or something."

Mack switched off the frying pan and the toaster and came over to sit in his favorite chair.

He must not have heard her before, because he whispered, "Who is it?"

Mina covered the receiver with her hand and told him, "Vasquez."

To the investigator, she said, "I appreciate that. What did you, uh…" She tried to brace herself for the inevitable bad news. "What did you guys learn?"

Vasquez cleared his throat. "Most of what we discovered was exactly what we all thought—Grey and some of his team got mixed up in a heroin smuggling network operating in and outside their base. The firefight in the village appears to have been a deal gone wrong, and the explosion at the pesticide warehouse a direct retaliation for that. The men on the ground were exposed to some nasty fumes, as I think you figured out. Nearly all of them have experienced some form of cancer, sterility, or lung disease since it happened."

"Jesus," Mina breathed.

"Yup. In the confusion afterwards, we suspected that some of the men in Grey's unit went back in and managed to get their hands on the original drugs, but we could never figure out who it was, or what became of the heroin. We assumed it got portioned out and sold off quickly, before it could leave much of a trail to follow."

"Let me guess," Mina said. "You assumed wrong."

The Marine let out a mirthless chuckle. "Not thrilled about that," he admitted. "But the people in on it didn't stop looking. We think they followed the trail to you."

"Me?" she yelped.

"Remember that red car you saw?" Vasquez asked.

"Yes…"

"Turned out it wasn't one of ours. We finally traced it to another guy on Grey's team, First Lieutenant Alan Moore." Mina didn't miss the implication that the Marines had been watching her, too, but decided to let it pass.

"Wait—I know that guy!" she said. "He came to Grey's funeral, I think."

"Yeah well, he's not going anywhere else for good long while," Vasquez muttered. "He confessed that he'd been trailing a couple others besides you. I hate to tell you this, but it's entirely possible he broke into your house at some point. He did it with the others. I doubt he would've hurt you, but still…"

She thought about all the times she'd felt like Grey was watching her, and about patio doors that blew open for no reason. Mina winced—not a ghost, it seemed, but a real flesh-and-blood man.

"I don't understand, though. After I called you about that box, I left the house. I was gone for three days—he could've broken in then and gotten what he wanted before you ever had a chance to see what it was."

"He's not that good," Scott said, and Mina could hear the smile in his voice. "Once I knew I couldn't get out there for a bit, I had some people that no one was going to get around guard your place."

Mina laughed. "That seems excessive. You didn't even know what I'd found!"

"Just covering the bases," Vasquez chuckled.

More seriously, she asked, "Do you think there will be others?"

"I don't, actually. For once, I think we've finally nailed down all the moving parts on this cluster."

"That's a relief," Mina said.

"Anyway, I thought you'd want to know that we also found out where Grey was during those two months he went missing."

Mina knew that wasn't going to be good. She motioned for Mack to join her on the couch, then scooted closer and squeezed his hand.

"Okay," she said into the phone. "Where?"

"It seems Mr. Whitney actually assumed a false name, travelled to Delaware, and worked as an airport baggage handler for a brief time. In that way, he was able to secure the heroin when it came into the country on a transport, then disappear with almost no one the wiser."

It was hard to miss the way the Marine had omitted Grey's former rank. Mina let out a long breath. She'd long since passed disappointing husband territory and headed right into *So, I Married a Villain*.

"Oh my God," she breathed.

"It gets worse," Vasquez admitted. "The name he used was 'Skip O'Connell.' Does that mean anything to you?"

"God *damn* it," Mina snarled, abruptly incensed. "Why couldn't that asshole have just made something up like a normal criminal?"

Vasquez laughed. "I take it that's a yes?"

"*Yes*. It's my dad's name," she snapped. "Don't get me wrong, he's no pillar of the community, but come on—he's still a real person. In my *family*."

Mack was scowling mightily now. His grip on Mina's hand had gotten hard enough to be uncomfortable, so she worked her fingers free, then shook some blood back into them. He sat back, crossed his arms over his bare chest and looked only somewhat sheepish.

"All right," Scott said. "I was hoping you weren't going to say that. Just to clarify, we're talking about your father, Stephen Michael O'Connell, right?"

"That's him."

"I'll be sure to note that in the records, so no one goes looking for him inadvertently."

"I'd appreciate that. He's no angel, so it's hardly like he needs any extra help getting mixed up in messes. I don't think any of them have been as bad as this one, though."

"I hear you," the Marine commiserated. "That being said, is there anything else we can do for you at this time?"

"No, I don't think so. Should I tell my dad what happened, just in case?"

"If you'd rather not, we can do it."

"No, let me. We don't want to spook the guy." Mina might have conflicted feelings about the man who'd sired her but setting the Marine Corps on him seemed a tad extreme.

"Fair enough," Vasquez said. "Once again, thank you for turning over that box. Between that and the guy in San Diego we managed to flip, we were finally able to connect all those dots."

"I'm glad I could help," Mina told him.

"Ms. O'Connell…on a personal note, are you going to be okay? If you need something, the Corps has resources that we could—"

"You know what?" Mina interjected. "For once, I actually think I'm going to be fine."

Strangely, it was true. With the mystery solved and the case closed, she felt…free. The ugly door into her past had finally closed for good, divesting her of its burdens. Now Mina could head into her future with nothing to carry but hope.

"Good. If that changes, just give me or Kowalski a buzz," Scott said.

"Will do."

Mina disconnected the call and gazed at Mack. A peace fell over her that she had never felt before.

"Okay?" Mack inquired, his eyes searching her face for clues.

Mina beamed at him. "Very," she said.

A life with Mack was going to be the best thing that had ever happened to her, and Mina couldn't wait. She'd earned that gift, and she didn't plan to waste a single second of it.

Chapter Thirty-Six

T HE AFTERNOON AFTER the phone call from the investigator, Mack managed to corner Mina in his bed again. It wasn't like it had been hard—Mina had raced him up there and run so fast she'd nearly won. She'd been different all day, almost...ebullient.

He guessed not having to wonder anymore when the other shoe was going to drop was a relief. Mack was grateful for that, even before Mina's sweatshirt and leggings hit the floor and she stretched across his comforter.

"Well, well, well—what do we have here?" he drawled. "Hey, Mina...guess what?"

"*What?*" Mina sounded frustrated and exasperated from her position up on his pillows.

Mack grinned. "I found a four-leaf clover, *right* when I was about to get lucky," he told her.

"You don't say," she growled. "Funny, it never brought me much luck."

Mack licked the tiny tattoo on her hip with the tip of his tongue and watched her buck halfway off the bed. Who would ever have guessed that a woman as resilient as Mina would be so ticklish? God, it was just too good.

"It's like I can *feel* my luck changing," he smiled against her skin. He ran his tongue lightly along the crease between her thigh and her hip, to test things out. As he expected, Mina writhed and squeaked, unable to stay still.

"Stop teasing, Mack," she demanded. But she threaded her fingers into his hair to hold him tightly in place.

He huffed out a laugh, and the feel of his warm breath against her skin had Mina contorting again.

"No...I don't think I will," Mack smirked. Then, just for good measure, he nipped the inside of her thigh.

"Mack!"

He held Mina's legs wide with his hands but shifted up slightly, so he could plant one careful kiss right where her pubic bone met the creamy skin of her lower belly. Then he raised his head and watched the shiver wash across her body.

"*Mack*, what?" he inquired.

"Mack..." she threatened. It was hard to take her seriously, given her position.

"Is it, *Mack, please*? Or *Mack, more*?" he asked. "Or maybe you meant the ever-popular *Mack, you're a sex god*?" He knew he was taunting her, but he still dropped three more kisses in a line, right across her abdomen.

Mina's head jerked up from his pillow so fast she'd be lucky if she didn't get whiplash. She glared at him, "Mack, I swear to God—I'm going to kill you."

He tried not to laugh at her, he really did. When was the last time he'd had so much fun? Had he ever?

"Oh. Well, if that's how you feel..." With that, he finally put Mina out of her misery, and ran his tongue firmly along her cleft, stopping at the top to press firmly where she probably wanted him the most. Damn, she tasted amazing.

Up near the head of the bed, Mina inhaled a huge lungful of air like she might be getting ready to let out a horror-movie shriek. *Huh*—something else to shoot for.

Mack flicked his tongue.

Life with Mina would never be dull, he thought. It would glow and pulse and roar, and Mack was going to love every second of it. He was going to love *her*.

Epilogue

MINA CLOSED THE accounts payable screen on the computer and pushed away from the receptionist desk in the main room of Bolton Engineering—which also happened to be the ground floor of the house she now shared with Mack.

She'd been pitching in for him temporarily, while she looked for a full-time paralegal position there in St. Michaels, and it was…nice. Comfortable. So far, none of the staff they'd interviewed to help Mack had seemed quite up to snuff. Just like none of the jobs she had interviewed for seemed like quite the right fit. Mina didn't think either of them would mind if their current arrangement lasted a lot longer.

Since she'd returned from her weekly breakfast date with his mother, Mack had been closeted in his office for the better part of the morning, glaring at his big computer screen like it had killed his favorite dog. She'd bet her last dollar that he was out of coffee in there, but he was probably too focused on his work to get up and get himself some more. It was obviously time for her to deliver the "mail." She got what she needed from the top desk drawer, then stood and shoved it into her pocket.

A quick jaunt down their brick front walk brought her to their mailbox. Mina had planted mounds of black-eyed Susans around the base, but they'd need to install a bigger box on the pole soon, if business kept up like it had. As it was, on many days the mailman had to cram their mail into the box and leave the overflow on the ground below. Mina gathered it all up, then carried the pile through the office and into their kitchen at the back of the house.

She filled Mack's backup travel mug with coffee, added milk for him, then arranged the mail in order of importance. Mina pulled the most significant item of all from her pocket and placed it right on top. Then she lifted everything in her arms and went to peek in his door.

Mack looked up immediately, and his expression cleared.

"The legal community will never love you like I do. Please stay with me instead." It had been his daily refrain for weeks now. He was wearing her down with his devotion.

Mina smiled. "The mail came. Here." She set the pile in front of him and waited to see what he'd say.

Mack pushed it aside and stood, moving around his big desk to reach for her.

"Uh—" She put out her hands to hold him off, but there was never any denying Mack Bolton. He wrapped her in his arms and planted an enthusiastic kiss smack on her lips. Laughing, Mina broke it off. "You might want to take a look at that envelope right on top," she said.

"Later."

"*Now.*"

"All right, fine," he huffed. He kept one hand on her arm to keep her from sneaking away, then twisted back to retrieve it.

He read the return address aloud, "Dr. Diane Davis and Associates—Obstetrics, Gynecology, and Fertility." Mack froze, and his grip on Mina tightened. His eyes flicked up to hers, searching.

She bit her lip and tried not to let her excitement show. "Open it."

His hands were trembling—the paper shook in fine little tremors as he read it. When he looked up at Mina again, his eyes were wide and hopeful.

"So, we can start trying?" he confirmed.

"Well…" she shrugged, "I thought you could make an honest woman out of me, first."

"Yeah. Of course. But *then* we can start trying?"

Mina smiled. She was happy they would have a chance at conceiving naturally, but no matter how they ended up having a family, Mack was going to make the best husband and father in the world.

"As soon as the ink is dry," she told him.

Mack pulled her in close again and nuzzled her neck. "How do you feel about justices of the peace?"

"I'm sure they are very nice people."

"Great. I'm free this afternoon. What about you?"

Mina laughed and tried to fend off the barrage of kisses Mack was attempting to settle on her face and lips. "Been there, done that," she drawled.

"*Mina*," he complained. "Are you seriously going to make me wait a whole year to knock up your pretty little behind?"

Oh God. He was too much. "No, nothing like that. But we could pull off something small in a few months, I bet."

Especially once his mom and siblings got in on the act. Based on how baldly they'd been lobbying for this exact outcome, they were going to flip their lids, they'd be so excited.

"A few *months*!"

Mina nodded. "Hey, it's better than a year."

Mack stroked her hair and cupped her skull, so he could examine her face. His expression turned more serious.

"Is that really what you want?"

She nodded. "Yes. I want to do this right, Mack. I want to walk down the aisle wearing a big, fluffy white dress and ridiculous heels. And I want to smash cake in your face."

His face scrunched up, but at least he laughed. "Then that's what we'll do."

Mina wound her arms around his neck and kissed him. "Thank you," she smiled.

Mack turned her toward the door and spanked her on the ass. "You've got some calls to make, honey. This better be the fastest trip to the altar this town has even seen, if you don't want your dad showing up with a shotgun," he joked.

"Mack, my dad wouldn't know what to do with a shotgun if it crawled into bed with him."

"Don't care. Go on, get out of here. I'll come see how you're doing in a little while. Right after I head upstairs and throw out every piece of birth control in this damn house."

Mina giggled, but Mack was actually pushing past her and heading for the back stairs.

"Mack? Mack!" she yelled after him. "What're you—"

His voice called down the stairs, "Call that church, Mina O'Connell. No backing out now."

No, he was right. There was no backing out now. Mina was going to marry that man upstairs. She was going to be his wife, and this time, it was going to be forever. She couldn't wait.

Review

Did you enjoy **Finding Forever**? If so, please consider leaving a review at the retailer where you purchased this title.

Book reviews can be as simple or as detailed as you wish, but all of them help authors sell more books, and assist other readers in finding the stories they want to read.

Almost any book can be reviewed by simply logging into the website where you purchased the title, then scrolling to the bottom of the title's product page to find an area called "Leave a Review."

Up Next

Forever and a Day

Lost & Found, Book 4.5

If you read Finding Forever, then you know…*never* is a very long time.

When Dimitri said that he was never going to get married again, he was dead serious. After all, he had to focus on raising his small daughter Lilly now that he was her only parent. Besides, there was no way he could endure another broken heart like the one his first wife's passing gave him.

Too bad life had other plans—Lilly's new teacher Emily is too young, too pretty, and too untouched by life's darker moments to make any sense at all for him. She's also too perfect to ignore. What's worse is that Emily wants him just as much as he wants her.

If you loved Finding Forever, then you know…you have to discover what happens when *never* becomes Forever and a Day.

Includes the bonus short story **Forever Starts Now**!

The Flynn and O'Connell sisters have gone through a lot to secure their happily-ever-afters. Now, one weekend and two big milestones will finally bring them all together again—in this sweet and funny conclusion to the Lost & Found series.

Forever and a Day

Chapter One

DIMITRI FIGURED HE must have been dead to the world when his alarm sounded for the second time that morning. Not only had he not registered the first go-around, but a quick glance at the clock on his nightstand showed that he'd overslept by half an hour. Which sucked.

Most days, he tried to meditate in his room for fifteen minutes before heading downstairs. After that, he could usually work in about 45 minutes of *tae kwon do* in their tiny back yard before Lilly woke up. Time to himself pretty much evaporated after that, since he had to switch gears into straight Dad duty for her, and *man* did that kid ever wake up hungry. And talkative. And happy. And so, so ready to *go*. The meditating and martial arts every morning kept him sane in the face of it all, but only barely. Not being able to do either was going to seriously screw up his head that day.

Out of habit, Dimitri sat up and folded his legs into position, then closed his eyes once more. After only three deep breaths in and out, it was clear the meditation thing was a lost cause—he was too aware of how late he was already running. So, he pulled on a t-shirt and a loose pair of sweats and padded as quietly as he could downstairs. As he went, he tried to concentrate on small things to keep himself grounded—like the way the air felt subtly cooler at the bottom of the stairs, and the way the textures under his feet changed from smooth wood to woolly rugs and back again.

They hadn't had any rugs at their old place in DC. Anna hadn't liked them, preferring the spare, modern look of bare floors.

Dimitri hadn't minded back then. Even though it was louder in the house, it was a happy sort of loud—Anna and Lilly's laughter and love reflecting around the rooms until their whole home was filled with it. He supposed he must have been laughing, too, but it was so hard to remember that. When he joked around with Lilly now, it felt like there was a dismal underside to it—a sad nostalgia that he hadn't quite been able to shake.

When Anna had passed, and he'd realized—once and for all—that they weren't ever going back to their old life, Dimitri had sold off the DC house and almost everything in it. The townhouse he'd rented in Annapolis for himself and Lilly was small and cozy and had soft rugs everywhere because, especially in those first several months, he hadn't been able to bear the empty echoing. It had been deafening—devastating. Worse than spending every day in his wife's hometown without her.

The loose board outside the kitchen creaked from his weight when he walked across it. The back door squeaked when he slid it open and again when he closed it. Even though Lilly shouldn't be able to hear those small sounds from upstairs and behind her closed bedroom door, Dimitri knew that she would. She had an almost preternatural sense of hearing when it came to these things. Which meant that—at best—he had ten or fifteen minutes before she scampered down the stairs, primed for the day.

Out in the yard, Dimitri flexed his toes in the grass and began putting himself through a brief warmup and some basic poses. He was rushing, but it still felt good—normal and natural. Despite being competitive in high school and college, he'd given it up for years afterward. He could no longer remember why.

By the time Dimitri had met Anna, he'd been full into the gym and running scene. They'd even run a few 10Ks together before she got pregnant. But after she got sick, then died…well, Dimitri hadn't done much of anything for a while there. He supposed he ought to thank Dr. Mercer for suggesting he give *tae kwon do* another try. On some days, it seemed like the therapist and her bright ideas were the only things saving his life.

Dimitri phased into a more rigorous routine, beginning to work up a sweat in the spring humidity. Any minute now, Lilly would be banging on the glass, begging for his attention. He had to hurry. He kicked, spun, kicked again—then glanced up at the back door. There she was, his feisty little sprite in pink cat pajamas, mimicking him in the frame of the sliding glass door. Dimitri smiled. Her form wasn't half-bad. Maybe he could start teaching her a few things.

He walked over to Lilly and made a goofy face, and his little girl rewarded him with that silly giggle of hers. Even though she was so like Anna, there *were* some differences—and that laugh was one of them. Anna's chuckle had been restrained and throaty, something that he'd loved. In contrast, Lilly's laugh was giddy and unfettered, and she doled it out generously. To Daddy only, he amended—with almost everyone else, she was incredibly shy. And everyone knew she got *that* from him.

Lilly hopped back from the doorway as he stepped through, chirping, "Did you see me, Daddy?" She punched at the air, her pudgy little fists and fierce frown making him smile wider. "I fight like a girl!"

Well, that wiped the grin right off his face. "Fight Like a Girl" had been something of a catchphrase for Anna, after her old coworkers had given her a t-shirt with that motto when she'd taken a turn for the worse and finally had to quit her job. His wife had worn it all through her chemo, and in some fit of...*whatever*, Dimitri had cut up the shirt and framed the words once she'd passed. Then—because he was almost certainly a glutton for punishment—he'd hung it in Lilly's room when they moved here. She couldn't read the words herself yet, which meant that his daughter remembered it from *before*.

Which was further proof it was going to be one of *those* days for him. Dimitri turned on the coffee maker, then stared into the fridge—buying himself time while he schooled his expression. So many "befores" and "afters", every day. His whole life could be divided into those two awful categories, and there didn't appear to be any end in sight.

"How about some eggs for breakfast?" he asked Lilly.

She hung on his leg and swung around so she could see his face. His daughter stuck out her tongue and gagged comically, even though last week she'd been all about the scrambled eggs with cheese.

"Waffles?" he tried.

"No!" she laughed. *Preposterous*, her tone implied.

Dimitri shook himself. Why was he even doing this? Too many choices for a kid her age led to total anarchy, a fact he'd learned fast and well rather recently.

"Cereal it is," he told her, grabbing the milk. That was good—it was an easy and fast enough choice that he might now have time for more than a five-minute shower.

Lilly ponied up to the table without complaint, and Dimitri pulled out her chair. She climbed into it before he could help and kicked her little bare feet back and forth under the table.

"I can has blueberries?" she asked him sweetly.

"Yes, you may have blueberries," he agreed, subtly emphasizing his grammar the way Anna might have done. He supposed she would have, anyway—Lilly had been too young for that kind of thing when his wife had died. As with everything else, it was all up to him, now.

He grabbed a bowl for himself and joined her at the table. Dimitri told her a little bit about what he was going to do at work that day, and Lilly chattered about the baby animal project they'd been working on all week at school. He sent her up to get dressed while he rinsed the breakfast dishes and packed her lunch, then headed upstairs to see what kind of crazy outfit she'd cooked up.

Luckily, it wasn't too bad that day—simply a t-shirt and hoodie over some sparkly leggings. True, everything Lilly wore was a competing shade of light blue—her newest sartorial quirk—but Dimitri wasn't going to attempt any adjustments, not when the time he had left to get ready himself was rapidly evaporating. At least her clothes were clean. No one could take Lilly away from him for that.

He brushed her wispy hair into a reasonably neat ponytail, tossed her a pair of coordinating socks, then led her into his room to she could watch a cartoon on his bed while he shaved and showered.

The fan in the bathroom was lousy, and the steam from his shower turned the space into a virtual sauna, fogging up the mirror and leaving a faint dew on the countertop.

Dimitri cracked the door to release some of the humid air while he dressed and caught the first notes of the theme song for Lilly's favorite show. He sighed, knowing he'd probably be whistling the tune for the rest of the day. And yeah—that was pretty much fatherhood in a nutshell. No room to be a badass when you were walking around town singing kid songs to yourself.

His hair was still a little damp when they trooped back downstairs. Lilly sat on the floor to put on her shoes while he grabbed her lunch from the fridge, and then they were on their way. Her school was only a few blocks away, an easy walk for her. It was a pretty one, too, the road lined with big shade trees and the spring day not too hot yet. Dimitri adjusted his long strides to her little ones and reveled in the feel of her tiny hand in his. He might not have much left, but at least he had that.

"Is today a Miss Emily day?" Lilly asked, hopping and skipping along.

Oh, yes—Miss Emily. Dimitri reached up and kneaded his neck, which had gone oddly tight at his daughter's question. Three times a week, his little girl started her school day with the reading specialist. Miss Emily had only recently taken over from the prior lady in the position, and Lilly loved the young woman to distraction.

Lilly was making much better progress under her tutelage, too. Maybe because his kid seriously looked forward to the mornings she spent with Emily, or perhaps because Emily was a better instructor. Either way, Dimitri wasn't going to split hairs—he was just happy that Lilly was finally getting fired up about reading and wasn't so discouraged anymore.

"It sure is," he told her with a smile. Lilly let go of him, whooped, and executed a funny little victory kick.

He couldn't exactly quibble with her. Even *he* kind of looked forward to reading days. Miss Emily was indisputably young and pretty, with pale blond hair and blue eyes the size of dinner plates. She had a spray of freckles across her nose and cheekbones that made her seem even younger, and she always smelled terrific. She was efficient and no-nonsense, kind and cheerful, and the perfect person for the job.

For some reason, Emily also had a weird way of making Dimitri feel twitchy and ill-at-ease, like his skin was too tight. He couldn't seem to hold still around her. And he really didn't *want* to notice things about her, but damn—Emily's lips and her body were like something out of his wildest fantasies. The fact that he knew that about her, without any doubt, made Dimitri even more uneasy. Like he was some dirty old lecher, or something.

It wasn't like Miss Emily dressed provocatively, either—she was working with little kids all day, for crying out loud. Still, it was hard for a grown man to miss the way her jeans snugly cupped her ass and her hips, or the way her soft, oversized sweaters obscured some parts, but still managed to outline others perfectly.

Unlike Anna, she wore very little makeup that Dimitri could see. But when Emily smiled up at him, it was a like a neon blast of crystalline eyes, long lashes, and lush, kissable lips. The fact that a guy wouldn't have to navigate past a truckload of cosmetics made her seem disconcertingly…accessible. Her warm, inviting demeanor only added to the impression.

Which was wrong and bad, because his kid's teacher was off limits for so *many* reasons. Among other things, Emily was too young, too innocent, and too important to Lilly's well-being. Dimitri wished sometimes that he could slap some dorky glasses on her, maybe get her to stop washing that slightly messy hair for a week or two. He could cocoon Emily in some grandma clothes and spritz her with mothball scent, and then he could move on.

If Miss Emily weren't so all-fired enticing, then Dimitri might quit noticing irrelevant details about her, and get back to focusing on what was important—which was Lilly, and Lilly's happiness. And…that was about it. His daughter was all he had, and all he needed.

Dimitri blinked. It was a noble sentiment. Right and good, considering he was currently all *Lilly* had. Except, that wasn't entirely true, was it? Lilly had school and friends and playgrounds and her abiding love of ducks—both stuffed and real. She had take-out pizza on Friday nights, Sunday morning pancakes, and the hope that she might get a surprise cupcake here and there.

They approached the tall wrought-iron gates of school, flung wide for the day ahead. His daughter drifted back to grip his hand again, her previous exuberance tempering into a sort of quiet resolve. He wished it wasn't that way, but at least she didn't cry and cling when he dropped her off anymore. After Anna died, Lilly had needed to know he was close—and so he'd given her that, without a second thought.

For the first time, Dimitri paused to wonder if he was getting the things *he* needed, too. He had a throw-away job that he could do in his sleep. Mina was the only friend that he could really stand the sight of, but she was currently thick in the middle of new love and not terribly available anymore. He had his baby girl and the few minutes that he stole for himself when she was asleep, and…his list petered out. Perhaps the time had come for a hobby or two. Even Dimitri could see that his life was looking a bit thin.

He and Lilly made their way across the wide lawn of her school, sticking to the brick pathway that led to the small building beside the kindergarten wing. Which circled him right back around to thoughts of Miss Emily again.

There had to be a way to find out how old she actually was. When he considered the fact that Emily apparently sported a master's degree and years of impressive work experience, Dimitri realized that she couldn't possibly be as young as she first appeared. Despite that, there was probably zero chance a woman like her hadn't been snapped up by some enterprising asshole or another. Looks and smarts aside, Emily was just so goddamn *nice*.

He and Lilly arrived at her door and let themselves into her serene classroom. Next door, the kindergarten was housed in a big two-story space, airy and sunny and filled with windows and nooks for reading and science and art projects. They'd stuck the specialists like Emily in a similar room—still spacious, but more open and definitely quieter. Emily immediately looked up from her desk with a smile when they entered.

Well, there were those glasses Dimitri had been hoping for, but their chunky tortoiseshell frames only made her look cuter—sexy and bookish. Emily's jeans were faded and tight from top to bottom, and she wore a soft-looking black sweater that buttoned up the front. Cashmere, he decided. It had that look, but he didn't dare find out for sure.

In the split second that Dimitri let his eyes pass over Miss Emily, he noticed several things: the freckled triangle of skin exposed by the sweater's deep v-neck, and the little silver necklace glinting there. Her short, pink, newly-polished nails, peeking out below those too-long sleeves. And the flash of more skin exposed at her ankles, between the unhemmed edge of denim and her red suede flats. How she managed to be both excruciatingly appropriate and totally devasting was beyond him.

Dimitri figured he must have some kind of lowered immunity, what with his epic drought and all. At this point, he'd probably find any woman sexy—not just the one who was crouching down to hug his daughter like she'd been looking forward to it for a year. He forced his eyes up to stare out the windows, so he wouldn't check if Miss Emily's jeans were riding low at her back. Dimitri was suddenly, irrationally glad that he hadn't worn his handyman coveralls over his clothes that day.

It hadn't been done out of vanity, only to save time—he'd shoved the jumpsuit in his bag on their way out the door. Since he hadn't gotten much of a workout that morning, he'd worn a t-shirt, gym shorts, and running shoes, hoping he could take a run around the school's track on his lunch hour, if there wasn't a PE class using it or anything. But wearing normal clothes at least made Dimitri feel like he was just another dad in Emily's eyes, and not the modern-day equivalent of the Cockney chimney sweep in that old children's film.

Miss Emily laid a soft hand on his arm, startling him out of his thoughts. Dimitri tried not to jump like a scared cat, but his hand went up to steady him of its own accord, landing on the back of her slim shoulder. That sweater was even softer than it looked. Definitely cashmere.

"Did you need anything else?" she inquired.

Yup, he sure did—a cold freaking shower. Lilly looked expectantly up at him, too, worksheets and flashcards already spread in front of her on the pint-sized table.

"Nope, all good," Dimitri managed. "Have fun, you two."

He reached down to tug his daughter's ponytail—but not too much, lest he mess it up and annoy her. He gave Miss Emily an anemic wave, and then he skedaddled out of that wicked den of temptation. Because, yeah—that was exactly where a dad wanted to leave his little girl for the day.

Jesus. It was nine a.m. and he already wanted a beer. Or a scotch. Or…anesthesia.

At least Dimitri had exactly the right cure for this kind of shit-show. A *literal* shit-show, courtesy of the constantly-clogging toilets in the upper level boys' bathroom. God only knew what the little menaces flushed down those things, but today was the day Dimitri intended to find out. By the time he had to pick Lilly up at the end of the day, his head would be right and tight, and back in the parenting game.

To read more, please purchase *Forever and a Day* from your favorite bookseller!

FREE BOOK

Get a glimpse of Morgan, Meg, Molly and Mina — *before* their happily ever afters take place!

Sign up for the author's Reader's List and get a free copy of the Lost & Found prequel novella "Girls Night Out."

Also by Kristen Casey

The Triple Threat Series

The Titan Was Tall

The Doctor Was Dark

The Hero Was Handsome

The Masquerade was Magic

The Hero's Brother

The Triple Threat Box Set

The Black Watch Security Series

False Flag

Heat Seeking Missile

Brothers in Arms

Fight or Flight

Search and Destroy

Squared Away

Acknowledgements

When it comes to editing and beta reading, no one beats the lovely, indefatigable Helen, who searches out all my missed words, extra words, and awkward words with the same cheerful enthusiasm that she tackles jokes about DEFCON levels and whether the hero is acting sexy or...*not*. I'm grateful for how she makes my books better, but even more for how she brightens every table I've ever shared with her.

Deborah at Tugboat Design has designed another gorgeous cover for Mina and Mack's story—as she does. The skill and creativity she brings to my books are always deeply appreciated, and I am so thankful for her help and insight.

To my readers—a huge thank you! I love to hear your thoughts on my characters and my stories, and I love it even more when you take the very thoughtful extra step of putting those ideas into reviews. When you message me to tell me things like, "I bought your book for my mom and she loved it!", it makes this job the best and only one I could ever imagine doing.

Speaking of families...there's mine—the most loving, understanding, adorable fans an author could ever hope to have. They're always right there with a high five or a pep talk, and I am grateful for every day I get to share a life and a home with them. Love you guys!

About the Author

Kristen Casey writes the kind of heartfelt, steamy books she loves to read—full of relatable characters and delicious dialogue. She lives in Maryland with her husband, kids, and assorted cats, and in her free time, she enjoys all things crafty—especially projects she finds on Pinterest.

Sign up for her newsletter to receive exclusive free content and the inside scoop on sales and new releases—all emailed right to your inbox.

You can also follow her on social media for behind-the-scenes tales, character and setting inspiration, book reviews, and more:

Goodreads: Kristen_Casey
Facebook: AuthorKCasey
Twitter: AuthorKCasey
Pinterest: KristenCase0461
Instagram: Kristen.Casey.Books
BookBub: Kristen Casey
TikTok: KristenWritesRomance

Reading Order of Kristen's Books

The Lost & Found Series

Girls Night Out (Prequel exclusive to subscribers)

Finding Home (Book 1)

Finding Love (Book 2)

Lost in Love (Book 2.5 – Includes *Lucky in Love*)

The Flynn Sisters Box Set (Includes *Christmas in Cambridge*)

Finding a Husband (Book 3)

Finding Forever (Book 4)

Forever and a Day (Book 4.5 – Includes *Forever Starts Now*)

The O'Connell Sisters Box Set (Includes *Heroes & Husbands*)

The Triple Threat Series

The Titan was Tall (Book 1)

The Doctor was Dark (Book 2)

The Hero was Handsome (Book 3)

The Triple Threat Box Set (Includes *The Masquerade was Magic* and *The Hero's Brother*)

The Black Watch Security Series

False Flag (Book 1)

Heat Seeking Missile (Book 2)

Brothers in Arms (Book 3)

Fight or Flight (Book 4)

Search and Destroy (Book 5)

Squared Away (Book 6)